SWEET COUNTRY ROMANCES

AUSTRALIAN OUTBACK ROMANCES - VOLUME 1

SUZANNE GILCHRIST

CONTENTS

Australian Outback Romances
Sweet Country Romances
Volume 1

By

Suzanne Gilchrist

BOX SET TITLES

Cowboy Under the Mistletoe
Dance in the Outback
The Cowboy's Gift

Sweet Country Romances – Volume 1 © 2019
Mallee Star Enterprises
ISBN: 978-0-6484510-2-0
All Rights Reserved

This is a work of fiction. Names, characters, places, and incidents are either the product of the author's imagination or are used fictitiously, and any resemblance to actual persons, living or dead, business establishments, events, or locales is entirely coincidental.

Published by Mallee Star Enterprises
P O Box 224
Rutherford NSW 2320

After three long years, Rachel's ex-boyfriend returns to Sturt's Crossing, to compete in the Christmas Rodeo. Despite all her best efforts at replacing him in her dreams, and her heart, she's never succeeded. Perhaps this might be the perfect opportunity to sate an itch that never really faded away. Then she can get on with her life. But Chris has plans of his own; one of which is proving to Rachel he's no longer a footloose cowboy. The other involves a sprig of mistletoe.

~

Years ago, Melanie Black was rescued from a burning house by her best mate, a fellow foster child. When he begs for help to save his marriage, she can't refuse and is soon living on a cattle station as a nanny for his children. Dirk Tanner can't believe his eyes when his brother-in-law's 'friend' alights from the plane. He recognises her as the do-gooder who gave his ex-wife advice on 'living her own life'. No way will he allow Melanie to meddle in his sister's affairs too. When disaster strikes, Melanie faces her worst nightmare. But will she face it alone or can Dirk overcome his prejudice and stand by her side?

~

Rosie Turner is done with denying her dreams and good-looking men who make her knees weak. To pay-off her two-timing ex-husband's debts, she'll sell Blackbird Tor, and set up a guest house to give her son and herself financial independence. She also has high plans to put Sturt's Crossing back on the map and breathe life into this failing, small town. Maybe then she'll be free of her past.

Luke Williams is resolved to turn heavily mortgaged Flat Rock Station into a thriving property and bring a spark of life back into his dad's tired eyes. But his options are limited as he must find additional collateral to obtain another loan. When Rosie catapults into their lives, Luke's father reveals the myth of a rich opal seam located on Blackbird Tor.

This could be the answer to both Rosie and Luke's problems. But they're not the only ones desperate to discover the hidden treasure.

COWBOY UNDER THE MISTLETOE

BY SUZANNE GILCHRIST

CHAPTER 1

Rachel slipped the bolt and entered the pen of the prize-winning sow of the Sturt's Crossing Christmas Rodeo and Show. Piglets scattered and tumbled about her feet when she approached the snuffling animal. It sniffed the air, must have caught her scent for the sow lowered her head and returned to nosing amongst the hay on the ground.

"You remember me, don't you girl." Rachel grinned and ran a gentle hand along the animal's spine.

The pig grunted.

"How are you feeling after giving birth to twelve babies? If it were me, I'd be in bed for a month."

"Who are you talking to Rach?"

The sudden voice made Rachel jump and the sow flinch from her touch. "Gosh Rosanne, couldn't you have called out or something? You almost gave me a heart attack."

"Rubbish." Her sister grinned around the top of the straw poking out of a Coke can and sucked nosily.

"Should you be guzzling that lolly water in your condition?" Rachel straightened from where she'd been checking the sow's belly and waved a hand towards her sister. "Gestational diabetes is no picnic."

"Duh. Doc said I was in perfect health when I saw him yesterday."

"That doesn't mean you should slacken off."

"Give over, Rach." Rosanne rolled her eyes. "The way you nag everyone, you'll never snag a guy."

Rachel hunched her shoulders and returned to her examination. "I'm quite happy with the way my life is, thank you very much." Her thoughts immediately winged to one guy in particular and his twinkling blue eyes. *Liar, liar, pants on fire.* Apparently time had done little to douse the ache and the *'may-have-beens'* whenever she thought of him.

"One of us has to be responsible," she added through a clenched jaw. She finished with the pig, gave the animal an affectionate pull on its cute little ears then crossed to her sister's side.

"I'm the eldest so you should take my advice." Rosanne crumpled the empty can in her hand, her rosebud mouth puckered into a childish pout that had garnered her everything she'd ever asked for when they were kids.

Pity it no longer worked on Rosie's husband. A fact Rachel had recently discovered much to her horror. *What am I going to do?*

Goaded, partly from irritation and partly from anxiety, Rachel sniped, "Maybe I will. When you grow up and face reality."

"Did you get out of the wrong side of bed this morning or what?" Rosanne blew out a noisy, dramatic sigh.

"Sorry sis." Rachel pressed her fingertips to where a pulse of tension pounded into her temple. "You're right. I'm being a total bitch today. Forgive me?"

"Of course." She stepped away from the gate so Rachel could walk through. "I know something's been worrying you for days. What is it? Can I help?"

The genuine concern in her sister's voice twisted the guilt Rachel felt for being snarky. She'd spent the past three weeks stewing over the problem that had haunted her day and night with the result here she was taking it out on Rosie. *Should I fess up?* From under her lashes, she eyed her sister while she re-fastened the bolt and ensured the sow and her family were safely behind bars.

If only I knew what to do for the best. I wish there was someone I could talk too. However, after years of their family looking to her to solve their problems, Rachel felt unable to voice her own concerns. She'd always kept her thoughts and feelings to herself; unlike her sister who had no qualms about gushing forth even to total strangers on everything and anything. Carefree, optimistic and completely impervious to the realities of life, Rosanne appeared to live in a fantasy world where everything and everyone was perfect and rosy. Although lately, Rachel had caught her sister staring into space, a fixed expression marring her pretty features, as if she didn't like the direction of her thoughts. Or was contemplating a difficult decision.

But perhaps she'd imagined those shadows in Rosie's normally clear eyes? There certainly was no indication now her sister had anything more serious in her mind other than enjoying the day.

Rachel twitched her shoulders, as a cold shiver flashed down her spine. She was the go-to girl; the practical one, the tough one. The one who saw the world for what it was – challenging and fraught with difficult decisions. She was the one with her life all mapped out in front of her. *Yeah, and look at the mess I've made of it so far.*

Rosie squinted before tossing the empty can through the air, laughing when the can landed neatly inside a plastic garbage bin. "And she scores!"

Rachel sighed. *I can never tell her. It would destroy her. Besides, she has, what, two or three weeks to go before her baby is due? With luck I'll have a solution and our lives will be back to normal.*

But why did she have the distinct feeling it wasn't going to be that simple?

Leading the way out of the shed, she muttered, "It's been a busy week what with the rodeo and the cattle injured in that road train crash last week."

"Oh, yes. I forgot. That was terrible." Sounding genuinely upset, Rosanne waddled along beside her, a hand resting on her rounded belly.

"Yeah, it was."

Far too many animals had had to be put down. It had been a difficult job and one that had fallen to Rachel seeing how she was the only vet in this small town south of the Queensland border and literally kilometres from anywhere of any significance. The moment she'd finished her training in Sydney, she'd returned home and been taken on as old Tommy McDonald's assistant. Gradually, she'd taken over more and more of the business until a little over six months ago Tommy decided to embrace his retirement fulltime. He was currently fishing off Cape York leaving Rachel in charge of a busy and wide-spread practice.

Some days her job was enough to break her heart.

The chute opened and, like a cannon ball, out shot the cowboy riding the worst, the meanest, the angriest bull of the circuit.

In the stands, Rachel sat transfixed, her eyes never leaving the drama unfolding in front of her. The bull bucked and snorted and twisted and spun around the small arena. Its pounding hooves stirred up clouds of rust-red dust that puffed into the stifling, hot summer air and drifted downwards to settle on anything and everything. The cowboy held onto the pommel of the saddle, the bull rope wound around his left hand. His right hand, he held high in the air, clutching his white Akubra.

Should his right hand, at any time, touch the bull or any part of the saddle then he'd be disqualified.

With each savage movement of the bull, his blue-denim clad body jerked and swayed in the saddle. His butt more off the leather than on.

Eight seconds.

Eight seconds the cowboy had to remain astride that heaving, muscled mass of fury in order to qualify for the next 'go round'. If Rachel lived to be a hundred she'd never understand the lure of what had been branded 'the most dangerous eight seconds in sport.'

Her fingers gripped the programme so tightly, her nails bit through the paper in small crescents.

It was him.

He was the reason she was perched in the stands instead of doing her rounds checking on the animals in the petting enclosures, her heart beating wildly, her stomach one huge knot of tension.

"OMG! Rachel, is that who I think it is?" Rosanne squealed and jabbed her elbow sharply into Rachel's ribs.

Rachel shifted further along the hard, timber seat to evade any further onslaughts from her sister. Deciding perhaps ignorance would be her best defence she tried the *I-have-no-idea-what-you're-talking-about ploy.*

"What? Sorry, I was miles away thinking about what roast to cook for Christmas dinner."

"As if! Tell it to the Marines."

Rachel should have known her attempt at deflection wouldn't work on Rosanne; the woman would put an inquisitor to shame.

Bobbing and weaving, Rosanne craned her neck to see past the fellow in the row in front of them who'd failed to remove his hat. "I knew it. I knew you had something on your mind and this proves it!"

Oh Rosie, if only you knew the truth.

Her sister was correct in one thing though, the moment Rachel's disbelieving eyes had spotted his name in the local rag under the list titled 'Riders', no force on Earth could have kept her away. She wanted to see for herself.

Who was she kidding?

She needed to see him.

Chris Atkinson. The one guy who she'd been unable to shake from her thoughts or her dreams for the past three years, eight months and twelve days.

But who was counting?

She'd done her best to erase him from her mind. She'd gone out with every man who'd asked, some of whom she hadn't even liked.

It had turned out that when she'd pushed Chris out of her life, she hadn't realised how hard it would be to push him out of her heart.

The seconds counted down to zero.

Chris remained on the maddened bull's back.

The buzzer sounded, and the flagger signified the eight second mark. The crowd surged to their feet and roared while the commentator screamed out Chris's name. He'd survived the first 'go round' in one piece. Now all he had to do, was ride in another two 'go rounds' and he'd be eligible for the final round.

And after the end of the 'short round', the cowboy with the most points would win the trophy and prize money.

"Woohoo! Attaboy!" screeched Rosanne jumping to her feet.

Rachel yanked at her arm. "Sit down, Rosie. And for heaven's sake stop bobbing up and down like a jack-in-the box. You're supposed to be taking it easy."

"I know, I know." Rosanne subsided onto the timber

bench and squeezed Rachel's hand. "Are you going to talk to him?"

Like a homing pigeon, Rachel's gaze returned to the arena and landed on Chris who had bailed off and was racing out of the way of the still bucking bull. The two barrelmen, or rodeo clowns as they were also known as, darted about to distract the bull. "I don't know. I'm not sure it would be a good idea."

"I think you should go for it. I think he's good for you. He makes you laugh."

"Oh Rosie." Unexpected tears welled. Rachel blinked them away furiously. "There's more to a relationship than having fun."

"See! That's your problem. You're twenty seven in February, not eighty seven. At least think about it."

As if I've been thinking of anything else! Rachel shot to her feet. "Sure thing. Stay here and rest out of the heat. I need to do my rounds and when I've finished, we'll go to the CWA hall and have lunch. I don't know about you, but I've sweated five pounds off me since I got up this morning."

Rosanne laughed. "Don't be too long." She fished inside her handbag and retrieved her mobile. "I'm gonna talk up some Christmas cheer."

"I'll come back and help you down the stairs."

"Don't sweat, Rach." Her sister gave an exaggerated eye roll. "Maggie will meet me here in a few minutes. We'll catch up with you in the hall."

Rachel smiled then froze as Chris turned his head as if searching the people milling about in the area between the arena and the two stadiums.

Settle down. There's no way he'd be looking for me.

*Still…*Anxious not to be seen, her emotions rioting inside her like a protestors march, Rachel ducked her head and edged along the row of seats, heading for the exit. Why had Rosie insisted they sit near the top? It seemed to take forever to climb down the steps. She was at the last three steps when she couldn't stop herself from sneaking another peak.

Her senses drank him in greedily.

Chris leant against the timber railings that fenced off the arena, hat held high in response to the adulation of the cheering crowd. He'd always been popular with the spectators; both men and women, giving good value for their entrance money, since he always chose to ride the craziest bulls.

It also helped he was very easy on the eye.

Too easy for she'd fallen hard the first moment she'd laid eyes on him; same town, another rodeo. Even now the memory of his heavy-lidded, cobalt eyes and the teasing, sensual curve of his wide mouth sent her pulse fluttering and her body quivering.

I should be over this; over feeling like I want to spend my life in his bed.

He placed his left hand on the top railing, then turning around, stared directly up into the stands where Rachel was hurrying to the exit.

She stumbled, caught herself just in time before she pitched head-first down the remaining steps.

Her heart pounded frantically in her ears. Across the distance separating them, their eyes locked.

He's seen me.

CHAPTER 2

It's her. Bloody hell. I'd know her anywhere. Chris forced himself to look away, forced himself to climb between the two lower railings and walk from the arena. Instead of giving into his instinct and bounding up the stairs and tossing her over his shoulders.

Flexing his left hand to increase the blood flow from where the leather reins had wrapped around his wrist, he shoved his Akubra on his head, grimly keeping his back to the stands.

Absently, he fished out a clean, red and white checked bandana from his shirt-front pocket and mopped his forehead of sweat and red dust. He stuffed it into his back jeans pocket, his stride slowing while memories and disjointed thoughts swirled through his head.

Her blonde hair was shorter now, only to her shoulders but from where he'd stood, she'd hardly changed since the last time he'd seen her. Still a little bit on the plump side, exactly the way he liked her. The long-sleeved, brown cotton shirt and baggy-looking cargo pants she wore didn't do her sexy body any favours. Not that he was complaining, the less competition he had from other blokes sniffing around her, the better.

That is, as long as she didn't have another bloke on the scene. But Macca would have given him the nod if she'd hooked up with some other guy and he'd only spoken to him last week.

In fact, Rachel was the reason Chris was back in town.

Rachel and the Sturt's Crossing Christmas Rodeo and Show prize money.

Frowning, he rubbed his chin as he recalled the moment when their eyes had met across the arena. She hadn't looked particularly impressed when she noticed him. In fact, he'd received the distinct impression she was rushing away as if anxious to avoid his detection.

A sick feeling in the bottom of his gut forced bile to his throat. Appalled, he recognized the emotion clawing inside was fear; fear that he'd lose her a second time.

Or worse, fear that he'd already lost the opportunity for a second chance.

He'd done a lot of growing up these past three years.

He'd had to; becoming a single daddy did that to a man.

He was ready to man up and embrace a different future away from the rodeo circuit. And damned if he wouldn't do whatever it took to convince Rachel he was no longer, a care-for-nothing cowboy.

Chris nodded to a passing fellow rodeo rider and wished him luck before quickening his steps. Word was Rachel worked as the vet for this town now and if so, then the odds were she'd be heading to the animal holding pens.

With the crowds being entertained by the rodeo clowns for the next fifteen minutes that area would be quiet and empty.

The perfect place for a showdown.

Three minutes later he ran her to earth. Resting his arms on the gate of the llama enclosure he watched while Rachel meticulously performed her inspection of the male and female llamas. He could tell she'd sensed someone behind her, by the way her movements became stiff and jerky.

Sweat prickled uncomfortably under his armpits as he waited. Finally, she straightened, appeared to take a deep breath then turned to face him.

Try as he might, he couldn't read her facial expression. Her sherry-coloured eyes were shadowed, her normally full lips compressed in a thin line. He had to hand it to her, not by a flicker of her brown eyelashes did she portray any emotion. But then, she'd always been a prickly little thing with a tough protective shell that challenged him to crack.

His eyes swept over her, absorbing the fullness of her breasts beneath her cotton shirt, her trim waist, her lovely curvy legs that had gripped his back with surprising strength. His manhood rose to the occasion, as sexual tension crackled between them.

Yeah, the sex had never been the problem.

"Finished looking?" Rachel raised her eyebrows in a mocking fashion that irritated the hell out of him and made him want to kiss her until she couldn't breathe let alone think. That was her problem, always thinking, over analysing, stressing over stuff out of her control, unable to go with the flow.

"Sweetheart, I'll never finish looking at you." He shrugged. Grinned lazily, knowing it would annoy her. Sure enough, she frowned and hunched her shoulders as she ripped off her disposable gloves with a snap.

"Unlike some of us who have a real job to do," she shot back at him, eyes flashing. "A job that doesn't entail risking your life every day."

There we have it people, the major issue that had severed their brief but oh so mind-blowing relationship. I can't wait to tell her but, damn if I won't have a little fun first.

"All work, no play…" his voice trailed off suggestively.

Her checks flooded with bright pink, her tongue darted out to moisten her lips and the aching hunger that had made his life unbearable since they'd parted thundered through him. His hands fisted. By employing superhuman control, he stopped himself from charging into the enclosure like a rampant bull.

Rachel honey, you have no idea what you do to me.

"I'm surprised to see you back here." Slapping the gloves against her palm, she walked to where she'd placed her large vet bag on a stool and stuffed them into a side pocket. Viciously she zipped it shut.

"I'm after the prize money." Strewth, how he loved teasing her.

"Naturally. What else? Apart from another trophy to add to your collection, of course," she drawled, hoisting the heavy bag. She nodded towards the gate. "Do you mind? I need to get a move on before the petting enclosures are swamped with people."

He stuffed his hands into his pockets to stop himself from taking the hefty bag from her. She wouldn't appreciate the help – she'd always been too independent for her own good. "How many more to go?"

"Five."

"No worries, then." He opened the gate for her then closed it securely behind her. "I'll wait for you outside the CWA hall."

She began to walk away, fast, as if she couldn't wait to be shot of him, saying over her shoulder, "What for? A gossip session of do-you-remember? No thanks, I've got better things to do with my spare time."

"You always did have a smart mouth," he said mildly before raising his voice to add, "You need to hear this Rach. It concerns Neil."

Her quick strides faltered. With interest, he noted the pink flush of colour flooding what he could see of her face when she turned slightly side-on.

"Fifteen minutes but not the hall. I don't want people to see us together and add us into a twosome. Inside the feed shed should be nice and private. Don't keep me waiting." She ducked into the next stall and disappeared from his sight. He could hear the soothing tones of her voice as she spoke to the animal.

Chris sighed and scuffed at the dirt with the toe of his boot. *That could have gone a whole sight better. Dammit.*

Fifteen minutes.

I need more than fifteen minutes to win her over to my way of thinking. Rubbing a hand along his clenched jaw, he walked off.

Out of sight, Rachel scrubbed angrily at the tears scalding her cheeks feeling distinctly rattled. Neil. Did Chris know? But how? Could they have been seen? In small towns like these, gossip travelled fast. She guessed it was possible someone had spilled whatever he'd seen or heard over a pint of beer in the local pub.

No, it wasn't possible anyone could know.

But if they did? *I couldn't bear it if people were talking about me. Worse, how long before someone blabs to Rosie? Shit. I should have told her, shouldn't have left it this long hoping against hope that I'd think of some way to fix this mess.*

Mechanically she went about her job then took a few minutes to write up her notes about the animals she'd examined so far.

Fifteen minutes.

No, down to twelve now. She continued her rounds, working faster, egged on by the sick churning in her stomach. Exiting the last pen, she checked her watch. Two minutes to spare. Squaring her shoulders, she grabbed her bag and trudged, head down, toward the amenities block at the western end of the showground.

I need to find out exactly what Chris knows and deal with it before the rumours spread. What a shit Neil is, if only Rosie had never married him.

A family of five passed her, calling out almost in unison, "Merry Christmas, Rachel."

She smiled and managed a response in return, envying the way the couple held hands and the excited faces of their three children skipping beside them. There'd been a time when she'd thought she could have it all; a successful, fulfilling job and a family. But when Chris entered her life and his face superimposed over the fantasy figure of her husband that dream had been well and truly splintered.

Anyone less husband or father material, she couldn't imagine.

And that had been the crux of it – she'd wanted a commitment he couldn't or wouldn't make.

The sun beat down strongly searing her shoulders through her shirt and making her thankful her tan Akubra protected her head. On such a hot day, it wouldn't take a great deal of time outside to develop heat stroke.

Her quick strides brought her up to the shady side of the shed where the wide doors stood open. Lounging on a bale of hay was Chris, flat on his back, arms linked behind his head, his beautifully toned body splayed out like an offering.

Could he be teasing her on purpose?

She dropped her bag with a loud thunk, and waited.

Chris rolled onto his side, propping himself up on one arm and looked her up and down.

Despite the heat inside the barn, she shivered, her flesh prickling in edgy awareness of the predatory hunger blazing from his eyes.

Then he lowered his eyes, a tiny smile playing about his lips.

Wow, looks like he sure missed me! Why, oh why did he have to turn up out of nowhere and put a spanner in the works? The only thing his re-appearance in her life had proved had been the depressing realisation she still wanted him.

Badly.

Maybe it's like a chocolate addiction or something. If I gorge myself, I'll never want another bite again.

Who was she kidding? She'd spent far too many hours regretting her decision to oust him out of her life. Could fate have given her another chance?

Even if it had, what made her think it would work out this time?

Chris was still an adrenaline junky, living for the moment, loving life on the road, never in one place for too long.

She was still the staid, anxious one wanting an old-fashioned life; a husband, a family, roots.

"Well?" she demanded. "What's so important?"

His smile disappeared. He sat up, running a hand through his flop of dishevelled brown hair, overly long as usual but still downright sexy. She sighed at that enticing line of day-old stubble enhancing his square jaw with a cleft which she'd spent a lot of time in the past kissing.

Rachel mentally willed her fantasies to the devil.

He looked over at her and the moment their eyes met, the clamouring demands of her stupid hormones and girlish day dreams vanished. There was no mistaking the serous expression on his face. He patted the hay beside him.

Deciding it would be safer to keep her distance, she stayed where she was and shook her head. Clearing her throat, she prodded, "You mentioned Neil."

"Yeah. I've heard he's having an affair," Chris said bluntly.

Even though she'd guessed this was what he was going to

say, the raw shock of hearing those words took her breath away.

"You don't look surprised." Chris looked at her with assessing eyes.

"I'm not," she croaked and walked slowly over to the hay bale. She sat down before her legs gave way from under her.

"Shit. I'm sorry. Does Rosie know?" He slung a comforting arm around her shoulders.

Blindly she turned to him and he hugged her against his hard angles. As before, their bodies fitted perfectly together, one piece, one heart. If only they were one mind. She cleared her throat. "No. Do you know who it is? Someone local? Or a fly-in from the mine?" Holding her breath, she waited for his answer.

"Nope, sorry." He frowned and seemed to consider his next words before asking, "How long have you known?"

Fear. Worry. Loneliness. Doubt. Myriad emotions weighted her, sank into her soul, pressing down with a heaviness that was unrelenting. Her shoulders slumped. *I'm tired of dealing with everything by myself.*

"A bit more than three weeks but to be honest, I've thought for the past year they were having problems. Every time I asked though, Rosie told me I was imagining it."

"Your sister doesn't like facing the truth, Rach. You know that," Chris pointed out.

Should I tell him the rest of the dirty mess? She chewed the inside of her mouth and folded her arms across her chest. On one plane, she was soaking up the familiarity of his embrace; on the other, stewing over what his reaction would be once he knew the truth. Would he believe her?

Chris sighed noisily, his breath stirring tendrils of her hair. "I can practically hear the gears in your brain clanking over. What's up, sweetheart?"

"Everything." Rachel straightened out of his hold, shifted away from him and stared out the open doors. In the distance she heard the blaring of the loudspeaker and the indistinguishable excited babble of the commentator, the mooing of cattle, baaing of sheep, the raucous craw of a massive black cockatoo gliding overhead in the stark blue sky.

"I think it's me. I think I'm the mystery woman."

CHAPTER 3

"What do you mean *you think*? How the hell couldn't you know?" Chris sprang to his feet and paced up and down in front of her.

She shrugged. "I can't remember."

"You mean you were drunk?" His voice resonated with disbelief. "No, Rachel, I don't buy it. You never get on the turps. You always stop after two drinks, tops." He did some more pacing, muttering, "I can't believe it. You and Neil. Shit, what were you thinking?"

"Bloody hell, Chris. Will you listen? I'm telling you there was no 'thinking' involved. I'd never, ever be interested in Neil, even if he wasn't married to my sister."

Shaking his head, Chris thinned his lips and stalked to the other side of the barn. Then stopped.

She saw the exact moment the penny dropped.

His face slackened, drained of colour for thirty seconds before a surge of blood turned his tanned skin dark red.

"I'll kill him!" he bawled, slamming his right fist into his open left palm.

Rachel jumped to her feet and held her hands out

beseechingly. "Stop shouting! Do you want the whole town to hear us?"

"They should. Geeze, Rach, that dickhead slipped you a mickey."

"Tell me about it. I was there, remember?" Rachel spread her hands.

Five quick strides and he was standing in front of her, his gaze scrutinizing her face. "Are you okay? Did he … did he hurt you?"

"I'm fine."

"What about the cops? Why is this jerkbag still walking about town? I saw him outside the Post Office this morning before the rodeo started. Not to mention last night when he was spouting off in the pub." Chris squeezed his eyes shut while he struggled for control. The muscles in his neck stood out like ropes.

She remained silent.

Opening them, he pinned her with his flat stare. "You haven't told anyone, have you? Why the hell not?"

"Because I'm not certain anything actually happened. I don't really have any proof he gave me a roofie. It'd be his word against mine." Rachel pressed her hand over her shaking mouth for a few moments, then regained control. "Look. It was Rosie's birthday and a whole bunch of us were at their house having a barbie. I had two drinks when Neil handed me a glass of champers and told me to drink up. I drank about a third, maybe half the glass then tipped the rest out. You know I'm not a big drinker and I remember thinking it tasted funny."

She sighed and rubbed her face. "It was late at night when this happened. Most people had left already. I felt dizzy and sick but didn't want to spoil Rosie's special day."

"Then I bet the bastard offered to drive you home." Tight lipped, Chris crossed his arms.

"Yes. I don't remember a lot of the trip back to my place."

She smiled wryly. "I'm renting the Ferguson's house. I'm not sure if you knew them but it's about three kilometres out of town. Too far to walk on a hot night, especially when I was feeling so unwell. I have a vague recollection of being in my lounge room and Neil kissing me. My dogs were barking. I don't remember anything else until about ten o'clock the next day. I'm fairly certain I punched his ears because in the morning I noticed my knuckles had abrasions and were sore."

"Geeze." Chris did some more raking through his hair and more pacing. "Go on."

"I still had my jeans and shirt on. Every button done up ..." she hesitated, heat blooming over her face and neck. "Um, you know, I didn't physically feel as if anything had happened. You know, no soreness, no bruises or marks on the rest of me. Plus, I was lying on the couch and Snap and Dragon were sleeping on the floor."

Chris appeared to relax slightly at the mention of her dogs. "Still have those two flea bags? Somehow I can't see them not raising hell if you were attacked."

"Exactly. You know they're the best in the watch dog department. Plus, they don't like Neil. This is the only good part about the whole disgusting mess." Rachel wagged a finger, laughing suddenly. "When I spoke to Rosie a day later, she told me that Neil must have been bitten by a stray dog because he had bruises and bite marks on his ankles. I suspect Snap and Dragon went for him after I hit him and then they must have chased him out the door."

"He can't be allowed to get away with it." Chris planted his hands on his slim hips and glared.

"Rosie is due to give birth in two weeks' time. I can't upset her now. I'll deal with it later."

"Later may be too late. He's bragging down at the pub, Rach. Telling anyone who cares to hear that he's the man, the one with a blonde piece on the side. And that she's the best lay this side of the Queensland border!"

Horrified, her blood chilling in her veins, Rachel stared at Chris. "It could be some other woman."

Chris ticked off his fingers. "One, blonde, that's you babe."

"I'm not the only blonde in town."

"Nope, but you're the vet and according to Neil, this chickie-babe has a way with animals. It didn't twig with me at first, not until now. If I've guessed, it won't be long, and others might do the math."

"I need some time to think."

But he was already shaking his head. "What you need is a bloke by your side tonight at the Bushman's Ball."

"Chris …"

"Don't interrupt." His jaw worked for a minute before he bit out, "I've got a plan. A simple one. It's where my fist meets Neil's pretty-boy face."

Rachel threw her hands in the air. "As if that's not going to make the town start gossiping!"

"Trust me. Your name will never be mentioned."

"So, your solution is to brawl like a school boy."

Face grim, Chris promised, "It'll be nothing like a kids' fight, I promise you. I intend to beat the crap out of him."

"Fighting is not the answer."

His chin lifted.

On seeing that firm jaw and the cold glint in his normally warm blue eyes, Rachel slumped back onto the bale of hay. *Stubborn. Pig headed. Protective.*

"Ugh! No. Absolutely and categorically, no. I'll deal with this problem myself. I mean it, Chris. Stay away from him. And me." Rising, she stalked to her bag, scooped it under her arm and hurried from the barn.

Dressing for the Bushman's Ball later that afternoon, Rachel was consumed with fear. Fear that somehow Rosie would find out and the shock would bring on a complicated birth. Fear that something terrible would happen to either her sister or the baby or both. Fear that Chris instead of beating on Neil would end up the loser.

An image of Chris lying on the ground, broken and bleeding refused to leave her mind. Of course, he could end up the victor and behind bars, too.

Round and round her thoughts went until her head pounded and she wanted to sink onto the bathroom floor and stay there all night. No, wait…for eternity!

Too agitated to check her appearance in the mirror, she picked up her bulky leather handbag that contained an assortment of animal first aid treatments, a hairbrush, her wallet and car keys and a tube of coral lipstick. She'd fed her pets earlier and ensured they were all secure with plenty of fresh water, either in their yard enclosures or inside the Queenslander room off the back of the concrete block house.

Taking a deep breath, she left the bedroom and walked down the hallway towards the lounge room, only to come up short on the threshold.

Sprawled in the armchair with her dogs, Snap and Dragon panting adoringly at his feet, was Chris. He waved the longneck beer he held in his hand in her general direction, took a slurp without removing his gaze from her.

Inside her two-inch, strappy nude-coloured heels, her toes curled.

If I were a match, I would ignite into flames.

"You were worth the wait, sweetheart," he said in a slow, deep voice, placing his beer onto a small side table.

Somehow, she gained the impression he wasn't talking about how long it had taken her to shower. Or throw on the gossamer thin, tangerine sun-dress with its sweet-heart neckline and full, knee-length skirt.

Raw heat flashed over her skin.

He dug about in the gap between the seat cushion and the arm of the chair for a moment then held aloft a small red and green arrangement.

"I brought my own." He smiled and waggled it invitingly. "Check it out. Mistletoe."

Rachel pursed her lips to stop from bursting into laughter. Her sister was right. He could always make her laugh. "Don't get any ideas. We won't be using it." But heavens, the mere idea of having his lips on hers shot sparking tingles to all her womanly bits.

"Is that a dare?" Grinning, he rose in one fluid motion to his feet and tucked the concoction into the breast-pocket of his white dress shirt. His dimple appeared in his chin. "We've got all night. I can wait."

With his sleeves rolled up to his elbows and the buttons undone a good third down revealing smooth tanned skin with a sprinkling of ginger-fair chest hair, he was mouth-wateringly attractive.

And he knew it.

Sternly repressing the lure of tugging him down onto the pseudo sheepskin rug and having her wicked way with him, Rachel marched to the door. Her fingers curled into her palms wanting nothing more than to wind their way through those soft curls that covered his chest and arrowed down to a place that promised...and delivered...heaven.

At least, for her.

"Since you're here, I guess you can ride along with me," she said gruffly.

"Honey, I thought you'd never ask."

"My car and I'm driving."

"Yes, ma'am, two bags full ma'am."

"Lock the door behind you, please Chris." Grinning, Rachel pushed out the door and trotted down the steps. "It's common sense. This isn't a date. And I don't have to rely on anyone else to get home. You piss me off, Chris, and you are walking."

"The last thing on my mind, honey, is arguing with you. I have other plans for tonight." His voice reeked of amusement and inuendo.

Her pulse raced. *Don't look at him.*

She looked.

He smiled, that damn slow smile that made her heart flutter and all her good intentions to remain aloof take flight.

What could it hurt to have one last sex fest with him? *I could get rid of this itch once and for all.*

The thought was depressing.

She crossed the short expanse of dry yellow grass that crackled underfoot to her car, a Ford ute with its two animal cages bolted in the tray. A few seconds later, they were underway.

The drive to the Country Women's Association hall where the Bushman's Ball was being hosted was mercifully quick.

"Running from someone, honey?" asked Chris, cocking his left eyebrow quizzically as they pulled up in the parking lot in a spurt of gravel.

"I don't want to be late," she excused her uncharacteristic speeding.

He hooted and swung out of the car, closing the door gently behind him.

This is going to be a long night. Without bothering to lock the car, Rachel headed to the hall entrance, doing her best to appear as if there wasn't the hottest guy this side of the equator prowling behind her. She fielded the curious glances that darted from her to Chris and back again and exchanged pleasantries with the people milling about near the front entrance – no doubt enjoying the faint evening breeze.

This was a close-knit community where everyone knew everyone else's business. Three minutes tops and the news that Rachel Brown was out and about with a rodeo rider would be bandied about to all and sundry.

Behind her, she heard them greeting Chris, heard thumps signalling the blokes were clapping him on the back to congratulate him on his success that day, heard the flutter of soft sighs from the women as he spoke to each and every one. There was no doubt about it, he was a real people person. He had the gift to engage with all kinds of personalities. But he always acted like he was genuinely interested.

Not like her sister's husband with his smooth charm and snake-oil lies.

She climbed the four wide timber steps and passed through the open doors, into the stifling heat of the hall. The building made of timber cladding and an iron roof had high ceilings and small windows which meant it was a cool as being inside a pizza oven. Ceiling fans buzzed frantically causing the gaudy tinsel, colourful balloons and glittering baubles that adorned just about every surface and hung from the rafters, to tinkle and rustle with every sweep of their blades.

Nothing adorned with glitter, thank heavens. Rachel knew the devastating effects glitter had on the wildlife when the damn stuff was let lose outside. She'd given quite a speech the year she'd started work here and it looked the CWA organisation had taken her homily to heart.

The hall was packed with people. Not just townsfolk but station owners, jack and jillaroos, linesmen working on the roads, miners, farmers – everyone eager for an excuse to put their troubles in a box for a few hours and enjoy the moment. On the stage at the far end of the hall, the local country and western band was in the throes of testing the loudspeaker and twanging their guitars. Although how anyone would be able to dance with the amount of people here, had Rachel beat. The drummer, no less than Snake who now ran the local pub, twirled his sticks through his fingers and nodded in her direction as their gazes met.

Chris crowded behind her and placed his hand on her waist. Her flesh simmered beneath his touch and memories of long, hot nights where they'd lain together flooded her mind.

"Better this way. A smoke screen in case anyone links you with Neil and his bullshit," growled Chris close to her ear. "Speak of the devil."

He jerked his chin to the right where a close bunch of people had turned around at their entrance. Rachel followed his gaze, a tight smile forming on her lips as she spotted Neil standing beside her sister. With a sigh, she recognized two of Neil's drinking mates were with them.

Rosanne, looking smashing and cool in a pink and white smock that flattered her pregnant figure, waved vigorously, her face bright with interest when she stared at Chris.

Hesitating, Rachel sent a longing glance towards the trestle tables groaning with finger food and jugs of ice-cold punch. Ever since the night of the barbeque, she'd done her best to avoid Neil and had succeeded. Now there was no getting away from the son-of-a-bitch. Her stomach knotted.

What would he say?

More to the point, what am I going to say? How can I act as if nothing happened?

"Stay sweet," murmured Chris. "Remember, I've got your back. I'll always be here for you, Rach."

Her eyes burned.

Will you? Will you really be here for me? What about tomorrow? And all the tomorrows after that? The questions clogged her throat, questions she was terrified of asking in case she didn't like his answers.

She stared into his intent face and the world bled away. His blue eyes were like fathomless, cool pools, soothing and peaceful. *I could look at him forever and I'd never get tired of seeing him.*

Chris stroked her left cheek with his forefinger. "You don't have to do this, honey. I'll drive you home. Let me deal with this dickhead."

"You mean it, don't you?" Rachel searched his face, recognized the steadiness of his eyes, the resolution in the squareness of his jaw.

"I'm not the same bloke I used to be, Rach. Trust me. Give me a chance."

Could it be true? Her heart leapt. Her hand found his, their fingers interlocked. Slowly, she nodded. She'd missed him so much. "Let's make tonight about us. No one else."

"Sounds like a plan." Chris glared over her shoulder toward her sister and Neil. "I still intend to deal with him, honey. And that's a promise."

"Not now. Not with Rosie here. Please."

He sucked in a deep breath, his chest expanding in such a way, Rachel couldn't help noticing how the women close by almost drooled.

Eat your heart out, girls. This one is mine.

For tonight anyway.

He smiled, the tense lines in his face fading. "Okay, Rach. Tonight, it's just you and me."

CHAPTER 4

"I knew it. I knew it. I knew it," squealed Rosie.

Praying for patience, Rachel hissed, "For heaven's sake, keep your voice down. He can hear you. And keep still. You just spilled your punch over my dress." For the past hour, she'd managed to avoid speaking to her sister and had managed to avoid Neil altogether. But she should have known better; nothing could stop Rosie when she put her mind to it – and it seemed trapping Rachel in a corner so she could interrogate her had been Rosie's plan since the moment she'd set eyes on her with Chris.

Tutting, Rachel swiped uselessly at the damp patch near the hem. Another droplet splattered on the lino splashing her shoe. Hastily, she stepped back a pace then rolled her eyes as her sister followed. There was no getting away from her now.

With the strength of an eagle's talons, Rosie gripped Rachel's arm to stop her from moving any further. "I'm so happy for you, Rach. He looks like he'd be a cracker in the sack. I wish you'd share the details."

Rachel groaned as heads turned, knowing smirks spreading across her friends' and neighbours' faces. She flapped a hand uselessly in front of her burning cheeks. "Rosie!"

"Give over. You're such a prude." Rosie grinned. "Fess up. You never told me before. Is he as good as he looks?"

"I'm better." Chris winked as he appeared, elbowing his way to where they stood off to the side, having departed in search of refreshments. He handed over a glass of punch, which Rachel received with a quiet word of thanks.

She pressed the cool glass against her hot cheeks. Fresh whispers erupted from the watching crowd.

A man slid through, two others on his heels. Neil.

This was a mistake. I should have stayed home. With difficulty Rachel kept her gaze averted from Neil's flushed face. The way his lips were twisted into a sarcastic snarl sent all her senses quivering into alert mode. He was up to something.

"It's been years since we've seen you, Chris. What have you been doing?" Rosie said.

Good question, thought Rachel, feeling as if her ears were popping out from beside her head as she waited for his response. Had he met someone? Someone special?

"Keeping busy." Chris took a long swallow of his bourbon and coke.

"Yeah?" drawled Neil, rocking back on the high heels of his cowboy boots.

Rachel eyed her brother-in-law. He looked the part, narrow, blood-red neck tie, pale-blue and white checked shirt, moleskin pants. Pity this paper cowboy had never sat on a horse in his life.

"I've been asking around about you," Neil continued. "The other guys on the circuit say this is the first time you've turned up for a rodeo for three years."

"What's it to you?" Chris wrapped his arm around Rachel's waist and cuddled her close.

Neil's eyes narrowed. He puffed up his chest. "Seeing

how I'm Rosanne's husband, I stand in as head of the family. It's my duty to ensure Rachel is taken care of."

Chris bit out, "Rach, can take care of herself. She's one hell of a woman." Dropping his arm from her waist, he stepped forward until he was right there in Neil's personal space. "Let me spell something else out for you, mate. Keep your nose out of my business." He shot a quick glance to Rachel then fixed his glare on Neil.

"Or what?" blustered Neil.

"Seriously? You're that thick you can't work it out for yourself?" jeered Chris.

Blood infused Neil's face in an ugly puce colour.

Oh no. Fight alert! Rachel darted a look at Rosie. Her sister's jaw was sagging as she stood off to the side staring from one to the other. Quickly, she snatched the glass out of Chris's hand and shuffled his and her own glass off to her sister. Ignoring Rosie's protest as she juggled three glasses, Rachel said, "Let's dance."

"Honey, I thought you'd never ask." Smiling, Chris allowed her to tug him away from the danger zone. They struggled through the press of people until they reached a small clearing near the stage. The band burst into the first stanza of a popular country rock song.

"You promised," she whispered under cover of the music.

"He did it, Rach. He assaulted you. No way will I let him get away with it."

"Men. You're all the same, never grow up. I told you, I'll deal with it." *No idea how, but I better think of something fast before this implodes in all our faces.*

"I don't like the way he keeps watching you. Rach, I have a bad feeling about him. He's acting more like a zealous boyfriend than a brother-in-law."

"Shush." Rachel stopped, glanced around then winding her arms about his neck she leaned in close to say, "I know. It's making me feel sick inside. If Rosie finds out…"

Chris sighed, lowering his head until they were cheek to cheek. "Yeah. She's such a sweetheart. When I first met her, I could never believe she was the eldest. She never seems to have a clue about the real world and she sure hasn't changed."

"You do understand then."

"Yeah, but, honey, you can't protect her forever. She'll have to find out eventually. It'll be better coming from you before that dickhead decides to tell her his skewed version. Lying bastard."

"Maybe. Oh, Chris, I don't know what to do but fighting won't solve the problem."

"Well, honey, nothing needs to be decided here and now. I suggest we sleep on it."

Rachel reared back and examined his twinkling eyes. His sinful smile was enough to make any girl's head whirl. Smiling, she quizzed, "Sleep?"

He laughed. "Sweetheart, if I have my way, neither of us will get any sleep tonight."

Snuggling closer and happier than she'd been in years, she half-closed her eyes. *Tomorrow. Tomorrow, I'll work out how to deal with Neil.*

Chris spun her around, his arms strong and warm against her back. *I've missed this so much.* Her fingers splayed over his shirt, her right hand over the steady beating of his heart. His body was hard where she nestled her softer curves and all she could feel, all she could think of, was him.

A round of applause suddenly erupted around them.

Startled, Rachel raised her head and met Chris's grinning face. He jerked his chin.

She stared upwards.

Dangling down from the rafter was a bunch of plastic green and red mistletoe.

"Kiss, kiss, kiss," the crowd chanted.

"I hate to disappoint my fans," murmured Chris with a wink.

"Oh, what the heck." Rachel smiled.

His mouth came down to meet hers.

Dimly, she was aware of the cat-calling, whistling and laughter that resounded through the hall. But as the kiss went on, she became blind and deaf to everything but the dance of his lips and the heat from his body.

Lust unfurled its heady wings deep in the pit of her belly.

She strained against him, pulling him close, closer. Images of him lying beneath her while she rode him hard and fast flared inside her mind. Her blood pumped thickly through her veins while she kissed and kissed him.

Or was he kissing her?

One thing was certain, there was no mistaking the raw hunger in the power of his touch.

"Rach. Rach!" Someone shook her shoulder roughly dragging her back to the present.

Giddy, she pushed back, her lungs struggling for air.

Chris lessened his grip on her.

The glazed expression on Chris's face was balm to all the lonely nights she'd suffered through since they'd parted.

"Rach!" inserted the strident voice at her side. Her sister pinched her upper arm.

"Ow! What are you doing?"

"What am I doing?" Her brown eyes as round as saucers, Rosie pointed out, "Everyone is watching. You two need to get private. And, I'm talking, like now. Whew! You almost had me on fire, too." She flapped her hands dramatically.

A quick glance around, confirmed her sister's words.

They were the centre of attention.

Apart from Rosanne and Neil, who had his stare fixed in the direction of Rachel's chest, they were the only couple on the small dance floor. Her ardour shrivelled when he wet his lips. She had a horrible feeling he wasn't thinking any 'brotherly' thoughts.

Bile, mingled with fury, rose until she thought she'd choke if she didn't release the pressure. By the way Chris had bunched his hands into fists, she knew he'd caught Neil's disgusting glances.

"I need to get out of here," she forced through her gritted teeth.

"I agree." Chris flung his left arm around her shoulders and turned her around, ensuring his body was between her and her brother-in-law. He brushed past, deliberately knocking into Neil and sending him a staggering pace backwards.

"Hey! Watch it, cowboy," snapped Neil.

Chris lowered his voice and leaned closer to Neil. "No, you're the one who needs to watch it." Straightening, he looked at Rosanne. "Can we give you a lift home, Rosanne?"

"Actually, I think I will go home. I'm a little tired."

The sudden stiffness of her sister's expression, sent a shiver along the fine hairs of Rachel's neck. There was a coolness lingering in Rosanne's eyes that worried her. Immediately, she twisted out of Chris's hold and linked her arm through her sister's. "Let's go then. How about we have a cup of hot chocolate at your place?"

"I'd like that." Rosie's bottom lip trembled, and she rubbed a hand over her swollen belly.

Appalled, Rachel exchanged a glance with Chris. Did she know?

Two hours later, Rachel pulled up outside her house. She switched off the engine. The familiar night sounds of the Australian bush flowed through the open window. The far off howl of a wild dog, the whisper of the wind over the paddocks, the rustling of lizards as they raced through the shin-high, dry grass. She breathed in a scent that was as familiar to her as her own reflection.

Now what do I do?

Chris touched her hand gently where it rested on the steering wheel. "I can leave if you want me to."

"No. I need you. I need this time together. Just the two of us. No one else." With the realisation came a sense of peace; of surety. She turned to him in the dark, trying to discern his expression in the gloom and was relieved by the flash of his white teeth when he smiled.

"Always happy to oblige a lady."

She laughed, feeling the stress of the past few hours slough off her shoulders. "Do you?" she teased.

"Do I what?"

"Oblige a lady." Suddenly she wanted to hear his answer. How many other women had there been in his life since she told him to walk away?

"Rachel, you know you're the only lady I ever oblige."

"What? Not ever?" Half laughing, half crying she turned her hand and curled her fingers through his.

"Since the first moment I saw you, there's never been anyone else for me. What about you? How many legions of admirers have you left by the roadside?"

"I dated but nothing serious. I tried oh so hard to get rid of you from my life, but it didn't work." Her voice sank to a whisper.

"We have a lot to talk about. I know I sure have a lot to tell you." He raked a hand through his hair. "But let's leave all the nitty-gritty stuff for the morning. Honey, I want you now."

"I want you, too. Tomorrow sounds a good idea. You know, for a minute there back at the hall, I thought Rosie..."

"Me too. I'm certain she would have said something

though, Rach, if she'd heard any rumours. She's never been one to keep quiet."

"True." She opened the car door. "Come on, cowboy. Time to show me your moves. Last one inside has to muck out the stables in the morning."

She'd reached the verandah when Chris picked her up by the waist and slung her over his shoulder.

Laughing, Rachel cried, "We need to unlock the door and the key's in my handbag."

From the rear of the house a volley of shrill barking ensued. Not the deep-throated growls that Dragon made when strangers approached but the *'don't-forget-about-me'* excited yaps both her dogs treated her to every time she came home. It didn't matter whether she'd been gone five minutes or five hours; her reception was always the same.

"I guess you better settle them down first," grumbled Chris setting her on her feet.

Rachel dug in her bag and retrieved the key. Inserting it into the lock, she smiled up at him. "It'll only take a minute."

"Love me, love my zoo." Chris gave an exaggerated *hard-done-by sigh* as they entered.

Leaving him in the lounge room, she hurried to the Queenslander room to speak to her pets. When she returned, Chris had been busy. The lamp with the rose-coloured shade sitting on the coffee table near the cold fireplace had been switched on, the curtains pulled wide over the big, double window and the four pillows from her bed tossed onto the rug. The effect was intimate and cosy.

Her pulse quickened, and a delicious thrill tickled her spine like dancing butterflies. *He's had the same fantasy as me.*

Over near the entertainment unit, Chris pressed a button. A haunting Celtic instrumental tune thrummed softly from the speakers. Turning around, he transfixed her with the intensity of his gaze.

"I've been waiting for this moment a long time."

"Me too," she admitted.

His right hand extended towards her, Chris strolled across the room, his slim hips swinging slightly in an erotic fashion.

Heart thudding wildly, she stepped forward to meet him.

Their fingers gripped and held.

In time with the music, they swayed from side to side. With every movement, they edged in exquisite slowness a little bit closer until her breasts brushed against his firm chest.

Her body felt like it was on fire.

Her blood thumped in heavy pulses through her veins. All she could think about was the memory of his touch and the magical way they'd come together in the past.

Would it be the same?

What if they'd lost the thrill?

No. That would be impossible. Not when I still love him.

"Strewth, you're beautiful, babe," he growled. He lowered his head to rest his forehead on hers. Their hands linked together.

Words of denial sprang to her lips but she bit them back. Who was she to disillusion him? Besides the knowledge she had this power over him, was headier than any drug.

Dip.

Sway.

Still holding her left hand in his, he swept his arm behind her and pushed her lower body close.

She could have wept.

His touch burnt like flames through the thin material of her dress.

"I guess you're bearable for one night," she said hardly recognizing the breathy voice as hers.

He snuffed out a short laugh. "That's big of you, sweetheart."

"I know. Maybe you'll give me a medal or something."

"No medal from me, I'm afraid. But I damn well know what I will give you." Open mouthed, he trailed his lips down the line of her neck and across the edge of her dress over the rounded tops of her aching breasts.

Arching her back, she surrendered to him. Her fingers curled into her palms as ecstasy rippled over her skin.

"You have too many clothes on."

"I'm not the only one." In response, she tugged her hands free from his and attacked the buttons on his shirt.

Chris craned his neck, peering over her shoulder while his fingers fumbled about her back. "How do you get this damn thing off?"

"Zipper. On the side. Here let me." She was up to the last button anyway. Yanking the ends of his shirt from his trousers, she released the last button then twisted around to pull at the zipper on her dress.

"Got it," Chris said with satisfaction as if he'd found the zipper all by himself.

"That's my hero," drawled Rachel.

Chuckling, he tugged the zipper down the side of her body. When he reached the end, he didn't bother ridding her of her dress. Instead he slipped his hand under the material to stroke her flesh.

Her breathing stuttered in her throat. "Not bad, for a greenhorn."

"This is nothing, sweetheart. I have some moves I haven't shown you yet."

"You sure you're not all talk and no action? You're taking your sweet time here." She splayed her hands wide over his chest. His soft hairs tickled her palms.

Flinging back his head, Chris roared with laughter. "That's my girl. Struth, I've missed you, Rach."

Unable to speak, she decided the time for words was past. She tugged his shirt off his shoulders. Obligingly, he held his hands away from her body while she pulled it off his arms and tossed the shirt onto the floor.

Greedily her hands closed over his upper biceps, loving

the firmness of lean muscle beneath her touch. No steroid enhancement here, no this was all honed by a lifetime of hard work either on the land or the rough life of the rodeo circuit.

His knuckles nudged her chin. His other arm held her tight as an iron band.

She met his plundering mouth eagerly, opening for his questing tongue, relishing the almost frantic pace of his kiss.

He pulled her dress down off her body and she kicked it away. Clad only in her lace-edged knickers she trembled, her flesh pebbling in anticipation of his body covering hers.

He didn't disappoint, in fact, he never disappointed. He'd always been a considerate lover. It had been too long. And she'd missed him so much. "Chris, please."

He stared into her upturned face. He feathered butterfly kisses over her brow and down her cheek, whispering, "I know, babe, I know. I feel the same."

When his arms hugged around her back, she smiled.

Oooh yeah, the magic was still there.

CHAPTER 5

*E*yes closed, hands braced on the tiles, Chris stood beneath the shower, enjoying the cool wash of water beating down his back. Now was the moment. He couldn't delay it any longer. He had to tell Rachel what he'd been doing these past three years. How would she take it? Not many chicks would be able to accept a ready-made family.

Would she understand?

What will I do if she tells me to piss off? I've made my decision, sunk all my savings in this venture. If she can't accept me as a husband, then I'll have to live with being her friend.

Decision made, he turned off the taps and reached for a towel. After a brisk dry down, he wrapped the towel around his waist and padded out of the bathroom.

Nose twitching with appreciation, he followed the tantalizing smell of frying onions and sausages into the kitchen.

Three people turned as he entered the room.

"Ahh, sorry folks. I would have dressed if I'd known we had company." He pinned a polite smile on his face for Rachel's sister's benefit. His sharp gaze quickly assessed the tension crackling like a downed power line between the two sisters and that jerk-off.

The smug sneer Neil was sporting snapped the hairs on the back of Chris's neck as straight as a flagpole.

"What's going on?" he asked, his smile fading at the stony expression on Rachel's face. Dragon growled from outside the kitchen. Chris could see both dogs pacing up and down the short porch, their eyes fixed on the screen door.

Rosie dragged a chair out from the table and levered herself down onto the seat by hanging onto the edge of the table. She wailed, "I don't feel very well."

Her face was paler than usual with dark smudges beneath her eyes.

Typically, Rachel rushed to her sister's side, placing a protective hand on her shoulder. She scowled at him. "You did this, she's disappointed in you."

The ice in her voice chilled Chris to his bowels. Her unspoken words hung in the air – *I'm disappointed in you.*

Shit! What the hell was happening here?

"It's quite simple," stated Neil, his smirk widening until Chris wanted to punch it off his face. "I've told Rachel the truth. I've told her you've got brats. No idea what you've done with their mother, though. But no doubt she'll turn up soon." He produced his mobile from his jeans pocket with a dramatic flourish and the screen lit up revealing the image of Chris walking hand-in-hand with two small children.

"Rachel, I can explain."

"Huh! Wow, talk about original!" Rachel presented her back to him and marched to the stove where she grabbed a spatula and hacked at the food in the frying pan.

Chris winced with every grating jab she made.

Scrap. Jab. Poke.

"You lied to me." She attacked the pan some more.

"What a load of crap. I didn't lie. Dead set, I intended to give you the drum this morning."

"Oh, yeah, right." Rachel spun around and yanked open the cutlery drawer. A spoon clattered onto the floor.

"I asked you to trust me."

"I'm such a fool. I shouldn't have caved."

"Are you saying you regret last night?" Feeling as if he was waiting to be kicked in the gut by a brahma bull, Chris held his breath, waiting for her answer.

Finally, Rachel whispered, "Maybe." When she turned to look at him, he hated seeing the tears of pain and of what she thought was his betrayal glistening in her eyes.

He held his head high. "You don't think I'm fair dinkum," he said slowly.

She broke the connection, turning back to the stove, her shoulders hunched. "I want to believe you, Chris. But this … " she admitted.

Sweat beading on his forehead, Neil shouted, "Honest to God, Rachel, it's true. You need to piss him off, like you did the last time instead of allowing him to come sniffing about like a dog in heat."

Snap and Dragon let forth a volley of barks and snarls. One of them scratched frantically at the door, no doubt anxious to get to Rachel's side.

In three steps, Rachel was across the room and in Neil's face. Inches from his nose, she said, "Don't you think you've stirred the pot enough for one day? I want you out of my house and never step foot in here again."

"I'm family!"

"No, you're not. You're nothing to me. You're the one that can't be trusted. I should never have kept quiet."

"What are you talking about Rach?" Rosie frowned.

Ignoring his wife as if she didn't exist, Neil glanced wildly from where Chris watched him carefully then back to Rachel. "You want trouble, then I'll give it to you. Your precious, holier-than-thou, sister made a pass at me Rosie. She begged me to have sex with her."

"Neil? Are you sure? Rach would never do such a thing to me or anyone else. She'd never date a married man." Rosie gaped at her husband.

Doing a good impression of wringing her hands, Rachel cried, "Neil! For heaven's sake!" Her eyes glistened with tears.

Chris' hands balled into fists at the sight of Rachel's distress. "Right, that's it. It's not true, Rosanne. He's the one that tried to force himself on your sister by using a roofie."

Rosie gasped, pressing a hand against her mouth.

"Lies! All lies," howled Neil.

Chris grabbed Neil's arm and twisted it behind his back making the other guy yelp with pain. "One more word and I let those dogs inside. I bet you a hundred bucks, they remember what you tried the last time you were in this house."

"Get off me, you shit." Sweat trickled down Neil's forehead. He struggled to free himself from Chris' tight hold.

"Rachel, is this true?" Then Rosie caught her breath, scrunching up her face. The way she suddenly clutched her belly, made Chris forget about her dumb husband and rush to her side. Rachel beat him to her by a hair and crouched down beside the chair.

Rosie panted, "Oooooooooh! I think the baby's coming!"

"What? Now?" Rachel said.

"Strewth! Are you sure?" exclaimed Chris.

"But you're not due for another two weeks," croaked Neil, falling back against the kitchen wall.

Arching her back, Rosie gave a blood-curdling shriek. Her waters broke, gushing onto the kitchen floor.

"What a mess." Lip curling, Neil stared at the puddle.

"Rach, I'm so sorry you had to deal with my fool of a husband." Rosie sucked in another long breath through her nostrils and expelled it through her mouth noisily. She raised her head and glared at her husband while she patted her stomach and hauled in loud gasps of air. "I've put up with your affairs for too long. But this? How could you Neil? Get out. I don't ever want to see your face again."

"It's the hormones, making you crazy."

"I know you only married me to get your hands on the dosh my godmother left me. You tired of me pretty quickly once it was all spent." Rose's lips twisted bitterly. "It's over. I want you to leave and never come back."

"That's the kind of spitting the dummy I needed to hear." Chris grabbed Neil's arm again and propelled the dirtbag from the room, down the hall then through the front door. Releasing his hold, he gave Neil a push that sent the other guy stumbling down the steps.

"Listen, you no-hoper of a bludger..." blustered Neil turning around.

Bad move. No one calls me a bludger and gets away with it. Chris balled his fist and ploughed into Neil's face. The guy floundered backwards, tripped over the garden hose and landed on his backside in the dirt. Blood dripped from his nose.

Standing over him, Chris jabbed his finger towards the road. "If you know what's good for you, you'll leave town and never come back."

He wiped his hands together as if to rid himself of any lingering germs and raced back into the kitchen.

"Is he gone?" Still on her knees beside her sister, Rachel examined Chris critically from head to toe. No marks, no obvious bruises, no bleeding. Thank heavens.

When he nodded, she smiled, holding out her hand toward him.

His fingers closed strongly over hers. Lines of tension furrowing his forehead and bracketing his mouth disappeared. She even saw the shadow of his usual twinkle flicker in his deep blue eyes.

"Shall I phone for the ambos or will we drive to the hospital?"

Rachel shook her head. "I don't think we can wait for the ambulance to get here from Bourke."

Chris looked at Rosie doing her breathing and panting thing. "Waddayreckon I get a blanket for your sister? If we've got time I'll grab some towels to help clean up."

"Chris." It was all she could manage given the flood of emotions swelling in her chest when he gave her fingers a gentle tug before striding down the hallway in the direction of the linen closet. Dazed, she stared after him. Far from running at the first sign of trouble, he'd manned up, taken her side and apparently intended to stay right where she needed him. Then she remembered the picture of two young kids and frowned.

"Gaaaaaaaah," groaned Rosie, recapturing her attention. "This baby is coming fast!"

"Then we need to leave now for the hospital. Let me help you up." Rachel scooped her hands under her sister's armpits and helped her off the chair. "I'm so sorry about Neil."

Rosie blew hair from her eyes, breathed through a contraction before saying in a strangled voice, "If you're talking about his tom-catting around town, don't stress sis. He's been like that for a long time. I'm the one who is sorry for what he put you through."

"No, Rosie. This one is on him."

Chris rushed back into the room, his arms laden with towels and with a folded blanket wedged under his arm. Hesitating he glanced from the floor to Rachel and quirked his eyebrows.

She said, "We're off to the hospital in Bourke."

"You go then. I'll clean up here and make sure your animals are secure."

"Thanks, Chris." Rachel smiled and wiped away a couple of stray tears with the back of her hand.

"Will you come to the hospital, Chris?" Rosie scrunched up her face while they shuffled to the door. "Rach will need you."

"I'd like to, if I won't be in the way." Chris studied Rachel's face as he handed over the blanket and helped her wrap it around her sister's shoulders.

Rachel drew in a deep breath, knowing the moment she said the words, she'd be taking a leap of faith that may well end up breaking her heart. *I have to trust him. No, I do trust him. He's a good man. I can see it in his eyes.* "Please, I'd like you to be there."

"Now, that's a date." His grin was dazzling and sent her pulse jumping crazily. He smacked a noisy kiss onto her lips and said, "That's for believing in me."

They hurried as fast as possible out to Rachel's ute where Rosanne slid awkwardly onto the passenger seat, holding her belly.

"What about your over-night bag, Rosie? Do we have time to swing fast your house and fetch it?"

Rosanne shook her head. "It was in our car and Neil's driven off to who-knows-where."

"No matter. Once we're at the hospital, we'll make a list and I'll get you everything you need." Rachel secured the seat belt over her sister then closed the door. Turning to Chris, she slipped her arms around his neck. "Don't be too long."

"I won't." He nuzzled her neck. "Drive safe. I'll secure your animals too before I leave. Rach, about the kids..."

Rachel glanced through the window where her sister was making frantic 'hurry up' signals by thumping on the window. "I have to go. But, Chris, you owe me an explanation. I hope it's a good one."

"They're my niece and nephew. Dan died in a car accident

three years ago. I took them on when their mum re-married six months later," he said in a rush.

"I'm so sorry," whispered Rachel, tears stinging her eyes. All this time she'd believed Chris to be enjoying a carefree and footloose lifestyle and he'd been coping with the responsibilities of full-on parenthood. "Where are they? Are they here, in town?"

Rosie wound down the window and screeched, "Come on!"

Chris cupped her elbow and hustled Rachel around the car to the driver's side where he opened the door. "Yep. Lou's misses is minding them. They've got a girl about six years old. Rachel, I won't abandon them. They're mine now. And I want you to be a part of our family." He pushed her inside.

Head whirling, Rachel snapped on her seat belt and started the engine. She hesitated, uncertain how to respond.

Rosie ground out, "Rach, unless you want this baby born right here, right now, you need to drive!"

"It's a boy!" exclaimed the midwife. The maternity room of the small district hospital was rent with the sudden squalls of a baby. "He's perfect. Congratulations, Mrs Turner."

Wiping tears from her cheeks, Rachel gently squeezed her sister's fingers.

"Oh Rach!" Rosie began to weep.

"It's okay, Rosie. Everything will be okay, don't worry." Rachel plucked tissues from the box on the side table and pressed them into her sister's hands. Surreptitiously, she checked her mobile. She'd sent texts to their parents and also, after a hard ten minutes of thinking, to Neil.

Zilch from the dirtbag.

She opened the only message and smiled. "Mum and dad

are on their way. They say they'll arrive here this afternoon around two o'clock instead of tomorrow morning."

Her sister mopped up her wet face. "Oh God. What am I going to tell them?"

"If you mean Neil, I guess you need to tell them the truth. They'll support you, no matter what you decide to do."

"If only it was that easy," wailed Rosanne before blowing her nose. She held out a sodden mess of tissues.

Grimacing, Rachel plucked them from her hand and disposed of the remains in the toxic-waste container.

Behind them, the midwife and nurse bustled about the room and one minute later a blue-wrapped bundle was laid carefully into Rosanne's arms. She hugged him close, staring down into the wide blue-eyes of her son.

"Oh Rosie, he's beautiful." Rachel leaned over and touched his little face with her forefinger.

Her sister pressed a soft kiss to the baby's forehead then smiled up at her. "He is, isn't he?"

"I texted Neil. I thought he should know what's happening."

Rosanne shrugged. "He won't care. It's not like he's the father."

Rachel gaped for one long minute. Swallowing, she found her voice. "Seriously?"

"It wasn't long after we married that I realised Neil was only interested in bagging the most sought-after girl in town who just happened to have inherited money from her godmother." Rosanne's mouth trembled. "That wasn't the worst thing though, Rach. Oh Rach, then he told me he could never have children. I wanted them so much."

"I know." Rachel nodded remembering how they'd played together when young. Not interested in being princesses of some fantasy castle, they'd both pretended to be mothers and their numerous dolls had been their children. Of course,

Rachel's family had included an assortment of animals, including one plastic elephant and one soft-toy tiger.

"I sucked it in for ages, pretended I was happy with our hectic lifestyle travelling and seeing the world. Then last year, something broke inside me." Her sister gazed lovingly down at her baby. "I went on line and found a sperm donor."

The hospital staff were going about their business so quietly Rachel just knew they were holding their breaths and listening. She wondered whether she should stem her sister's confidences to another time. But it looked as if once she'd started, Rosanne couldn't stop.

"I sold Aunty Claire's double-strand pearl necklace which I'd hidden from Neil. I was lucky. It worked straight away, like it was meant to be." Rosie sighed. "And here he is, my gorgeous little boy."

"And Neil?" croaked Rachel.

"I'll divorce him. There's more but I'll save it for another time. I've got a lot I need to sort out first."

"Rosie, you never said anything to me. Why didn't you come to me?"

Her sister turned her head and met Rachel's worried gaze. "I had to deal with my own mess, myself. Everyone thinks I'm this scatty, ditzy princess who'll shatter if I'm dropped and couldn't think to save her life. Trust me, sis. I can take care of myself."

"I know this now." Rachel's throat closed over the burn of emotions welling like a tsunami. "I've been too bossy, too eager to take charge. I'm sorry."

"It's cool, Rach. I like you just the way you are, and you are going to make the best aunty. You'll keep my little boy and me in line."

Perfectly in accord, they smiled at each other.

"Do you think they'll let me out for tomorrow? I really want my baby's first Christmas to be spent surrounded by family."

"I hope so. I'll stay another hour then I'm gonna rush to the shops. This little guy can't miss out on his first Christmas present."

Rosie popped a kiss to her son's rounded cheek before grinning mischievously at Rachel. "It sounds like you need to buy more than one present. I'm so happy for you, sis. Chris is awesome. Give him a chance otherwise I may be tempted to take him off your hands."

Slipping carefully off the hospital bed, Rachel laughed. "No way. This guy is mine."

EPILOGUE

CHRISTMAS DAY

The loud knock from the front of the house sent her heartbeat into overdrive. Snap's and Dragon's claws scrabbled over the worn timber floor as they shot through the lounge room in their frantic dash to the door. Rachel could hear them whining and snuffling; no barks that would warn her of a stranger or her soon to be ex-brother-in-law.

The absence of her pets' hostility could mean only one thing; Chris and his new family were standing on her verandah.

Carefully, Rachel placed the roasting dish she'd retrieved from the oven, onto the counter. Her movements jerky, she tugged off the oven mitts, tossing them near the sink.

Above the dogs' excited panting, came the unmistakable noises of children, whispering and giggling.

This was it.

Her first meeting with the kids Chris had taken on as his own. And, hopefully, the beginning of something new, something precious and the one thing she'd longed for her whole life.

A family with the man of her dreams. What she hadn't

dreamed would happen was the man of her dreams coming with a family of his own!

In a nervous gesture, she smoothed the soft folds of a cool, white linen dress overlaid with a pattern of bunches of small, red cherries nestling amidst shiny green leaves. She'd bought it yesterday as she thought the bright and cheerful colours gave her a Christmassy look.

A quick check in the shiny, metallic surface of the toaster reassured her hair remained neat and her lippy unsmudged after her labours in the kitchen.

She'd risen at six, performed her checks on her animals then over to the surgery where she checked the couple of convalescing animals, before returning to organize her home for the onslaught of her family. Old and new.

Her breathing seized as she walked to the door.

Through the shade-cloth she'd used to re-screen the door, she could see Chris's outline and the two much smaller figures popping up and down beside his legs.

"Finally," Chris exclaimed. His white flashed as he grinned broadly. "I thought Christmas would be over by the time you answered the door."

"Patience." She could feel her answering smile spreading wide over her face. Her heart gave a happy skip as their eyes met and held.

Chris yanked open the door and pulled her into his arms.

The dogs pushed past her legs and raced around the children, barking madly, much to the kids squealing delight.

Then the world shrank to the feel of his warm lips claiming hers and the reassuring strength of his arms holding her so close. She sank into his kiss, returning his ardour in equal measure.

"I missed you," he murmured when he raised his head. "Last night was the last night we'll ever spend apart."

Rachel bit her lip and gazed at the little girl and boy now squatting on the verandah floor and being thoroughly welcomed by her dogs with extra dashings of slobber. "Chris, what if they won't like me?"

"Aint gonna happen, honey. They're like me; desperate for someone to take over the cooking before we starve." Like a dingo scenting the air, he sniffed. "Smells good. When do we eat?"

Laughing, Rachel whacked his shoulder. "I was hoping you wanted me for something other than my cooking."

"Only your body, sweetheart." Chris lifted her and twirled her round and round.

The kids jumped to their feet.

Grinning, Chris lowered her to the ground. Holding her hand in his, he crouched down to their eye level.

"Kids, meet, Rachel. Rachel, meet Jim and Milly. Rachel and I are getting married. Jimmy's four and Milly's seven."

"Wow, you're really sure of yourself," muttered Rachel under her breath to him.

Chris just grinned.

Rolling her eyes, Rachel knelt. "Hi." Smiling she held out her free hand.

The little boy, Jim, transferred a battered, one-eared teddy to his other hand and shook hers gravely while his sister inspected Rachel's face warily as if she scented danger.

"Are you going to be our new mum?" Milly's smooth forehead wrinkled as she added, her voice rising with anxiety, "Our real mum didn't want us when she got married. She said we cramped her style."

Geeze, what a thing to say to your daughter! Rachel gazed from one child to the other, taking in Jim's flop of ginger-brown hair and the dimpled chin so like his uncle's and Milly's lop-sided mousey-blonde ponytail with a straggling red ribbon dangling down. The clothes they wore were crumpled but clean and their feet bare and dusty.

Their stiff little bodies and glum faces she realised contained their fear of being rejected by another woman. Her heart swelled and expanded painfully as the blossoming of love for these two innocents bloomed.

"If your uncle Chris asks me nicely then, yes, I will be your new mum. Or if you prefer, your aunt. Either way, you'll live with us forever."

"We call him, dad," pointed out Milly gravely.

"I'm sorry, my mistake," murmured Rachel.

Milly tilted her head and thought for a few minutes until a brilliant smile spread over her face. She stared at Chris then back at Rachel. "I want a mummy, please."

"Oh, honey," choked Rachel. "May I fix your ribbon?"

Milly nodded solemnly.

A few deft tweaks and Rachel had Milly's ponytail centred and her ribbon tied into a perfect bow.

"I lost my tooth. Look!" Jim bared his lips to reveal the gap at the top of his mouth.

"Has the tooth fairy been?" Rachel smiled at Chris who wiggled his eyebrows, as if to say…*don't go there.*

Too late.

The little boy's mouth trembled. "It fell down the drain."

"Well, the tooth fairy knows all, so don't worry. I'm sure she'll work something out tonight. Let's go inside, shall we?" Rachel stood up and opened the door invitingly.

"Yay!" shouted Jim, springing up and down and making the boards underfoot creak.

"We've got presents and food." Milly pointed to the two eskies and the three large shopping bags where gaily wrapped bundles protruded out the top.

"We'll put them under the tree then, with the others." Rachel looked at Chris who unfolded his body in one graceful movement. "My parents will arrive shortly. They're picking Rosie and the baby up from the hospital. She's got a three-hour pass. My brother's already here. He flew in late last night from Mount Isa. He's in the shower."

"Here doggy," sang out Jim, trotting over to Dragon, who

stood almost as tall, and tugging at his collar. "I like this one. Can I have him?"

Dragon swept a long pink tongue over Jim's face and Jim screamed with joy.

"It gets a bit noisy," said Chris raising his voice slightly.

"I like noisy."

Milly picked up a bag and skipped inside the house. A second later she squealed out, "There's a present here that says my name!"

"Where's mine?" Yelling, her brother charged through the door to join her, the two dogs trotting happily on his heels.

"God, you're gorgeous." Chris hugged Rachel. "I've got something else to tell you."

"More surprises?"

"You'll be impressed with this one." He grinned and puffed out his chest. "I bought the local livestock feed store a month ago - with the help of the bank of course. If I win the bull-riding competition, I'll have enough dosh to tide me over until I can get the business up and running."

"A permanent job." Wide-eyed she stared at him.

"Told you I was settling down." He sounded smug.

"Oh Chris. You know what I think about rodeo riding." She touched the side of his face with a gentle finger.

"Yeah, I know but I need the money."

"We you mean. We can make do, if you'll let me help. And I hope you will. I want a proper relationship. A partnership. You're a father now, you shouldn't be risking your neck for the sake of a few dollars."

He rasped a hand along his jaw. "Maybe."

"Please," she insisted.

"I guess I could get the solicitor to draw up an agreement. I'll pay you back, Rach."

"Seriously?" She planted her hands on her hips and looked down her nose at him. "I thought you and I were going to be a team."

"Are we?" His serious eyes searched hers.

Face flushing, she nodded.

"Now that's a different kettle of fish." He cupped her face with his big hands. "Rachel, you have no idea how much I've dreamed of this moment. Well, are you going to make an honest man of me?"

"Look up." Breathless, she jerked her chin towards the roof.

Hanging from a verandah rafter was a familiar cluster of bright red berries and deep green leaves.

"My cowboy under the mistletoe. Aren't you going to kiss me?" she teased.

"I never say no to my honey." He swept her into his arms and his mouth came down on hers.

Sweet, warm and tender the kiss they shared promised a future they couldn't wait to begin together.

Someone tugged at her hem.

Leaning back within Chris's embrace, Rachel gazed down into Jim's face.

He held the present she'd bought for him yesterday in one hand, partially opened as evidenced by the ripped wrapping paper revealing part of a bright red fire engine. Chocolate smeared his mouth. And covered the fingers still pulling at her dress.

Little Jim grinned, revealing the gap of his lost tooth. "I need to pee."

"Welcome to the family," laughed Chris.

DANCE IN THE OUTBACK

BY SUZANNE GILCHRIST

The plane banked slowly to the right, gliding lower over the wide expanse of flat, red earth. Fascinated at the scene spread out below, Melanie Black craned her neck to stare through the plane's small window. With no buildings in sight, the harsh landscape was as foreign to the urban neighbourhood where she lived, as Mars.

Anticipation bubbled in her veins, making her head spin. So much depended on the outcome over the next few weeks. Finally, perhaps she could repay the debt she owed to the man who had saved her life all those years ago.

Sunlight flashed off the plane's wing. A bright flare of blinding white. Reminding her. Squeezing her eyes shut, she forced back her nightmare and took deep breaths willing the panic to subside.

Her eyes opened as the plane dipped then jolted and the landing gears engaged. Across the aisle, her best friend smiled.

"Everything okay, Mel?" asked James.

"Fine, I've been thinking about how busy the past couple of months have been."

He heaved a sigh. "I wouldn't have made it without you.

But I can't help worrying over my wife's reception. And my kids? Especially Tammy, she's old enough to worry about what's going on. Hell, I've missed them all so much. I don't know what I'll do if this scheme of yours doesn't work."

"Think positive, James. Catherine's bound to take one look at you and be wowed all over again. Just like the first moment when you two met in college."

"I hope so. If only we didn't have to meet on *his* turf."

"Catherine's brother can't be that bad." Melanie braced herself as the plane angled again. After lifting her handbag out from the pocket of the seat in front, she foraged for her compact and checked her makeup.

James gave a dramatic groan. "I forgot you've never met him."

"Well, if you guys had organised a formal wedding, maybe things might have been different," Melanie teased.

"Nothing like a shot-gun ceremony to really rile the in-laws." James leaned across the aisle and beckoned Melanie closer. "The bloke's a bit of a control freak. Super protective of his sister and seems to forget she's my wife. Worse, he's one of those *I-can-handle-anything* blokes. He lives out here in the middle of nowhere without a qualm and likes nothing better than telling everyone his opinion. Whether you've asked for it or not."

"Errr, James, are you talking about your marriage or the vineyard?"

Face grim, he said, "Both."

"Well, I'm sure Catherine is mature enough not to pay too much attention to him."

"I hope so or this will be another failure to add to my list." He shifted in his seat and looked away.

Melanie frowned as she stared at the back of his head. As soon as he'd phoned her for help, she'd packed her bags and landed on his doorstep. Re-scheduling her business appointments to cram them into three days had enabled her to stay the majority of the week at his vineyard.

Under her encouragement James had thrown off the depression he'd sunk into when Catherine had left him. Melanie had gently bullied him out of his infrequent bouts of drinking, pointed out the error of his ways and hauled him in front of a mirror. There she'd bluntly informed him that no woman wanted a man who had no respect for his health or hygiene. Then came the counselling sessions she'd insisted he participate in – not too difficult considering she ran a small but successful relationship counselling service in the lower Blue Mountains.

The final result - she had James and Catherine not only speaking again but willing to spend one-on-one time together in an attempt to save their marriage. Hence this journey to outback Queensland where Catherine had taken their two children.

But now it looked as if another fly in the ointment had materialised. If James were correct, she would have to think of some way to stop Catherine's brother from interfering. At least until James and Catherine made a final decision.

"It'll all work out fine, you'll see, James. And do you know why? Because I know that both of you love each other." She snapped shut her compact and re-zipped her handbag. "I also know that you're like me, you value having a family above all else."

Even she could hear the wistful note in her suddenly husky voice.

James turned around. Concern lined his face but when he met her eyes he flashed a grin wiggling his eyebrows in that funny way of his that always made her smile. Her moment of self-pity faded as she remembered their difficult childhood.

I owe him so much. He'd always stood in front of the skinny, awkward little girl she'd been, protected her from the bullies and the meaner side of their sterile life in the foster system, comforted her when time after time prospective parents passed her by and picked another child to take home.

After that terrible night, both he and Melanie had fled the system and he'd looked out for her on the rough streets of the Rocks. When they'd found their way to Father Brian's Refuge at Blackheath, it had been James who had encouraged her to strive for an education. Even now, he was still her best friend.

Melanie straightened and returned his smile.

I'll do anything to help him. And no one is going to stand in my way.

Dirk Tanner sighed at the growing mountain of luggage *(mostly pink.)* piling on the hard-baked red earth beside the double-engine Cessna. Even from where he stood the cheerful sound of the pilot's whistling reached him. The sound somehow adding to his irritation as he shifted his stance with restless feet taking note of the careful way the other man stacked the items on the ground. Usually Ted threw everything off the plane with a callous disregard for the contents.

For the umpteenth time that day, Dirk checked his watch, and glanced up at the blazing sun. *What on earth's taking so long? And who travels with this many bags anyway?* This was supposed to be a short break, not a permanent visit.

The day was already half over and he still had the northern fences to check before dinner. A small rivulet of sweat trickled down his temple. He swiped off his Akubra and used the sleeve of his faded chambray shirt to mop his brow, then slapped his hat back on his head.

The pilot placed a peculiar shaped box gently onto the ground.

Baffled, Dirk jerked his chin in the direction of the unknown item. "*What* is that?"

"I think that's Muffin," his sister, Catherine, said as she walked over to join him with her two-year old daughter nestled in her arms.

He shot Catherine a quick look but her attention was riveted on the plane. His ears were suddenly assailed with a series of high-pitched yaps. He gritted his teeth. "Strewth, sis. Are you sure this is a good idea?"

"Honestly? I have no idea, Dirk. But I've decided I'm not giving up yet."

At the withering look in her eyes he hunched his shoulders in defence and clamped down on the words he wanted to say.

"For the sake of my children I'm willing to give my marriage another chance." Catherine laid a gentle hand on his sleeve then resumed patting her daughter's back. "I do appreciate what you're doing for me. And I know it's an awful big ask landing you with our kids while James and I are away, but this is important. That's why I asked Melanie to help out."

Sharp spikes of guilt prodded his conscience. It had been a long time since there'd been a young child running about under his feet and the past couple of months hadn't been easy for everyone living at his homestead. Catherine had spent her days either crying or promising dire retribution. It had been hard extracting any information on exactly what had caused the rift. Catherine was either evasive or too emotional to speak coherently.

If it hadn't been for his housekeeper and his son keeping his nieces amused, Dirk didn't know how he would have coped. Having them land on his doorstep unexpectedly, had also meant many of the daily chores of running the cattle station had fallen by the wayside. But Catherine had always run to him to sort out her problems and she knew he'd never turn her away.

Speaking of kids. He turned around and spotted his eldest

niece several yards away poking at an ant's nest with a stick. He smiled. Nine years old and the spitting image of his sister at the same age. There had only been the two of them. He'd always wished for more brothers and sisters but that was something their footloose parents had been unwilling to provide for them. They'd been far too involved in their carefree lifestyle which had ended one drug-fuelled night on the Capricorn Highway, leaving Dirk and his sister in their grandfather's care.

"But a stranger? You hardly know her."

"She's James' best friend," Catherine said simply. "I know she's not family. I did think of asking Maggie, but Aunt Lucy broke her leg a couple of weeks ago and I know she'll need Maggie's support for a while. They still run that grocery store in Sturt's Crossing."

"Thought Aunt Lucy and Uncle Grant would have retired by now."

"I believe that's next on the cards as soon as Aunt Lucy is on her feet."

Dirk sighed, scuffed the dirt with the tip of his boot. "Sis, you know I'll help in any way I can, even if it means I have to put up with a yappy mutt and your husband's *friend*," he admitted gruffly.

Catherine jerked her gaze back to his and bit her lip before saying, "Shush, Dirk. Will you stop referring to Melanie in that cynical tone of voice?"

"I know all about those so-called friends of the opposite sex." *Yeah, I sure do, considering my ex-wife now lives with a bloke she'd insisted for years was 'just a friend'.*

"You're over-reacting. She's my friend too and Anabelle's godmother." She sighed and added, "I admit I do feel a little jealous with the amount of time James spends on the phone or his laptop chatting to her. I can't help feeling left out even though I know they've been friends since childhood."

"I don't know, sis, sounds like they're more than 'friends' to me."

Obviously deciding not to respond to his goading, Catherine gave him a tight smile. "Do try to be pleasant." She sucked in an audible breath. "There's James."

"About time," he grumbled under his breath. He sensed the sudden tension in his sister and squeezed her shoulder encouragingly. He knew this wasn't easy for her.

"Daddy," shrieked a voice behind him.

A small figure waving a hand vigorously pelted past him and headed for the plane. Some of the tightness pinching his forehead eased at the sight of Tammy running towards the man who'd appeared in the shadowy doorway of the plane. Little spurts of fine red dust rose briefly in the air to settle over her shoes.

James sprang down the short flight of steps and ran forward to greet his daughter, who launched herself at him and wrapped her thin arms about his waist.

"Oh dear," murmured Catherine and sniffed.

Feeling his own eyes burn Dirk averted his gaze and cleared his throat from its sudden tightness.

Although he was dubious about Catherine's decision to give her relationship with James another go, he'd decided it would be a good idea to have all concerned on his turf. Hence, his agreement to house his two nieces and the family friend whilst Catherine and James jaunted off to spend quality time with each other.

At the sight of his sister's green eyes sparkling with tears as she gazed eagerly at her husband, Dirk's gut cramped and concern ate into his heart. He had learnt from bitter experience that sometimes all the good will in the world couldn't mend a broken marriage - especially when one side had proved to be unfaithful.

What else could the problem be? It made sense, his sister's

evasive tactics and another woman hanging around all the time like a bad smell.

Tammy emerged from her father's hug and with a wide smile on her face, tugged him over to where Dirk and Catherine waited at the edge of the dirt runway.

Catherine hurried to greet her husband with Dirk ambling along in her wake. No sense in rushing about in this heat.

James stopped a couple of yards away as if hesitant to take those final steps. At his side, Tammy began to jump up and down. Her eyes sparkled with excitement. "Look, Dad, here's Mum and Uncle Dirk."

Catherine said softly in a voice full of such hope that Dirk clenched his jaw so hard his bones ached and he had to turn away, "Hello, Jamie. I'm so glad to see you."

"Catherine." James cleared his throat and nervously fiddled with a button on his light grey jacket.

"You're looking well and that's a nice suit. I assume Melanie chose it. She has such excellent taste." Catherine hesitated a moment then reached up and bussed him on the cheek.

Dirk rolled his eyes. *Excellent taste – huh.* His sister's determination to treat that little home wrecker with friendliness was more than he could stand. He had every intention of ensuring that the 'family friend' was gone by the time Catherine and James returned. Regardless of what role she played in James's life.

James stepped forward and offered his hand.

After a brief hesitation, Dirk reached out and they shook. Biting his tongue on the recriminations he longed to fling at the other man, he said, "James, glad you could finally make it."

"Dirk, please."

What? Dirk's shoulder muscles bunched with tension as he folded his arms across his chest and weathered the glare his sister aimed at him.

"The girls have missed you, James," murmured Catherine.

James let out a noisy gust of air and suddenly looked lonely and miserable.

Maybe there is hope for this marriage. Frowning, Dirk stroked his chin as he stared out over the parched land that stretched endlessly to the horizon, paying no attention to the awkward silence that had fallen over their small group. *Bloody hell, I've still got those fences to check not to mention the homestead bore.* He shot an exasperated glance up at the sun now beginning its descent.

"Aunty Melanie, over here," hollered Tammy in such a high voice she could have been auditioning at the Sydney Opera House.

A dozing black cockatoo rose shrieking from its perch on a large mulga tree beside the runway. The huge bird flapped his long glistening, black wings and circled above their heads displaying the brilliant crimson-red feathers of his under tail.

The mutt in the dog carrier yapped hysterically.

Startled from his ruminations about what could be causing the bore's engine to misstep and his ears ringing from the racket, Dirk swung back towards the plane.

The pilot was handing down the few steps of the plane, a young woman who exuded an aura of warmth and gentle energy. Dirk noted with disbelief the fatuous look on Ted's face and the faint noises of encouragement he made to the woman as if she attempted a hazardous climb from the summit of Mount Kosciusko.

Dirk couldn't blame the young pilot for his obvious interest. Even from this distance, Dirk could see how shapely her legs were beneath the short skirt of her buttery yellow sun-dress fluttering in a teasing dance against her thighs.

His hands fisted involuntarily and he heaved a resigned sigh as Tammy danced off again.

The woman raised her head and directed a sunny smile towards them before turning away.

Unease prickled along the length of Dirk's spine.

Something about her...no, he must be mistaken. He was certain he'd never met the *family friend* before.

The woman spoke to Ted who then began to enthusiastically haul more luggage from the interior of the plane. Tammy reached her and the woman scooped the young girl into a big hug. Then, hand-in-hand they strolled across the red dirt, faces turned towards each other, chatting as if they had all the time in the world.

"Catherine, how lovely to see you again. And there's my darling Anabelle," the woman called out. Her voice as thick and smooth as treacle slid over Dirk's senses. "Tammy, be a sweetheart and let poor Muffin out of her carrier before she becomes traumatised."

"Okay, Aunty Melanie." Tammy ran off to fumble with the latch of the dog carrier.

An unearthly yowl split the air. "Oh poor Mister Gibbs," crooned the woman bending down. The movement caused her honey blonde curls to bounce and glow in the bright sunlight.

With an effort, Dirk wrenched his stare onto the box she carried; another animal carrier.

For the love of...not another pampered pet. My dogs are going to go ape-shit. Dirk directed an irritated glare at the woman. Their eyes met and all the air wheezed from his lungs as he received the shock of his life.

Her.

He stood and gaped, vaguely aware his sister was introducing the *family friend* but the words flowed over him like the background noise of waves on a beach. All he could think of was the last time he'd seen this woman.

Sure, it had been years ago but he'd never forgotten that day -- the day that had marked the end of his marriage.

Uncertainty flickered in the pretty, sky-blue eyes staring back at him.

"Dirk," hissed his sister as she whacked him on the arm. "If you're not going to greet Melanie, the least you can do is get all of us out of this heat."

"Sorry," he mumbled and sucked in a breath, immediately wishing he hadn't as her perfume filled his nostrils.

Summery and citrusy it stirred life into thoughts which given the situation didn't make sense. Shoving his fists into his pockets he shifted his stance into a more belligerent pose, deliberately scanning her up and down. She looked hardly more than in her early twenties with that trusting, wide-eyed look. But if what he suspected was true, she had to be around twenty-seven or twenty-eight years old.

At a little below medium height, the top of her head probably would fit quite neatly under his chin. Dirk's shoulders twitched irritably at the insane thought as he continued his perusal. She was small boned and subtly rounded with a tantalising peaches and cream complexion that made his mouth water.

Dirk watched her casually shrug the thin shoulder strap of her dress back over her shoulder and had a crazy urge to reach out and smooth the strap into place himself. Her face was heart shaped with delicately arched brows, a small nose and a very kissable mouth with full, pouty lips. He was vaguely aware that the others had finished chatting and now waited for his response. Dirk let his gaze slip lower, lingering over her full, high breasts and rounded hips.

He could certainly appreciate her obvious charms and understand if his brother-in-law had succumbed to temptation.

She was every man's fantasy rolled into one.

But for him, she was his nightmare.

Dirk dragged his gaze upwards to clash with her narrowed stare.

Tilting her chin skywards, she addressed Catherine. "I need to check with Ted about my bags. I won't be a moment."

She tossed her shoulder-length curls and turned away, the animal carrier swinging out in an arc as she moved. Her skirt fanned out revealing more of the line of her legs in such a manner it captured Dirk's gaze.

The hard metal box connected with a resounded thwack against his kneecap.

His leg buckled.

Pain shot up his thigh.

"Bloody hell." Dirk staggered to the side to keep his balance. "Are you blind? Any fool can see I'm standing right here."

"Oh, I'm so sorry. Are you all right?" asked the woman. She'd spun round and stood frowning with concern, while chewing on her lower lip.

"Do I look like I'm okay?"

The young woman raised her eyebrows and considered him thoughtfully. "Well, actually..."

Catherine butted in, glaring at him. "Dirk, for heaven's sake. It's not like Melanie did it deliberately."

He grumbled, "Okay, okay, it bloody hurt, that's all."

Gathering the remnants of his dignity, he rolled his shoulders releasing some of his tension. His older niece watched him with wide eyes, as she hugged the little dog, a ball of brown-coloured fluff its red tongue lolling as it panted in the heat. Dirk winced inwardly at the sight of a pink bow tied around a tuff of hair on the top of the dog's head. *Yeah, a pampered pooch and about as useful on a working cattle station as a snowflake in a desert.*

The dog squirmed and emitted a volley of shrill yaps.

Gritting his teeth, Dirk smiled thinly at his sister and her husband. Damnit, he suddenly felt ill used, sweaty, hot and uncomfortably in the wrong. With hard won determination, he turned to apologise, yet again, to his nemesis only to discover she must have decided he wasn't in imminent danger of collapsing to the ground. She'd walked over to the pilot and now stood near the plane, giving Ted directions regarding the luggage and boxes littering the ground.

He ground his teeth. His sister looked at him as if he had grown two heads. James, hands in pants pockets and rocking back and forth on the heels of his shiny, new, leather shoes, watched him with wary eyes.

"Let's all get in the car, shall we? I'm sure Mrs Weber will have some iced tea waiting for us." Dirk added under his breath, "Probably reached boiling point by now since this has taken so long."

Head reeling, not knowing if he was Arthur or Martha, he limped off to where his dusty Toyota land cruiser was parked and jerked opened the driver's door. Ted could see to organising the luggage; that was what he was paid to do. Dirk threw his hat onto the dashboard and collapsed onto the seat. Drumming his fingers on the steering wheel he waited for the rest of the party, ruthlessly resisting the urge to rub his still smarting leg.

It was her.

He was certain of it.

The same busybody who'd started a conversation with his wife in the hospital kiosk when they'd flown down to Sydney to welcome little Tammy into the world. He'd been pretending he wasn't acting gooey-eyed over the pink bundle in the tiny cot he could see through the protective glass in the nursery section when Valerie had marched up and demanded *'they talk'*.

The next thing he recalled they were standing in the hospital carpark and his wife was saying she was leaving him and their son. He remembered following the line of Valerie's pointing finger to a young woman jogging past and heading for the bus stop.

And to be honest, he remembered little else save the face that had been carved into his memory banks at the same time Valerie had sliced his heart in two.

Behind him he could hear the commotion of James and Catherine attempting to strap an indignant Anabelle into the toddler restraint. Then they all had to squeeze onto the back seat beside her, all chatting. Laughing even while he sat there feeling as if he'd been smacked up the back of his head and kicked in the gut while he was down on the ground.

The seating process took considerable time to organise, complicated by an irate dog.

"Can't someone please put that mutt back in its carrier?" Dirk swung round to frown at the chaos behind him and knocked his knee against the gear stick. He bit back the oath before it burst from his lips.

Pain throbbed up his leg.

"It's not Muffin's fault, Uncle Dirk. She's just cross cause she's been cooped up for so long. She'll be good I promise."

There were tears swimming in Tammy's eyes and her mouth wobbled and Dirk twitched his shoulders feeling as low as a flea at her obvious distress.

"I'm sure Uncle Dirk isn't cross with you Tammy. There's no need to be so upset, sweetheart." Stress and tension made his sister's voice sound strident in the confines of the car.

Sweat trickled down his back. It beaded under the lop of hair that had fallen over his forehead despite his best efforts to keep it swept back.

Feeling as if he had been outflanked and knowing he was in the wrong for acting like a moron, he muttered, "I'm sorry, Tammy. I just want to speed things up a little. It'll be pitch black soon."

Then the passenger door opened.

"Hello again, everyone. Sorry that took so long but I needed to organise our bags. It's so sweet of Ted to pack them in his ute." She slid onto the front seat gently positioning the cat carrier on her lap.

Dumbfounded, Dirk sat as if frozen. Her voice light and warm seemed to sooth his turbulent, bitter thoughts like beams of moonlight washing over the parched earth after the turgid heat of the day.

Her lips parted in a wide smile showing slightly bucked white teeth she turned to address the others and clicked on her seat belt, "Gosh it's hot. Everyone okay back there? Muffin be quiet."

Miraculously peace reigned in the four-wheel drive.

Warily, Dirk eyed her as she directed that warm, oh so sweet smile at him.

"We seem to have gotten off to a bad start," said Melanie. "It's so good of you to let me stay for a while, Dirk."

And from the backseat, James gave a short laugh.

"This is my first time in the real outback, so it's going to be quite a treat." Melanie continued blithely, "I've always wanted to visit a cattle station and I know we're going to have so much fun."

"This isn't a holiday camp," muttered the gruff man beside her as he started the car.

Sitting ramrod straight on the hard seat Melanie tried not to wince as the four-wheel drive bounced and bumped over a rough track of red dirt (*it could hardly be called a 'road'*) which wound its way between sparse prickly looking bushes in a raw, primitive land that stretched to the far horizon.

Everywhere she looked, the landscape was the same. There were no gentle rolling hills, no green lawn, no lushly branched trees to break up that stark blue sky. No buildings, no shops, no signs of civilisation. Only miles of red dirt, tufts of yellowed dry grass, clusters of the sparsely leaved, small mulga trees that appeared to be prevalent to the area. Not to mention those painfully spiky knee high bushes she'd already had the misfortune to brush her bare leg against. The entire land was blanketed with a heavy thick silence as if nothing dared to speak or move under the punishing summer sun.

And yet she found the quiet peaceful, fascinating even despite the fatigue washing over her and the tension headache slicing across her temples.

The glare of the sun's rays where it reflected off the car's metal stabbed cruelly into her eyes. Squinting behind her glasses she wished she'd been able to find lenses that were completely impenetrable.

Gosh it was hot.

Trickles of sweat prickled under her armpits and her hairline. Her dress stuck uncomfortably to her body. She longed desperately for a deep cool bath where she could wallow to her heart's content....and preferably far away from these flies.

She flapped her hand in front of her face and dislodged the annoying black dot that had perched on her nose.

Feeling rather worn out by the past weeks of 'toing' and 'froing' between her home and the vineyard on the outskirts of Orange, Melanie considered the last hectic few days. It had been a long trip made especially so by having to organise the travel arrangements, lock the house up and another re-shuffle of her personal affairs. Luckily old Russell who lived in a caravan on the vineyard in return for doing odd jobs was happy enough to help out with her animal shelter. No help had been had from James who'd driven off on some errand as soon as he received Catherine's call. He'd met up with Melanie in Sydney where they'd then flown to Brisbane airport before boarding Ted's Cessna.

Now, remembering James' sudden disappearance, Melanie wondered what had been so important to send him off as he was about to embark on a journey to see his wife and children.

But they'd made it. They'd finally arrived.

Here, in what James termed, the back of nowhere.

"How far are we from the nearest town?" she asked.

Dirk drawled, "Missing the bright lights already?

Longreach is the largest town and it's to the nor-east of us. It's more than a fair day's drive. I wouldn't go thinking you can take off for a coupla hours at the beauty salon and be back by lunch."

Irritating man.

"I was making polite conversation."

He laughed.

The deep sound did something funny to her insides. After clearing her throat, she asked, "Is this the Diamantina Country?"

She fielded the surprised glance he shot her by batting her long eyelashes and was rewarded with an upward quirk of the edges of his mouth.

Dear me, is that a smile I can see?

"I've always been interested in the Outback. It's so vast and untamed."

"It is all that and don't forget it can also be deadly. You must carry water on you at all times," warned Dirk. "The Diamantina Country is further south of us. We're on the edge of the Channel Country."

"Oh. Then I guess flooding could be a problem during the wet season."

"Sometimes, it depends on how much rain we get up north. Of course if a cyclone crosses the coast, anything could happen. Especially if she's a category four or five. There's a low pressure system churning about in the Arafura Sea at the moment."

Charming. Another fly buzzed about her face and she swatted uselessly at the pesky insect. *Heat, flies and possible floods. Sounds like a fun break. I wonder if I'll get to see an emu.* She sank back into her seat feeling the heat press in on her from all sides. Longing to rest for a moment, she resisted the urge to close her eyes, unwilling to reveal her weariness in case it was construed as weakness.

As if he was in tune with her thoughts, he asked, "It might

take some days before your body acclimatises to the heat. You'll need to take it easy for a while before you can start pulling your weight."

"Pardon?" Startled, Melanie turned to stare at his profile.

Dirk said in a smooth voice, "This is a working cattle station. Everyone has a job to do. We need everyone we can get to help with the mustering out in the western region. Probably only take about seven days. Ever ridden a horse? Or maybe a camel might suit you better."

Mouth open, Melanie shook her head. *Was he serious?* Visions of a female version of Lawrence of Arabia chasing a cow floated about in her head. She'd wear a pit helmet and a long floaty white scarf. She swivelled round and looked at James who nodded encouragingly.

James said, "You'll love it, Mel. Just think; no need to worry about bathing every day, sleeping under the stars with scorpions and meat ants and nothing but red dust for miles."

"You'll need to keep a sharp lookout for camel spiders too. Ever seen one?" Dirk turned on the car's fan and immediately hot air blasted from the vents.

Melanie shook her head again.

Dirk made a sweeping motion with his left hand. "There're bigger than my hand and can run about 16 kph."

"What?"

"I wanna go with Aunty Mel," demanded Tammy.

"They're teasing you, Melanie. Camel spiders are usually found in Iraq or Afghanistan, places like that." Catherine smiled. "No-one's going anywhere, Tammy, and keep that seat belt done up." She gave James a playful slap on his thigh and he grinned.

Relieved, Melanie sank back into her seat and smiled ruefully at Dirk who looked suspiciously deadpan. "You had me there."

He shot her a glance and for a moment, her breathing

seized at the laughter twinkling in his dark eyes. "Couldn't resist, although I wouldn't mind seeing you on a camel."

Melanie laughed.

"I for one can't stand them. They have the most peculiar gait and I never enjoyed it when Pops took us to Alice that winter," Catherine said.

Feeling more than a little envious, Melanie said, "It sounds like fun. How is your grandfather? Is he enjoying his retirement?"

"Catherine hasn't visited him in a while." Dirk slowed the car to circumnavigate a pothole that looked like it could swallow a town it was that deep.

"I've been busy."

"Have you met him?"

Melanie shook her head when Dirk turned his head to look at her. No, she'd always ensured she was absent from her friends' lives when they had family visiting; that way she wouldn't have to deal with her feelings of being on the outside.

"Pop's a good bloke; the best. I don't remember grandmum, she died a long time ago well before Pops brought us both back here. He's got himself a boat and spends a lot of time fishing off the coast near Airlie Beach. Always bragging about the fish he caught or the one that got away." A reminiscent smile tugged at his lips and Melanie found herself staring at his mouth spellbound.

"Does he still own the cattle station?"

And just like that the shutters came down. Face set, his eyes wary and cool, Dirk slanted another considering look over her and she froze. *What did I say?*

Voice clipped, he answered, "It's a family business."

Disappointed with his mood change Melanie fell silent. After a few minutes she lifted a hand and brushed aside a strand of hair that had blown into her eyes. It was gritty to the touch. She sighed. If she wound up the window to get some relief from the dry wind blasting into the hot cabin no doubt she'd turn into a spit roast and begin to cook.

"Doesn't this car have air conditioning?" The last word left her lips and she turned to encounter Dirk's watchful glance. The kind of look that made her suspect he hid something -- but what?

Unease tapped icy fingertips down her back despite the heat inside the car. She gulped. Her nerve ends tightened as his lids drooped lower as if he now stared at her bare throat. She sat as still as an endangered bilby.

And suddenly she remembered how he'd examined every inch of her body at the landing strip. She'd never considered herself a beauty and had worked hard to achieve the attractive veneer she now presented to the world.

But no man had ever looked at her as if he contemplated having her served up on a plate.

Certainly not a man that exuded that alpha-take-no-prisoners attitude from every pore of his skin. The recollection of those searing hot, thorough stares of his caused goose bumps to prickle over her skin. At the time she'd wanted to turn tail, run back to the plane and bolt the door behind her.

This was not a man to cross lightly.

"Feeling the heat already?" came the terse response from the man beside her. "The air-con's busted. But this is nothing. You're lucky you've arrived on the tail end of summer. Out here everyone dresses for the environment and that means covering up that fair skin of yours and wearing a hat on your head."

"No need to be so concerned, I'm sure I'll be fine," she said sweetly and was rewarded with a flash of irritation in those dark eyes.

"I'm the boss here, and what I say goes," he fired back.

Catherine said, "Stop acting all macho, Dirk. Melanie's very sensible. I would never trust her with my children if I thought otherwise."

Thankfully, the car lurched sickeningly to the side and his attention was diverted as he wrestled with the steering wheel. Tammy squealed with delight in the back seat while Melanie tightened her grip on the cat carrier. After sliding momentarily across the road, the car finally straightened. She released the breath she didn't realise she had been holding in an embarrassingly loud *whoosh*.

"Roads a bit rough, sorry about," he said.

The remote drawl so apparent in Dirk's voice had Melanie's spine snapping straight as if her bones had turned to well-tempered steel. All thoughts of her physical discomfort fled.

Why did she get the distinct impression he didn't trust her?

She lifted her right hand and admired her immaculate French polished nails as an interesting idea took hold. Adrenalin sizzled and popped through her veins.

She'd had to fight all her life for respect, there was no way she was going to let one oafish farmer, no matter how sexy he was, undermine all her hard work.

"Welcome to *The Golden Perch Station*."

Melanie fixed her attention firmly ahead as the car rattled over the cattle grid. Outwardly composed she was secretly aghast at how Dirk's voice as smooth as velvet and yet with that unsettling mocking undertone caused her stomach muscles to quiver and flutter. *Oh dear. This was not good. Nerves, that all it is....just nerves.* On this bracing thought, she lifted her hand and fluffed out her limp curls relieved that journey's end was merely moments away.

The car swept down the gravel road towards the homestead. Surprise had her brows arching high and her mouth dropping a little open at the sight of lush green lawn.

Several gum trees and clusters of woodland made up of the smaller mulga trees dotted the large yards defined by timber fencing. They provided an inviting area of valuable shade. But she was also amazed to note what appeared to be a small orchard of fruit laden orange trees running along the side of the property. In the middle of the expanse of neatly mown lawn, stood a massive magnolia tree and three or so grasstrees of varying heights, their dark ridged trunks contrasting with their long drooping thin green stems. Various callistemon bushes bristling with deep red and bright crimson brushes edged the house and down one side of the drive. On the other side grew low-growing acacias with thin, pale green leaves and an abundance of yellow, fluffy-looking flowers.

When the car sped past, a flock of green and yellow budgerigars rose in a cloud of colour to circle, squawking their annoyance in the air before settling down in the shrubs once they passed by.

"How beautiful."

"Yes it is, but most women don't see the beauty in this land. My ex could see nothing but hard work and isolation."

A swift frown puckered his brow and Dirk tapped his forefinger on the steering wheel. His clean-cut profile was grim, the square of his chin firm, the curl of his lips suggestive of cynicism as if his brooding thoughts were of a painful nature.

Whatever was bothering him must be serious for he was hardly the type of man to spend time on trivialities. Melanie wrenched her gaze back to the windscreen and looked her fill of where she'd be living for the next couple of weeks.

The main building was a soft creamy yellow built out of massive sandstone blocks and was a "L" shape. An array of various sized satellite dishes festooned one end of the roof. Wide, colorbond bullnosed verandahs encased the sides and looked extremely inviting with comfortable cushioned cane chairs and lounges. Several smaller similar structures were built close by and were connected to the main house by covered walkways.

Three windmills with huge water tanks on raised platforms dotted the lawn, their blades motionless in the somnolent heat of the day and etched high against the stark blue sky. Opposite the homestead and a good 800 metres away, were several other buildings, one also built of sandstone with a long porch at the front and the other structures made of colorbond steel.

A weird feeling of coming home settled deep in her soul as she stared at the homestead.

"Is that a wind farm?" Melanie pointed in the direction of a distant paddock. She blushed and pressed her shoulders back into the passenger seat. In her excitement she'd leaned forward so far, her nose had been almost glued to the windscreen.

"Yes," responded Catherine from the back. "It reduces our reliance on the generators for energy but of course only useful when the wind blows."

Twisting round Melanie meet the other woman's eyes and they exchanged a smile. Dirk changed down a gear and the car slowed onto the horse-shoe shaped carriageway.

Melanie's gaze ran over the house. "Oh, it looks perfect. I don't think I've ever seen a more peaceful and welcoming home. How can you bear to leave it?" Another pang of longing shafted through Melanie's heart making her wriggle on the seat.

"It's not often we do, running a cattle station means long hours and working twenty-four-seven some days when there's a problem. But I doubt if I could live anywhere else," Dirk admitted gruffly.

She peeped at the man by her side.

For some odd reason, she experienced a desire to needle him so in her most demure voice, she said, "Oh course it *is* very isolated and miles from any type of mall. Is there television reception out here? I can't miss the season's end of my favourite sitcom."

She met his narrowed gaze innocently and fluttered her dyed thick lashes rapidly to ward off his assessing stare.

"You could leave now," his voice was bland. "I can arrange for Ted to fly you direct to Brisbane and you would arrive later tonight. It's no trouble." His lips parted showing strong white even teeth. Casually he stopped the car and turned to face her, his hooded gaze sweeping with excruciating thoroughness over her body once more.

Melanie cursed the betraying heat that stained her cheeks. His head was lowered slightly, his dark brown hair with those fascinating blue-black highlights flopped over his forehead shielding his tanned features. It was impossible for her to read his thoughts on his impassive face. Not that she wanted to of course. His good opinion of her was not necessary for her to complete her job. And yet, she found herself wondering with a strange pang, what it would be like to have this complex man relaxed, those mobile lips quirking in a gentle smile, those chocolate brown eyes melting with warmth.

For her.

Horrified at the direction of her wayward thoughts, Melanie strove to keep her voice light and breezy and free from revealing the turmoil in her belly. She choked out a brief laugh. "That is so sweet of you, but I wouldn't dream of putting you to so much bother. Anyway, I was teasing."

The amused gleam in his eyes flustered her further, especially when he murmured, "I know."

Attempting to regain control of the conversation, she said

brightly, "I can't wait to see everything. I've been looking forward to our holiday."

"This is not a five star resort, princess."

Princess. Where did that come from?

Dirk pointed out with emphasis, "No one's going to be waiting on you. Here we all work....and that includes any so called guests."

Ah hah, now I get it. He thinks I've never done a hard day's work in my life. Well, he's going to be in for a surprise. But I do hope the work he's talking about does NOT include camel riding.

Car doors opened. A flurry of activity and noise heralded the exiting of the passengers. With a start Melanie realised she was the only one left inside the car, sitting like a stuffed grass turkey, busy chewing over Dirk's words.

The door beside her, jerked open with a loud creak of dusty hinges. She blinked owlishly at James who had a smile the size of the Great Australian Bight splitting his features. He handed her out of the car then frowned.

"You okay, Mel?" concern deepened his voice, his hands reassuringly familiar on her waist.

"I'm fine," she managed to choke out. Involuntarily her gaze drifted past his shoulders to encounter Dirk, his arms folded, his long legs braced wide, his expression inscrutable beneath the shade of his Akubra hat. The line of his mouth was straight and thin. He must have moved faster than a rampaging bull to gain the opposite side of the car so quickly. Why did she have the distinct impression he didn't intend to let her out of his sight?

That crazy desire to run.

Run fast and far, screamed through her mind again.

She smoothed her gritty hair and smiled at James. With a tremor rocking her legs she stepped away from him. Adjusting her sunglasses securely on her nose, she tilted her chin skyward and gripped the cat carrier so tight pain cramped her fingers, while she marched towards the house.

Every step of the way, she was certain Dirk's gaze bored into her.

She resisted the urge to turn around.

She resisted the urge to tug the hem of her dress lower.

Biting her lip, she finally reached the steps of the verandah and hesitated. There standing facing her, the hair at the back of their necks bristling and a low rumbling growl coming from their throats were four dogs. One blue heeler and three black and white border collies.

"Stand down," came Dirk's voice from behind her.

The dogs whined then slunk back into the shade near four large water bowls. Muffin bounded past and leapt onto the verandah to deliver a volley of high-pitched barks.

"Here Muffin. Stop!" shrilled Tammy scrambling up the steps. She tried to catch the little dog but it slipped through her hands and dashed madly back and forth barking.

The working dogs growled, the hairs at the scruff of their necks bristling in warning.

From inside the cat carrier came an eerie yowl.

The blue heeler snarled.

Dirk pushed past Melanie and ordered the dogs to 'stand down' again and tails between their legs, they subsided. With his longer reach Dirk grabbed hold of Muffin and thrust the dog at Tammy. "Hold this thing."

Two of the collies had their black eyes fixed on the cat basket in Melanie's hand and the other two dogs watched the frolics of Muffin squirming in Tammy's arms.

"Oh dear," said Melanie. Her heart thumped like a tom tom drum, so loud she couldn't hear herself think as she walked up the three steps.

Dirk pointed at the dogs and they slunk back to their beds. "You had better keep that cat inside the house while you're here."

"Yes, I will. He'll need some time settling into his new surroundings anyway."

"You can use the laundry to stash his litter tray." Dirk turned round and giving her another once-over look. "Don't worry, your pampered pets will be safe."

She nodded. "Thank you."

Dirk side-stepped and waved her ahead.

On shaking knees she trotted past, admiring the abundance of hanging baskets of fuchsias, gerberas, verbenas and various succulents. The shade was a welcome relief from the oven-type temperature out in the sun.

The others were busy arranging themselves with a great deal of noise and laughter around a laden table further along the verandah. As if once released from the confines of the car, everyone had relaxed.

Melanie tottered to the nearest chair, placed the cat carrier gently onto the floor and collapsed. When Dirk lowered his lean frame into the chair beside her, she bit back a squeal of irritation.

He moved the chair.

Closer.

"Can't take the heat, princess?" His breath lifted tendrils of her hair and whispered over her sensitive skin.

She stared at the table so hard her vision blurred. *Did he mean the sun's heat? Or his heat?* She didn't dare turn her head. He was *way* too close. She prayed he couldn't hear her galloping pulse, and gave thanks when, with an irritated grunt at her lack of response, he scraped the chair across the timber decking.

Giving her some space.

Melanie gulped air.

"Why do you call Melanie, princess, Uncle Dirk? She's not a princess. Don't you know?" Tammy said in her shrill treble. Barely pausing for breath, she continued, "Can I take Muffin for a walk? Did you bring my books and dolls, Aunty Mel? Can I take Aunty Mel to see the horses, Uncle Dirk? I promise we won't go too far."

Dirk gave a shout of laughter and lifted up a hand in protest. "Stop, chatterbox. I'm certain your mother will let you show Melanie around after we've all had something to drink and eat."

Tammy grinned. She sat swinging her legs with youthful energy, her arms full of panting dog.

Melanie's lips formed a small circle, her gaze riveted to the laughter lines crinkling beside his eyes and the line of his smiling mouth. Heat that had little to do with the summer sun flared bright and searing through her body. She snapped her mouth shut and quickly removed her gaze when he turned towards her. That cool impersonal appraisal of his shook her to her core. Her lips wobbled into a smile at James and she wished she had thought to sit beside him instead of at the opposite end of the table.

"First, I'll lay out the ground rules to the newcomers." Dirk rapped his knuckles on the table to gain everyone's attention. Melanie reluctantly looked at him.

"No one leaves the main paddock. I repeat, no one. All of you will stay within the boundary of the homestead and be on the lookout for snakes. When I've got time, Tammy, I'll take everyone for a tour of the station. There's a great lagoon nearby where we can go swimming."

"Yay," shouted Tammy.

Melanie repressed a groan at the thought of more time spent inside that rocking can on wheels, boiling like a pot on an open fire.

After a brief pause to let his words sink in, he continued. Melanie rolled her eyes at his authorative tone. The man seemed to love giving orders.

Melanie almost bolted from the chair like a cornered brumby when he turned his attention back to her.

"And I call Melanie, princess, because she is one – pampered and more at home with the bright lights of the city.

Just like that mutt there." He jerked his chin at the dog in Tammy's arms.

His derision chilled Melanie to the bone. *But why?*

Tammy's brow wrinkled but before she could question his meaning, the screech of the screen door opening had her looking up to see a woman approaching the table carrying a heavily laden tray. Dirk pushed back his chair and rose to take the tray from her hands. He placed it on the edge of the table.

"This is Mrs Weber. She's the housekeeper here at *The Golden Perch Station* and does a marvellous job. We'd be lost without her." Dirk then introduced Melanie and James.

Melanie rose and shook hands with the older woman who looked kind and motherly with faded twinkling blue eyes, a bone thin frame and sun-weathered features.

"Wow, this all looks delicious." Melanie smiled and eyed wistfully the offerings as Mrs Weber whisked the gauzy pale blue coverings off delicate bone-china plates of cakes, slices and cut sandwiches. *Probably Royal Albert and worth a fortune. Oh, I do hope I don't drop anything.*

Frowning she cast her gaze over the food and glumly considered her recent decision to do something serious about her figure. But her growling stomach reminded how long it had been since she last ate. *Forget the diet.* "That caramel slice and those pink iced butterfly cakes look far too good to resist. They're my favourites."

"That's very nice of you to say so, miss."

A hideous yowl split the air. Melanie hid her amusement at Dirk's wince.

Mrs Weber beamed. "Oh a cat too. Well that will come in handy. We always have a bit of a problem with mice in the summer when feed gets too thin in the pastures. I'll get a nice saucer of milk for your kitty. Would you like me to take him inside?"

"I'll do it if you could show me where he won't be in your way."

"It's not a problem, miss. You stay here and have a nice, cool drink. I'll take him in with me to the kitchen. You can settle him into your room afterwards."

"Thank you, Mrs Weber." Melanie bent to undo the cage. Lowering her voice she crooned to the wary Mr Gibbs to entice him onto her lap.

"Pampered animals are not much use on a cattle station," grumbled Dirk.

Mrs Weber winked at Melanie. "Oh I don't know about that, boss. I'm sure he'll do just fine."

"He's hardly pampered. Mr Gibbs spent the first four years of his life as a stray but he is an excellent mouser." Melanie grinned at the expression on Dirk's face, as the cat sauntered out, tail erect, fur on end and hissing a warning for everyone to keep their distance.

"That has to be the ugliest cat I have ever seen" he said in an awed tone as the animal stalked past him.

His steps as finicky as a Victorian lady when confronted with a foul smell, Mr Gibbs padded beneath the table legs. He jumped onto an empty chair and began to lick his mud-brown fur.

Melanie rounded the table and scooped the cat into her arms. "I guess that depends on what you call ugly. He's loyal, affectionate, he's gentle with the girls, gets on well with Muffin and he's really good in a fight."

Dirk held up his hands in mock surrender. "Hey, don't eat me. I expected some kind of pedigree."

"I know exactly what you expected, Mr Tanner." Her voice was cool. "Sometimes it doesn't pay to make assumptions based on prejudice. Because then you have to eat crow." She smiled triumphantly, feeling exhilarated as his expression of good humour wiped from his face in an instant. Then wondered why she wanted to annoy him so much.

Head high, she handed Mr Gibbs over to Mrs Weber who began to tickle him under one ear. *Obviously a cat lover.*

"He'll be fine, miss," Mrs Weber said, and cat wrapped in her arms, re-entered the house.

"Would you like some iced tea?" Catherine nodded towards the glass jug in the centre of the table, the ice cubes clinking against the crystal. Nestled against her mother's chest, little Anabelle yawned and her eyes drooped. Catherine rubbed her back in soothing gestures. "You must be hungry, Melanie, have something to eat. Then afterwards I'll show you around the house and let you unpack."

"Lovely although I'll need to spend some time with James." Melanie reached for the jug and poured a glass, ignoring the way Dirk's brows had met in one straight black line at her words.

Dirk thrust his chair back with a clatter and rose fluidly to his booted feet, his lean form towering over Melanie. She didn't dare look up.

"I've got work to do." He nodded to the gathering in general, snatched a handful of sandwiches and strode with long measured strides the length of the verandah, jumped off onto the lawn and headed for the land-cruiser. The others fell silent and watched him leave.

The car shot down the drive, crunching over the gravel and spitting stones in all directions.

"I wonder what's eating him? He gets worse each time I see him although I bet I know what he needs." James wriggled his eyebrows dramatically and winked.

"Ugh. Enough, please." Catherine hesitated then placed a restraining hand over his arm. "I'm really glad that you're here, James."

He covered her hand with his and over the top of their youngest daughter's head, their eyes met. "Yeah. Me too."

Melanie noted their expressions with deep pleasure and quietly finished her slice and iced tea. Pushing out her chair, she rose and held out her hand to Tammy who had been sitting stuffing both herself and Muffin with cake.

"How about we find Mr Gibb's litter tray and bed, Tammy? Then we can take a walk. Muffin needs to stretch her legs and you can show me the horses."

CHAPTER 3

*A*fter Melanie unpacked her suitcases that had been deposited in her bedroom by a flatteringly helpful Ted she organised her pets' needs, then sought out James. She found him with Catherine standing on the front verandah. By the way Catherine's hands were planted on her hips and the flush on James's face, it wasn't difficult to tell they'd been fighting. *Oh dear.*

Waving the Japanese paper fan she'd unearthed from her suitcase in front of her face, Melanie smiled brightly and walked past the now silent couple to stand on the top step.

"I'm surprised at how cool it is inside the house." Melanie indicated the wide double-screened doors behind her.

Catherine walked over to her side and placed a hand on the verandah post. "Yes, Dirk has spent a lot of money on insulating the house. Together with the controlled ceiling vents and the whirly birds on the roof it helps keep the temperature bearable. It was Dirk's idea to extend the homestead by adding on bungalows for any visitors."

Pity, he'd done little with the decor - so oppressive and sombre. "I like how the extensions are connected to the main house by covered breezeways. How do you keep the grass so green in this heat?"

"Bore water and there is an automatic sprinkler system set up. Be careful though, the water from the outside taps is unfiltered. I wouldn't go drinking any water unless you get it from the house taps."

"Thanks, I'll remember. Where are the girls?"

"Tammy's in the kitchen with Mrs Weber and Anabelle is asleep. I haven't told you yet how much I appreciate what you're doing for us." Catherine sighed and leaned on the railing, staring down at the grass below.

Melanie shrugged. "You know how much I love them, so it's not a huge deal."

"But what about your business?"

"That was a little tricky juggling my appointments but I've re-scheduled everyone with thankfully not too many complaints. Besides, it's not forever. You and James will be away, what, three weeks?"

"That was the intention." Catherine straightened and glared at James. "Sometimes, I wonder why I even bother to speak to him."

Forcing herself not to give her exasperation expression, Melanie's gaze travelled beyond to James, standing hands in pocket and glaring moodily at his shoes. "How about we have a proper couple session?"

"I'm sorry, Mel, but I find I can't talk to him right now." Catherine whirled round and stormed inside the house. The door slammed shut behind her.

Now what? "Sorry if I said something wrong," said Melanie fiddling with the handle of her fan.

"It's not you, Mel. Cate's a little bit angry about what I told her." James sent Melanie a hunted glance then ran a hand through his hair. He shrugged off his suit jacket and tossed it onto a nearby cane chair. "Maybe this was a bad idea."

"Rubbish." She waited a moment for James to reveal this

latest problem but for the first time in their long acquaintance, he remained silent.

Finally, Melanie marched over and took hold of his arm. "Come on. Let's find somewhere more private and you can practice your wooing skills. If you ask me, you are seriously rusty in that department."

James choked off a short laugh. "It won't work if the other partner isn't interested."

"Now, that I don't believe since I'm not blind. I had a great bird's eye view of Catherine's expression the moment you stepped off the plane. Don't forget, anything worthwhile is never easy. Come on."

Rolling her eyes, Melanie towed him along the verandah until they reached another set of steps. Arms linked, they strolled along a flag-stoned path that meandered across the lawn then through a small, woodland of mulga trees.

There under the shade of a weeping mulga tree they sat on a stone bench. They then spent a rather exhausting hour, on Melanie's part, and lack of co-operation on James' part, going over conflict resolution tricks. Winding up, she began a tactful dissertation on the physical aspects of a relationship.

James hooted with laughter. "Since you're hardly an expert, what do you know about making a member of the opposite sex hot for you?"

Although his words hurt, Melanie retaliated, "How would you know? We haven't seen much of each other since you married Catherine. Apart from emails and phone calls, you only know what I've told you about my life. Anyway, relationship counselling *is* my job."

"Yeah? I thought you were into anger management programmes."

Melanie averted her face. "I branched off into relationships a couple of years ago, after I did a course in Sydney. That's now my main business."

"Well, I don't think your counselling is going to work

here. Not every marriage can be saved," James said gruffly. He rose to his feet and strode off, arms swinging by his sides leaving her staring after him and feeling as if he'd slapped her in the face.

What on earth was going on? What had James said to turn his wife against him? And why wont he confide in me?

Grumbling to herself, Melanie flounced off to find Catherine then hustled her off to the orange grove for a quiet discussion. The older woman had not been particularly receptive to her advice and gentle questioning about her feelings for her husband. After a few pithy comments, Catherine stalked off leaving Melanie unsettled and remorseful. She should have known better than attempt any serious discussions until the couple had had a couple of days to relax and get used to each other's proximity.

Instead she had charged in -- a woman on a mission.

And she well knew the reason why. There was something about the rich, red earth and the waiting stillness of the landscape that called to her soul.

Made her feel as if she'd come home.

And that certainly couldn't be right. No, what she wanted was a return to her normal, life where she could forget this place and the man who belonged to this quiet, brooding land.

Hah. What I really need to do is take hold of both Catherine and James and shake some sense into their thick heads.

Couldn't they see how much they had to lose?

Distinctly rattled, Melanie wandered back to her bungalow and ran a deep, tepid bath. She lit a vanilla scented candle and flopped into the tub, closing her eyes and delving deep for the special place that calmed her.

But today it eluded her.

Finally, she stepped out of the tub and dried herself, then spent far too much time in her room dithering over what outfit to wear. She hoped the strapless sheath of thin silk the colour of a ripe plum ending mid-thigh, would pass muster.

Her hair she left loose and curling around her shoulders. Slipping on slinky high heels to give her an extra two inches, she did another twirl in front of the full length mirror on the wardrobe. *Perfect.* Sophisticated and slimming.

Smiling she left her room and walked over to the main house.

From where they stood in an awkward tableau near a drinks counter, everyone turned as one to watch her entrance into the formal dining room -- a long narrow room with a wide, heavily curtained window at one end and a white, damask covered table that ran almost the full length of the room. Their stiff postures, the weighted silence that she splintered with her cheery greeting. It was obvious they'd been arguing.

Dirk made a big show of shoving up his sleeve and checking the time on his wristwatch before saying, "At last, we can eat." His eyes raked her body with a thoroughness that shattered her composure.

Her cheeks on fire, she mumbled some excuse, but glad she'd taken the time over her appearance as she viewed everyone's formal attire.

The men had changed into dress pants with crisp, open necked shirts although to be honest she barely noticed what James was wearing. He could have been clad in a loincloth for all she cared, her mind and body too busy wrestling with her reaction to Dirk's amazing transformation from rough cowboy to debonair man about town. The superbly cut jacket he'd donned over his white shirt did nothing to hide his lean hard body but rather seemed to accentuate the breadth of his wide shoulders. The soft material of his pants appeared to mould the thick muscles of his thighs.

To her dismay, the whole effect did something destructive to her breathing process.

Catherine, in true hostess style stepped forward and linking arms, led her to her place at the table.

"Your dress is gorgeous," said Melanie as she admired the other woman's ankle length, red dress that showed to perfection her dark brown hair and porcelain skin.

"Thank you." Catherine smiled and added, "You look lovely too. I wish I had your figure."

A remark, that had Melanie inwardly be-moaning another flush of heat that crept over her face as her host's stare bored into her.

"You haven't met the last member of my household. This is my son, Harry." With a wave of his hand, Dirk indicated the teenager who gave a jerky nod in response.

"Hello, Harry. I'm pleased to meet you." Melanie smiled and wondered where the boy had been all day.

"This looks magnificent, as always, Mrs Weber," Dirk said to the housekeeper as she entered the room and took a seat.

"Thanks, boss. Well, don't go waiting on me now. Eat up while it's hot," Mrs Weber said.

Melanie murmured a greeting and picked up her glass of spring water.

By the time dinner had finished, she was wound tighter than a champagne cork.

With Dirk being studiously polite, like a host who was enduring guests who had long outstayed their welcome, his son shyly uncommunicative, James and Catherine responding to each other as if they were strangers, the meal seemed to last forever.

Mrs Weber was enthusiastic about the addition of a cat at The Golden Perch Station and spent the remainder of the dinner talking about her daughter and her forthcoming operation. Tammy peppered her cousin with questions about his horse and Anabelle played with her food. Both girls oblivious to the tension crackling round the table.

As soon as the meal ended, Melanie placed her napkin neatly on the table and made her excuses as quickly as possible. She escaped to her room, unhappily aware from the disconcerting glint in his eyes that Dirk considered her departure as a retreat on her part.

After closing the door of her bedroom, she leant against the wall and closed her eyes. *What a day. I so could use some sleep.*

~

Three hours later, a light breeze lifted the curtains, billowing the cream lace and sighing like a lover's touch, cool and tantalising over her still far too warm body. In the darkness, Melanie shifted restlessly in the queen bed with its sinfully soft mattress and crisp, cream sheets. Curled up near her feet, her little dog, Muffin, raised her head to stare at her but gave a sigh and settled back to sleep.

Moonlight flowed over the floating timber floorboards, muting the harsh outlines of the solid timber furniture. It would have been a beautiful room if there had been more colour. In fact the whole house, in Melanie's opinion needed more colour.

More warmth.

With its stark white walls, brooding dark furniture stiffly arranged and the heavy brocade curtains wreathing the rooms in shadow, the house fairly screamed out for a makeover. Melanie's hands itched to bring the house to life.

She couldn't help but think how the house mirrored its owner.

Melanie kicked irritably at the sheets wound round her ankles and Muffin growled her irritation at being dislodged. The dog jumped off the bed and lay down in her basket positioned next to Mr Gibbs who was worn out from his travels.

Drat the man. Melanie glared into the darkness. She was spending far too much time thinking about him. Reaching over, she lifted her mobile phone from the bedside table to check the time. Almost midnight and the heat was only now beginning to leech from the baked earth and dissipate into the depths of the night. The soft scents of the outback drifted into the room on the back of the breeze. She filled her lungs deeply with the clean unique scent and willed herself to relax.

It was no use.

She was far too tense.

Her mind teemed with splintered thoughts, random snippets of conversations and the events of the day. She knew the longer she lay there ignoring her stress, the longer it would take her to fall asleep.

Decision made, she rose and crossed the room to the oak chest of drawers to rummage amongst its contents. Soon she was attired in a pair of candy pink spandex shorts and a wispy-thin, white cotton tank top. Her hand had hesitated over her bra but she cast it back in the drawer. It was far too hot for such constriction and besides no-one would see her. She thrust her feet into a pair of well-worn volleys.

The French doors were already open and led from her bedroom directly onto the verandah. After ordering her little dog to 'stay', Melanie left her room as quietly as possible then tip-toed along the timber decked pergola.

She stepped onto the grass and headed towards the orange grove. Above her, the stars hung like glistening diamonds pinned to black velvet. Laughing softly, she marvelled at how close they looked and raised her hands as if to reach out and grasp them. Her hair lifted off her neck in the light breeze.

An amazing feeling of freedom flooded her mind. She tossed her head and broke into a run, skipping over the uneven ground, arms outstretched. The scent of citris mixed with a richer, older smell of deep, primitive earth filled her nostrils as she ran beneath the trees.

She stopped in a small clearing, her breasts rising and falling with her rapid breathing, her heart slowing its race.

She stood for a few moments with her eyes closed, listening to the sounds of the small nocturnal creatures, revelling in the wildness which pulsed an age old urge through her veins. She swore she could feel the heart of this ancient land beating beneath her feet.

Flexing her fingers, she jiggled her arms and legs to loosen the muscles. Then, taking a deep breath she raised her arms skyward and with practiced ease flowed fluidly into the first of her exercises *'Grasp the Sparrows Tail'*. Her mind emptied of everything bar her concentration on her movements and tenor of her breathing, as effortlessly she went through the motions of her routine. It wasn't until she neared the end and was performing the movements of *'Drawing the bow to shoot the tiger'* that she became once more aware of her surroundings. Automatically her body flowed into the final positions, while pin pricks of sensation tickled her spine.

She was not alone.

Someone watched her.

The clearing where she stood was awash in moonlight. The shadows were deep beneath the branches of the orange trees. The leaves above her rustled as a light breeze lazily stirred the branches.

The world had ceased to move.

Even the small night creatures had fallen silent.

Perhaps it had not been such a good idea to come out here in the darkness of the night. She glanced in the direction of the homestead but its outlines could barely be seen at this distance. All she could see was yellow light from three windows. How far would sound travel? Would they hear her yell for help?

And if it was her imagination, she could just imagine Dirk's derision with her panic over nothing.

Her stomach turned over and churned with anxiety. Goose bumps rippled over her skin. She bit her lower lip as she wrestled with her desire to open her mouth and scream blue murder.

It could be some kind of animal....a feral pig with huge tusks that would gore out her intestines? Were there dingoes here? Would they attack a human? This was their territory and it would be only natural for an animal to defend what it thinks is his.

Or could it be something worse?

The crack of a dry branch underfoot made her jump and the very person she'd been attempting to block from her thoughts, stepped out from the shadows.

"Sorry, princess. I hope I haven't scared you."

"What are you doing out here?" she hissed. *Apart from spying on me.*

Dirk held something up in his hand and moonlight glinted off a bottle. "Having a cold one before I hit the sack. Why are you out here dancing? Which by the way was very sexy. I certainly appreciated it."

His deep, amused voice plucked at tiny strings inside her belly making her muscles all tight and tingly. She moistened suddenly dry lips and as casually as possible mumbled, "It wasn't for your benefit. And for your information it's not a dance, it's tai chi."

"No matter, the end result was still the same."

The innuendo in his voice made her body turn molten. Melanie forced herself to re-trace her steps, her breath catching in her throat, her mind begging her to run.

He walked closer until he strolled beside her. "Having trouble sleeping, princess?"

"It's just a very hot night."

"True. It should cool down a little soon. Wait, please." His hand on her arm stopped her march back to her room. "Why did you come here?"

And somehow she knew he was not referring to her exercise. She shrugged off his touch. "You know why. I'm looking after the girls while James and Catherine take a break together. With Mrs Weber heading off to her daughter's, you'll need someone here or your cattle station will grind to a halt."

"Tsk, tsk." Dirk clicked his tongue in an irritable fashion. "That's not what I'm talking about as I'm sure you already know. I won't let my sister be hurt, Melanie."

Where was this coming from? Melanie sucked in a breath and fixed her hands on her hips. "I have no intention of hurting her or anyone."

"No? But you can't deny how close a friend you are with her husband."

"Why would I? James and I have been friends since we were kids. I'm Catherine's friend too." No need to explain any further she decided. It was none of his business.

"Are you certain? I've watched you and James together and there's a closeness there that's a bit too warm and intimate for *'friends'*."

"What the hell are you driving at?"

"It wouldn't be the first time, friends turn into lovers. I've had first-hand experience at the so-called, *we're just good friends*, bullshit. My ex-wife now lives with one."

Certain steam was rising from her ears Melanie said through clenched teeth, "I'm not your ex-wife."

"Finally a truthful statement."

Melanie poked a finger on his chest to emphasise each word. "I...do...not...lie."

"And I don't know you well enough to accept you're telling the truth. But I'm warning you, princess. I'll be watching your every move. You will *not* ruin my sister's life like you ruined mine."

Dumbfounded, Melanie gaped as he stalked off.

It felt like forever until her mind bade her legs to move. Head whirling she stumbled along a flagstone path. When she reached the relative haven of the paved covered breezeway connecting the guest wing with the main house, she broke into a sprint raced along the verandah and flung through the French doors latching them securely behind her.

Heart pounding, palms flattened seeking reassurance of a barrier between herself and Dirk's crazy words, she pressed her face against the glass and peered into the night.

But he was gone.

What was he talking about? As far as she was aware, she'd never met his wife. And as for his insinuation she was angling for an affair with James! That thought made her feel distinctly creeped out as if she'd been accused of lusting after her brother.

Troubled Melanie moved away from the doors and cast herself onto the bed, drawing the sheet up to her neck. She stared wide-eyed at the patterns the faint light from the full moon cast across the ceiling.

Rolling onto her side, Melanie pounded her pillow with her fist. She didn't think she would ever sleep again.

CHAPTER 4

A truce was declared by all the next day, mainly engendered by Melanie and her fierce determination not to let all her hard work be sabotaged. And rather surprisingly, by Dirk who displayed a courteous manner at the breakfast table before leaving the house.

Long hours lying staring into the darkness the night before had hardened Melanie's resolve.

She would rekindle James' marriage.

Then as soon as she'd returned home, she'd do something about her longing for a family of her own. She'd join those dating sites her friends where always onto her about and maybe some bushwalking groups. She'd be bound to meet a nice, considerate, kind bloke if she really made an effort at putting herself out there. And if that bloke happened to have dark hair and eyes like hot chocolate, then she for one would not complain.

She'd also come to the conclusion that the failure of Dirk's own marriage had made him more suspicious than most men in relation to her role. Really, she couldn't blame him. He'd obviously loved his wife and found it hard that she had left him for another man.

And when she had a spare moment, she'd find out why he was under the impression she'd ruined his life.

After helping Mrs Weber clear away lunch, she sought out Catherine and found her on the verandah reading a romance novel and sipping iced tea.

"Catherine, I'd like to lighten the mood of your house. Do you mind if I make some improvements?"

Curious, the other woman laid down her book. "Like what?"

Melanie waved a hand in the air. "Oh, just some cushions and a few throw rugs to brighten up the main living room. I found them shoved in the back of the linen press. I thought I'd also take down those heavy brocade curtains. They make the room appear hot and stifled."

"I'd forgotten how you're into all that feng shui stuff." Catherine smiled. "It's Dirk's house really, not mine. Although I have a smaller portion of shares in the station just like Dirk has shares in the vineyard but here, this is my brother's domain."

"Do you think he'll mind? Perhaps I should wait."

"No, don't wait, I'm sure he'll love whatever you do." Catherine grinned as if her thoughts pleased her.

Melanie narrowed her eyes in sudden suspicion. "Why are you smiling like that?"

"Like what?"

"Like a cat with a saucer of cream," Melanie said dryly.

Catherine laughed and waved her book in the air. "Sorry, it's nothing really. Reading romances, gives me all sorts of crazy ideas."

"Now, that sounds promising. How about we discuss these ideas?"

"No way. But I will tell you this, Mel, my husband is going to be very happy."

Melanie laughed as Catherine pulled a suggestive face.

Apparently whatever had upset Catherine yesterday wasn't an issue today; or perhaps she'd moved past it.

"Do you realise how strange it is that you've never met my brother before now?"

"I guess our paths never crossed."

"Mmmm. I can't help feeling that was for the best." A broad grin on her face, Catherine sat up and swung her legs to the floor.

Puzzled Melanie slanted a look at her friend who merely smiled. "I'll see if Tammy and Anabelle would like to help. Where are they?"

"That's a great idea. They're with James playing on the swings." Catherine placed her book on the chair and stood. "Let's find them. And if you wouldn't mind keeping them amused for a few hours that would be wonderful. I feel a need to spend some one-on-one time with my hubby."

Inwardly rubbing her hands in glee, Melanie called Muffin who'd been sniffing at the dogs' empty feed bowls. Together they all strolled along the verandah and down over the soft grass.

Leaving Catherine and James alone, Melanie herded the girls back inside the house. Ably assisted by a giggling Tammy and a not particularly helpful Anabelle, Melanie hauled down the thick brocade curtains, leaving the heavy cream lace in place. She re-arranged the furniture into small groupings of comfortable chairs and tables. With her helpers, she threw gaily patterned shawls and cushions over sofas, with no thought to symmetry. Laughing they unpacked the girls' toy boxes and placed them with their overflowing contents on the play rugs they had brought with them. A task that took some considerable time, as Anabelle wanted to thoroughly examine each toy. And chew it.

Next, Melanie tacked some of the girls' brightly coloured art works to the walls. She sat back on her heels and admired the effect. With Muffin's toys and rug added the room was transformed. It exuded that 'lived-in' air of a true home.

They spent an hour or so playing *'barbies'* before Catherine strolled into the room to shoo the girls off for their bath.

Melanie headed off to her bedroom where she loitered near her open French doors, until the rattle and roar of Dirk's car sent her racing back to the living room. Grabbing a magazine, she curled up in an armchair and held it close to her face, giving an excellent impression of indolence and unconcern. Muffin raced to the front door, yapping at the dogs whose claws scrabbled over the floorboards as they headed for their bowls. Next, came the sound of boots being kicked off and the front door closing.

"Evening," said Dirk. "Well, you've certainly been busy."

Pretending surprise, Melanie peeped over the top of the magazine, braced for his response. Dirk stood silent for several minutes gazing his full at the main living area before inclining his head slightly and padding off in his socked feet in the direction of his rooms without uttering another comment. He'd looked tired with dirt smudging his face and staining his clothes following a long day toiling under the broiling sun, doing who knew what with his cows.

She refused to admit to herself how much she wanted his approval.

And how fascinated she was about this life he led. She longed to trail after him and pepper him with questions but she restrained herself.

Instead, she wandered off to the kitchen to tend to her pets and assist Mrs Weber.

At dinner that night Dirk embarked on an easy discourse about the art exhibition that featured works from prominent past and present outback artists and was currently on show in the State Art Gallery in Brisbane. He kept the conversational ball rolling smoothly from one innocuous topic to another not allowing a hint of discord to disrupt the table.

Not that it was needed for Catherine and James kept exchanging melting glances and held each other's hand under the table. A fact Melanie had discovered when she dropped her napkin onto the floor and had to retrieve it. She excused herself early again only to spend the night tossing and turning, beset by strange dreams in which Dirk loomed like a ghostly presence.

Her eyes heavy from lack of sleep she staggered into the breakfast room the next morning after letting Muffin out to do her business on the grass. Mr Gibbs streaked past her and on into the kitchen. No doubt heading for his saucer of milk.

One hand covering her mouth as she stifled a yawn Melanie blinked at the other occupant of the octangular shaped room. *Dirk.*

Not expecting anyone else to be up at such an early hour, she had dragged on a short peasant skirt in a bright sky blue that hung low over her hips and a tiny white anglaise top with thin straps.

Those chocolate brown eyes of his after lingering several agonisingly slow heartbeats on her dishevelled hair curling about her shoulders zeroed onto her exposed midriff and stayed locked on the indent of her belly button where a paste purple gem glittered.

Melanie poised like a deer transfixed by headlights, her gaze on his tanned face, her ribs constricting her lungs until she could barely breathe. His lips parted. The tip of his tongue darted out and slowly licked his lower lip.

The silence lengthened.

Time ceased.

Through the open French doors and into the small room

heat pulsed. Outside dawn was breaking over the horizon in a riotous cauldron of pink, orange and gold. Shafts of sunlight lanced across the earth duelling and vanquishing the shadows of the night.

The raucous cries of a lone crow echoed eerily as the cycle of an outback day stirred once more into life. From the yard beyond, an excited yapping erupted.

Dirk lowered his gaze to his empty plate.

"I'd keep an eye on that dog of yours, princess. You won't want it to go wandering off and get attacked by a dingo. Although it's more likely to get lost and I have better things to do with my time than waste it searching for your fluff ball."

As if liberated from a spell, Melanie released the breath she'd been holding and flittered like a wary butterfly over to the sideboard. For one long bewildering minute, she had entertained the strangest image of holding his face close so she could feel his tongue delve over the contours of her belly.

"Muffin never goes far from my side." Her hand shook as she lifted the silver lids to peer blindly at the contents of the dishes. An aroma of freshly fried bacon hit her nostrils and her stomach rumbled.

Mortified at her body's wayward reactions, her mind a morass of confusion she kept her back to him and refused to turn around when his footsteps padded up behind her. She almost leapt out of her skin, when hard warm fingers trailed her lower back across the top of her skirt before falling away.

"You sure are jumpy princess. Anything I can do to help?"

The lid slid from her boneless hand to clatter onto the polished teak surface. His soft chuckle dark and deep stirred the tendrils of her hair. Then he was gone. The quiet click of the screen door heralded his departure.

"Is everything okay, miss?" Mrs Weber said as she bustled through the doorway with a tray of steaming pots of tea and coffee. Tail wagging, Muffin pranced about her heels.

"Yes, thank you. Here let me help you." Melanie hastened

to her side and took charge of the tray. The older woman nodded and departed.

After lowering the tray onto the sideboard, Melanie tottered to a nearby chair for support and fought to regain her composure. She flapped a napkin in front of her face waiting for those quivery feelings to subside. *Talk about smoulder.*

But what was he up to? One minute warning her away from his sister and brother-in law and the other flirting with her like there was no tomorrow. Maybe this was part of a plot. Rattle her nerves confuse her with his intentions, while secretly working on getting her on the first plane out of here. For who knew what reason.

Well, I'm not going anywhere until I've done the best I can to help my friends.

On this invigorating decision she bounced out of the chair and lavishly helped herself to the food. She was warned now and there was no way she'd fall for any of his tricks. In record time she demolished her breakfast, her mind busy with planning her next move.

Over the next few days, a rough routine soon emerged. Each morning Dirk would disappear with his stockmen and not return until late in the day. After breakfast, the girls had riding lessons on a small fat pony. Dirk had allocated this job to his son and it was obvious to Melanie how much Harry enjoyed the role of instructor.

Under Catherine and James' watchful eyes, Harry would lead the pony around the small paddock closest to the homestead with one hand on the lead and the other holding tight to a clutch of Tammy's clothing on her back. For Anabelle he mounted the pony and held the little girl clasped to his chest while she squealed and shrieked with delight.

Sometimes Melanie watched for a while then returned to the house where she helped Mrs Weber to clear up the kitchen before loading up the washing machine. After her arrival she had sought out Mrs Weber and offered her assistance.

Together with Catherine, she now helped as much as Mrs Weber allowed with Melanie taking on the task of attending the needs of the dogs and Mr Gibbs.

Afterwards she spent some time reviewing her case notes and studying her texts, then took an hour of alone time performing her tai chi routine in the sanctity of her room. It would have been lovely to breathe the scented air of the orange grove but she had no intention of risking a repeat occurrence of that first night.

In the afternoon, when Anabelle was down for a nap and Tammy was busy playing with her dolls in the living room (which somehow often involved Mr Gibbs being dressed in baby's clothes), Melanie would hold a group session with James and Catherine. The first one had been gruelling, with both of them unresponsive and she had begun to despair at ever making progress when after one of the longest hours she had ever experienced, Catherine had suddenly burst into tears. An action which had James bounding to his feet and taking her into his arms, incoherently babbling his apologies. Melanie had gathered her folders hugging them to her chest and hurried away, a gleeful smile on her face.

The second session went even better and ever the optimist, her hope bloomed. This was going to work.

Four days later, Melanie entered the breakfast room to find everyone already seated at the table. Her humming froze on her lips as she encountered the smiling faces turned towards her. Silently she made her selection from the sideboard and carried her plate to her place at the table. She had not missed that dark glance Dirk had slanted at her as his eyes slid over her body drinking in the expanse of skin left exposed by the candy pink sun-dress she wore.

"Nice dress. Make sure you don't wander about in the sun

for too long. It's going to be scorcher," Dirk said quirking an eyebrow at her.

"It's so sweet of you to care," Melanie murmured. With deliberate precision she placed her napkin over her bare thighs and forked scrambled eggs into her mouth. Under that amused regard, the food tasted like the ashes from a long dead campfire. She chewed with grim determination.

"If you get sunburnt or sunstroke, I don't have time to play doctors and nurses, princess."

Melanie choked.

A grinning James, who sat next to her, reached over and pounded her helpfully on the back. Melanie dabbed at her mouth with the napkin and waved him away.

Tammy jumped up. "Can I play, Uncle Dirk?"

"Sure you can, honey but you'll have to make do with Melanie."

Eyes watering, Melanie glared at Dirk who lifted his hands and said in a voice too innocent for her to believe, "What did I say?"

Melanie turned her shoulder to him and asked, "I'm sorry, James, what did *you* say?"

"We're leaving after lunch." James nodded towards Catherine who was attempting to coax a defiant Anabelle to open her mouth to receive her spoonful of rolled oats.

"So soon?" said Melanie. "I thought you would be leaving at the end of the week."

"Cate and I think it's best if we go it alone from here on in. Not that we don't appreciate your counselling sessions, Mel."

He twiddled with a strand of his short sandy hair, a telltale giveaway. *Oh dear, something is bothering him.* For some reason she recalled the argument between James and his wife when they'd first arrived. Unease sent a shiver prickling over her skin.

"What? All of you?" Harry said through a mouthful of cornflakes.

James responded, "No, just your aunt and I. Mel and the girls will remain here at *The Golden Perch Station* until we return."

"How long is that gonna be?" Harry frowned.

Melanie quietly attending to her breakfast marvelled at his sudden resemblance to his father. Why the sudden hostility to her presence? Did he perceive her some kind of threat? Or had he merely picked up on his father's wary attitude?

James shrugged and smiled awkwardly. "We're not sure. A few weeks."

"Strewth. That means I'm tied to the house until they're gone. I wanted to ride out on the bike and help look for stragglers." Disgust laced Harry's voice. He threw his spoon onto the table.

"Harry, watch your language," said Dirk. "Next time, son."

"Sorry," muttered Harry, his face flushed a bright red picked up his spoon and shovelled porridge in his mouth at a great rate.

Anabelle watching goggle eyed at this display of rudeness from her adored cousin threw her spoon across the room.

"Anabelle, that's no way to behave at the dinner table. For heaven's sake. James. Dirk. One of you do something." Catherine balled her napkin in her clenched hand and glared at both men in turn.

"She's your daughter," Dirk said calmly. He mopped up the last of his eggs with a slice of toast and popped the morsel into his mouth.

The little girl hurled a nearby fork at the wall. Melanie raised her napkin quickly to her mouth and pressed hard to stifle the absurd giggle that threatened to escape. Catherine sat like an outraged hen fluffing up her feathers. James sat mute biting his lip to hide his smile, his gaze swivelling from his wife to his brother-in-law to his errant daughter. Tammy sat on the floor ignoring the chaos erupting above her head.

She was far too busy feeding Mr Gibbs and Muffin strips of bacon.

Over the cloth, Melanie's eyes met Harry's. They burst into laughter.

Catherine forced a reluctant smile and said, "I suppose I overreacted. I guess I'm a bit anxious about leaving my girls."

Melanie placed her napkin on the table and leaning over, patted her friend's hand. "I'll look after them, but I know they'll miss you."

Tears glistened in Catherine's eyes. "Oh, Mel. You're such a good friend to us."

"Isn't she?" James rose to his feet and retrieved the spoon and fork. On the way back he gave Melanie a tight squeeze around her shoulders.

Dirk glared as James resumed his seat. Melanie flicked Dirk a quick glance, noting how a vein pulsed rapidly at his temple.

"How long did you say you two have been friends?" he asked in a cool voice that gave no indication to whatever was on his mind.

"Oh, about forever." James dropped into his seat and handed over the utensils to his wife before reaching for the BBQ sauce bottle. He drowned his scrambled eggs in a sea of brown liquid.

"Forever could mean anything."

"Geez Dirk, persistent bloke aren't you." James forked eggs into his mouth, chewed and swallowed. Then rolled his eyes when he caught Dirk still staring at him. "Since we were kids. You were what, Mel? Six or seven years old? I was ten, I remember that much."

"I was seven," said Melanie. Her blood cooled to ice in her veins and she shivered. *As if I could ever forget the year my mother ran off and left me alone in that crappy apartment. I never saw her again. It took a week before Social Welfare came knocking on the door.*

A strange darkness surrounded her as their voices faded away. She was no longer listening. Her eyes were glued as if in contemplation of the food on her plate. But her mind was far away.

Back in that cold building that housed her past.

Back where she had buried so many childish hopes and dreams.

Back where she'd been rejected so many times.

Sitting here in this warm room surrounded by people who were obviously close and cared deeply for each other only served to remind her of what she had missed out on her entire life.

Something warm enclosed her hand and gripped hard. With an effort she dragged herself out of her lonely fog and realised it was Dirk's hand covering hers. Looking up she found him staring intently at her, concern etched into the compressed line of his mouth.

He lifted an eyebrow and said softly, "Okay?"

"Of course." She pulled her hand out from under his and glanced around the table. Harry was pretending to filch strips of bacon off Tammy's plate, much to her squealing excitement as she defended her food with a fork. James was busy addressing his breakfast and Catherine...*oh dear*...Catherine was looking at both her then Dirk then back again that weird, smug smile on her face.

"How about we have the riding lessons now?" said Harry shoving his empty plate away. He chugged down the remainder of his orange juice.

"Harry, I need you to oil the windmills today as well as check out the spark plugs on the Honda motorbike."

Harry nodded and rose. "No worries, Dad. I'll get on it after the lessons."

"Good lad. I'll be away all day. The dingo fence to the west needs to be repaired."

"Well, that's all settled then." Catherine rose in haste from the table and plucked Anabelle into her arms. Mumbling a farewell, she hurried from the room, herding Harry and Tammy in front of her.

The noise of the general exodus from the room roused Melanie from her dark thoughts and with a start, she realised that if she didn't move fast, she'd be left alone with Dirk. Before she could escape however, his hand clamped over her arm.

"Before you run off again princess, I'd appreciate a few words with you."

James opened his mouth but Dirk cut in before he could object.

"I'm sure your wife and children need you outside, James."

After darting an uneasy glance at Melanie, he gave an abrupt nod and walked out. But not before he'd cast another look over his shoulder.

Melanie waved him on his way mentally encouraging him, *your place is with your family now, go.* Staring down at the darkly tanned hand holding her so firmly, she gathered her shaky confidence and waited.

CHAPTER 5

*D*irk loosened his grip, his fingers sliding over that silky soft skin, gently smoothing the area where he had gripped her so tightly to prevent her departure. She was far too pale he reflected. And tense. Her lashes fluttered and swept over her cheeks betraying her inner turmoil. Her blue eyes as they met his warily were shadowed with secrets and hidden depths he itched to explore.

And banish.

But more than that, he needed desperately to find out the reason why she would sabotage a complete stranger's marriage. Then he'd put a stop to whatever game she was playing with James. *For his sister's sake of course.* His determination had nothing to do with this foolish urge to comfort and claim that pounded through him every time his thoughts turned to her.

His movements slow and deliberate, carefully hiding his fascination with the smoothness of her skin beneath his callused hands, he released his hold to cradle his teacup. Leaning back in his chair with a deceptive casualness he watched her from hooded eyes.

"We've met before."

He suppressed his deep satisfaction at her reaction, noting the warm colour that flushed her face and the militant sparkle that re-appeared in her eyes. Withstanding her glare, he was uneasily aware that she was the last person he should want to protect.

"Rubbish. I'm certain I would remember."

"Not exactly met but my ex-wife pointed you out at the hospital when Tammy was born."

"Seriously, I have never met either you or your wife." She spoke loudly as if he was hard of hearing and he hid a sudden grin.

The chair creaked under his weight as he shifted position and his amusement faded as he recalled that day.

"Apparently you struck up a conversation with Valerie in the kiosk and gave her a whole pile of unwarranted advice about how she should live her life."

Her hand flew to her mouth and her eyes widened. "Oh, I remember her now. A dark haired woman about twenty-five with an olive complexion. She looked so unhappy I asked her what was the matter."

"Unhappy! Valerie wasn't unhappy."

Irritation flared when Melanie rolled her eyes at him.

"Duh. She told me she felt trapped, that she was living a life others had mapped out for her. I couldn't turn away from her, not when she reached out and asked me to listen."

"Maybe not, but you didn't have to tell her to leave her husband and child."

"I did no such thing!"

"Really?" he drawled, feeling a surge of that old resentment he'd carried inside for so long boil his chest until he thought he might explode. "Funny that, because the next thing Valerie did was seek me out and announce our marriage was over. Shit. We hadn't even made it to the car. I can still see her standing there in the carpark and pointing to you as you ran for a bus. Your hair was in a ponytail and reached down to your waist and you carried a bulging bright purple backpack."

"Oh my gosh." She slumped back into her chair and her mouth wobbled. Those lovely blue eyes of hers went all watery.

Crap. She wasn't going to cry was she? He hated it when women cried. Made him feel as mean as a wild bull. With difficulty he clamped down on the words of comfort that wanted to spill from his lips.

She was the one in the wrong.

"I was in my first year at uni, studying for a counselling degree and full of desire to help people. When this woman said she was at a crossroads in her life, I sat down and listened to her." Melanie poked strands of her hair behind her ear and there could be no denying the earnest expression on her face as her gaze didn't waver from his.

She sighed. "The woman went on and told me how she'd always had a dream to design clothes for the unfashionable full-figured women. She described how she'd grown up with her family expecting her to make a match with the grandson of a neighbouring cattle station owner. How the entire district talked about nothing but their wedding day. She did say how much she cared for this man who she'd known since she was a child. But she'd always sensed something was missing from her life; that there was something waiting for her elsewhere. I'm sorry, Dirk, but she also said how much she hated living here."

His jaw worked and he tore his gaze from Melanie to stare blindly through the window. *Why hadn't Valerie told me?*

"I suggested she talk her problems over with her husband but she wouldn't listen. Kept saying how no one was interested in what she wanted to do. So...," Melanie hesitated.

Dirk swung back and glared through narrowed eyes. "What did you say then?"

Voice defiant, she continued, "That a person has only one life and that she should look for a way to meet her needs and those of her family."

"Right, and ten minutes later I'm getting slapped in the face with a divorce proposal."

"I'm sorry. I never thought she'd react that way." She pleated the tablecloth between fingers that shook and made him feel like a louse.

Melanie's response certainly cleared up a lot of unanswered questions that had plagued him through the years, but instead of feeling a sense of closure, pangs of remorse squeezed his heart. He must have been blind not to realise how Valerie had felt. Instead, he'd charged on with his eyes set firmly on his goal; making his grandfather proud. Unfortunately, that had included marrying his reluctant, childhood friend. *What a mess. If only Valerie had talked about her feelings. I probably wouldn't have listened, too busy being the dutiful grandson.*

But at least he had set Valerie free with no recriminations on his part only a hope that she'd include their son in her new life.

Pity though, the first thing she did after moving out was move in with a *'friend'* she'd been corresponding with through the internet.

Dirk raked a hand through his hair. His anger had fled, and he now wondered how long their marriage would have lasted if Valerie had stayed. Would he have woken up one day and realised she wasn't the love of his life too?

Well, there is one thing I've learnt and that's to be damned careful of whom I let into my life. And it certainly won't be another woman with ties to a city life.

His nostrils flared. Through the increasing heat in the room, he caught the scent of her subtle perfume. *Crap.*

She was sitting so still, with those big, blue vulnerable eyes that played such havoc with his thoughts, and made him long to sweep her up into his arms and keep her safe. Those eyes that caused uncomfortable twinges inside his heart, made him wish she really belonged here in the Outback.

And that she was only a friend to his brother-in law not someone waiting in the wings to step into his sister's shoes.

Damn it. She was sitting too still.

She was hiding something. But what? Was there more she hadn't told him about Valerie? He went over their conversation in his head. No, he was certain everything there was kosha. So it must be to do with James.

And I do love a challenge. Dirk swept his hair back from his forehead as he pondered his next move. Her furtive glances signalled the depth of her tension. *Perhaps it was time for him to back off for a bit. Give them both a bit of space to chew over her revelations.*

She straightened. Her voice spilled over him like sweet mellow wine. "I can offer you a counselling session if you wish to talk about your feelings. Help you move on. I've built up a nice little business from very satisfied clients."

"What?" *Forget backing off. Huh. It'd be a cold day in hell before he gave this filly any slack.*

He leaned forward until his face was inches from hers and had the gratification of seeing her eyes widen, those silky lashes sweep down trying to shield her reaction.

He said, "Clients? Tell me, were they all male?"

"Of course not. Relationship counselling requires a couple." She rolled her eyes. "But for my anger management programme, the clients are mostly male. Statistically men have more problems with anger management than women."

"Is that right?"

She nodded her head. Her curls bounced on her shoulders.

Dirk gave into temptation, reached out, wove his hand

through the heavy mass to rest, cradling the nape of her neck. His thumb slid with sensuous stealth over her soft skin. A pulse was beating rapidly in the indent at the base of her throat. He stifled the urge mounting within him like a steam engine about to explode, to press his open mouth against its frantic flutter. Jealousy ate inside his gut at the thought of other men in her life.

"I just bet you were a great success with all those male clients of yours." His quiet remark had her jerking away from his touch.

"Oooh, I can't believe you said that!"

He watched with hard won detachment, her fight for control. She drew in a deep shuddering breath which had his eyes drifting with appreciation over the neckline of her dress, before she placed her utensils gently onto her plate of half eaten food and rose with commendable calm. Only the blue sparkle of her eyes and the apricot blush staining her cheeks gave an indication of her feelings.

"If you'll excuse me? I have work to do." Head held impossibly high, she stalked from the room.

It wasn't until that straight little back had disappeared down the hall that Dirk realised he still sat at the table. He should be concentrating on the tasks that awaited him instead of loitering here in this irritating way.

Fantasising over a woman who had no place in his life.

And never would.

The man was impossible.

Her mind seething with images of Dirk apologising, Dirk begging for forgiveness, Dirk chained to a windmill; Melanie stomped into the main living room. She sank into an armchair and curled her bare legs under her. Mr Gibbs who had followed her, jumped onto the arm and gazed unblinking into her face. Muffin darted into the room, snatched her favourite stuffed toy from the pile then scampered off down the hall.

She scratched Mr Gibbs under his chest. The cat's loud familiar rumble which was his version of purring, gradually soothed the rioting butterflies in her stomach and calmed her galloping heart. Dirk's opinion of her was pretty well rock bottom, she decided glumly. Not that she could blame him. It was only natural for him to resent the person he held responsible for his wife's departure. She only wished it didn't matter so much.

How strange that all those years ago their lives had interwoven with such dramatic results.

She sighed and propping her elbow on the armrest, cupped her chin in her hand, turning over the conversation with Dirk in her mind. He must really hate her. Tears pricked painfully behind her eyes. *Why was his good opinion so important?* It was a source of constant worry to her, how her thoughts kept returning to him. She'd never had this problem before with either her clients or their families.

The room was warm and quiet apart from the sonorous ticking from the old grandfather clock that graced one corner. She could have stayed there all day, mooning about, dreaming impossible dreams.

Her absent gaze fell on the clock face, sharpened and with a muffled exclamation she leapt to her feet dislodging Mr Gibbs. The cat hissed and gave her a baleful glare then settled onto the cushions.

Time for her to help out in the kitchen.

Melanie bustled into the kitchen glad to see the housekeeper was elsewhere. She needed time to attain her usual serenity. She needed time to throw off the despondency, that had darkened her spirits after the conversation with Dirk. She located the plug for the sink and turned on the taps after loading it with detergent. After peering cautiously into the breakfast room to check it was deserted, she started to stack dishes.

The heavy tread of a man's footsteps walking down the verandah had her whirling to face the French doors.

"Oh it's you, James." Her brow wrinkled. Was that disappointment or relief she could hear in her voice?

"Who did you think it was?" James sent her a searching look as he stepped over the threshold. "Look, we haven't got much time. There's something I need to tell you before Catherine comes back to the house."

Alarm bells rang. Melanie stiffened. Her movements became jerky and wooden as she carefully carried a stack of plates into the kitchen to place on the bench near the sink. She recalled his actions at the breakfast table and remembered how she had thought for some time that he had withheld some information from her.

"Can you stop that for a second?"

There was a sharpness she had never heard before in his voice. Troubled Melanie turned to face him. James' face was drawn tight with tension as he crossed the room and placed his hands on her shoulders, his fingers digging into her skin.

She gave a shaky smile of encouragement.

"Mel, I'm in trouble." A shuddering breath rattled from his hoarse throat. "It's the vineyard. What with the recent drought and the overseas market palling, I've had to borrow more than I can afford to pay back. I thought I'd recoup my losses by placing bets with a bookie I know in Sydney, but I've sunk further into debt."

Melanie gaped at him for several moments until she found her voice. "Gambling? Oh please don't tell me, you're mixed up with Roscoe and his mob?"

"Sorry, Mel, but yeah."

"Was that where you went before we flew up here to Queensland?"

"Uh huh. Now I've got my bank manager hounding me

every five seconds. If I don't come up with a solution, we'll be bankrupt. We'll lose everything."

"Have you told Catherine?"

James shook his head. "Kinda. I told her about the issue with the bank, but she'd already guessed as much. She was angry that I hadn't told her about our problems. How could I? I feel I have to continually prove myself to be better than a kid from the streets."

"James, you have to learn to share both the good and the bad with Catherine. That's what makes a marriage."

"Maybe. But I can't tell her about Roscoe. Shit. There's stuff in my past I don't want her to know about, she'll ditch me for sure if she finds out."

"She may well ditch you if you keep on holding her at arm's length. You need to show you respect her strength and tell her everything," Melanie pointed out dryly.

"How can I? I just can't do it. I can't tell her anything about my involvement in that gang or about how I now owe money to a kingpin of the underbelly." His voice rose with panic. "Roscoe is not going to wait forever. He's talking about a partnership, for heaven's sake."

Melanie cupped his face in the palms of her hands. "Why didn't you tell me before?"

A wry smile lighted his features briefly and he shrugged his shoulders. "'Course I thought I could find a way out of my problems. And because you'd think I was a failure. Like Catherine does."

"I refuse to believe she thinks you're a failure." Melanie stood on tiptoe and pressed a gentle kiss on his cheek. "I'd never think that, you're the best thing that ever happened to me."

"Well, well. What a cosy little scene. Don't let me interrupt you." The drawled voice from the doorway had Melanie's heart jolting in shock before thundering into a gallop. She thrust her hands behind her back, as if she had been touching a live snake and ducked under James arms to stand like a guilty schoolgirl waiting for punishment to fall on her head.

Dirk was propped against the door jam, arms folded across his chest. The hostility in his eyes hit her with the force of a sledgehammer.

How much had he heard?

CHAPTER 6

The Cessna soared into the cloudless sky of a blue so bright it hurt her eyes. The plane banked to the side and rose higher, the drone of its engine fading as Melanie shaded her face to watch the plane dwindle into little more than a black speck.

Then it was gone.

The sky was empty.

Loneliness assailed her. Unexpected tears pricked her eyes. She wished fervently she was on that plane and on her way home. This new mess James had gotten himself into made her head ache. If only he'd confide in his wife but despite Melanie's continued pleadings James had turned pigheaded and avoided her attempts to manoeuvre him where they could speak unheard. Now he was gone leaving her reeling and wondering how on earth she could help him.

Still there was no way she could let him down. She would have to find a solution but how she could manage that stuck on a cattle station and so far from the city, boggled her mind.

She raised her hand again and waved at the disappearing plane. With Mrs Weber departed to visit her daughter and grandson in Rockhampton and Catherine and James off on a 'honeymoon', Melanie was left here with Dirk as the only adults. She'd have full charge of cooking and cleaning. Not that she minded. In fact, she relished the thought she'd have physical work to occupy her days. For one thing, it should keep her out of Dirk's way and give her plenty of time to plot and plan.

Thankful for the shield of her sunglasses, she blinked away betraying moisture and swooped down to pick up a snivelling Anabelle. Whooping and imitating the swoop of a plane's wings with her outstretched arms, Tammy skipped around in ever increasingly large circles.

"Ready, princess? Or shall we continue to stand here and fry in this heat while you weep over the absence of your *friend*?"

The emphasis on the word *friend* stiffened her backbone. She shot an irritated look in his direction and slogged her way through the red soil to the waiting four-wheel drive. Her lips pursed in mild annoyance at the fine red dust coating her sandals and her bare ankles. She shifted the little girl more firmly onto her hip so she could open the door. To her surprise, Dirk's large brown hand reached past her and closed over the handle.

"Do you need a hand there?" His gruff voice so close to her ear, startled her as he yanked the door open.

She stammered slightly, feeling strangely short of breath. "Nnnno....no I'm fine." Melanie added a reluctant, "Thank you."

His, *"Not a problem, princess"* feathered across her warm cheeks. Heat scorched her from the body standing so close behind her.

Her teeth sank down into her bottom lip to stop the whimper that trembled to escape. In desperation she reminded herself he was only trying to rattle her cage.

And succeeding.

She bent slightly to strap the little girl into the child

restraint and could have died from mortification when her bottom bumped into his groin. His dark chuckle scraped across her nerve endings like a maestro plucking a violin.

"Mmmm, very nice."

Melanie wrestled blindly with the clasp, the wriggling Anabelle not helping in the slightest. With every movement she made she seemed to brush against him causing her body to begin to thrum with a deep pulsing vibration.

"Tsk, tsk. You've got the belt way too tight. Here let me."

To her horror, Dirk's arms imprisoned her and dealt with the fastenings with cool efficiency. He was bending over her his legs braced apart trapping her within their arc. The muscles of his long hard torso flexed and bunched through the thin material of her pink dress as he leant against her.

"There, see that wasn't so hard," he murmured. His hands settled firmly over her waist, his fingers splayed wide over the curve of her belly as he pulled her against him.

Her knees buckled. Her head whirled as she sucked in air and drew in the scent of his spicy masculine heat. Ever so slowly he stepped backwards one step at a time inching Melanie out of the car.

"You can stand up now, sweetheart." The hint of laughter in his voice brought her to her senses.

Heat flashed over her from the tip of her toes to the top of her head. She just knew her face glowed that tell-tale red. Grabbing his hands she flung them from her waist and marched on unsteady legs around the car to check Tammy's seat belt. Her blood was making so much racket racing around her veins the young girl's chatter flowed and ebbed like a tidal lake in the background.

She supposed she could clamber over the little girl and take refuge in the back of the vehicle. But that would be sheer cowardness and Dirk's probable reaction was enough to cause a shudder to rack through her frame. Racing back to the passenger side she found he'd remained leaning against the hot metal, the expression in his eyes hidden by the shade of his hat. She circled around him out of arm's reach, than darted towards the car, feeling like a fool. He moved with the stealth of a hunter to block her path before turning and opening the door. Dithering, she shuffled her weight from one foot to the other. The sound of Tammy's shrill treble rising in accusation, finally penetrated her abstraction.

"Aunty Melanie, you're not listening to me."

What was she doing, jumping about like a jackrabbit on a hot tin roof? Chin lifted high and wishing herself miles away, she stepped towards the open door.

"Problem, princess?" Those chocolate brown eyes were glinting with suppressed laughter as he shifted his body with a swiftness that caused her to gasp and lifted her into the car.

Melanie swatted fruitlessly at his possessive touch, breathing an audible sigh of relief when his hands slid away, and the door slammed. She twisted round and fixed a smile to her hot face. "Sorry, Tammy. Would you mind repeating yourself?"

The driver's door slammed shut but Melanie refrained from looking at him fussing with her seat belt. The young girl rolled her eyes dramatically then regarded her thoughtfully. "You look awfully hot Aunty Melanie, doesn't she, Uncle Dirk?"

"She sure does honey. I guess she needs a swim to cool down." He turned the key and set the car into gear.

If they had been alone, she'd blister his ears with a pithy account of his shortcomings of which in her opinion he had many but with two little girls hanging off every word they spoke she'd have to restrain herself.

She said sweetly, "A swim would be lovely but as there's nothing here for miles but dirt it's out of the question." The sound of the irritated drumming of his fingers on the steering wheel was her reward.

Triumphant that she had gotten a under his skin, enabled her to relax into the leather seat.

The drumming stopped.

She sneaked a peek at his profile. A faint smile was lifting his lips at the corner. She tensed. *Oh, oh, now what?*

"I guess I could re-arrange my afternoon and take you ladies for a swim."

Had there been an emphasis on the word 'ladies'? While Melanie sat chewing over his comment squeals of delight emanated from the rear seat.

"Can Harry come too, Uncle Dirk?"

"I don't see why not. The nearest lagoon is too far for us to go there today. The bore tank will do just fine. So how about it, princess, feel like cooling off in one of my er .... tanks?"

Her tummy lurched up and down like a roller coaster when she met the challenge in his eyes. His face was alight with sheer devilment. Melanie managed to nod, her voice having disappeared to points east on its own holiday. *Now what was he up to? Why was he suddenly being so charming?* Maybe he was biding his time before he started the twenty questions about the scene he'd interrupted in the kitchen.

The touch of his warm hand covering her clenched fingers where they were clasped together in her lap startled her. "Relax, princess. I think we should cry truce for a while. Mmmm?" His deep voice flowed over her churning senses, soothing her.

Dismayed at the warm glow of comfort his touch gave her, Melanie stared out the windscreen as the car hurtled down the track.

Dismayed, also, at the spring of joy flowing from the thought of spending hours in his company.

His hand left her lap to brush a knuckle down the line of her cheek before returning to the gear stick. Her lips trembling, Melanie flashed a quick glance at him. He was frowning and his mouth set in a stern line.

The desire to cast herself onto his chest and cling to his strength came out of nowhere and was enough to bring an independent woman to her knees. *What was happening to her? Whatever it was she didn't like it.*

"A swim sounds like a very good idea," she said primly and decided it would be wise to ignore his latter comment. She vowed if it killed her, she would treat him like she treated the members of her other clients' families, in a professional and polite at-arms-distance manner.

Why did she have the feeling then, that this time, it wasn't going to be so easy?

Surprisingly enough the remainder of the day turned out pleasant. More than pleasant Melanie mused as she bustled about readying Anabelle for bed that night.

The soft scent of the night mingled with the comforting smell of baby powder as she fought Anabelle into her leaf green cotton pj's. Dirk had been true to his word and had reverted to an easy casual attitude - one that she was more familiar with receiving from members of the opposite sex. An action which had confounded her completely and now viewed from a safe distance from his disturbing presence, one that reeked of a cunning plot.

Melanie bit her lip as she considered how she had responded by lowering her guard so much so, that she had acted naturally around him for the first time. She had found herself enjoying his company not even taking umbrage when he laid down his order for them to swim in the tanks by themselves. Or his other order in hustling everyone out of the strong sun's rays when he considered they had all had more than their fair share of UV exposure

All in all it had been blissful, to float around in the cool water so high above the ground a new experience for

Melanie, even with an excited Anabelle firmly ensconced in her floatation device shrieking with joy. Dirk had kept a watchful eye on Tammy who had loved splashing and practicing her 'duck diving' with her cousin.

Melanie had been very wary at first, staying as far away from Dirk as she could but she need not have wasted her efforts, as Dirk had coolly ignored her. His swift impersonal glance over her bikini clad body had left her with the strong impression she could have been wearing an atmospheric pressure diving suit or be painted purple and he would have remained unmoved.

Afterwards they had eaten a noisy late lunch on the verandah consisting of cold meats, salads and the mouth-wateringly iced cupcakes Mrs Weber had baked early that morning. It had been a very long luncheon, with Dirk giving both him and Harry time off from their constant work for once. Later Melanie and Dirk had leant against the railing fence side-by-side while they watched Harry give riding lessons to his cousins. Not once by action or word, did Dirk evince any sexual interest in her.

This blowing hot and cold on his part was enough to make a woman want to scream. It was if he couldn't make up his mind what he wanted...or how he felt about her.

Not that she cared one way, or the other Melanie told herself as she plonked Anabelle onto her bed and plumped the pillow with vigour.

"Story," demanded Anabelle, her round brown eyes fixed entreatingly on Melanie.

Melanie smiled gently at the little girl and brushed a kiss over her satiny cheek.

"Tammy, would you mind getting the book, '*Wind in the Willows*' from the living room please?"

"Okay, Aunty Mel," sang out Tammy. She stopped jumping up and down on her bed and raced out of the room, Muffin yapping at her heels.

Briskly Melanie tucked the little girl into bed and sat beside her, settling against the dark wooden headframe. While she waited for Tammy to return, she entertained Anabelle with how they could re-decorate the gloomy room. Melanie sighed. The whole house was a misery in her opinion.

She looked up with a welcoming smile when Tammy danced back pulling her grumbling cousin by the hand. Harry shot a quick glance in her direction then allowed himself to be dragged over to Tammy's bed. He flung himself down on his back and covered his eyes with his arm.

Tammy and Muffin jumped onto the bed and snuggled up to Melanie's other side, the little dog crawling into the girl's lap.

"Here you go, Melanie."

"Thank you, Tammy. Now where are we up to?"

"Oooh, I know. Mole & Rat have just found Mr Badger's house.'

Melanie opened the book and began to read. Her voice though soft was clear and soothing and she read well, putting just the right amount of expression in her tone for her young listeners. Anabelle stuck her thumb into her mouth, her eyelids drooping as she sucked and Tammy wriggled closer.

She read for some time until her voice was dry and beginning to sound hoarse. Melanie raised her eyes from the pages to see Dirk leaning against the doorframe. She wondered how long he had been standing there. Across the width of the room, the impact of his dark eyes pulsed her relaxed body into urgent life.

"Time for bed I believe," Dirk drawled. He straightened and strode with a lean grace towards the bed.

Mesmerised Melanie watched his approach, her heart fluttering madly in her throat, barely noticing Harry's muttered goodnights as he left the room. She longed to leap from the bed and escape but she was hemmed in on both sides by the girls. Upon recalling her undignified scurrying about at the runway earlier that day a mortified heat stained her face so hot her skin could have been on fire. Laughter sparkled in Dirk's brown eyes as he planted one hand on the bed beside Tammy to balance himself and swooped over them to plant an affectionate kiss on Anabelle's forehead.

Great, just great. She should have moved when she had the chance.

Now she was trapped.

Children either side of her.

Dirk hovering centimetres from her body. Tempting her sinful wickedness. Or at least within the privacy of her fantasies.

Her eyes squeezed shut as she struggled to regain her composure. She breathed in the faint scent of musky aftershave lotion mingled with warm male. His arm brushed against her as he carefully moved tendrils of hair out of the little girl's eyes.

Melanie froze.

If she moved her breasts would come into contact with all that hard wall of muscle that made up his chest.

With difficulty she banished that wicked little voice whispering in her head to do just that.

She concentrated on keeping her breathing nice and steady.

"Goodnight, Anabelle." His deep voice rich with affection caused havoc to Melanie's rioting senses.

She cast him a fulminating glare. White teeth gleamed as a grin split his tanned features. *He was doing it deliberately. Drat the man.*

Melanie spoke in her most haughty tone, "Please move out of the way Dirk so Tammy and I can get off the bed."

"Sure thing, princess."

A sigh of relief escaped her when he grabbed Tammy and tossed her, squealing, over his shoulder as he strode across the bare floorboards. Paws scrabbling, Muffin pursued them. With quiet efficiency Melanie tucked a light cotton sheet over the little girl and raised the bars on both sides of the bed.

A quick glance over her shoulder reassured her that Dirk had gone. She crossed the room to give Tammy a cuddle and goodnight kiss, patted the little dog that had taken up residence on her bed, before turning out the lamps, making sure she left the door slightly ajar.

Her fingers closed over the handle of her bedroom door. Perhaps she should spend some time unpacking some clothes, although the thought of rearranging Catherine's belongings to make room for her own, was somehow distasteful. It had seemed the logical thing to do, to move into Catherine's bedroom that not only lay across the hall from where the girls slept but was also located in the main homestead. A tiny frown wrinkled her smooth brow. Melanie wished she were back in her own little building. For one thing it was the furthermost dwelling from the main homestead....the furthermost away from Dirk's domain.

Now, she was under his roof.

"Coffee or a pot of tea? A nightcap perhaps?" murmured Dirk from the shadowy depths of the long hallway.

Her heart skipped a beat. Her hand jerked back from the door as if it was on fire. "Oh, you startled me." The breathless anticipatory tone to her voice, made her want to squirm with embarrassment.

"Sorry, princess." He moved towards her, his footsteps muffled by the faded mud-brown hall runner covering the length of the hallway. In the dim light, his white teeth gleamed from his mocking smile. Cupping her elbow with his strong fingers Dirk turned her around and led her willy-nilly down the hall and hustled her into the living room. He thrust her into a surprisingly comfortable armchair and stood over her, eyebrow raised in silent query.

Finally, Melanie found her voice. Clearing her throat delicately, she muttered, "I was about to go to bed."

"You read my mind princess."

Furious with the hot blush that washed over her face, she choked out, "I meant alone."

Dirk quirked his other eyebrow. "Now, what made you think that was an invitation?"

Melanie drummed her fingers on the armchair. Words tumbled about in her head, as her irritation soared to dizzying heights. A lovely fantasy of her jumping up and boxing him smartly on his ears floated enticingly in front of her eyes.

"Now, now. Temper, temper." Dirk wagged a finger in front of her nose. "There's a woman I know who runs anger management classes. Perhaps I should give you her name?" His chocolate brown eyes were alight with merriment.

Unable to help herself, Melanie broke into a peal of delighted laughter.

"I guess that makes us even." She grinned at him cheerfully, then wondered at his suddenly remote expression that wiped all traces of amusement from his face.

"I guess it does."

Melanie's teeth sank into her bottom lip and nibbled uncertainly. His response was courteous no more, their moment of rapport vaporised as if it had never existed.

"What would you like to drink?"

"Iced tea would be lovely, thank you," she answered soberly.

In bewilderment she gazed at his broad shoulders as he departed the room. She turned her head and met the unblinking glittering stare of Mr Gibbs from his cosy basket beside the coffee table. Her hands spread wide and she shrugged, doing her best to hide her sharp disappointment. The man was a complete enigma.

For one wonderful moment she had thought he actually liked her.

Ordinary Melanie Black from nowhere in particular. Now he was back inside his perfect host persona.

And she was back where he obviously considered she belonged – at best the unwelcome guest....at worst the intruder.

She only wished it didn't hurt so much.

To be back on the outside.

Looking in.

CHAPTER 7

The afternoon sun beat down onto the earth, radiating intense heat while she strolled beneath the orange trees and brooded over the past three days. The hours had flown with so much to do in the house and occupying the girls. And yet Melanie had found herself spending far too much time thinking about her host.

And far too little worrying about James and his financial woes.

She kicked moodily at the dirt with her open toe black leather Grecian sandals with the leather ties. Red dust drifted up into the late afternoon air and settled over her feet. She sighed at the result and dreamed wistfully of an ardent Dirk who would tenderly remove all traces of the red soil before running those strong brown fingers all the way up her legs, her inner thighs....her thoughts skidded to a halt.

I'm thinking about him again.

After worrying and fretting over Dirk's motives she was emotionally wrung out. Suppositions warred a constant daily battle with silly impossible daydreams and she was exhausted. Now that she knew the reason why he resented her interference in both his and his sister's lives, she was at a loss to explain his current actions.

He'd curbed his tendency to flirt and now maintained his courteous host persona. No, it was more than that for this new Dirk displayed a disquieting consideration for her wishes and her every comfort.

Polite in his manner and conversation, always staying on impersonal topics, always including her in the lively discussions he encouraged at the dinner table with the children.

He kept his face carefully expressionless his voice remained steady and bland.

There were no more sexual innuendoes.

There were no more probing questions about her life. Instead, he evinced what appeared to be a genuine interest in her ideas and opinions.

It was a pity, he now kept his hands to himself.

Had he forgiven her? Had he decided he no longer wanted to know if there was a relationship brewing between her and James? Perhaps he no longer cared either way. Certainly he had made no further reference to the scene he had interrupted in the kitchen. It was if he had something else he considered far more important on his mind.

But that wasn't the worst of it, for she caught herself wistfully daydreaming of a return to his flirting and challenging manner. And longing for the fizz and buzz of life that bubbled under the barest whisper of his touch.

Waiting for him to revert back.... and if she was going to be honest with herself, wanting him to revert back.

Really it was all most annoying.

Even more worrying was with her thoughts tied up with Dirk, she'd failed to come up with a solution for James' problem.

Annoyed, she tilted the Akubra's brim to a better angle against the burn of the sun. The same Akubra hat Dirk had presented her with on her first day at *The Golden Perch Station* with the terse instructions to wear it at all times.

Now she was thinking of him yet again.

"Aunty Mel." Tammy's yell splintered her fantasy into a thousand shards. "The mail's here."

Melanie turned around to see a figure waving madly from the edge of the orange grove. Startled she realised she had walked further than she had realised, lost in her daydreams. At her feet Muffin slumped, her tongue hanging down from her panting jaw, her round black eyes reproachful. Remorse twinged at her heartstrings. Melanie scooped the little dog up and tucked her under one arm and turned around. Her pace quickened as hand in hand with Tammy, she headed back through the dappled shade of the fruit trees the young girl skipping along at her side, bubbling over with chatter.

"There's a postcard from Mum and Dad. Isn't that great? I wish I was with them. But it's good fun being here too with Uncle Dirk, Harry and you, Aunty Mel." She grabbed the hat off her head and tossed it one-handed into the air. Her bright green eyes squinted at Melanie in the late afternoon sunshine. "Ted wanted to see you. He brought the mail in his plane. But Uncle Dirk said you were too busy. Are you busy, Aunty Mel?"

"Put your hat back on your head please, Tammy." Melanie cut in when the young girl paused to take a breath. "Is Ted still here? I would like to see him again. He was so helpful when we arrived, that I'd like to thank him."

Tammy slipped her hand from Melanie's grasp and began to skip around her. "Nope, he's already gone."

"No not nope, please Tammy. Ooops." Their legs tangled together but quick action on Melanie's part stopped their downward fall. "I think we should walk not skip to the house."

When they reached the main homestead, Tammy jumped up the steps and raced along the verandah yelling over her shoulder, "The mail's in the office. Hurry up, Aunty Mel." She disappeared into the house.

Melanie set Muffin on the ground and the dog shot off after Tammy.

It wasn't only the mail that was in the office Melanie found when she entered the room and Dirk's dark gaze did his slow sweep of her body. He waved the small packet of envelopes in the air and quirked an eyebrow. There was curiosity as well as speculation in his hooded gaze.

"You've got quite a number of letters here, princess."

Melanie reached out and took the proffered envelopes. She quickly skimmed through them, her heart faltering when she recognised that long sloping scrawl on the last one.

"Well, aren't you going to open it? Or do you want to be alone? You have only to ask, princess." He spread his hands wide, the mocking tilt to his lips fuelling her irritation.

Really the man was impossible. Was he teasing her? Or was there a bite of jealousy underlying his tone?

Somehow, she managed to dredge up a composed response. "That won't be necessary Dirk, there's no hurry. I can read it later." She cast a swift look at him from under her lashes, and carefully hid her amusement at the flash of frustration which furrowed his brows together. He shifted on his feet then rocked back on his heels. Melanie marvelled how at times, she could read him so easily and braced herself for his next onslaught.

Again, though he took her by surprise, replying in casual tones, "I noticed some of those envelopes looked like business correspondence. You're welcome to use my office facilities if you need to respond."

A jolt of heat surged over her bare skin when his hard fingers closed gently around her upper arm. Obedient to his silent command she allowed him to push her into the plush black leather chair manning the sturdy timber desk.

With smooth efficiency he offered instructions in the use

of his computer and printer. The letters clutched tightly in her hands she barely registered the words he was uttering, her attention was focused on that deep voice and the now familiar disturbing reaction of her body.

"You're not listening to a word I'm saying are you, princess?" he sighed. "Never mind, I'm sure you're techno smart. Internet is up and working should you need to send any emails. Don't forget, if you need anything, you have only to ask. I won't be that far away."

Aghast Melanie stared at him. Colour mounted in her cheeks at the laughter dancing in his eyes. Her mouth watered with sudden forbidden images. She had always been weak where dark chocolate was concerned.

"What...what do you mean?"

With a sweep of one hand, he indicated a haphazard pile of varying sized envelopes lying on the desk. "Work, princess. I also have a business to run."

What a fool she was, of course he'd have correspondence. She bit her lip with such savagery the metallic taste of blood spurt into her mouth. With dismay she watched him scoop up the pile of letters and saunter over to an armchair by the open window where he settled himself with the air of a man who had no intention of moving for some time.

"Where's Tammy and Anabelle?" Melanie squashed a feeling of guilt as she remembered her charges.

Dirk said in an absent voice over the rustle of paper, "Don't fuss. They're with Harry."

Melanie bowed to the inevitable. Well if he was able to ignore her presence than she would ignore his!

Deciding to leave James' letter for last, she picked up an envelope and read the return address. Oh good, an update from her personal assistant. Quickly she slit open the envelope and scanned the contents. Nothing to worry about on her business side of things and no problems with the small animal shelter she ran. Still, she'd better advise Lauren internet access was available and to use her Gmail account in case she needed to contact her urgently.

A few taps on the keyboard and she had her Gmail up on the screen. It didn't take long to send her message. Next, she checked her inbox, sighing at the number of unread mail waiting for her attention.

"I do appreciate the use of your computer, Dirk. I wish though I'd thought to ask you sooner." Her fingers hovering above the keys, she peered round the monitor at Dirk.

Dirk looked up and grinned. "No, that's my bad, princess. I should have thought to mention it. Have a lot of mail, do you?"

Melanie gave a theatrical groan. "Only about a million messages."

He chuckled.

Smiling, she returned to the task of dealing with her inbox. Sometime later, she sat back in the chair and finally opened the last letter. Inside, James had detailed the contact information for Roscoe together with a brief message advising he'd requested his solicitor to keep both of them informed on the precarious state of the vineyard's finances.

Very conscious of the man sitting within feet of her, she composed an email back to James' yahoo address re-affirming her willingness to give whatever assistance possible.

But what can I do? After a few moments thought, she sent out emails to five former foster friends with whom she still maintained contact. It was possible one might have some information which she could use to persuade Roscoe to be more forbearing with his repayment demands. While she waited in the hope a response would ping back straight away, she admired the workmanship of the timber desk.

"This is a beautiful desk," she said running her fingers over the intricately carved pattern dug along the desk's edge.

"Cheers. Glad you like it. It's a hobby of mine."

Startled she stared at him.

Dirk smiled and indicated the three bookcases that lined the wall. "I'm an enthusiastic wood turner and carpenter in my spare time."

Secretly impressed and feeling unaccountably shy at his easy reply, she said, "I didn't think you would have any spare time. A cattle station as big as *The Golden Perch Station* would take a lot of effort to keep solvent."

"It does, but everyone needs their down time. I make sure the stockmen get sufficient time off too."

"How many people are employed here?"

"On and off, anywhere from three to eight. Depends on the season and obviously, when mustering time comes around, we need more boots on the ground. A lot of blokes travel from station to station all year round offering their expertise."

"And at the moment?"

"Apart from my housekeeper's husband, Bill who's also leading hand, two others and they're both working in the south-western corner of the property. We've got some fool cattle that have ventured into the National Park area and need to be returned to the main mob."

"Oh." Melanie fiddled with her hair. Then with the stockmen elsewhere on the property, she really was alone with him in the homestead. She looked out the window at the empty landscape that stretched to the far horizon and recalled the news she'd scanned before bringing up her inbox. Despite the heat of a raw summer's day she shivered. "What if there's an emergency?"

Dirk sighed and placed the letter he'd been reading onto the side table. "Like what?"

"You know." She hesitated, gnawing at her inside cheek. "An accident or what about a bush fire?"

"Well, it is bush fire season, but I don't think we need to worry too much about that at the moment. Not with all the rain we've had up north. A coupla days and that rain will be down here on our doorstep and filling our creeks and rivers to overflowing. Although *The Golden Perch Station* is on the outskirts of the channel country, we still get our share of the wet season."

"I'm sorry. I guess I'm being silly thinking of stuff like that."

From across the room, his gaze zeroed onto her hot face. She lowered her head from his frown waiting for him to bombard her with some sarcastic comment.

"I don't think you're being silly at all. This is a big country and we're fairly isolated out here. It's important to know what to expect and what to do in an emergency."

Relieved he'd not taken the opportunity to de-ride her anxieties, she lifted her head and peeped at him. His expression was serious and dammed if she didn't read a faint question in the darkness of his eyes.

Feeling as if she should give something back since he was being so nice, she admitted, "I've got a bit of a thing about fires."

Dirk nodded. "They can be terrible events but don't worry too much about them. As I said, the rain heading our way should alleviate any danger of a fire in our area." His gaze left her as he picked up his letters. "You'll be comforted to know, we have a small plane in the out buildings plus a helicopter we can use in an emergency. And Harry and I can fly both."

"Oh, good." Melanie placed her hands on the desk. *Wow, he sure is capable.* "It would be wonderful if the rain reached down south. There're a couple of fires burning out of control in Victoria and New South Wales."

"I know. I've been keeping an eye on the news. Those poor bastards working the containment lines have their work cut out for them."

"Maybe we should dig a trench all the way down western New South Wales to the Victorian border."

Dirk grinned. "I'll get my shovel."

She smiled back. Their gazes locked for one long breathless minute.

The computer pinged an incoming message and broke their connection. Flustered, Melanie ducked her head and tapped the enter button. But instead of Gmail, Outlook opened on the screen.

Ooops. I've accidently logged into Dirk's email account. She peered round the monitor but Dirk had returned to his mail. She stared up at the ceiling. Shifted her gaze to the window. Grabbed a bunch of her hair and examined the ends without really seeing them. *Oooh, I have to look. Just one quick peek.*

How irritating, she huffed. No steamy message from a woman, no spicy message that would give her an insight into his private life. Nothing but a reminder from the Country Women's Associate about a forthcoming rodeo and dance. Would Harry and Dirk attend? It did sound like it might be fun. The girls would certainly enjoy the carnival rides that were bound to be there. Should she ask?

Another ping, this time from Gmail. Her breath caught in her throat when she read the response from James' solicitor.

A private buyer had made an offer to take over the debt on the vineyards.

Was it Roscoe?

It appeared she would have to work fast, if she was going to save her friend's livelihood.

CHAPTER 8

fter placing her mail inside her suitcase and shoving the bag back under her bed, Melanie wandered outside in search of the children. An easy feat as all she had to do was follow the sound of Tammy's laughter and Muffin's crazed barks. Beyond the lawn lay a small enclosure shaded by a stand of mulga trees and two ancient eucalypt trees. Here she found Harry riding a stockhorse, one arm anchoring a squealing Anabelle in place where she sat in front of him. Tammy yelled encouragement from where she leaned on the fence, her arms dangling over the top railing. Muffin lay in the dust, panting.

As she approached, Harry kicked the gelding into a trot. Anabelle shrieked with delight while Tammy whooped waving her hat in the air. Beneath the shade of his Akubra, Harry's mouth curled into a grin so similar to Dirk it made Melanie's heart stutter.

On seeing her, Harry slowed the horse to a walk and reined to a stop near the fence. Melanie ducked under the railings and lifted Anabelle off the horse and into her arms.

"Anabelle and Tammy love riding. It's good of you, Harry

to continue their lessons." Melanie stood smiling up at the young teenager.

Harry shrugged, tugged the brim of his hat lower then swung down out of the saddle.

Determined to crack his shy veneer, she persevered. "I bet you're a really great rider. Are you going to the rodeo?"

"Most people out here can ride." He shot her a quick glance then tugged on the reins, leading the horse behind him as he walked away.

Melanie rolled her eyes. *Really. He's such a typical teenager.* Of course, she had no intention of letting go of the subject easily, so she fell into step beside him, repressing her grin at the hunted look he shot her. He quickened his pace.

"Where are we going, Harry?" piped Tammy trotting at his side.

"Ajax needs a rub down and a drink after all his hard work," said Harry.

"About the rodeo, I hear there's a dance afterwards. Now that sounds like fun and a great excuse to meet up with your friends from the other stations." Melanie shifted Anabelle into a more comfortable position on her hip.

"I'm not going."

"What? Neither of you?"

They'd reached the lean to at the other end of the enclosure. Harry loped the reins around the railing and un-cinched the saddle girth. Moving with swift efficiency he soon had the saddle off the horse and began to rub the gelding down with the blanket. Tammy ran off to rip up tufts of grass then raced back to offer it to the horse, who nibbled the strands from her open palm.

"That tickles," she said giggling.

Melanie said in a demure voice, "I know Tammy and Anabelle would love to see a rodeo. And ride the merry-go-rounds."

"We're not going. We hardly ever go," admitted Harry

gruffly as he draped the blanket over the fence. Slipping his hands under the horse's neck he undid the buckles and eased the bridle of its head. Ajax snorted and ambled off to the water trough.

"I want to go on the merry-go-rounds. So does Anabelle," trilled Tammy. "I'm gonna ask Uncle Dirk." Clamping her hat back on her head, she skipped towards the house.

Melanie smiled and turned from watching her retreating form to find Harry kicking clods of dirt with the tips of his riding boots and scowling.

"Why? What's so important about us going?" he mumbled.

She shrugged and jostled Anabelle a bit higher in her arms. "I thought it would be fun for everyone including you. You must get lonely out here with no company your own age."

"Not everyone's a fan of crowds."

"Hardly a crowd and I would have thought only the locals would attend the rodeo."

"Hah! Rodeos are considered one of the major highlights of the year out here. But not by us. We're not going and we're fine with things the way they are now." He tipped the brim of his hat lower over his face as if to hide his expression. "Tell Dad I'm off to do a water run."

His thin shoulders rigid, he strode off in the direction of the outbuilding Melanie had learned housed the motorbikes leaving her staring after him and wondering what lay behind those gruffly spoken words.

"Come on Muffin," she said and walked back to the house where she fed Anabelle, changed her and laid her down for a nap. Worn out by her busy morning, the toddler fell asleep instantly. After turning on the baby monitor, she left the bedroom and headed for the office.

"Harry said to tell you he's off on a water run, whatever that means," she announced as she entered the room.

Dirk spared her a brief glance before returning his attention to his computer screen. Melanie continued her march until she stood next to the desk. Folding her arms across her chest, she tapped her fingers against her elbow.

"Means he's checking the troughs and tanks have plenty of water and the windmills and pump-jacks are working," he muttered.

"Oh." She stood for a moment considering his bent head and admiring the glint of blue-black strands in his hair. "Harry says, you're not going to the rodeo and dance."

Sighing, Dirk leaned back in the chair and linked his hands together in his lap. A tiny smile tilted the corners of his mouth. "I take it, you're the one responsible for Tammy bursting in here moments ago babbling about merry-go-rounds."

Melanie smiled. "Maybe."

"Maybe, nothing." He snorted. "Don't worry, princess. I've already said yes to her."

"It sounds like it will be so much fun." She hesitated then added, "Thank you. Harry will come too, won't he?"

"Probably not. He's not that keen on socialising."

About to leave, his comment had her turning back and frowning. "A boy his age should be hanging out with his mates, not skulking behind sand hills."

This time it was Dirk's turn to frown. "He isn't skulking. If he doesn't want to go I have no intention of forcing the issue."

"No. You'd much prefer he stayed here the rest of his life. Hiding from the world, like you."

"What." Dirk pushed to his feet and glared, his face looked thunderous with his straight mouth and his dark stormy eyes.

Melanie didn't back down. She waved an airy hand. "Useless to deny it. You both exhibit classic symptoms of recluses and anti-social behaviour. No doubt a knee jerk reaction from your wife leaving you, but that was years ago. You both need to emerge from your cave."

"You're treading on thin ice."

"Pwush. And you have your head buried in the sand." She planted her palms on the desk, leaning forward. "If this is the life you have chosen that's fine, well, actually it's not really, but your son needs a chance to live his life. To experience the turmoils and excitement of being a teenager. You should encourage him to get out there and be with others his own age."

Dirk rocked back on his feet and narrowed his eyes. "Why does it matter so much to you what happens to me and my son?"

"Surely you haven't forgotten this is my job, counselling people," she lied.

Dirk sighed and muttered, "Sometimes you completely bewilder me."

Heat flamed over her face. But he merely stood there, frowning and staring at her as if he sought the secrets of her soul.

The minutes ticked by until finally, he said, "I'll think about it." Running his hand through his hair, he broke eye contact to gaze out the window. The lines around his eyes appeared sharper making him look tired. "I know I've taken the easy way out with, Harry. Simpler to bury myself in running the station and leaving the boy to his own devices. He takes it hard that his mother rarely contacts him or visits. At first Valerie was keen to maintain communication but Harry hasn't heard from her in months."

"It works both ways you know. She could think he doesn't need her anymore given his age. Harry may not like to ask to visit in case you feel he's deserting you. Of course, it could all boil down to his self-esteem issues," she mused. *Yes it could be a bit of everything but I'm sure his lack of confidence is at the root of the problem. For his attitude is so similar to what mine used to be. And I've got a good idea what's behind it too.*

"Huh?" Dirk looked at her completely bewildered as if she'd suddenly taken it into her head to speak Chinese.

Honestly, men they really don't notice what's under their very noses.

"Yes, and in relation to your marriage breakup maybe he blames himself."

When his eyebrows lifted so high they could have taken flight, Melanie lifted her hands, palms out. "Most children do in similar situations."

Dirk shook his head then in her view, deliberately changed the focus of their conversation. "You sound like you speak from experience." He added, "Is that what happened to you, princess? Did your parents split up?"

Melanie breathed deeply for a moment, hiding her clenched hands behind her back. Her voice so low Dirk had to lean forward to hear she said, "No. I was an orphan. Abandoned on the doorstep of a children's home, actually."

"I'm sorry." He began to walk around the side of the desk, purpose etched in the straight line of his mouth.

Terrified he intended to give her sympathy and hold her in his arms, she backed away. For she knew once she was in his arms, then she would never want him to let her go. She whirled round and ran from the room.

Melanie spent the remainder of the day in the kitchen baking. With Tammy an eager helper plus Anabelle once she'd woken from her nap, the girls kept her busy and her mind occupied. Now she surveyed the groaning kitchen table with satisfaction. Cooking had always been a favourite pastime of hers and she loved nothing more than losing herself sourcing new recipes and flavours.

And trying them out, she decided as she patted her tummy.

"Bath time I think," she said. Hands on hips she ruefully examined her helpers. Anabelle looked as if she'd been rolled in flour and some sticky mess covered Tammy's hands and tee-shirt. Even Muffin had clumps of soggy flour dotting her back and wedged between her hairy toes. Tail wagging she licked the muck covering the floor.

"Oh dear, it looks a bit like a war zone." Melanie debated whether to clean the kitchen or clean her helpers.

"Uncle Dirk and Harry are gonna love our cookies, won't they, Aunty Mel?" Tammy stuffed another Anzac biscuit into her mouth.

"I'm positive they will." Melanie gently prised a wooden spoon from Anabelle who instantly opened her mouth and howled at being denied her new skill -- drummer of pots extraordinaire.

"Mine. Mine. Mine." she yelled and kicked her heels against the lino floor causing a cloud of flour to rise in the air and Muffin to sneeze.

Mmmm, definitely children first.

"Later." Melanie helped the toddler to her feet and repeated, "It's bath time young lady."

"Bath," repeated Anabelle instantly forgetting her desire to be a rockstar. She placed her sticky fingers on Melanie's bare leg and grinned up at her.

Not for the first time, did Melanie realise how much she would miss these two once she'd returned to her own life. What would it like to have children of her own? A sudden vision of a dark-haired infant cradled in her arms flashed inside her mind and her eyes blurred with sudden tears.

"Well, I can see you've been busy this afternoon," came Dirk's voice from the doorway.

Blinking, Melanie glanced up to spy him standing hands stuffed in his faded jeans pockets and surveying the carnage that was his kitchen. But he didn't look angry, rather amused, as a wide grin lit his dark features. Harry edged his way around his father's tall figure, to gape then sniffed the air.

"Roast lamb," he said, smacking his lips. "I'm starving, when's dinner, Mel?"

Wow, that's the first time he's called me anything. So that old adage about the way to a man's heart was via his stomach must be true. Melanie glanced at the kitchen clock and smiled. "About half an hour. You'll have time to shower."

He gave a quick grin and ducking his head went to leave the room.

"Wooah, just a minute, Harry. How about you give me a hand cleaning up the kitchen while Melanie sees to washing these two little chefs?"

"No worries, Dad."

"It's not a problem, I can see to the kitchen. Both of you have been working hard all day," Melanie said, her gaze travelling from father to son then back again.

"It's non-negotiable. Anyway, the sight of these two is putting me off my food."

Melanie chuckled. "They're not that bad. Okay, well your help will be very much appreciated. Thank you. I'm afraid we got a little carried away."

"A little?" Dirk laughed.

Harry, his eyebrows raised so high they disappeared into his flop of brown hair, stared hard at his father.

Feeling that annoying heat bathing her cheeks once more, Melanie swept Anabelle into her arms. "Come on Tammy."

Dirk walked to the broom cupboard and Melanie herded Tammy and Muffin down the hallway to the bathroom. By the time the girls and Muffin were denuded of the afternoon's efforts, Melanie needed a wash herself.

After checking the time, she left them playing dolls in the living room and had a super-quick shower before donning a sleeveless white cotton dress with thin straps, a moulded bodice and a lovely floaty, knee-length skirt. A dash of lipstick and a quick brush of her hair and she was ready. She padded bare-feet to the kitchen to pause for a moment near the table marvelling at the changes Dirk and Harry had wrought. The ding of the timer on the stove had her hauling on an apron then opening the oven door to inspect the contents.

She was arranging the roast vegetables on a serving dish when damp-haired Dirk entered. Bemused she zeroed in on the tanned flesh of his chest exposed by the open-necked shirt. Clad in a clean white short-sleeved shirt tucked into fresh linen pants, he looked good enough to eat.

"I'll give you a hand." He crossed over and began slicing the roast shoulder of lamb. "This smells fabulous. Have you added something different?"

"Different?" Not daring to look up again, Melanie dished up vegetables as if her life depended on it.

"It smells different to Mrs Weber's baked dinners."

"Mmmm, I'm not sure how your housekeeper cooks it but I've added a glaze of honey and herbs plus I've poked garlic cloves throughout the meat."

Dirk groaned. "I don't know why but I never thought you'd be a good cook."

That got her attention. Melanie planted her hands on her hips and glared. "Why? Is that because you don't think I'd be good at anything?"

"Hey." He raised his hands in the air. "It's just that I never thought of you as a home-body."

"Right, so how exactly do you think of me?"

Dirk compressed his lips and transferred his gaze to the table. A pulse ticked beside his tight mouth.

"Well?"

"I think it would be best if we leave this topic for another time. The dogs and your cat have been fed by the way. Sounds like a riot going on in there." He indicated the doorway from where shrieks echoed from the living room.

Raising his voice, he called, "Harry, stop teasing your cousins."

"Fine, but don't think I'll forget about this, because I won't. It's about time you told me what's eating you." Melanie grabbed the serving dish and carried it into the dining room. She supposed she should be grateful he'd helped out especially as he'd been working on the land during the afternoon but damnit she was tired of his suspicions and wary attitude.

Not that there'd been any sting behind his words this time, rather his tone had been teasing and his voice full of warm appreciation. Had he mellowed towards her? It horrified her, how much she wanted his good opinion. Pushing her confused thoughts aside, she concentrated on setting the table.

~

The meal was a resounding success and well worth the time she's spent in the kitchen. Melanie glanced around at the others then leant over to wipe gravy from Anabelle's mouth with a napkin.

Harry placed his knife and fork on the table and heaved a satisfied sigh.

"Full?" Melanie asked. She smiled. "I hope not, because there's lemon meringue pie for dessert. It's in the fridge."

"Awesome," said Harry and raced into the kitchen to return a moment later with a covered pie dish. Brown eyes sparkling, he carved himself a hefty slice.

"Don't forget the cookies Tammy and Anabelle made," said Dirk grinning.

"They are the best, Uncle Dirk," said Tammy. She slipped a slice of meat under the table to Muffin.

Dirk sipped his merlot then said, "Everyone will be pleased to learn we're off to the rodeo next weekend."

"Bonza!" Tammy clapped her hands and bounced in her seat.

"I'm not going," muttered Harry as he shovelled pie into his mouth.

"I said, everyone, Harry." Dirk placed his glass down.

Harry glared across the table at Melanie who gave him a sunny smile in return.

"And tomorrow, we'll take a few hours off to show the ladies the lagoon. Once that rain reaches us it may be several weeks before the road is safe." Dirk lifted his slice of pie onto a plate, picked up his spoon. He raised the laden spoon and opened his mouth. "Heavenly," he said, closing his eyes as if to savour the tart flavours.

Her heart rate galloping along at the notion of spending more time in his proximity, Melanie picked at her tiny portion of pie pondering the use of his word, *ladies*. Said casually, no inflection in his tone. What was he up to? She looked up to find his intent gaze on her face and heat washed over her. No, more than heat, she realised as her skin tingled as if a million feathers had brushed over it. Beneath the table, she pressed her trembling knees together.

She forced herself to eat the dessert.

After dabbing at her mouth with her napkin, she said, "I need to take a trip into Brisbane. Is that doable?"

Dirk tapped his forefinger on the table and considered her. "Any particular reason?"

"I have business to attend to." No way could she admit it was James' business. "I wondered whether Ted could fly us there."

"Us?"

"I thought I'd take the girls and Harry with me. That is if he'd like to come. After I've concluded my business, we could spend the remainder of the day at Sea World."

"Sea World?" squealed Tammy. "Come on, Harry, please come."

"That is not fair tactics," said Dirk, nodding towards an excited Tammy who jumped out of her chair and raced around the table to pull at her cousin's arm.

Melanie lifted her shoulders and attempted a look of innocence.

"All right, princess. You can have your way. But," he lifted a finger in the air, "there will be conditions. One, I will go with you." He watched her with the intensity of a hawk.

With great difficulty Melanie managed not to twitch under his regard.

"I've got to see my financial manager anyway, so this will be a good opportunity. The other condition is we will need to stay overnight. There's no way we'll be able to cram everything in one day after we factor in flying time."

Wordless, Melanie nodded.

"That's settled then. I'll contact Ted and arrange the flights."

Melanie bunched the napkin into a ball.

Now how am I going to wriggle some alone time?

What had seemed like a good idea had morphed into a very difficult situation.

CHAPTER 9

It took some time to settle Tammy and Anabelle after dinner. The older girl was so excited by the treats in store she wound up her younger sister until neither would go to sleep. Not even a story read by their cousin worked and Melanie ended up resorting to threats of cancelling all merry-go-round rides unless both closed their eyes immediately.

By the time she exited their bedroom, she wanted nothing more than the sanctuary of her own space and time to unwind. The lure of the orange grove beckoned like a siren's call but she resisted. For she had resolved that tonight it was time to clear the air.

Feeling rather militant she marched in to the living room, where Harry who'd had his head buried in a video game, looked up and upon catching sight of her, mumbled some excuse, grabbed his game control and fled.

An action Melanie regretted for his presence would have acted as a nice, safe buffer between her and Dirk.

"Sherry?" Dirk held a bottle high.

"Yes, thank you." She crossed the room and sat down in

an armchair. Mr Gibbs jumped from his perch on the fireplace onto her lap and kneaded her legs. "Ouch." A gentle push from her and the cat curled into a ball on her thighs and closed its eyes.

"Spoilt," said Dirk handing her a sherry glass filled with amber liquid.

"I know, but he had such a terrible life before I rescued him."

Dirk raised his eyebrows. "I believe you've mentioned something similar in a previous conversation."

She shrugged, took a sip of the sherry before saying, "Rescuing animals is my passion. I run a small shelter for abandoned and stray dogs and cats. The shelter isn't very big as I can't afford much but James and Catherine allow me to rent space at their vineyard for peanuts. Their odd-job man, Ned, looks after them for me during the working week. Even Muffin was a rescue. She'd been abused by back-yard breeders and made to have litter after litter. It was appalling the conditions she lived under. I had to threaten the owners with court action plus hand over a *'bribe'* but it was worth it."

"You harbour very strong feelings towards animal welfare. Well done you for taking action." Dirk swallowed his finger of whiskey. After setting the tumbler down on a side table he sat down in the armchair next to her. "I think I'm beginning to understand."

Understand what? Melanie frowned into the distance for a few minutes before she realised he called her name. And not for the first time.

"I'm sorry, my thoughts were far away." She placed her forefinger behind Mr Gibbs right ear and stroked his coarse fur. It wasn't often she opened up to virtual strangers so why did she feel the need to share a piece of herself with this man? *Be careful,* warned the wary voice that lived inside her heart.

Willing herself not to retreat to her room, she turned her

head and gave Dirk a friendly smile. He was leaning back, looking extremely comfortable with his legs crossed at his ankles and his arms lying on the armrests, fingers loose. No sign of any cynical twist to his mouth. In fact, even his lips looked relaxed. And tempting. What would they feel like against her skin?

Focus.

Clearing her throat delicately, she said, "Actually I'm glad we have a few moments alone, Dirk. I want you to understand exactly what James means to me and how we came to be friends. I fear we could be at cross-purposes. Or perhaps you have misunderstood the situation?" She made the last statement into a question deliberately defusing the comment so he wouldn't misconstrue it as an attack.

"I admit these past few days it has crossed my mind that perhaps I may have been mistaken and allowing my past to prejudice me against you."

Startled she gaped at him. Her heart clenched at the warmth in his eyes as his gaze held hers.

"Why don't you give me your version?" he prompted.

Voice tart, she said, "It's not a 'version', it's the truth. But very well, provided you don't interrupt me."

His mouth quirked at the corners as if he suppressed a grin. When he murmured an agreement, she averted her eyes to stare down at the purring cat. Somehow, she it was easier to reveal her bleak past if she didn't look at him.

She said in a matter-of-fact voice, "James and I met in a children's home after I'd been placed there by Welfare. My mother, who was, I think, about eighteen at the time, decided she couldn't cope with being a single parent. Apparently, I was the result of a one-night stand. She took me to this building and told me to sit on the step until someone came outside. It was a horrible place and I was very lonely. James was the first friend I ever had."

Dirk stifled an exclamation then said softly, "Go on."

"I'm not saying all this to garner your sympathy." Melanie shot him a glare. "But you need to know the world where both James and I come from forged a strong bond between us. There were about twenty of us in that place. It was clean but run more like a prison than a home. Occasionally we were fostered out and many were very rough places; especially the last house." She drew a shaky breath. "The son didn't take it very well when I smacked him on the nose for getting too friendly with me. He waited until I was alone before extracting his revenge. But James arrived."

No need to tell him the specifics of that horrible day. She spread her hands wide. "And that's it really. I met your sister through James, and we were lucky enough to become friends too. James called me for help when they had problems, so I came. He knows I run a successful practice in relationship counselling and thought I could help. I understand your view of opposite sex friendships has been tainted by your own experiences. I suspect you think I'm a threat to your sister's happiness, which I assure you I'm not."

"You're right I did believe that but these past few days have shown me how much integrity you have; there is no way you'd be so underhanded. I can understand a bond that's formed through difficult circumstances." Dirk captured her gaze again and this time she didn't look away. "Our parents may have stayed together, however they weren't particularly interested in family life. They lived the *'free and easy'* lifestyle of hippies with people of similar ilk running about the vineyard which they allowed to run into the ground. I remember lots of wild parties with drugged up strangers wandering through our house. After one rather frightening night, I put locks on our bedroom doors."

Dirk ran a hand through his hair, his expression grim.

"Life was...difficult. But we were lucky. Our grandfather took us in after Welfare contacted him and he realised what was happening. He became the only real parent we ever had and when retired he made the station over to me. Catherine inherited the vineyard when our parents were killed in a car crash. Both were high on drugs at the time. We were in our teens then. It took quite a deal of good management and hard work by Pops to make the vineyard a profitable concern once again."

"And I thought you'd had an easy life," Melanie tried a shaky smile. *Oh boy. What will he do, if he finds out the vineyard's about to be signed over to a crooked bookie?*

"Assumptions can often be wrong," Dirk agreed.

She picked up Mr Gibbs and holding him close, rose to her feet. "Well, thank you for listening. I think I'll turn in, it's been a long day." *Before I cave and blub out my problems all over those broad shoulders.*

Dirk also stood. He stepped closer. Right up into her personal space and placed the knuckle of his right hand under her chin.

"Pleasant dreams, princess." Then he placed a feather-soft kiss on her lips.

Surprisingly, Melanie slept like the dead that night, waking in the early morning to find a day that promised heat and endless sunshine. She stretched languidly and lay a moment pondering that kiss. A kiss that had ended way too fast and yet it had seared straight to her heart.

So brief but it had soothed away a little of her childhood nightmares.

She found herself smiling as she scrambled out of bed before pulling on a cotton kimono over her cotton tank and shorties. Hugging herself at an entire day spent in *his* company she left her bedroom. Then she checked on Tammy and Anabelle, thankfully both still sound asleep. With Muffin, scampering about her feet, she headed for the kitchen and switched on the coffee percolator.

A panting noise interrupted her daydreaming and she

approached the screen door where Dirk's working dogs sat, tails wagging and waiting for a feed. They whined and pricked their ears and she laughed. After filling their feed bowls that resided on the verandah, she emptied the heavy metal bucket and re-filled it with fresh water for them. Not the least bit intimidated by their size, Muffin squirmed her way through the mass of bodies wolfing down food, to gobble her share from the bowls.

"You are going to become fat if you're not careful." Melanie smiled and shook her head at her little dog.

Back in the kitchen she laid out bacon, eggs, chipolata sausages and tomatoes then commenced cooking breakfast. It wasn't long before the room was redolent with the smell of frying food, making her stomach growl.

There was nothing like coffee and bacon to wake the taste buds.

It wouldn't be long before everyone else followed their noses into the dining room. In fact, she was certain she could hear Dirk's deep rumble intermingled with Tammy's excited squeals. She quickly placed the full serving dishes on top of the warmer and hurried to her room to change.

A feat which took her longer than usual as she dithered over the contents of her suitcases for quite a while before shaking out an A'line leaf-green, cotton dress, a long-sleeved white, cotton cardigan to protect her arms from the sun and her favourite sandals. She braided her hair, dabbed a tiny dot of *Joop* under each ear lobe and rushed into the girls' bedroom only to find Dirk had been there before her and room was empty.

After a noisy breakfast, Harry and Tammy cleared up while Melanie packed sandwiches made from leftover roast lamb and salad.

"Tammy, don't forget to put your bathers on under your clothes and a towel in your backpack," she reminded the little girl as she shoved into the hamper the Anzac biscuits the girls had 'made' and chopped up fruit for afters.

"No worries, Aunty Mel." Tammy raced from the kitchen.

"Thank you, Harry." Melanie smiled at the boy who mumbled a gruff, *'not a problem, mate'* under his breath and also departed.

Dirk strolled in with a chuckling Anabelle in his arms. "Almost ready, princess? It'll be sundown at the rate you're going before we even leave the house."

"Very funny. Why don't you pack the hamper into the car while I organise a change of clothes for Anabelle."

"Sure thing, boss lady."

The teasing warmth of his grin remained in her mind as she scurried from the room with the same haste as a lizard fleeing from a wedge-tailed eagle.

Two hours later, the land-cruiser coasted to a halt beneath the shade of a tall, weeping-mulga tree.

"This is lovely. Who would have thought there'd be water out here in all this barren dirt?" Melanie gaped through the windscreen at the view.

Set in the heart of a large woodland of mulga and eucalypt trees and smaller growing acacia bushes, the lagoon spread out the size of a football field. An expanse of muddy sand made up its shores and a wide wooden deck had been built out to the centre where a flock of five pelicans drifted in majestic slow-motion. A faint breeze rippled over the surface, disturbing the mirror-like image of the blue-sky above.

Dirk snorted. "It's not barren, princess. This land supports an abundance of wildlife as well as my cattle. But it is a fragile environment."

"And hard." Melanie turned and looked at him.

He nodded. "Nothing worthwhile is ever easy."

One of my favourite sayings. Melanie picked at the polish on her nails, stewing over that realisation.

"You blokes can sit and yak if you want but I'm boiling. Tam and I are outta here." Harry unbuckled his seat belt and opened the car door. Tammy scrambled after him. He strode round the back of the land-cruiser and let the dogs out. Barking hysterically, they raced for the water and dived in, splashing noisily and causing the pelicans to turn their bright-eyed gaze towards the shore. Muffin yapped and frolicked about the other dogs' heels.

"Let's join them, shall we?" Dirk opened his door and swung out. He leaned back in and said, "We've been lucky this year with rain about a month ago. Before that the last time we had any water in the lagoon was three years ago."

Under his steady regard, Melanie fumbled with her seat belt. "I guess once the rain that's coming down from the north hits, the lagoon will become a lot larger."

"Yeah, we'll have a lake with multiple streams running quite swiftly into it. Harry and I and any of the stockmen who are around at the time, will bring out the kayaks and have a ball. You'll enjoy it." He smiled.

But by then I will be long gone. The thought sank like a stone into the bottom of her belly.

After slamming the door shut, Dirk, whistling a merry tune, unloaded from the roof several folding chairs, a table, containers of water and a bucket for the dogs' water.

And all the while, Melanie sat like a stuffed bush turkey dreaming an impossible dream.

Harry appeared at the door and jerked it open. "I'll supervise the girls if you like, Mel while you and Dad get everything organised."

"Cheers, Harry." Roused from a bitter-sweet fog, Melanie gathered her composure and smiled.

Working together, it wasn't long before they had a miniature camp set up under some shady weeping mulga trees. With a tarp spread on the ground, chairs and a table with the hamper, the scene looked quite inviting, but not as inviting as the sparkle of sunlight on water.

Squeals and shouts came from the lagoon where Harry paddled a blow-up canoe with his cousins sitting side-by-side in the front. Anabelle with floaties around her chest and upper arms, ripped her hat from her head and threw it into the water. She shrieked with laughter when Harry groaned loudly as he attempted to fish it out with the end of a paddle.

"They look like they're having a good time," Melanie said as she wriggled out of her clothes to reveal her one-piece pink swimsuit. Unscrewing her suntan lotion, she began to slather it over her exposed skin. Dirk's lack of response caused her to eventually glance up and find his gaze following the motion of her hands up the side of her leg.

Her throat seized at the heat blazing in the taut lines of his face and the darkness of his eyes. He'd shed his clothes and stood, feet apart clad only in a pair of dark blue board-shorts that hung low on his lean hips below a wash-board hard stomach.

"Why don't I help you with that," he murmured and stepped so close if she'd moved she would have brushed against his bare, brown chest.

The next instant, he'd removed the bottle from her nerveless fingers and pushing her hand aside, smoothed the lotion of her thighs. Round the back of her legs then up over the long line of her spine left bare by her low-backed swimmers. The glide of his warm, calloused hand over her soft skin sent shivers of delight dancing like ballerinas deep down low in the pit of her belly. Breathing hard she closed her eyes for a moment, imprinting his touch on her memory until the sound of childish laughter brought her reluctantly back to the present. *Not the time or the place to indulge her craving for this man.*

He pressed his warm lips against her bare shoulder,

lingering in a kiss that said more than an entire conversation and made her feel her bones were liquefying inside her shaking skin.

Her low, "Thank you," was husky and it took considerable effort to step away from the temptation he presented. She swept him a quick glance then looked towards the children. Mouth trembling she forced herself to place a cloth hat on her head and walk off.

He's teasing me, that's all. It means nothing. And yet the image of his tightly controlled features remained in her mind throughout the proceeding hours they spent together at the lagoon.

It wasn't until well after lunch which they'd spent lolling about in the shade and munching their way through the contents of the hamper, that Melanie managed to procure a moment alone with Harry. He'd raced up from the lagoon to where she sat on the tarp beside Anabelle lying on a small foam mattress sound asleep. Shaking water in all directions much like the dogs bounding along at his side, he flopped onto the ground and reached for a water bottle before chugging down its contents. Out in the middle of the lagoon, Dirk encouraged Tammy to practice her freestyle strokes.

The dogs headed for their bucket of fresh water and jostled each other as they slurped.

Harry indicated his sleeping cousin with a jerk of the water bottle. "I don't mind watching her for a while, if you want to take another swim."

"No that's fine, thank you, Harry. Actually, I'm glad you're here as I want to show you something." Melanie picked up her digital camera, flicked through the photos stored on it for a moment before handing it over.

He cast a questioning glance but obediently looked at the

image depicted on the screen. After staring for a few minutes, his frown cleared and he looked over at her. Incredulity loud in his voice, he said, "Is this you?"

"Yes."

"Why are you showing me this?"

"Because I thought a picture would speak more clearly than words." Melanie shrugged, titled her head on the side and smiled. "My ears used to stick out as much as yours. I was so self-conscious I never wore my hair pinned away from my face."

She heaved a dramatic sigh. "Then there were those terrible freckles, well laser surgery got rid of them. Plus, I did have a tiny nose job."

Harry's goggling gaze dropped to her chest and she snorted out a laugh.

"No, those are all mine, I'm afraid. I love my food too much to watch my diet. I know I should be a lot thinner."

"Nah, you're good as you are," he forced out and red-faced, swallowed as he hastily averted his stare. Whacking the empty bottle on the tarp, he mumbled, "Did it hurt?"

"Having my ears pinned back? No, it was relatively painless and quite a simple procedure. I know of a really good cosmetic surgeon if you're interested. It usually takes anywhere between one to three hours, and of course, you have to be careful for about a week until the stitches dissolve. And even better, he's located in Brisbane."

The hope shining in his brown eyes when he finally met her gaze again, had her heart clenching painfully. Shyly he said, "Do you think you could make me an appointment? I mean, I could just go and see what the doc has to say."

"Oh Harry. But first, you need to talk it through with your father. I'm certain he wouldn't stand in your way." She reached over and squeezed his hand. Beaming she said, "Leave it to me."

"Leave what to you?" asked Dirk striding up, his lean,

hard body glistening from where the sun's rays gilded his wet skin to glittering bronze.

Tammy ran up and collapsed into a chair, but Melanie barely noticed her. Her tongue cleaved to the roof of her mouth as she drank him in.

Beside her, Harry said quickly, "Nothing Dad. We're talking about our trip to Brissie next week."

"Mmmm, well, about that trip. There's been a change in plans. I've arranged for Ted to fly us out in two days' time. I don't want to risk flying once that weather hits us. Hope that suits you, princess."

"Huh?" *What was he talking about again?*

"Aunty Mel, Aunty Mel." sang out Tammy. "I need to go...you know."

"Oh, of course. Here, put your sand-shoes on first." Face on fire beneath two pairs of amused brown eyes, she rose and pulled on her volleys. Holding her hand out to Tammy, they walked away from the camp-site.

"I'm having so much fun. Are you having fun, Aunty Mel?" chattered Tammy. "Oooh, look over there! Emus."

The young girl dropped Melanie's hand and raced off in the direction of a flock of emus that stood with their inquisitive faces and beady black eyes turned in their direction. Puffs of red dust rose around Tammy's feet as she ran.

"Tammy, wait," called Melanie as she hurried after her charge.

Suddenly, Tammy screamed and fell to the ground. Her heart in her throat, Melanie closed the distance fast only to stop three feet from Tammy's legs. The little girl lay prone on the dirt her hands braced either side of her small body. From where she stood, Melanie could see her eyes were open and she was breathing quickly.

Coiled on the ground in a sinister thick, olive-green circle right in front of her head was a snake.

Even as Melanie watched with terror turning her stomach upside down, the reptile rose a metre into the air and swayed, hissing, from side-to-side. There was no mistaking that cream, unmarked belly.

The mulga snake or otherwise known as a king brown.

One of the deadliest in Australia.

CHAPTER 10

"Don't move," Melanie whispered and Tammy blinked to show she'd understood.

Oh God, please no. Had Tammy been bitten? What to do? All she could remember from the documentaries she'd watched was to remain still. Don't make any sudden moves.

Or noise.

Ahead, the snake continued to hiss and sway. Its tongue flickered.

It began to rear backwards.

What if I pull Tammy's legs? Can I get her out of the way in time? The reptile's eyes slitted. *Shit. It's going to strike.*

Melanie dived forward, placing her body in front of the little girl's. At the same instant a shot rang out. Melanie landed on the ground and the snake exploded into a mess of blood and tissue.

Shuddering she crouched over Tammy while moist bits landed on her hair and remained protecting the small girl until Dirk gripped Melanie's waist and lifted her to her feet.

"Melanie. Have you been bitten?" The hoarse words were shouted at her as Dirk set her down on her bottom and ran

172

his hands over her head fingering her scalp and over the tops of her shoulders looking for puncture wounds.

"I'm fine. At least I'm fairly sure I am. Check Tammy."

"I'm okay," said Tammy. "I saw the snake then tripped and fell to the ground. It was asleep and I woke it up." She burst into noisy tears and scrambled into Melanie's open arms.

"Oh, thank heavens," Melanie whispered, clutching her close. Her gaze alighted on the rifle lying on the ground and the gory mess that remained of the reptile and she burst into tears as well.

"It's all right, everything's all right," Dirk wrapped his arms around both of them and pulled them against his chest. He murmured the words over and over into Melanie's hair as she trembled and Tammy sobbed.

At last, Melanie pulled away from the haven of his arms. She gave a terse-faced Dirk a watery smile then cupped Tammy's face in her hands and looked into the little girl's still terrified eyes. Tammy hiccupped.

"It's okay. Look your Uncle Dirk killed it."

"I don't want to look," said Tammy, her slight body shaking under Melanie's hands.

Voice harsh, Dirk said, "I wouldn't normally shoot but I had to in this instance. We're too far from medical help and I couldn't risk one of you would be bitten."

Through wobbly lips, Melanie said, "Do you always carry your rifle with you?"

"Always." He sat back on his haunches, allowing his hands to fall from her waist. "When I heard you call for Tammy to come back, some sixth sense made me grab the rifle from the cruiser and follow."

That must have been one amazing shot.

Her eyes filled again. "Thank you," she mouthed.

Dirk passed a hand over his eyes and averted his gaze.

"Dad?" Harry, with Anabelle in his arms, walked up to

hover near his father who immediately rose to his feet and slung an arm around his son's shoulders for a quick squeeze.

"All good, mate."

With his eyes glued to Melanie and Tammy, Harry said, "I told the dogs to stay and locked Muffin in the cruiser. The windows are part way down so she shouldn't get too hot."

"Thanks, Harry," said Melanie. Hoping to drive away the horror still staring out of Tammy's white ridged eyes, she added, "I need another swim. I'm covered in snake goo."

Tammy sniffed then giggled. "Oooh, yuk." She wriggled out of Melanie's hold to throw her arms around Dirk's legs. "Thanks, Uncle Dirk. Just wait 'till I tell Mum and Dad. Oh, can I use the internet tonight, Uncle Dirk? I want to tell my bestie, Georgia what happened. She's so going to wish she'd been here."

Her knees feeling as soggy as over-cooked pumpkin, Melanie stood up and followed a now recovered Tammy holding onto her cousin, Harry's hand as she trotted beside him chattering nineteen to the dozen.

"Feeling better, princess?" Dirk asked, his rifle slung under his armpit and his forearm supporting the opened muzzle.

Too spent for words, Melanie nodded.

Dirk linked her hand in his and together they returned to the lagoon.

After a subdued dinner that night, everyone departed for their rooms. By the way Tammy and Anabelle were acting up, Dirk knew Melanie would have a fight on her hands getting them to settle for sleep. But for the life of him, he had no energy to offer to help. He knew he should, but he was too shaken with not only the events of the day but with the life-changing realisation that had hit him with the force of a lightning bolt.

With one arm draped along the mantle-piece above the fire, he stared down into the empty hearth, reliving that moment when he'd believed his world had come to an end.

At first, he'd thought his niece had been bitten and he'd experienced such a gut-wrenching fear, if he hadn't kept running he would have fallen to the ground.

What happened next would remain with him all the days of his life.

Like a movie on constant replay, he recalled the moment Melanie placed herself in front of an aggressive mulga snake to protect a child that wasn't hers.

Saw the snake rear back.

It's mouth open.

The glistening fangs, the dripping saliva.

The smooth deadly metal of the gun had been cold in his hands, as he lined up the sights, squeezed the trigger and the rifle had bucked into his shoulder as he fired.

And all the time, there'd been no air in his lungs, so tight had been his chest. His heart had slammed like a canon ball against his rib cage.

Inside his soul, denial had screamed to the heavens above for mercy.

For he knew if he missed, there would be no second chance.

He'd once seen a mulga snake latch onto the hind leg of a Brahman bull. Unlike other snake species, the damn thing had hung on chewing into the cow's leg as it injected massive amounts of highly toxic venom. Needless to say, he'd put a bullet to the bull's head. The only thing to do and in the circumstances, the kindest.

His hand shaking, Dirk formed a fist then straightened and left the house. He bid his dogs stay on the verandah then strode to the barn where a small gym had been set up in a room off to the side. After binding his hands and wrists with cloth, he pounded into the punching bag until sweat dripped off his brow and coated his back.

Finally, he stopped. Clutching the bag in both arms, he leant his head against the leather. *When had she become so important to him?* He couldn't say. He'd known an instant physical attraction which he'd constantly fought since the first moment he'd set eyes on her; despite his resentment at her intrusion in his life all those years ago. Then that sneaking desire to protect and care for her had penetrated his defences every now and then when he let his guard down. The gentle aura that surrounded her drew him like a magnet. And he'd been nothing but impressed with the love and attention she showered on his nieces.

But love? Could he? Did he?

He knew so little about her.

But one thing was certain she was the woman of his heart.

But could she live out here? A woman who knew nothing but city life – his ex sure couldn't hack it and she'd been born here.

Doubts gnawed at him.

"Sorry, princess, but I need to sort this mess my sister and brother-in-law are in first. Then maybe sweetheart, just maybe we can work something out," he muttered to the punching bag.

"Dad? Who ya talking to?"

Dirk stepped back and turned around to see Harry standing in the doorway, hands in jeans pockets.

"Myself," Dirk said ruefully. "Come in and give me a round."

"No worries." Harry grinned and headed for the equipment cupboard for the boxing gloves. He a pair over to Dirk then pulled on his own.

"Mouthguards," Dirk reminded him.

"Awe, yeah. Forgot." Harry opened a new box and tossed

him one. Before slipping his over his teeth, he said, "That was pretty cool thing, Mel did today."

Dirk grunted and stretched his neck from side to side, jiggling his shoulders to loosen the muscles.

Harry persisted, "She's a bit of an all right."

Surprised, Dirk removed the mouthguard and said, "Yeah? I thought you couldn't stand her."

Shrugging, Harry jogged in one spot to warm up. "At first, I didn't but that's only 'cause I thought she was a prissy city girl and Uncle James' sheila. But anyone with one eye can see they're the best of mates. Plus, she fits in, like she'd meant to be here."

Dirk frowned into the distance thinking over his son's words. It seemed his son was maturing fast. He'd certainly discerned the true nature of matters far more quickly than Dirk.

"Mel says she knows this great doc. She says this bloke is really good at cosmetic surgery. I want to go see him, when we're in Brissie and have a chat about my ears."

"What?" Feeling like he'd been punched in the ribs, Dirk gaped over at his son standing beside him. *Where the hell had this come from?*

"I've got a bit of a thing about them, Dad. I figure once they're fixed, I could start going to the rodeos and maybe heading into town more often."

Head reeling, Dirk muttered, "I had no idea you felt like that, son."

"Mel says it's okay to have doubts about yourself. She says it's better than being cocky and arrogant. Mel says the trick is to not let your doubts hold you back. But to face your fears and take control of your life."

Hardly daring to believe the words coming from his son's mouth, Dirk managed a mumbled, "Really?"

"Yep. So you're okay with the doc's?"

"I'm okay." Dirk reached out and rubbed his gloved hand

over his son's head. *Bloody hell. He's shot up fast. He's nearly as tall as I am. In a few years he'll be a man. And I've been so blind to his needs. Well that's going to change and it's not the only thing that's going to change around here.*

"One round or two?" Dirk grinned at his son.

Harry snorted. "Come on, Dad. You're getting old. Let's make it three."

~

Worn out, Melanie and the girls slept through breakfast. It wasn't until Tammy jumped on her bed and tapped her shoulder, did Melanie drag herself from the depths of an exhausted slumber. Groggy, she stared at a still pyjama clad Tammy for a moment then wordlessly held out her arms and gave the young girl a hug. Those terrible moments of yesterday were too fresh in her mind.

"Good morning, sweatpea," she said.

"G'day, Aunty Mel. What are we gonna do today?"

Melanie eyed Tammy, shuddering at the barely-restrained energy bouncing off her in waves. "Something quiet. Is Anabelle awake?"

"Yep and she's been changed. Uncle Dirk did it. He said to tell you to take it easy and not rush. He said he's fed the dogs and Mr Gibbs and he and Harry have gone out on the bikes to move cows to higher ground."

Higher ground? Melanie frowned. To her untrained urban eyes, the land around here was as flat as a pancake. She made a mental note to query Dirk on his return. "Okay, how about we both get dressed and do something about breakfast."

"No worries, Aunty Mel." Tammy jumped to the floor and raced from the room, slamming the door behind her.

Where did this sudden penchant for *'Aussie slang'* come from? Possibly gleaned from her cousin whose shadow she'd become.

A super quick cold shower did wonders to wake Melanie up and when she left her bedroom dressed in a pair of high-top cotton shorts and a lime green tank top, she was ready for whatever the day would throw at her.

On entering the living room, she found Tammy playing 'dolls' with her younger sister, dolls clothes and furniture strewn over the rug where they sat. Mr Gibbs raised his head and stared at Melanie through his bottle green eyes, then stood up and turned his back to her before settling down again. Oh dear, that's someone who isn't happy he didn't receive his good morning treat along with his breakfast.

Silly perhaps to feel hurt over a cat's actions but she'd always considered her animals like family. She walked over and opened the screen door to admit Muffin into the house and who'd been basking on the verandah in the bright morning sun.

"Let's do some cooking this morning, shall we?" Melanie said.

"Bonzer!" shouted Tammy springing to her feet.

"Then we'll attack the pile of washing in the laundry."

"Ooooh, yuck." Tammy made a face as she held out a hand and helped an unsteady Anabelle to her feet.

"Perhaps pancakes with maple syrup will make you feel better, Tammy."

"Eureka."

Smiling at the young girl's excitement, Melanie herded her charges into the kitchen where she found a note with her name on it attached to the refrigerator with a galah magnet. In his bold black script, Dirk had written: *Stay close to the homestead today and keep your pets close at hand. Wind and rain is forecast for the afternoon.*

The realisation he'd considered the welfare of her animals, caused her heart to swell. And the forecast gave her the perfect excuse to loll about and watch a dvd. Melanie heaved a pleased sigh at the prospect of some nice, *quiet* relaxing time.

"Hurry up, Aunty Mel!" hollered Tammy from inside the pantry. She emerged with all sorts of food stuffs clutched in her thin arms.

Bang, bang, Anabelle had found her 'drum' kit and sat on her bottom under the table wielding a wooden spoon.

Okay, quiet time is definitely not now. Melanie pressed her index finger to her forehead for a moment and indulged in a brief fantasy of a facial, a massage and a pedicure in a nice, *quiet* day spa. But when her gaze met the young girl's trusting eyes, her fantasy vanished. No, playing Mum was definitely more rewarding than her solitary, single life. Melanie swooped down and lifted Anabelle into her arms, planting a gentle kiss on her soft hair.

She pointed to the pantry door. "Put an apron on this time please, Tammy. Now, let's get started shall we?"

"How was your day, ladies?" asked Dirk the instant he strode through the front door and entered the living room.

Wow. That's such a domesticated greeting, I can't believe he said it. Owl eye-ed, Melanie stared at him from where she sat on the lounge, a sleeping Anabelle lying with her head in Melanie's lap. Her dog and cat curled up at her feet and Tammy lying full length on the rug on the floor, her head propped in her hands as she watched a Disney movie.

Melanie mumbled, "Fine thanks."

Across the room her gaze locked with his and a tiny smile curved the edges of his mouth. Dust smeared his cotton-drill trousers and long-sleeved faded blue cotton shirt. He'd already removed his Akubra and his tousled hair gave him an air of easy approachability.

It took every grain of resolution she possessed not to rush over there and wrap her arms around his neck.

Without turning around, Tammy piped, "Hello, Uncle Dirk. Are the cows okay?"

His mouth twitched and Melanie sighed, admiring the sexy curve and fullness of his lips.

"The cows are fine, Tammy." Straightening from where he leaned over the armchair he said, "We've had to move our plans forward a tad, Melanie."

What happened to calling me 'princess'?

Dirk continued, "That weather system I mentioned previously is moving a lot faster than the bureau predicted. If we want to make that trip to Brissie before it hits, we need to limit our stay to one day. I've arranged for Ted to pick us up at six in the morning and he's scheduled our return flight to leave Brisbane Domestic at seven thirty tomorrow night. Will that cause any problems to your plans?"

"No, I should be able to make alternate appointments." She nodded towards the girls. "What about Sea World?"

"If we organise our personal business for the morning that would leave the remainder of the day, say after a late lunch, the kids' treat time."

"Sounds like a plan. Do you mind if I use your office now?"

"No worries. I'll take a quick shower and spend some time with my girls, here." He sent a slow smile in her direction, one that hit her like a punch to the chest.

Breathless, she hurried off trying not to dwell on her quivering stomach muscles and how much she'd wanted to trace the line of stubble that edged his jaw. And how impressed she was with how he'd arranged matters to ensure his son and nieces still enjoyed a few hours of fun.

This man ran deep.

～

Later that evening, Melanie strolled out to the verandah. Resting her hands on the railing, she stared out into the darkness, allowing her mind to empty of all her concerns. The girls were in bed with Muffin and Mr Gibbs occupying the ends of their beds. Harry had disappeared into his room after a gruff, barely audible explanation. The night was still early and the novel she'd brought with her would be a good way to unwind but it remained unopened on the coffee table. She admitted she was reluctant to end the day without snagging a little more time with Dirk.

And if she was truly honest, what she really wanted was a kiss. Or even better, more than a kiss. To feel his arms wrap around her, his body hard against hers and pretend for a little while, they were together. A couple.

She could then take a few special memories with her when she departed. It might not be much but it was all she dared to snatch.

Behind her, the french doors opened and closed, and ice cubes chinked against glass.

Anticipation tightened her nerve ends, sent her heart skipping a demented beat as she sensed his presence close behind her. *Would he act on the signals she'd sent him all evening? Or would he reject her?*

Fear closed her throat in a tight choke hold.

Maybe this was a bad idea. Wouldn't it be better for her dreams to remain just that? Dreams? Her thoughts chased around her mind like a flock of birds while she gripped the railing so hard her hands cramped.

Dirk cleared his throat softly. "I've got us both an iced tea garnished with lemon. Thought you'd prefer this to alcohol."

Taking a deep breath, she flexed her fingers and turned. At the sight of his smile, her indecision fell like a discarded cloak to the floor.

"I do, thank you." Melanie took the proffered glass. "Cheers." Raising the drink to her lips, she sipped, keeping her gaze fixed on his face. Elation filled her, as his eyes darkened and dropped to stare at her mouth.

I wasn't wrong, he does want me. But she wasn't such a fool as to think physical want was anything more than that, an attraction of the flesh. For how could he feel anything more for her given the circumstances? *And that will suit me just fine too.*

Another wave of goose-bumps brushed over her skin. *Should I make the first move, or should I wait? Oh, why is dealing with the opposite sex so difficult?*

She licked her lips, soaking up the refreshing lemon tinged taste. He stood completely still, tension radiating from his body.

Somewhere out in the darkness a dingo howled.

Using the glass held in her hand, Melanie indicated the vista beyond the homestead. "He sounds lonely."

"Dingos are actually very social animals and usually belong to packs as many as twelve. They mostly hunt alone though."

Both fell silent.

"I think it's beautiful out here," Melanie finally blurted.

Dirk stepped closer. At the last minute moved to stand beside her. Even through the darkness she could feel the intensity of his gaze. Leaning his tall body against the verandah post, he said, "Not everyone can handle the quiet. Or the hard work. At times, it can be a lonely way of life."

"Do you get lonely?" she asked quietly.

He shrugged. "On occasions. But I keep busy. Plus, I have Harry, friends from neighbouring stations, mates who live in Longreach. I make sure Harry and I get away from *The Golden Perch Station* at least once every twelve or sixteen months to the coast for a break."

"What about Harry's mother? Does she visit often?"

Dirk gave a short laugh. "Valerie has been back, oh about four times since we separated. She grew up here you know.

On the station to the west of us. I thought she'd want to stay, that she loved this life as much as I do but she couldn't wait to leave for the bright lights."

He reached out and took the glass from her suddenly nerveless fingers. Her pulse soaring to the glittering stars above, she watched him deposit both drinks onto a cane table before he walked back to stand in front of her.

His fingers trailed down her left cheek, across her lower lip where he smoothed his thumb over its curves. He whispered, "I don't blame her for leaving me, but I hate it when she disappoints Harry. And what about you, princess? I thought you'd be a real whinging willy demanding to be taken into town every other day."

"Shopping malls are overrated." Her body thrumming with want, Melanie placed her open hands on his chest. His heat warmed her palms instantly. Tingles tickled her fingertips and sizzled like fizzing firecrackers along her veins until every inch of her trembled.

Deep inside her heart, she took a tiny virtual step forward and choked out, "I love it here."

And not only because here is where you are.

"Yeah, I really believe you do," he said, awe and surprise deepening his voice.

Too wound up to wait any longer, Melanie raised herself on her bare toes until their mouths were mere inches apart.

"You sure you want this, princess? Once we start, there'll be no turning back."

With clear emphasis on each word, she said, "I want this."

Dirk lowered his head and his lips met hers. Silky soft, pliant they moved over hers in a gentle caress more question than demand. A question she was more than ready to answer.

Her blood roaring in her ears, Melanie pressed closer and kissed him back with an ever-increasing hunger. His hands gripped her waist, pulled her square against him. Her breath caught in her throat as she relished the glorious sensation of his hard muscles beneath her fingers. His sex was hard against her belly and her muscles dissolved into molten honey. When his hand closed over her swollen right breast, a quiver ran through her limbs. She closed her eyes murmuring her approval deep in her throat. This felt so good. His skin was rough against her smoothness and sent a delicious sensation tingled down her legs to her curling toes.

He pulled back and mumbled near her lips, "Strewth, you feel good. I'm not going too fast for you, am I?"

"No, everything's perfect, just the way it should be," she said in a breathless voice she hardly recognised as her own. By angling her head a fraction, she captured his lips with hers in a kiss that lasted an eternity.

Dirk finally wrenched his mouth to her chin and nibbled his way along her jaw-line to swirl his tongue around her sensitive ear-lobe.

Sucking in air as if she was a swimming going down for the last time she wove one hand through his hair, allowing the silky strands to glide between her fingers. With the other hand she held on tight to his shoulder as his mouth moved down her throat then lower to the neckline of her cotton singlet top.

Dirk followed the edge with this tongue and she shuddered, heat blistering over her flesh and boiling her senses to fever point.

His face turned aside, and he rested his cheek on her breasts, breathing heavily. His arms were like iron bands around her giving her the impression he would never let her go. Dirk mumbled, "I don't fool around. Sex is like....you know....like a kinda commitment for me. Just thought you should know."

Oh my goodness. Does he mean it? Laughter bubbled like champagne popping inside her heart.

Smiling she opened her eyes and whispered, "I'm fussy

too about who I go to bed with, so I guess we have that in common."

He pulled back and stared down into her upturned face as if searching for an elusive gold mine. His grip tightened. "Yeah, we do."

His lips nibbled along the line of her shoulder trailing fire over her skin. He was all heat, all hard-packed muscle and yet his mouth was tender and his hands so very caressing with his touch. *I want him so much.* She ran her fingers teasingly down his spine to the waistband of his linen cargo-pants and slipped one hand under to explore the tight contours of his buttocks.

"Cheeky," he mumbled against her mouth before claiming her lips in another long kiss that flipped her heart upside down.

The next moment, he scooped her up into his arms. Nuzzling her hair, he whispered near her ear, "No sneaking off afterwards. I want to wake in the morning beside you. Your room or mine?"

"Yours," she said, snuggling closer and laying her head against the heavy thump of his heart.

His teeth flashed in a wide grin as he carried her into the house.

CHAPTER 11

Over the expanse of a grey Formica and metal-legged desk, Melanie fielded the curious gaze of Roscoe who, courtesy of Skype, stared shark-eyed back at her from the computer screen.

Keeping her shoulders straight she resisted the urge to sweep another glance around the Internet Cafe in the heart of Brisbane CBD, just in case someone was watching. *I'm becoming paranoid.*

For what sounded like the hundredth time, Roscoe repeated, "Seriously, Mel I don't see what Jimmy's money hassles have to do with you."

Melanie adjusted her earphones a trifle. "That's not the issue here, Roscoe. I understand an offer has been made to take over the debt on his vineyard. I need to know if it's you."

How will James take it, if the offer is from Roscoe? It would be just like him to kick James when he's already down. Roscoe could then use the vineyard as a means of laundering his grubby money. Another slap in the face to James for daring to leave his gang all those years ago. Bile burned in her belly as she considered Dirk and Catherine's reaction to this mess.

An oily smile spread over Roscoe's face and she sighed inwardly. Roscoe had always been unpredictable.

"Why should I tell you?"

"Because we were friends once."

Roscoe snarled looking frighteningly like the near-animal he had become. "Those days are long past. I owe you nothing. I don't owe anyone, anything."

"You're not the only one who had it bad there, Roscoe." Sudden sympathy softened her voice.

"Spare me the details. I'm not interested." He leaned back and straightened his pale pink silk tie with what looked like perfectly manicured hands. "Check me out, Mel. I'm no longer the ugly, fat kid with a deformed arm. I've made it. I've got this swish apartment on the North Shore, a wardrobe of designer clothing and a long, line of beautiful women begging to date me."

"Only because you used people to get where you are now."

"Mel, is that any way to ask someone for a favour?" He tilted his head on the side and lifted his eyebrows. There was no light in those curiously flat grey eyes and she shuddered.

She'd been there; she'd witnessed most of what he'd had to live through. They'd all been so young, so helpless...so alone. But she and James had found refuge at the youth community with Father Brian.

Roscoe? Well Roscoe had found something else.

"Can't you stop your games? I don't have a lot of time. Really Roscoe, it's a simple question and I don't understand why you won't answer me." Melanie took a deep breath. "I don't know why you'd shaft James like this either. You were good mates."

"He left my gang."

"So? That's his choice to make and you shouldn't hold it against him. He's never grassed on you, that's something."

Shadows flickered deep in his eyes, but Roscoe's gaze didn't waver from the screen. "I'm glad he left. I'm glad both of you made it out."

The pain of the past stung and she blinked away tears, words choking into a jumble in her throat.

Roscoe passed a hand along his jaw. The sleeve of his white linen shirt slipped back and revealed the scars criss-crossing his wrist.

"It wasn't me," he said abruptly. "Not that it hadn't entered my mind, but someone got in before me. I put out feelers but haven't been able to come up with a name."

"Oh no."

"Forget it, Mel. There's nothing you can do. I know you don't have the dosh to pay his debts and that's something you shouldn't do anyway."

"I realise that," Melanie said. She squeezed her eyes shut for a moment.

"Yer stressing over nuthin.," said Roscoe dropping his pseudo tosh accent. "I'll give Jimmy boy a call 'n work out an arrangement."

Her eyes snapped open.

And he grinned. "Take a chill pill, Mel. It'll be sumthin' legit."

"Why? A minute ago you were speaking about breaking legs," she hissed leaning closer to the screen.

"I aint forgotten. Catch ya." And he was gone.

Her fingers touched the monitor and she whispered, "I haven't forgotten either, Ross."

How could she when she'd received such a beating from the senior carer, she'd been unable to walk for four days. Still, she would do it again. Anything to stop Roscoe's tormentors. The next thing she knew she'd been farmed out to *that* foster home. On reflection she'd come to the conclusion, the carer had deliberately sent her into the house of another abuser.

Quickly, she logged off, took a moment to delete cookies and slung her handbag over her shoulder.

Seconds later she walked out of the cafe.

Heart thumping, she scrolled through the contacts on her phone, found the number she was searching for and hit the 'call' button. Three rings and the phone was answered as she clattered down the short flight of stairs to the pavement.

She needed that answer. Perhaps she could approach the prospective buyer and talk him or her out of the sale.

"Lewis, how are you?" Turning right, Melanie hustled her way through the busy street, heading for McDonalds where she'd left the girls under Dirk's and Harry's supervision. "I need a favour."

In a few words, she quickly outlined her problem and hung up. Lewis, a mate from their Refuge days, wouldn't fail her. Melanie was certain he'd have the information she needed in record time.

She paused at the traffic lights waiting for the *'Walk'* signal. Heat beat down from the sky above and bounced off the concrete beneath her feet, making her feel she was stuck inside a furnace. Not a breath of wind stirred the sultry air. She waved a hand in front of her face hoping to cool her flushed skin to no avail. Her light, loose flowing blue midi-dress felt as if it stuck to every inch of her sticky body.

Oh, how she hated humidity.

A quick glance to the sky before she stepped onto the road revealed grey clouds scudding across the little patch of blue she could see between the high rise buildings. The change was coming. It couldn't come quick enough for Melanie.

Another three minutes of brisk walking and the golden arches signified her goal. She pushed through the doors into the welcoming air-conditioning, and Harry, with Tammy beside him, waved at her from across the crowded room. Sinking onto the bench seat opposite him, she heaved a sigh of relief.

"Bit of a scorcher," said Harry grinning over the top of his extra-large choc-whirl frappe.

Too spent to speak, Melanie gave a brief nod.

"I've eaten two cheese-burgers, four nuggets, a pack of fries and Uncle Dirk promised me an ice-cream," chirped Tammy.

"Oh, for the appetite of youth." Dirk had arrived at the table, Anabelle snug in his arms. He handed the cone to Tammy and slipped onto the seat next to Melanie. Heat swept over her face and neck as her body tightened in immediate response to his presence. He wriggled closer until the line of his thigh pressed against hers. Memories of the night before, danced like tantalising sugar plums inside her head. Despite his protests though, she'd left his warm bed and returned to hers just as the first beams of dawn streaked across the sky.

There she'd spent the next few hours staring at the ceiling and wondering what would happen next.

What *had* happened, was Dirk treating her as he'd done the day previously; friendly, courteous, responsive to her needs almost before she was aware of them. Except now, he'd brush his hand against her cheek, soothed her hair, pressed his lips against the side of her neck when they'd passed in the hallway, placed a lingering hand on her waist as he assisted her in and out of the car, in and out of the plane... Really it was if he was eager to take advantage of any opportunity to touch her.

Not that Melanie had any intention of complaining.

She could feel him staring at her profile.

"You look hot. When was the last time you drank some water?"

"I have no idea," she answered honestly. She flicked a quick glance at him, registering the intentness of his gaze, then looked away.

"Here, hold this munchkin while I go and get you a drink."

Melanie received Anabelle and Dirk rose from the seat and stalked off. "Ugh. Anabelle what have you been doing? You're awfully sticky." The little girl patted Melanie's face with tiny brown-smeared fingers.

"That's 'cause she stuck her hands into a chocolate milkshake and spilled it all over the floor." Tammy craned her neck over the back of the bench and indicated where a morose-looking young McDonald's employee pushed a mop to and fro.

"I can see you've been having fun."

Harry rolled his eyes. "You have no idea."

Melanie laughed.

A large cardboard cup was placed on the table in front of her and ice cubes clinked.

"Drink up," said Dirk sitting back down. "As soon as you've finished, we'll be on our way to Sea World."

"Yay." shouted Tammy who looked as if she was about to spring to her feet and dash out the door right then and there. "I wanna see the polar bears."

"Bears." squealed Anabelle.

"I'm off to Castaway Bay." Dirk waggled his eyebrows. "I've always had a hankering to be a pirate. Think of all the pretty wenches I could capture on raids."

"It's got over eighty water cannons," chimed in Harry, setting down his empty glass. He turned to his little cousin, who stared open mouthed at him. "You'll love it Tam."

Melanie picked up a napkin and attempted to clean Anabelle's fingers. "That's a lot of cannons."

"Here, let me." But Dirk ignored the little girl's hands and leaning closer, slid the napkin over Melanie's cheek instead.

Doing her best to avoid gawping at his face so near to her own, Melanie struggled to suppress the tingle of excited need flipping through her belly like somersaulting seals. Through the fog of a sweet fantasy that involved Dirk and the privacy of her bedroom tinkled the bell message tone of her mobile.

"That's me," she mumbled, breathless.

Dirk plucked Anabelle from her arms and turned his attention to his son and other niece. Melanie fished her phone from her handbag and scanned the screen. She read, then re-read Lewis's message. In the background, Dirk's voice reminded everyone to use the bathroom before they left and Melanie found herself concentrating on his words.

On anything rather than the astounding information, Lewis had unearthed.

"Melanie. Is anything the matter?" Dirk's sharp voice penetrated her daze.

She switched off her phone and avoided his gaze by fooling about, stowing it inside her handbag. Hoping her hurt and bewilderment didn't reflect on her face, she said, "Everything is fine. Let's go, shall we?"

Keep it together. Don't spoil the kids' afternoon.

It certainly looked as if the days of playing happy families were numbered.

~

Afterwards, Melanie couldn't remember much about the rest of that day. She knew she'd laughed and played and enjoyed as best she could the time she'd spent with both Dirk and the children. But the memories were blurred as if she viewed them through a distorted lens from a great distance.

The flight back to *The Golden Perch Station* hadn't helped either.

Turbulence had rocked the plane from side to side and even dropping them downwards several times much to Melanie's horror. Tammy had been quiet, her little face pale as she gripped her cousin's hand and poor little Anabelle, locked in Dirk's arms, had screamed the entire trip. Before they'd boarded in Brisbane, Melanie had stolen a few quiet moments to send a text message to James. He needed to know what she had found out, as soon as possible.

With the Big Wet roaring towards them it was possible communications could be cut at the homestead for some time.

Now Melanie stood on the verandah looking out into the dark night. No stars lit the heavens. The bush had fallen quiet as if the land waited in tense anticipation for the deluge heading their way. Even way out here, the air hung heavy and thick with muggy moisture.

What to do?

Could the intell Lewis had given her be incorrect? But the more she thought about it, the more sense it made. The desire to hurtle accusations burned like the flames of hellfire. The knowledge she could well be trapped here for several days until the rain eased only made her more anxious.

Nausea cramped deep in her belly, making her sweaty and she rubbed the palms of her hands over her dress. Fear crowded her mind swallowing her hope and leaving her on the verge of panic. She turned again and paced from one end of the verandah to the other. The dogs lay quiet on their hessian beds, their eyes tracking her movements.

The fact she'd fallen in love with her host made her wonder whether to laugh with joy or cry with grief.

All she knew was that she couldn't stay. She had to run from this man and this land that felt like home.

She wouldn't give Dirk the opportunity to reject her. If he did, she didn't think she would ever recover. And it was obvious, that scenario was on the cards for he sure as hell didn't trust her. What a fool she'd been indulging in a foolish dream she'd be accepted for who she really was when even her mother had abandoned her.

But Dirk didn't make it easy.

He now included her in the caring, protective attitude he extended towards his nieces and it bewildered her. It had her bringing up that damned text message at least a hundred times to check she hadn't imagined it and re-read.

Who was he really? A control freak, determined to rule all aspects of his sister's life? Including her inheritance? Was their night together all part of some calculated plan to manipulate her against James?

Or was he simply a brother, over-protective sure but driven by his own past to shield his sister from anyone and everything life dared throw at her?

And if that was the case, where in his schemes did Melanie fit in, if at all? He'd said he didn't have casual relationships but how could she believe him now?

Since that day when they'd discussed the role she had played in Valerie's decision, he'd never broached the subject again. Had he forgiven her or did he still hold resentment for her actions?

Round and round her thoughts tumbled until Melanie collapsed onto a cane lounge and covered her face with her hands.

"Problems?" Dirk's smooth voice tumbled over her senses, firing her body into wanton life. His hands covered hers, pulling them down into her lap.

She raised her head and met his dark eyes, serious, searching. A tiny frown pulled his brows together. He had crouched down and their gazes were almost level.

The quiet magnified and cocooned them in a world of their own.

"Sharing may help." He took a breath that strained the fabric of his shirt over the impressive sculpture of his chest and her insides melted into liquid marsh-mellow. "And I'm not the kind of bloke that runs from trouble."

"What makes you think I'm in trouble?" she whispered, her heart pounding loud in her ears.

He lifted her left hand and pressed her knuckles against

his warm lips. She felt the brush of air fan over her skin when he said, "You haven't been yourself since you received that text message today."

Did he know? Did he suspect that she knew? She wished she could cast herself onto his strong chest and have him take charge and fight her dragons.

But her past reared its head.

The number of times, she'd been rejected by prospective parents, foster homes even, all ensuring she remain in the cold, terrible institution ruled by a monster who'd delighted in his power. She'd never told anyone, not even James that two years ago she'd tracked down her mother. Living in Melbourne and with a husband and a new family, the woman's reception of Melanie had been frosty. She'd advised Melanie to never contact her again.

Hope and fear fought a bitter battle inside her heart.

Fear won.

Drive him away. Make him angry. Reject him first.

Melanie tugged her hands free. "You've sent out feelers to take over the mortgage on the vineyards."

In the distance, thunder rumbled.

Finally, Dirk spoke. "Now how did you find that out?"

"How I know is not important." She kept her chin high, hiding her clenched hands in the folds of her wide caramel-coloured linen skirt. "But I see you're not bothering to deny it."

"Why should I? The vineyard is more than Catherine's, it's also Tammy and Anabelle's inheritance. I have a small stake in it but it's my nieces' future I'm concerned with. As soon as my sister landed on my doorstep, I made it my business to investigate exactly what kind of problems she faced."

"Does Catherine know what you've done?"

"I haven't told her." Dirk compressed his lips and looked away for a moment. "I hoped I wouldn't have to, that James would divulge the precarious state of the vineyard's finances."

"But you would have told her, wouldn't you?"

"Of course."

"And you'd use that information to ensure this marriage reconciliation would fail."

"Bloody hell." Dirk reared back. A ferocious scowl transformed his face into the man who'd greeted her at the landing strip so many days ago.

Hard, remote, cold.

"Just what kind of bloke do you think I am?"

Sick to her stomach, she ploughed on. "That's what I'm asking because I am really confused. I'd hoped you were a kind and good man who was genuinely concerned for the welfare of his sister. But now...all I know is you've secretly planned to grab control of the vineyard from under James' nose and that you've had a private investigator look into my life. Do you have any idea how intrusive that is? Not to mention it screams exactly how suspicious you are of my actions."

Dirk flowed to his feet, reached down and grabbing her shoulders, jerked her upright. Fury pulsed from him in waves.

Melanie struggled to free herself.

He merely tightened his grip. "That's not it at all. At least, give me the chance to explain."

"Why? So you can manipulate me?" Her voice rose as she continued, "And you did this after we spent the night together. I can't be with a man who doesn't respect or trust me."

Lowering his head until their noses were a scant inch apart, he bit out, "For a prissy princess, you know how to pack a punch. And how to condemn a man without a hearing. Thanks for nothing, sweetheart."

For one wild, insane minute Melanie thought he would

haul her into his arms and kiss her. But no, his hands fell from her shoulders as if he'd been holding onto a hot branding iron. His face shuttered, he stalked off and opened the door, slamming it shut behind him.

Alone, outside the house, Melanie choked back her tears as fat raindrops fell onto the parched earth.

CHAPTER 12

*R*ain drummed on the homestead roof with relentless monotony. After three days cooped up with two girls, a moody teenager and an aloof man simmering with contained emotions, Melanie was frantic to escape.

Neither Dirk nor Melanie had broached the twin subjects of the vineyard and his actions. Nothing could exceed the politeness with which he treated her, but Melanie knew the children were not indifferent to the tension between the adults.

They reacted in various ways. Harry had withdrawn into the sullen teenager he'd been when she'd first arrived. Tammy's energy could have fired an entire nuclear plant, and nothing seemed to please Anabelle who was fractious and whinging.

Even the pets were wound up with Mr Gibbs hissing and spitting as he leapt over the furniture and Muffin chasing him, yapping in such a high pitch Melanie thought her head would explode.

By the end of the third day, the rain eased. Melanie looked out the kitchen window. *This is it. I have to go now.*

Dirk had sought her out the morning after their confrontation and in frigid tones had laid out his plans for the vineyard. The money would be on loan only and on the guarantee a trust was set up to ensure the girls' interests would be looked after in their inheritance. He'd pointed out his proposal of installing a semi-retired vineyardist he'd found and who was prepared to act as a mentor as well as a manager to assist Catherine. James, too, if he still remained in the picture.

"It looks like you've left nothing to chance," Melanie had responded. "But this scheme you've organised is your plan. It's not Catherine's. Not James' and worse you've worked it all out behind their backs as if they're incapable of proposing any alternate arrangements. Of thinking for themselves. You've taken away their control and their self-worth."

Dirk had paced to the window and stood staring out at the rain. The tense set of his shoulders had signified how deeply disturbed he was by her words. "That wasn't my intention."

Melanie had sighed and said softly, "I know you have your family's best interests at heart and for what it's worth, my belief is they would have jumped at your proposal. But I think it would have been better to discuss your plans with them. Mind, I also think it should have been only an offer. Give them the opportunity to voice their concerns and have some input. The opportunity to say, no."

"Our grandfather worked hard every day of his life to build up this station. He called in favours and loans from friends to keep the vineyard afloat after my parents passed away. I can't and won't stand by and let all his efforts be for nothing."

"I understand." Her voice shaking with suppressed tears, Melanie added, "James is a good man."

Dirk turned around. With the window at his back, the gloom cast by the overcast sky and heavy furnishings made it hard to discern his expression. "He has no business sense."

"Possibly but he tries hard."

"He should have contacted me as soon as he realised the business was turning sour."

"Would you have run to your in-laws for help?"

Dirk barked out a harsh laugh. "Probably not. At least, not in the beginning." He ran a hand over his hair. "Yeah, I would've tried to dig my way out of my own mess."

"What are you going to do?"

"Tell them. As soon as we get satellite connection again."

"That sounds like a good plan."

Both had remained silent for five minutes, each waiting for the other to broach the more important subject that hung like a pall of black smoke in the air between them.

Finally, he asked in a cool voice, "And you? What are your plans?"

There'd been no hint of any interest in her future doings, no indication whatsoever he cared one way or the other, so she'd managed a carefree laugh and an equally carelessly spoken response. Knowing full well, her words would infuriate him, she'd said, "Oh, I'm going on a world cruise as soon as possible. Maybe I'll met a rich man and marry him."

There, that should do it.

"Can't wait to shake the red dirt off your shoes, huh, princess."

It'd been more statement than question and uttered in that hateful remote tone so reminiscent of that first day. So much so, that Melanie choked back the refuting comeback her heart screamed at her to voice. "You betcha."

Head held high, she'd left the room.

Pushing her bitter-sweet memories back into the past, Melanie turned away from the window closed the pantry door in passing and marched down the hall into the office where Dirk was knee deep in tax papers. Or at least attempting to give that impression. No sooner had she entered the room, then he switched his gaze from the wall to the papers on his desk.

"I have to leave. How soon can you arrange a flight?"

Dirk lifted his head and gazed at her, his eyes inscrutable. "You're in a hurry all of a sudden. Where's the fire?"

"I do have a business and a life of my own."

"Not to mention your cruise and the rich bastard you intend to round up." Bending his head, he picked up his pen and began to write. Voice vague, he added, "You picked your timing perfectly. Internet and my satellite phone came on line this morning. I've checked the weather bureau and the rain system is easing. Provided Ted is free, you can be out of here tomorrow."

"Perfect." She waited, twisting her hands together but he remained silent, seemingly engrossed in calculations and figures. "I can take Tammy and Anabelle with me."

"No way, princess. Those munchkins are no longer your responsibility. Mrs Weber will be here in three days' time and my sister is due back at the end of the week. Until then, I'm sure between the two of us, Harry and I can cope."

Still she hesitated. "Then, I guess there's nothing more to say."

"Nope."

Longing to throw something at him, Melanie fled the room.

Melanie had never been more miserable in her life.

Dirk had bundled her and her belongings into Ted's plane and waved her off without a word of sorrow, of reluctance and certainly no mention of seeing her again. Despite the hugs received from her friend and business PA when she stumbled off the plane in Sydney, she felt as if her heart was encased in ice.

Four days of sobbing into her pillow each night, thinking of how she could have handled the situation better had left her feeling isolated and bereft. A multitude of succinct responses, which would have put Dirk firmly in his place without once indicating her feeling whirled about her head. Even Muffin and Mr Gibbs acted sulky, moping about her cottage and being unusually quiet.

There'd been so much work to do when she arrived home and even though she made sure she filled every hour of every day, it didn't work.

It was if Dirk had carved out a niche inside her soul that would remain forever empty now that she'd left him behind.

However, he wasn't the only one she mourned.

She missed the girls and Harry's shy presence. She missed the wide, endless blue skies; the heat baking up from the ground, the unique scents of dry dust, rich red earth and the beat of the outback that seemed to throb through the soles of her feet and through every inch of her body.

It called to her; called her back.

She found herself imagining a life where she was part of that land. Where she worked side by side with Dirk and his son and with cheeky, miniature Dirks running around.

With every hour that passed, what had once popped into her mind as a whisper grew louder.

Take a chance. Stop acting like a frightened child. Show him your love: for him, his family and his way of life.

Friday morning, the moment she'd woken, she knew something had changed inside her soul. For the first time in years, she felt freer, stronger.

A future called to her if she was willing to take a chance. *I'm going to do it.* And she bounced out of bed fired with a sense of purpose.

Nothing worthwhile is ever easy.

Armed with her mantra she browsed the internet, doing her homework on Longreach and the surrounding communities.

Then made her decision. She phoned several real estate agents and queried the possibility of renting out her cottage for twelve months. A google search found a lovely property in Longreach available for rent immediately. It was a stand-alone, single storey building with an office fronting off one of the main streets. Even better there were basic living quarters to the rear and a massive back yard with laneway entrance. Plenty of space for her animals. Business would be slow at first, the community may well be reluctant to use the services she could offer but the rent from her house here would help with living expenses.

Best of all, I'll be close to The Golden Perch Station.

Then she'd put into practise what she taught her clients. Dirk was not going to know what hit him.

First, though, she needed to resolve the final impediment that stood in the way of James' happiness. She picked up her mobile and wandered through her garden to a wooden bench positioned under the shade of a tree and sat down and dialled. Even walking that small distance caused sweat to bead on her forehead.

It was scorching. Forty degrees Celsius and climbing.

A hot breeze ruffled the leaves of the mango tree behind her and brought with it the acrid stench of bush smoke.

James answered on the fourth ring. He sounded out of breath as if he'd been running. In the background burbled the incomprehensible mumble of a loudspeaker.

"What's up, Mel?"

Taking a deep breath, she dived in and told him he needed to tell Catherine everything and that included his debt to Roscoe. *Time he took responsibility for his actions.*

"Don't burst a gasket, Mel. It's done. I've fessed up and Catie has already called me an idiot. We're gonna work it out together. I've even told her about my record when I was running with Roscoe's gang."

"Thank heavens. I'm so glad, James."

"I've worked it out with Dirk too. He's a real stand-up bloke and has offered to help us. But I wouldn't have this chance if it wasn't for you. I owe you one, mate." He drew in an audible breath then continued. "I'm selling the dodge to a collector. Since it's almost fully restored, I should get a pretty penny for it."

Wow, it sounds like he's already taking responsibility. That car had been his dream since he was sixteen years old. He'd been so obsessed with it when he'd finally raked in enough cash to buy one when at uni.

"As soon as I can, I'm off to Sydney to settle up with Roscoe and that'll be an end to that problem."

She entertained a brief notion of asking about Dirk then dismissed it. If all went well, she'd see him soon enough. "That's fantastic, James." Another jumble of words squawked. Foreboding pricked her skin and she asked, "Where are you?"

"In Brisbane airport. I'm waiting for a flight to Sydney. Haven't you heard the news?"

"No, I've been too busy to turn the telly or radio on lately." *Too lost in my own problems more like it.*

James said in a voice overlaid with a thin layer of panic, "Fires are closing in around Orange. I've left Catherine and the girls at Dirk's and I'm heading back to do my bit with the local mob. They're having difficulty in maintaining the containment lines and need all the help they can get."

Melanie's heart stuttered and icy sweat broke over her body. "Oh no. How bad is it?"

"Bad, Mel. I've asked a mate of mine, Bill, to drive out and switch on the automatic sprinkler system. If the fire gets close, then maybe the house and cellar doors can be saved. You better do something about those animals of yours. I doubt Bill will have time to do anything. He's in the rural fire brigade, too. He'll be on duty until the crises eases. Maybe call the local vets. Someone could drive out and pick them up and take them into town."

"I'll ask Ned to crate them up and drive into the vets. I'll pick them up from there and bring them home here."

"No, can do. Ned's sent me a text about an hour ago. Says he's off to his elderly mother's place to ferry her back to town. She's being stubborn and says she won't leave her farm."

Images rose of the five dogs, two cats (one of which was a recent mother of seven kittens), the rabbit with only three paws and the six guinea pigs that she'd saved from starvation and abuse. "I'll do it." The words burst from her mouth before she had time to think about it.

"Mel. No."

"It'll be fine. I'll drive out there now."

"Mel..."

"Gotto go. Take care, James." Melanie rang off and ran for her car.

Three hours later, Melanie flexed her fingers from where they gripped the wheel of her Toyota Yaris and checked the car's odometer. Another five or so kilometres and the turnoff to the vineyard should come up on the left-hand side.

Leaning forward she squinted out the windscreen. The smoke had thickened so much it now blanketed the sky and she'd switched on her headlights in order to see the road ahead. She'd also shut her vents a good fifteen kilometres ago being unable to stand the smell any longer. Inside her car, the air was warm and stuffy. The small engine struggled to hold back the searing heat from outside although the air-conditioning was on full blast.

The radio crackled and the local emergency commentator

continued his summary of the current situation. It didn't sound good.

In fact, it sounded downright terrifying.

Her heart pounding and sweat beading her forehead, Melanie battled her long-ago nightmare.

I can do this - I have to. I won't let those poor creatures face a fiery death. Spurred by lurid images dancing inside her head, she pressed the indicator and turned the car onto the gravel road. She pushed down on the accelerator. From memory, it should take another twenty minutes at a steady pace, but Melanie intended to arrive a lot quicker.

Stones spun from the wheels as her car sped forward. Vision was limited now to fifteen metres or so in front of her. Smoke swirled and billowed, and the small car rocked from the strong, gusty wind.

The warning signal blared from the radio and when it finished, the commentator issued another evacuation order.

Oh no. The fire was close. Too close.

She roared down the driveway, rocketed towards the house then braked to a halt. The sprinkler system on the house was working and spraying water over the roof and down the sides of the building. Grabbing the keys from the ignition Melanie swung out of the car, closing the door behind her.

She froze.

It was if she'd been dropped into a scene from hell.

Terror filled her mind as her past hit her with the force of a tsunami and she gulped in mouthful after mouthful of smoke-filled air as she attempted to regain control. Finally, she leaned over and retched out the contents of her belly.

Legs shaking, she straightened and stared round.

The fury of the wind filled her ears with so much noise she found it hard to think. Its force slammed into her, knocking her against the side of the car. The impact jolted her back to the present.

Heat seared the exposed skin on her face making her glad she'd worn a long sleeved shirt, cargo pants and taken the time to haul boots onto her feet. She pulled a woollen balaclava from her back pocket and covered her head, tucking her hair underneath with trembling hands.

Through the dense smoke, flames flickered like massive tongues of fire roughly five hundred metres away as the fire advanced with all the determination of a starving beast of prey.

I'm not going to get out of here in time. Her stomach rolled over and again, nausea hit her hard. Memories hit her. One after the other.

Fire licked the floorboards, closer and closer to where she huddled clutching the stray cat she'd befriended. She'd been unable to escape, since that horrible teenager had locked her in a windowless store-room. She could still feel the heat singeing her skin through her clothes, smell the smoke choking her lungs, hear the creak and fall of the burning timbers of her foster home. Then through the darkness of encroaching eternity, the door had burst open and James had appeared. His hand had closed firmly around hers as he led her away from the fires of hell.

Now there was no James to rescue her.

She was on her own.

Swallowing, she wiped cold sweat from her upper lip. *Maybe I should leave now.* She sent a quick glance over her shoulder back the way she'd come then in a momentary lull from the wind, came a volley of shrill barks.

I can't leave. What will I do? Then she remembered the bunker.

Melanie moved fast. Opening the car's rear door, she grabbed her backpack and shouldered it on. Next, she lifted out two animal carriers and raced around the back of the house towards a small building inside a fully wired enclosure.

Her rescue shelter.

Quickly she unlocked the gate and entered, making sure the latch was secured behind her. The dogs were howling, running frantically around the pen. The cats and kittens were scrunched up in the corner of the door-less shed. She placed the crates on the ground and scooped the guinea pigs out of their cage and shoved them inside one of the crates. After a bit of hunting she found the lop-eared rabbit quivering under a pile of straw. Murmuring soothing noises, she picked her up and stuffed her in her backpack and zipped it shut. With the help of treats she snicked leashes she'd had in her backpack onto the dogs' collars.

Dogs and Honey Bunny first.

Melanie slipped her heavy bag over her shoulder.

Seconds later she had the terrified dogs out of the enclosure and the gate latched. Her heart in her mouth, she raced along a pebbled path the dogs pulling so hard on their leads they practically dragged her along after them. When she neared an immense cement water tank, she yanked them to heel. It took considerable effort to restrain them.

To one side of the water tank there was a massive mound of dirt and wedged in the middle of the mound was a building, about the size of a large laundry room. Apart from the heavy metal door with a small, reinforced glass window, it was composed entirely of concrete. She offered a brief prayer of thanks James had installed the fire shelter four years ago after a series of bush fires had ravaged the south coast. He'd spoken of nothing else for months and she'd been privy to the long, detailed explanations on the lay-out and design.

She'd never been inside it before.

Now if only he'd left the key where he said he would.

Melanie wound the dogs' leads around her wrists and yelled at them to sit. Eyes rolling, they obeyed but she knew they wouldn't remain quiet for long. Reaching up, she fingered the length of the lintel above the door until her fingers closed over what she so desperately sought.

Within thirty seconds, although to Melanie it felt like thirty hours, she had the door unlocked. She pulled the heavy lever and entered sucking in a deep lungful of smokeless air. The tightness in her chest eased.

Cobwebs brushed against her face. She shuddered and, tugging the dogs along, hurried towards another similar, metal door with a similar reinforced glass panel. Opening it, she groped for the emergency lighting switch and flicked it on to reveal metal steps leading down into a fire-proof (hopefully) bunker.

At one end were shelves stacked with emergency rations, several torches and an old battery-powered transistor radio. A metal bunk, which did dual purpose as a seat, ran the length of one wall. Along the opposite wall was a row of cages. Seconds later the dogs were safely locked inside the cages.

Now for the rest. Thank heavens she had no cows or horses here.

She scooped out the rabbit and popped her into a small cage. Grabbing her backpack, she climbed up the stairs, closed the internal door and headed outside; to find herself in the middle of what had all the hallmarks of... a firestorm.

*T*error and panic screamed inside his head, as Dirk floored the rented ute along the driveway. His heart beat in time with his furious thoughts.

What had she been thinking? All he could do was pray and be thankful James had phoned him immediately after he'd spoken with Melanie. At least Dirk had been given sufficient time to call in a favour. His mate, one station over owned a helicopter large enough to make the distance in one flight without having to re-fuel. And he'd been keen to help.

Dirk had to admit though; he'd held his breath the last fifty kilometres. The gauge of the fuel tank had sunk so low they must have flown on fumes.

Nevertheless, they'd made it to the tiny airport on the outskirts of town. There Dirk had picked up the ute he'd arranged for and pointed the car in the direction of the vineyard.

Black ash rained down onto the windscreen and he flicked on the wipers. It only made it worse, smearing it into a sooty mess. Dirk unwound the window and stuck his head out the better to see where he was going. Smoke caused his eyes to water and his throat to close. He coughed as he brought the car to a halt round the side of the house.

To his left, a eucalypt tree exploded. Burning embers and shattered branches were picked up by the howling wind and hurtled in all directions; spreading the fire into an inferno.

The noise was horrendous, rent with the crackle and pop of fire and the thunder of the wind.

Sparks and embers fell onto the roof of the house, but he could do nothing to save it. He pulled a flash hood over his head, clapped his fire helmet on, and left the car. His volunteer fire fighting gear was definitely going to come in handy today.

An eerie reddish gloom illuminated the darkness caused by the smoke cloud.

Breaking into a jog, he switched on his torch and yelled, "Cooee! Mel!"

The wind seemed to catch his shout and throw it back in his face.

He did a careful circuit of the outside of the house but couldn't see any sign of Melanie. The building appeared shut up tight with no open doors or windows. Apart from her car still parked in the driveway there was no other indication she had been here.

There was no way in hell he would leave without her.

He yelled her name.

Again, and again. Over and over until his voice was hoarse as he fought his way around the property, through the smoke and the fury of the wind.

A burning ember fell onto his helmet. He shook his head and it dropped to the ground. Dirk ground the heel of his fire boot over the spark until it was extinguished.

No doubt pointless in the scheme of things but somehow, he felt he'd achieved a victory.

His hand shook so badly, the torchlight wavered over the hardi-plank clad, three car garage. Already flames roiled in a twisted, demonic dance over the roof. In seconds, Dirk knew the structure would be one huge fireball.

Desperation was seizing his heart to a standstill in his chest.

His princess had to be here...somewhere.

A monstrous roar came from his right. He spun round to see his sister's home engulfed in flames that leapt twenty metres into the darkness.

"Dirk."

He turned again to see his Melanie holding onto a crate with each hand, a bulging backpack hanging from her arm, running in a weird lurching way towards him. She was looking over her shoulder, back towards where fire licked gleefully over the tinder dry grass.

Dirk raced to her side and his gut spasmed at the look of hope and trust glistening in her eyes when she met his gaze. Ash covered the balaclava she wove over her head and shoulders giving her strange, other-worldy appearance. Her eyes were bloodshot and swollen. From tears or the smoke, he couldn't tell.

"Come on." he rasped, taking one of the carriers from her. "To the bunker. Now."

Coughing and visibly reeling on her feet, Melanie clung onto his arm with her free hand as they sprinted for the race of their lives.

The heat was so intense, it beat against his back, pounding, demanding to be fed. In his peripherals, wisps of smoke wafted from Melanie's shirt.

Thank God, she'd worn a balaclava and a woollen one at that.

He needed to stop and wrap her in his coat but he knew if they did so, the fire would melt the very flesh from their bones.

Then, the torchlight depicted their haven; the bunker.

Beside him, Melanie's breathing came in harsh, rapid sobs. They reached the door and Dirk wrenched it open. Pushed

Melanie inside and slammed it shut on the beast snapping at their heels. Stumbling they crossed the short space to the second door, and he held it open while she climbed down the steps.

Melanie set down her bag and the crate she carried and reached up to take the second one from him while he bolted the door shut. He jumped off the steps and reached over to rip the shirt from her back, then flung the smoking fabric into a bucket of water. It sizzled as it made contact.

In that instant a tremendous shudder shook the small building above as if the fire was enraged it'd been denied its victims.

Dirk stared at the thick metal door, but no smoke puffed from around the edges. The bunker stood firm against the battle raging outside. His knees quaked and his shoulders sagged as he released his held breath.

Now to see to his lady.

He turned around, his gaze searching the rows of shelves but before he could move, Melanie landed on his chest.

Her ears ringing, her head throbbing, her lungs burning from smoke inhalation Melanie flung her arms around Dirk's neck and clung, knowing she never wanted to leave the safety of his embrace. She'd tugged off her ash-covered balaclava and tossed it to the ground before launching herself at Dirk. She wept into jacket, still breathing too fast and too shallow but knowing if she let go, she'd fall to the ground.

Dirk muttered a curse and unwound her hands. "Easy sweetheart. Here sit down for a minute."

He swung her up into his arms, carried her across the room then set her down on the bunk where she gripped the edges to keep herself upright. Through streaming eyes, she watched him hasten to the shelves then return with an oxygen cylinder in his hands and a mask. He checked the tag, then fastened the mask over her mouth and opened the valve.

Melanie sucked in a breath. Then another and another. The shaking inside her chest settled as the tightness and burning sensation eased.

Dirk soothed a hand over her hair, pushing limp strands away from her face. "Does that help?"

She nodded.

Releasing a loud sigh of relief, he pulled off his helmet, flash hood, and wiped his sweat covered face with his sleeve. Concern had etched deep lines around his eyes and mouth.

A meow and a hiss came from one of the crates. Then a little furry face with whiskers popped out from the top of the backpack and scrabbled down onto the floor. Followed by several others. "Bloody hell. Guinea pigs."

His resigned tones made her give a choked giggle.

"Is that a goanna behind those boxes?"

"Yes. I wanted to save them all, but I couldn't." Tears clogged her throat as she remembered those last terrifying minutes when she'd attempted to catch hold of a baby wallaby, but he'd been too quick for her. She could only hope he'd made it to safety before the fire overran the paddock.

"Oh sweetheart, I'm sorry."

His face still etched with concern, he smiled, and her heart turned over. He'd come for her. She didn't know how he'd managed it and at the moment she really didn't care. All she knew was he'd been here when she'd needed him the most.

He'd slain her dragon.

And she would love him all the days of her life.

"As soon as the fire passes over and it's safe to move, I'm taking you to the hospital to be checked out," he said, ever the *'take-charge-kinda-bloke'*. He unscrewed a bottle of water and offered it to her.

Melanie pushed the mask aside and took the bottle. "Thank you," she rasped and drank. The liquid slid down her throat, though warm it was an instant balm. She drank until the bottle was empty.

Dirk offered her another while he chugged down his own bottle of water. When he finished, he took the empties, placed them on a shelf, and returned with the first aid kit and a large container of water. "Let's clean ourselves up, shall we?"

However, he attended to her needs first. Feeling unaccountably shy, sitting beside him she was glad she'd worn a tank top under her shirt, even though it was soft and thin with age. With a damp cloth, he wiped ash and grime from her face, neck and hands. His motions were gentle, reverent almost. His face serious and his eyes darker than she'd ever seen them. He put down the cloth and opened a tube of ointment, which he smeared over a burn on the back of her left hand.

"That was too close." Dirk opened another tube, this time of aloe-vera lotion and carefully spread it over her shoulders and down the length of her arms.

Clearing his throat, he continued, "About that private investigator thing. I know I should never have organised it, but I was certain you were hiding something. I was desperate to know what it was and hoped that perhaps you'd share when we were in each other's arms. When you didn't, I emailed a bloke I know and asked him to do a minor search."

Melanie gave a woeful sigh, too tired and too defeated to pretend any longer. *What did it matter now?* "Actually, I was hiding my fear; my stupid fear I'd love someone and be rejected."

There. It was out; everything that lay in the shadows of her heart.

"I love you."

For a full sixty seconds, Melanie truly believed she'd conjured up his words out of her own fevered imagination.

Then he repeated his declaration. "I love you and I'll never reject you."

This time she heard it. Heard the questioning lilt to his voice, heard the vulnerability behind his words.

And the hope.

"I want to spend the rest of my life making you happy. Giving you the family life you deserve."

"Truly?" *Did he mean it?* But there was no mistaking the earnestness in his eyes or the promise he offered.

Joy soared like a singing choir inside her heart. Her weariness fled. Melanie smiled through fresh tears blurring her eyes. She leaned close and murmured mere inches from his lips, "Pity you beat me to it. I intended to make you fall in love with me with a new dance."

"I could take it back, change my mind." The deep lines bracketing his mouth washed away and he smiled.

"Then I'd have to persuade you."

"Under the orange trees?"

"Oh, definitely. Where else?"

His voice roughened. "I can't wait."

Questions, answers, explanations, she had a thousand of them but they all could wait. Melanie cupped his face in her hands and said, "Then don't."

"Just so you know, as soon as my sister returned, I was coming after you. I have no intention of ever letting you out of my life, princess."

Dirk wrapped his arms around her and pulled her into a tight embrace as if he'd never let her go.

Melanie's last thought before his kiss swept her away was - *I'm home.*

THE COWBOY'S GIFT

BY SUZANNE GILCHRIST

CHAPTER 1

Singing along to *Jingle Bell Rock*, Rosanne Turner—better known to her family and friends as Rosie—sent her Toyota Land Cruiser racing down the gravel road. She flicked her almost two-year old son a quick smile, loving how his blond curls so similar to her own, framed his piquant, round face and baby-blue eyes. Strapped in the forward-facing child restraint seat behind her, Caleb trilled the chorus through a mouthful of arrowroot biscuit.

The Land Cruiser hit a pothole.

Bounced.

Caleb chuckled. A tiny dimple deepened in his right cheek.

Rosie fixed her gaze back to the front windscreen and changed down a gear. Clouds of red dust billowed up, obscuring her rear vision and seeping through the open back windows. The guy in the seat behind her coughed and flapped a hand in front of his sun-burnt face. The action did little to dispel the fine red dirt that covered the land from one horizon to the other and now was doing its best to cover everything and everyone inside Rosie's car.

This was north-west New South Wales, as close to Corner

Country as a person could get and a good three hundred and fifty kilometres east of Sturt National Park. Sure as hell was hot, the area wasn't known for lush green pastures and the sparkle of well-filled winding rivers. No, this was the outback —dry, harsh and pitiless—and to Rosie's way of thinking the most glorious spot on Earth.

Sturt's Crossing. A tiny town of a little under one hundred people that encompassed a fairly large region midway between Tibooburra and Bourke. The place she was born and bred and, God willing, the place where she intended to spend the rest of her life.

And it all hinged on sweet-talking Old Man Williams into signing a lease that would grant her the right of passage onto the one hundred acres she was desperate to sell. As soon as the ink dried on that bill of sale, she'd be able to clear the debts incurred in her name by the one man she'd thought she could trust—her husband. Then, if the tourist marketing programme she had planned was a success, she'd land a regular income—something that wasn't easy to attain out here in the outback.

Turning down the volume on the stereo, she said, "How you doing back there?"

"I've had better days. Strewth, I'd forgotten how hot this place could be. Pity your air-con's on the blink, but I'm not surprised considering this heap of rust you're driving. How much further?"

Wow! What a charmer. I sure hope he can deliver on the promise he made me. She raised her eyebrows and shot a quick look over her shoulder at Mason, her passenger, supposedly top of his game in marketing and who also just happened to be Old Man Williams' youngest son. "What? You don't remember?"

"It all looks the same to me. Besides, I was only twelve when I left." His tone disgruntled, he tapped onto his tablet. "Shit. I can't believe there's no reception here."

Frowning, Rosie turned her attention back to the road. "Hey, Mason, watch it. Baby on board."

"Sorry."

"Ception's shit," repeated Caleb, before ramming the remains of his biscuit into his mouth.

Her little boy was at that stage where he was beginning to test the boundaries. He only had to grin that dimpled smile and Rosie melted like a marshmallow on a campfire. Heaven help her once he reached school age. She repressed the laughter bubbling inside and pressed hard on the accelerator. The cruiser leapt forward, jostling everyone from side to side.

"Bloody hell. What a crap road!" grumbled Mason.

"Crap road," Caleb imitated.

Rosie rolled her eyes and checked the odometer. Another three kilometres and the turnoff to Flat Rock Station should be in sight.

A tiny sizzle tingled through her and her face heated faintly. Silly really, to still remember the teenage crush she'd had for Luke Williams, eldest son of the station's owner and two years ahead of her in school. And even sillier, for those long-ago daydreams she'd had when she was sixteen, to retain the power to thrill her.

She shook her head, sending her curls bouncing against her shoulders and admonished herself to stay focused. This was business, and her beautiful baby's future was at stake. Not to mention her own financial independence.

I can do this—prove to everyone I don't need a husband or a handout to survive. She smiled wryly and adjusted her large sunglasses. *Sorry, Aunty Claire, no disrespect intended.*

When her godmother died, Rosie had not long finished high school. She'd been astounded to learn she was the sole inheritor of Aunty Claire's estate, which consisted of a run-down house one street off the main road of Sturt's Crossing, a trust fund of almost half a million dollars, and those damn acres located smack bang in the middle of Flat Rock Station.

Unfortunately, there was no way of getting anywhere near those acres unless it was through Old Man Williams' land. He'd made it clear in no uncertain terms long ago, that no one, including his sister, Claire, or anyone associated with her, would obtain permission to step foot on his land. With the title of those one hundred acres now in Rosie's hands, she was in something of a pickle.

Old Man Williams wasn't the type of bloke to give something for nothing. According to gossip, he'd never given his sister the time of day if they should pass in the street. And he sure hadn't bothered to turn up for her funeral. Rosie should know, she'd been there, struggling with her grief for a woman who'd been her mother's best friend and a big part of her own life while growing up.

A spinster, Claire Williams, the only sibling of Old Man Williams, had been estranged from her family before Rosie was born. Although she'd treated Rosie like a daughter, she'd never mentioned what had caused the rift all those years ago. To this day, the family feud was a secret no one in their small community had managed to unearth.

Once the shock and grief of Aunty Claire's death had abated a trifle, gratitude and delight had overtaken Rosie upon learning of her inheritance. At first, it had been wonderful, magical almost. She had been in a position to help her family but being a girl who had always lived in the moment, the last thing on her mind at that time, had been furthering her education or training for a career. No, she'd wanted to see the world. So she'd taken off on a cruise to Hawaii, her first step on a world adventure.

Six weeks later she was married to Neil Turner, a guy she'd met while scuba diving off the Maldives. Now, twelve years later, she was stoney broke, divorced, and a single parent of the most beautiful baby in the world.

Funny how your dreams never turn out the way you envisioned they would.

Caleb kicked his cute little bare feet, banging them against the child seat, and shouted, "I want Jingle bells, batman smells!"

"Man, not again." Mason groaned.

Smiling, Rosie switched on the disc and joined in with Caleb's singing.

It wasn't long before the turn-off appeared. A metal letterbox formed in the shape of a sheep stood beside the cattle grid signifying the entrance to Flat Rock Station.

Rosie slowed the car to a crawl, only putting her foot down again once they'd rattled over the grid. The road leading to the main homestead was little more than a track and ridden with potholes. Rosie did her best to avoid them to no avail and the Land Cruiser lurched from side to side much to Caleb's squealing delight.

"Man, it looks like a pile of nothing," Mason said. "It's easy to see why mother couldn't stand living out here. Thank God she took me with her when she left."

Rosie snuck a quick glance in the rear-vision mirror. He was scowling out the open window, his face twisted into an expression of disgust.

"I remember the summer you left Sturt's Crossing. I think you were in your first year at high school when I was in year ten." Her thoughts winged back to that moment when Mason had slouched into the school yard—which, if truth were to be told, was little more than a dusty paddock with some lean-to's for shelter for those kids who rode their horses to school. But nowadays the site was abandoned, and kids were either educated through the school of the air or boarded in a larger town like Bourke. Another example of what happened to a community when the population died out or moved away.

She sighed, remembering. Mason's older brother, Luke, had led the way. Tall, with wide shoulders even back then, he'd had a presence that sent the other kids scuttling out of his way, as if he was Moses parting the Red Sea.

The late summer sun had glinted on Luke's dark brown hair, sending the streaks of red glowing like fire embers. As he'd strolled past, he'd swept his crystal-clear, grey gaze over where she'd stood like a dork clutching her backpack, her mouth gaping, and he'd said, "Hi."

He'd actually spoken to her.

For the life of her, she'd been unable to utter *one, single word.*

He'd beckoned to his brother and turned away. As far as Rosie knew, he'd dismissed her from his thoughts forever. But for her; it had been the defining moment when she'd left behind her childhood and taken that first, hesitant step over the threshold into womanhood.

"Hah!"

The explosive sound from her disgruntled passenger caused Caleb to call out, "Mummy!"

Rosie turned her head and smiled reassuringly.

Mason added, "I'd hardly call a two-roomed, iron building divided by partitions with pit dunnies out the back, a high school."

"Yeah, well, we did all right."

"If this car is what you call doing all right, then I'm not surprised the town is on its way out." His voice was sharp with scorn.

"Times are difficult at the moment. What with the drought, that terrible flood a few years ago, and the dwindling market for beef and sheep, our community is suffering. There's no work and we've got so few amenities to service the people who are still here. But you know all this. I've made no bones about how dire our situation is out here."

"Talking about something then actually seeing it with my own eyes, can be two entirely different things." There was an inflection in his voice Rosie couldn't pin down.

"You're not thinking about ditching the job, are you?"

Switching her gaze back to the front windscreen, Rosie frowned.

"I guess not. 'Spose its time I saw the old man anyway. My mother's been nagging me for months since she found out how sick he's been."

Rosie's shoulders twitched. She hoped that it wasn't the lure of a possible inheritance that had made Mason decide the time was ripe to rekindle a relationship with his father. Neither Old Man Williams nor Luke, for that matter, had the reputation of being a soft touch.

This sounds like it could get complicated, but I can't back out now. I need that sale.

They drove for a while in silence. Even Caleb had stopped singing. A quick glance, revealed his sweet little mouth drooped. Perhaps he was tired, or maybe he had sensed his mother's disquiet.

The stony ground was undulating, and Rosie could just make out the silhouettes of the flat-topped tors called *"jump-ups"* by the locals, far away to the west. And where one particular jump-up was her ticket to debt-free freedom.

Scrubby, grey-white salt bushes and wispy, grey-green coloured grasses populated the landscape interspersed here and there with a few stunted eucalypt trees, feathery mulga trees, and desert bloodwoods. Stunning dark-red Sturt desert peas with their coal black bulbs dotted the paddocks bearing witness to the last rainfall a month ago, sufficient to allow the wildflowers of the region to bloom.

She guessed, to Mason's urban eyes, the lack of paved roads crammed with smog-spewing cars and house-filled suburbs was as alien to him as the landscape on the moon. He'd been back only once since his mother deserted his father and older brother for a new life in Sydney. Surely though, not all his memories had been lost?

Doubt gnawed at Rosie. Maybe this wasn't such a great idea. Maybe she should have thought her plan through a bit more thoroughly. What if she and Mason were thrown out on their ears before she'd had a chance to expound on what she hoped the station-owner would find difficult to resist? Old Man Williams wasn't known for his geniality these days, especially since his heart attack last year. But surely the man couldn't and wouldn't refuse to see his youngest son?

"All I can see is a couple of crows."

Gosh, he sounds as whiny as Caleb when he's tired. The birds' cawing squawked above the thrum of the engine and the rattle and squeak of its springs as they jostled down the track.

"Wow! I just spotted an eagle. It's massive."

Rose craned her neck to look out the side window. "Look, Caleb, can you see the wedge-tail eagle? See its diamond shaped tail?"

Caleb looked. "What's eagle?"

"A very big bird, sweetie."

"That's one hell of a wing span. Tyler would love taking a photograph of him."

For the first time since picking him up at the bus depot earlier this morning, Mason sounded impressed and Rosie allowed a little optimism to lift her spirits. If she could keep him interested, then maybe her idea of promoting this small corner of Australia would work. And if she could get the bigger land owners in the district to donate some funds she'd be able to organize an international marketing campaign. All they had to do then was sit back and wait for the tourists to arrive. Tension seeped from her shoulders. Yes, this was going to work. Besides, what could possibly go wrong?

"Tyler?"

"Yeah." Mason hesitated then added, "He does the accounting side of things for our marketing business. Plus, he's my partner."

Oh man. I wonder how that's going to go down with his father. Maybe Mason's sexuality is part of the reason why he hasn't been back for so long. She cleared her throat delicately. "Wedge-tails can get pretty big. Sometimes their wing span is up to two and a half metres."

Mason whistled.

"Where bird, Mummy?"

"Sorry, darling, you probably need to see it out of the windows on this side of the car. Hang on!" Rosie peered over the top of her sunnies. "What's he doing? He looks like he's circling something."

"Probably roadkill. Or a dead roo. What's it matter?" Mason snorted.

"Out here it pays to be mindful of your environment." Rosie applied the brakes and clutch and the old four-wheel drive lurched to a halt. She switched off the engine and immediately the heavy silence of the outback flowed inside the car as thick and heavy as cheap red wine.

"Are you coming?" Rosie slipped off her seat belt and creaked open the door.

"Only if I have to," Mason muttered.

"Keep an eye on Caleb for me then, please. If you don't mind, hand him his water sipper-cup and make certain he drinks it. And whatever you do, don't walk far from the car."

"Trust me. I'm not going anywhere."

"Mummy will be back soon, Caleb." After snatching up her fawn Akubra, she placed it onto her head and set off in the direction where the eagle continued to stalk its prey. The ground was rough underfoot, making her glad she wore her hiking boots. The heat of the first week of summer steamed down from the sky and her bare arms began to sting and burn. Pity she was born with her mother's fair skin and not the light olive tan her father and her younger brother and her sister were blessed with. Sweat soon prickled her scalp and beaded her upper lip as she slogged over a rise in the ground. Pausing, she wiped the back of her hand over her mouth and examined the dam that lay before her. What had once been an impressively sized dam was now a mere quarter full of reddish, muddy water.

The eagle swooped lower, its talons outstretched.

A bedraggled, thin lamb, not more than a few months, old bleated pathetically from where it appeared to be stuck in the muddy dam. There was no sign of its mother or any other sheep for that matter.

Galvanised into action, Rosie grabbed her hat off her head, flapped it madly about in the air and bounded forward, yelling at the top of her lungs, "Get out of here!"

Her shouting and the rush of her approach startled the bird. It wheeled back into the air, screeching its outrage. Rosie kept running until she reached the dam's edge.

The small lamb bleated again and, frightened by all the commotion, thrashed about. Its little head disappeared under the water.

"*No!*" Without a moment's thought, Rosie dashed into the dam.

The heavy, water-logged mud that lined the bottom of the dam sucked at her boots. She trudged carefully forward so she didn't overbalance. Every step was a gigantic effort, straining her thigh and calve muscles as if she was attempting to wade through quicksand. She reached the spot where she thought the lamb might be and after ramming her hat back on, swooshed her hands through the water.

Nothing.

If she didn't find the poor animal in the next few seconds, it would drown. She leaned into water now above her knees, and delved deeper. Her searching hands felt soggy wool, then lost it. She groped frantically, located more wool, took another step, and bent lower. Her hands slipped around the animal's belly and she heaved.

The animal squirmed and kicked out with its feet. Rosie pulled again. The weight of the water and the flailing of the terrified animal as she dragged it clear caused her to stagger.

Her right foot wouldn't budge being stuck up to her ankle in clay. The lamb clasped tight to her chest, Rosie fell backwards with a huge splash. Warm water sloshed over her body and face. Coughing and spluttering while attempting to hold the lamb above the surface, Rosie fought her foot free of the clinging mud. She scrabbled about, hacking stagnant water and staggered up the incline to drier, firm land where she fell to her knees and finally released her hold on the animal. The poor thing lay on the ground, the whites of its eyes showing. The lamb made a pathetic attempt to scramble onto its tiny hooves before collapsing again. Its mud-covered flanks surged up and down rapidly.

"Oh gosh, don't die little fella." Rosie shuddered, shaking off a vision of having to give mouth-to-mouth to a sheep. She looked around, spied her hat floating near the edge, and retrieved it. Akubras weren't cheap and she'd had to learn to curb her impulsive spending habits since Caleb was born. She needed to look for his future and not live in the moment. It hadn't been easy though. Her ex had been a mastermind at buying whenever and whatever he wanted. His bad habit rubbed off onto Rosie who'd never planned for tomorrow anyway. Of course, he'd never been able to afford his many holidays and so-called business trips if it hadn't been for Rosie's inheritance.

At least her marriage had taught her to be more cautious when it came to good-looking guys. Next time, if there was a next time, she certainly wouldn't believe everything that spouted from a man's mouth.

Rosie drew in a deep breath, bent at the knees, and scooped the animal back into her arms. Her gaze fixed to where she could see her vehicle's roof, she set off as fast as she could walk, weighed down as she was by the lamb's wet, shaking body. By the time she reached the cruiser, Rosie's arms ached so much they were trembling, but she didn't let go.

"You look like you've been mud wrestling. What happened?" Mason gaped at her through the open window.

Gasping, her heart thumping, Rosie bit out, "Give me a hand, won't you?"

From the safety of the car, Mason shook his head. "Ugh. It's all wet."

"Geez, Mason. That's the least of our problems. I think the poor thing is in shock. It hasn't moved. Come on. I don't think I can hang onto it for much longer."

"Maybe it's dead."

"Don't sound so hopeful," she snapped as Mason inched open the door and cautiously stepped onto the ground. "Open the tailgate and shake out the blanket that's folded in the side pocket. Make a kind of bed."

Grumbling, Mason walked to the back of the Land Cruiser, unlocked the tailgate, and swung it open. A few seconds later, Rosie gently placed the lamb on its nest of blankets. It lay there panting, eyes half-closed.

"Is that blood on you?" Grimacing, Mason pointed to her arms where blood formed from the long scratches that crisscrossed over her skin.

"The little baby wasn't a happy camper when I picked him up. Come on. We need to get him to someone who knows more about animals than me."

"You mean we're driving back to town to your sister's place?"

Rosie's sister was Sturt's Crossing's vet and now happily married with two stepchildren and one handsome husband who managed the local produce and hardware store. Rosie shut the tailgate. "No. Your family's homestead is closer. They'll know what to do. Hop in and buckle up."

She hurried to open the rear passenger door and carefully scrutinised her little boy making sure he was okay if a trifle red-faced from the heat. She checked the level of water left in his container to ensure he'd been drinking and popped a kiss on his cheek before walking around the car to the driver's side. The next moment, she had the engine on and barely waiting for Mason to shut his door, she slipped the vehicle into gear and took off.

"I sure hope father and Luke don't blame us," Mason said as he snapped his belt on. "Farmers can get touchy over the subject of their stock. That much I do remember."

"Too true." Rosie twisted around and smiled. "But I don't think we need to worry. We'll be treated as heroes, you'll see."

Really, matters couldn't have worked out better than if she'd planned it this way. *That lamb is going to get more than my foot over the door. Courtesy dictates I'll get a hot cuppa and time for a good, long chat.*

Rosie grinned and changed gear. *Flat Rock Station here we come.*

CHAPTER 2

*L*uke Williams worked the throttle of the quad as he drove along the fence line, checking for breaks in the wire as he headed for the homestead. Perched on the bike in front of him, his blue cattle dog, Jet, barked furiously as they passed within fifteen metres of a flock of emus. The tall birds raised their heads, their beady eyes blinking with mild curiosity before resuming pecking over the hard-packed earth.

"Settle."

Immediately Jet stopped his yapping and began to pant.

Luke didn't blame him. Close to midday and Luke's long-sleeve, cotton button-up shirt was sticking to his back. It was a scorcher of a day and the rest of the summer promised to be even hotter with little chance of rain. Unless Queensland's wet season flowed down through the Diamantina area and trickled into New South Wales, odds were he'd be trucking in water to fill his tanks, and feed for his stock.

Again.

Things could be worse though, they could be six feet underwater like in '13.

Before long, what used to be called the singleman's

quarters came into view; a high-pitched corrugated iron-roof dwelling of fibro-sheeting and with a wide veranda on all sides that had been screened in for sleep-out accommodation. Nowadays, it housed only the seasonal shearers. The fencing, boundary checking, and just about every other labouring jobs required on the station were done by *yours truly*. Times were tough and they'd been tightening their belts for close on four years now. The price they received for their sheep barely covered the cost of feed, water and the repayments for the mortgage.

And recently the bank had begun sending in letters threatening foreclosure.

But there'd been Williams on this land for nigh on a hundred and twenty years now. And he'd be dammed if he would be the one responsible for the loss of their heritage and their history.

Somehow, someway, Luke intended to turn Flat Rock Station into a thriving property and hopefully bring a spark of life back into his dad's dull eyes.

Problem was, he was running out of options.

Fast.

For the past three months, he'd been researching various ideas on making their station viable again and with a little luck, he was fairly certain he'd hit on the solution. But crikey, he'd put off broaching the idea to his dad because he knew the old man was not going to like it. With the bank pressing hard for regular repayments on the overdraft, Luke knew the time for procrastinating was over. He'd use his usual drop-in at midday when he ensured his dad ate something and took his meds and he'd press his cause.

The old man wasn't going to like what he had in mind— moving into the camel trade. Luke grinned. Maybe his plan would press his dad's buttons sufficiently for him to get all fired up, just like he'd used to in the old days, before his heart attack. In his mind, he imagined his father's spluttering which could only intensify once he also realised Luke's idea meant they'd have to increase their overdraft and buy back his deceased aunt's land.

With luck, their finances wouldn't be stretched too far.

A month ago his bank manager had let slip that the new owner was not only deep in debt, but a gambler that couldn't wait to shake the dust of this town off his shoes. He'd be bound to sell it for a song.

Maybe the stars were about to align in Luke's favour.

He slowed as he passed the shearers' quarters and cruised past the massive barn until he halted at the back of the main homestead. The hairs on the back of Jet's neck bristled and he growled low. An unknown and red-dust covered Land Cruiser with a rusty grill stood parked in the thin shade of the old jacaranda tree Luke's grandmother had planted nigh on fifty years ago.

No lettering on the side of the vehicle, so not a government or business car.

And Luke knew for a fact that the local bank manager drove a Toyota hybrid, so thankfully, not another visit from her. He rode the quad over to the triple, block-work garage and glided to a stop in the shade. He killed the engine, and swung off the quad, automatically adjusting the brim of his Akubra to shade his eyes from the blast of the noon-day sun.

It was quiet.

Too quiet.

These days his dad usually hollered and cursed at any strangers that dared to darken their door, but today, not a peep could be heard from inside the house.

Frowning, Luke scooped up the deep ceramic dog dish and re-filled it with water from the tap before placing it on the shady veranda. Jet trotted over to the bowl and lapped vigorously.

He tousled his dog's head briefly and then opened the rear screen door, entering the mud room where he toed off his scuffed boots. In his socks, he stepped over to the deep sink where a bucket half-filled with water was positioned in the base. Using the least possible amount of liquid, he splashed dust and sweat from his face and hands before drying himself on the thin cotton hand towel hanging from a hook on the wall. He tossed his hat onto the top of the dryer and ran his damp fingers through his short hair then was annoyed with himself for even that mild show of anxiety over his appearance. Hell, he was a working man and a working man got his hands dirty every day. Whoever their visitor was would just have to suck it up if Luke's appearance displeased them.

Shoulders squared, he headed out along the hallway and into the front lounge room where three, un-curtained, wide bay windows framed the acres and acres of Flat Rock Station.

My land.

My home.

And I'm not going to give it up without a fight.

His father sat as he usually did this time of day, in a brown leather armchair positioned so he could have full view of the property, not that Luke believed the Old Man had much interest in it anymore. No, Dad normally passed the slow hours of daylight by simply staring at the floor. Refusing to use the walking cane pressed on him by his doctor. And refusing to just about do damn near anything. It was like his recent brush with death last year had been the final straw and he'd given up. Like he was waiting to just damn well die.

"Not if I can help it," Luke affirmed under his breath as he marched further into the room. His hands curled involuntary into fists as if he was getting ready for battle. His gaze swept over the occupants, noting a guy a few years younger than himself dressed in a designer short-sleeve shirt and chinos standing near the front door and a pretty blonde woman seated on the lounge with a toddler on her lap.

With lush curves barely concealed beneath a pale green T-shirt and khaki shorts, dark brown eyes, and lips like soft-pink rose petals, she was enough to stop any red-blooded man dead in his tracks. For some strange reason, she was covered in dry mud and there was a long scratch down one arm that looked recent and raw. Luke stilled, his gaze lingering on her face a tad too long as an unexpected heat shot through his body and to his intense embarrassment, he hardened.

There was something about those blonde curls and the tilt of her head that seemed familiar, but what man in his right mind could forget that ripe body?

The kid on her lap popped the drink bottle from his mouth and chucked it onto the floor. "Gone!" he squealed.

Geez, mate get a grip. She's obviously this guy's wife. He wrenched his glance away and deliberately ousted the blonde from his mind, grateful as his sexual attraction gradually cooled. He concentrated on his father, automatically checking for any obvious signs of distress.

Tension oozed from his taut shoulders. His eyebrows rose.

Unless the heat of the day had affected his mind, Luke could have sworn his father looked about ten years younger. Gone was the grey-tinged complexion, the bitter-twist to his down-turned mouth, the dull-glazed pale blue eyes and slumped posture. His father was sitting bolt upright and his cheeks were flushed with healthy colour and, by all that was holy, he was smiling as he stared at their visitors.

Astounded and not quite knowing what to think about his father's change in appearance and attitude, Luke followed the direction of his father's fixed gaze. It took an amazing amount of will power not to allow his eyes to stray back onto the blonde. Firming his jaw, he examined the guy who kept shifting his weight from foot to foot rather in the manner of someone who didn't know whether to stay or make a run for it.

Bloody hell but he looked like his younger brother. *Was it ...? Could it really be ...?*

"Mason?" Was that feeble croak really his voice? Luke carefully blanked all expression from his face. What the devil was Mason doing here?

"Hey, bro." His brother cocked a jaunty smile and surged forward, hand out-stretched to halt just in front of him, waiting.

Head whirling, barely knowing what to make of his younger brother's unexpected appearance, Luke stuck to banality to give himself time to think. "How long have you been here?"

"Dunno. I guess about six minutes. The drive out from Sturt's Crossing took like forever." Mason rolled his eyes in a dramatic fashion.

Not one word of concern for their father, no explanation about the lack of communication between them, and certainly no apology. The happiness that had surged in Luke's heart at his brother's appearance quickly became doused with doubt about his motives. The eager boy that had followed him around like a puppy had gone. In his place stood a stranger, clad in city-slick clothes with a practiced smile and what looked like salon-dyed hair. This was not the happy homecoming Luke had hoped for. The years that lay between them felt chasm deep.

Luke glared down at the proffered hand then back into his brother's face. "You've got a nerve, showing up now."

Mason quickly jerked his hand away and twitched at his shirt. "I wanted to come the moment I heard about Dad, but you know how it is with work. I couldn't get away."

"His attack was thirteen months ago." Luke all but bit out the words.

His brother's face darkened. "Mother warned me I wouldn't be welcome. You ever think that's why I stayed away so long?"

"This isn't on me, so don't pretend otherwise." Luke leaned in close. "One visit in fifteen years. Yeah right. You really care."

Mason looked away, a flush riding high on his cheekbones and he shrugged. "Believe what you like."

"Enough of that now, boys. Let bygones be bygones. I'm real glad you came home, son." Luke's father grinned.

There was a twinkle in his eyes that Luke hadn't seen since his mother and little brother had disappeared from their lives when Luke had been barely eighteen years old. Something vicious twisted in his gut.

His father rubbed his hands together then reached for the cane as if about to stand. Luke moved to his side and offered his arm for his old man to use as balance while he heaved to his feet.

"This is a time for celebration, boys. Not only has my youngest son come home but he's brought my first grandchild with him."

CHAPTER 3

*B*usily soaking up all that gorgeous testosterone oozing from Luke with his wide shoulders, narrow hips and solid-looking thighs, Rosie sighed. Her admiring gaze drank in what surely looked like firmly-toned chest muscles straining his thin cotton shirt. It took a few seconds for Old Man William's statement to penetrate her fuzzy fantasy. *"What?"*

"I've only met this woman once in my life!" blustered Mason, his eyes bulging as he rolled them from his father to his brother to Rosie then back again. "Besides..." Mason snapped his mouth shut over whatever he'd intended to say.

"Looks to me like once was enough." Old Man Williams stepped forward and chucked Caleb under the chin.

"Grandchild!" exclaimed Luke, pinning an icy glare onto Rosie's face. He took his time, looking her over with such clinical intensity she was hard put not to run out the door and keep running.

Suddenly he hissed in a breath. His sensual mouth with that full lower lip thinned in a way that made her heart sink. "I don't know what game you two are trying to pull here but it isn't going to work. I recognise this woman, Dad. She lives in town. This is the vet, Rachel Brown's sister, Rosanne Turner."

Caleb's bottom lip trembled. "Mummy, man angry."

"It's okay, sweetie. He's hot, not angry." Pulling her eyes away from Luke's fascinating face, she smiled appealingly at the older man. "There appears to be a bit of a misunderstanding, Mr. Williams."

Luke cut in. "Aren't you married to that con man? The one who weaseled Mrs. Jenkins into selling her 1940's two-seater for a paltry eighty dollars? Mrs. Jenkins is on the old-age pension. That was a pretty low act."

Poof! The last of her remembered silly schoolgirl daydreams evaporated. Cold reality had a way of doing that to a person. She ducked her head and soothed Caleb's silky soft hair with shaking fingers, eyes welling with stupid tears when her precious boy peered into her face.

Damn Neil and damn her silly empty-headedness. Dazzled by Neil's charm and flattered by his attentions, she'd fallen hard for his boyish good looks, too young and naive to perceive the self-centred, narcissistic man that lay hidden beneath his polished façade.

To a girl from a small outback town, his smooth sophistication was intoxicating. The life-style he introduced her to of hob-nobbing with the high rollers was a movie-like fantasy and to her eternal regret, she'd thought she'd found where she'd belonged—that those people were friends and not like starving dogs with their tongues hanging out for anyone who had fat purses and were stupid enough to believe them. She'd spent many sleepless nights filled with disgust for her actions. For the way, during those first, crazy months, she'd spent money like water, drank far too much alcohol, and revelled in the feverish excitement of gambling dens.

But she was done with wasting her life.

Done with denying her dreams.

Done with good-looking men who made her knees weak.

Her chin rose, and she stared Luke down. "We're divorced. And I had nothing to do with any of Neil's shady schemes."

"Hah! The whole town knows how devoted you were to him," drawled Luke. "You'd have to be, otherwise why stay married to him for so many years?"

"My marriage is none of your business!" Rosie glared. How could she have left her husband? She'd been too ashamed of her own stupidity and too weak to admit her mistake to her family. Instead, she'd played the part of a loving wife, while her husband continually departed on his so-called many business trips, busily wasting her inheritance as he chased his obsession with becoming super-rich. *Just one more, Rosie. That's all I need. One lucky turn of the wheel and we'll be made.*

And she'd kept hoping that somehow the empty charade her marriage had become could be turned into a marriage like the one her parents had.

Luke folded his arms over his impressive chest. His shirt was unbuttoned at the neck showing a small amount of tanned skin. "Too right. But it just so happens, Mrs. Turner, that when you turned up here with a pretend Williams on your lap, it became my business."

"This is ridiculous and you're crazy." Rosie shifted Caleb in her arms and struggled out of the cushy lounge to her feet. "We're here because there's an emergency." Under cover of her little boy's body, she crossed two fingers.

Old Man Williams waved his cane about. "I don't understand what the hell is going on here? Is this or is this not my grandson?"

"No, Mr. Williams, he is not. I have no connection with Mason whatsoever. I picked him up from the bus station this morning and that's the first time I've set eyes on him since high school."

"But he's the spitting image of my boys when they were his age?" The old man frowned.

Rosie waved a hand, airily. "Coincidence."

"Hang on." Luke stepped forward, took hold of her upper arm, and turned her to face him. "What emergency?"

Heat crawled over her face and neck as his touch branded her skin. She stuttered, "Out there. In my car. There was a lamb stuck in a dam. My car's not locked."

"Damnit. Yakking about nothing, wasting time. We'll discuss what you're really doing here later." Shaking his head, Luke rushed from the room, calling over his shoulder as he reefed open the front door, "Dad? See to Mrs. Turner's arm before it gets infected. Since you're here, Mason, give me a hand."

"Again?" Mason glanced down at his immaculate clothes then caught the sudden frown on his father's face. "Yeah, sure thing. Sit down, Dad, while we take care of it for you." He gave a toothy smile and departed in the wake of his brother.

Left alone with Old Man Williams who was now glowering and looked as if he was about to send her packing, Rosie fluttered her eyelashes and allowed a mournful sigh to slip past her lips. "It's so hot and Caleb is exhausted from the heat. If we could stay a little while so I can feed him…" She allowed her voice to trail off and even managed a little sway. At least her years with Neil had taught her how to act.

Old Man Williams stared hard at Caleb. "You better sit down then. I'll rustle us up some hot tea and a sandwich or two. Errr … what about your boy? What can I get for him?"

"A sandwich is fine. If you have a banana or some other soft fruit that would be great. Plus, I'll need to boil more water for our trip home."

The station owner nodded. Everyone out here knew about the dangers of small children and babies drinking untreated or unboiled water. Water-borne parasites that attacked the brain had been responsible for several deaths of young children over the years. It wasn't worth the risk.

"Kitchen's this way." He turned and led the way down the hall. "There's a first aid box on the counter."

Rosie dabbed at the sweat beading her forehead with a flannel she pulled from the massive, powder-blue baby bag she carted everywhere. A searching glance out of one of the windows revealed Luke carrying the lamb off towards the barn. Shoulders slumped, his younger brother trudged behind him.

She hoped the animal was going to be all right. After picking up the bottle from the floor, she stashed it inside one of her bag's side pockets. If her luck held, Luke should have his hands full for a good twenty or so minutes. Well, she didn't have Mason here to fill in any gaps with his fluid talk about marketing, so it was up to her.

Twenty minutes.

I can do this.

Hoisting her bag's straps over her shoulder, she settled Caleb on her hip and followed Old Man Williams into the kitchen.

She found him busily buttering bread and laying cold ham and tomato in between the slices. In silence, one-handed, she filled the jug from the tap, lit the gas stove, and shoved the kettle on to boil.

"Sit down and leave the rest to me," Mr. Williams said gruffly, without turning around.

So she sat, positioning her son on her lap, her bag at her feet and took a good look around the room. It was large with old-fashioned painted cupboards of buttercup yellow and laminate countertops that had obviously never been replaced, judging by the scratches and even one or two scorch marks. The square timber table where she sat, was positioned in the centre of the room and there were two wide windows and a screen door that led out to the veranda. Through the wire mesh, a blue cattle dog peered inside, tongue hanging out, ears pricked.

"Doggie." Caleb almost threw himself off her lap in his excitement. "I want to pat."

"He's having a rest now, sweetie. He's been working all morning, so he needs a sleep."

"Can I play after sleep?"

Rosie smiled. "We'll see." She loved animals, but her ex had always refused to have one either in the house or their property, citing allergies. As soon as she had her finances squared away, getting a pet was next on her list.

A few minutes later, Old Man Williams had food on the table, tea brewing in a pot, and a glass jug of hot water cooling on the sideboard for Rosie's return journey. He shoved a plate of fruit and another of sandwiches toward her, then positioned a bottle of disinfectant and some cotton wool balls close by.

Rosie offered a sandwich to Caleb who promptly began to pull it to pieces and spread it over the table. After inspecting his work, he picked up a piece of bread and offered it to Rosie.

"Thank you, darling." Chuckling, Rosie peeled a banana and left it on the plate for him as well. She then tended to her arm, wiping off the blood before adding disinfectant to the scratch.

"What happened?"

"I had a little trouble getting the lamb out of the dam." Rosie tightened the lid back on the disinfectant bottle and placed the soiled cotton balls into a brown paper bag which Old Man Williams then disposed of in the bin beside the sink.

After hooking his cane over the back of a chair, he sat down facing her. "Tea?"

"I'll wait until it cools, thanks. I no longer drink my tea hot in case I accidentally spill some on Caleb."

He poured tea as black as tar into a mug and took a sip,

staring at her over the rim. His straggling grey hair and bristly chin and stooped, thin frame was evidence of his ill health, but there was no mistaking the sharpness of his pale-blue eyes. This was no senile old man and shame turned Rosie's belly as she remembered her airy idea of sweet-talking him. He deserved the truth and for her Aunty Claire's sake, Rosie decided to give it to him.

"I guess you've heard, I inherited Blackbird Tor," she said referring to her deceased godmother's land.

Caleb decided to turn his banana into play dough.

Mr Williams nodded, the line of his mouth grim. The way he kept staring at Rosie's son was disquieting though and without knowing why, she tightened her hold on him.

"I've received an offer to buy the land provided I can secure a guaranteed right of passage through Flat Rock Station. I'm here to negotiate a lease but I'd prefer an outright sale of a narrow strip of land all the way to my boundary line."

"'Ain't gonna happen."

"You haven't even listened to what I can offer." Her voice rose.

"Don't have to. My boy's got the say now over this place. Gave him power of attorney after that close shave I had last year." The old man's smile turned crafty. "Here he comes now. Why don't you ask him yourself?"

CHAPTER 4

$\mathcal{L}$uke flung his filthy, bindii-covered socks from his feet, leaving them on the veranda as he pushed through the door and entered the kitchen. In his haste to reach the lamb, he'd neglected to haul on his boots. He'd been damned lucky there'd been nothing more lethal than a few prickles and sticky-beaks lurking in the yard. One bite from a king brown could well have finished him off.

Irrationally, he blamed her.

The blonde.

That gorgeous bundle of trouble now kicking back as cool as winter rain on his kitchen chair and eating ham sandwiches.

As if sensing his mood, Jet whined from outside the door then growled as Luke's brother walked past him and inside the house. That was another problem, Luke needed to sort. While they'd worked together to aid the exhausted animal, Mason had failed to throw any light whatsoever on why he'd turned up out of the blue. But at least his brother had helped.

It reminded Luke of better times, when they'd been young and Flat Rock Station a world filled with adventures they'd shared. Before their mother had upped and left and taken his little brother with her. Apart from cards on his birthday and at Christmas, Luke had never heard from her again.

Mason had written at first, but then gradually the communication fell away.

Luke supposed they were both to blame for that. He hadn't pushed to keep his relationship with Mason alive either. He could blame having to take over more and more of the running of Flat Rock Station, but he knew in his heart, he'd been hurt that his brother had forgotten him so quickly. So, he'd erected barriers to protect himself. After all these years, he guessed they were still solid and standing firm. It would take more than a couple of smiles and a helping hand with an injured animal to break them down.

"Is the lamb okay?" Rosie Turner pushed her plate further away from the grasping hands of her son.

He supposed he should give the woman a little credit for rescuing his sheep from the dam. It wouldn't have been an easy task seeing how small she was. *Bloody hell, I'm staring at her boobs again.* Well, as much as he could see with a kid in her arms.

Rolling his eyes, he moved to the sink where he filled a glass with tepid water and sculled it down. Luke turned around, leaning his hips against the counter. "He'll live."

"Poor thing, but I'm glad. What about his mother? I didn't see any other sheep near the dam."

He shrugged. "It's possible she's rejected him. I'll take a drive out and check the area this afternoon. Now, what are both of you doing here and how come you turned up together?"

His brother drew out a chair and sagged into it like a wet paper bag of wilted lettuce. Sweat had dampened his hair and his once-pristine shirt was limp and stained. His face was flushed red and he looked as sulky as a kindergarten kid. He finally resembled the boy Luke used to know so well and despite his best efforts, his defences cracked wide open.

Remember, his brother was up to something, for sure.

"Isn't there any air conditioning here?" Mason said, flapping a limp hand in front of his face.

"This isn't the Ritz." Luke grinned. One thing hadn't changed. His brother was still as whiny as he'd been as a teenager.

Mason snorted. "I can tell."

Rosie jiggled her son on her knee which made him chuckle. The Old Man appeared to be mesmerised, the way he stared at the two of them while Luke's brother chugged down a glass of water like he'd been in the desert for three days.

"Come on, someone speak. I don't have all day to waste sitting around a table. Well?" Luke ignored the questioning glance his old man flashed in his direction at the bite in his voice. But that damn sexual itch was prickling all over his skin just being in the same room as the blonde.

"It's a long story." Rosie fluttered long, dark eyelashes at him and heaven help him, if he didn't feel some of his irritation dissolve.

Yeah, trouble with a capital T.

Luke drawled, "Somehow, I figured it would be."

"Then take a load of your feet, son. Sit down and grab a bite to eat," his father ordered.

Luke smothered his surge of delight at the sudden, *I'm-in-charge* tone in his old man's voice. It was good to have his dad back even if every instinct he possessed warned him he wouldn't like whatever was coming next. He took the only chair left, the one next to Rosie Turner. As he reached for a sandwich off the plate in the middle of the table, his arm brushed hers. Hunger for more than food unfurled low in his belly as he wondered what her skin would feel like naked against his.

"Luke? What are you doing, boy?"

He glanced up and realised his hand was still hovering

mid-air above the table. *Shit a brick!* Heat flared over his face as Luke caught the sly glance his father sneaked toward Rosie then back to himself.

"Maybe he doesn't like ham," Rosie said by way of explanation. She was busy putting a sandwich back together that looked as if it had been dismembered by a trainee surgeon.

"Yeah, could be he wants something else to eat." His old man snickered and took a noisy slurp of his tea.

Luke shot him a dirty look and grabbed the sandwich.

"Maybe I could take a shower? I really need to change my clothes." A pained expression on his face, Mason plucked at his ruined shirt.

"Sit. Please," Luke added when his brother looked as if he was about to leave the table. "Give me the short version of this long story. If there is one."

Mason heaved a sigh and rolled his eyes. "The idea was Rosie's. It's really nothing to do with me."

"Are you sure about that? I thought you were anxious to check on Dad."

"Of course I am," Luke's brother spluttered. "But now that I'm here, Dad looks fine to me."

He was right. Luke couldn't believe the change that had come over their father. Still he needed to get to the bottom of whatever mischief these two had cooked up before he could get back to his chores.

Rosie popped part of a sandwich into her son's mouth. "That's mummy's clever boy."

She smiled at the kid, and even though that beam wasn't aimed in Luke's direction, he felt the impact cut through to his bones. Warm, loving, protective.

What would it be like having her smile that way at him?

This was going to be a long day.

Rosie waved a hand in his direction. "Short version is I'm

offering to purchase a right-of-way access road to my property."

Luke turned blankly to his father who said, almost gleefully, "Blackbird Tor. Your aunt's slice of Flat Rock Station."

The pieces fell into place and landed forcibly like pelting pebbles inside his brain.

"I've got a buyer lined up and waiting to sign on the dotted line." Rosie aimed her tempting smile in his direction.

Luke narrowed his eyes. "Sounds like this buyer has stipulated the access road as part of the deal."

She nodded.

His blood boiled. "No. Way."

Her kissable mouth fell open and a frown began to form. "You haven't heard me out. I have a sweetheart of a deal for you. For everyone living in Sturt's Crossing."

"Whatever it is, the Williams aren't interested in any of your scams."

CHAPTER 5

*W*as this what it was going to be like for the rest of her life? Living under the dark shadow of her ex's lies? For thirty seconds, defeat felt like nails pinning Rosie to the floor.

At first, she'd been oblivious to the means Neil used to fund their lifestyle after her money dried up. But one momentous revelation about Neil and the hope she'd held onto that propped up her little make-believe-world, had shattered.

It had soon become painfully obvious Neil had a gambling problem. Not knowing how to handle his addiction, she'd been unable to burden her family with her problems. The idea of seeking help, had reinforced her feelings of failure and she'd been determined to deal with her problems alone.

When the remaining layers of her marriage had peeled away, the true sordid mess that lay beneath had been revealed. But she was getting there, and intended to anything she could, to undo the harm her ex had done.

Caleb moulded his banana into a hill and stuck out his tongue before declaring, "Yucky crap."

That's my boy. And it was crap. She was leaving her past

behind her. "I'm not my ex-husband. I'm my own woman and don't you ever, *ever* dare accuse me again."

"Fair enough." Luke leaned back and eyed her narrowly. "Who's the buyer?"

"Malcolm Ford."

"Ford! Over my dead body!" Old Man Williams held a hand against his chest, his cheeks almost purple with his rage. "He had an affair with my wife."

"Chill, Dad. That was years ago, after mother left you." Mason unbuttoned a couple of buttons of his shirt and blew air down his neckline. "I think I have a fever. I'm so hot."

Luke stabbed the table with his forefinger to get everyone's attention. "You've got to be kidding! There's no way Ford could afford to purchase more land. He's like the rest of us, skint."

"My solicitor says it's a legit offer." She frowned as Luke exchanged a grim glance with his father whose colour Rosie was thankful to see was losing its lurid hue.

"He's probably backed by a Chinese consortium. Haven't you heard how they're buying up large tracts of land to feed their own population? If we're not careful, Australians won't own anything of our own country."

Mason and his father kept swinging their heads from Rosie to Luke and back again, like they were watching a tennis match.

Rosie gave a dramatic sigh. "Aren't you being just a little bit paranoid?"

"At least I don't live in some fantasy world."

It was uncanny how Luke's words hit the mark. She placed the fork onto the plate with trembling fingers. She may have lived with a forlorn hope she could salvage her marriage for too long a time, but now she was living in the present. "I've heard about that happening, but I don't believe our government would allow such an eventuality."

"Who knows what they'll do if our national deficit sinks any lower?"

"I'm not here to discuss politics. Maybe you should stop thinking about conspiracy theories and hear me out."

"You sure you're not deaf, Rosie?"

"My name is Rosanne."

"I thought it was Rosie."

"Only to family and friends." Rosie stuck her nose in the air.

Luke grinned. His eyes crinkled at the corners revealing beguiling laughter lines and a deep dent in his left cheek.

Fire sizzled through her veins straight to her core until her fingers curled into her palms. She felt like panting as loud as the dog on the veranda and inwardly bewailed her stupid teenager crush. Apparently, the years had done nothing to douse that particular idiocy. *But I don't have to act on it. I'll ignore it. Once this deal is done, I'll never have to set eyes on this guy again.* Strange how that idea did nothing to cheer her up.

Maybe it was better to keep ploughing ahead before he ejected her from the house. The words rushed from her. "International tourism. That's the market we're aiming for." She nodded toward Mason who had lifted one slice of bread and was now sniffing the ham, a dubious expression on his face.

"I think the meat's gone off," Mason muttered, obviously obsessing over the food in front of him.

"It's crap," Caleb agreed. "What narna?" He pushed a mush of banana across the table toward Mason who shook his head wildly.

"Gross. I mean, no. Thanks."

"Mason's a whizz at marketing. He already has a business plan in place." Rosie tried not to wince at her rising tone.

"You're going into business with him?" Luke sounded incredulous.

Scowling, his brother slapped the bread onto his plate, saying, "Why is it so hard to believe I'm good at what I do?"

"Mad man." Caleb crammed a pile of banana into his mouth.

"Is it because I'm gay?"

"*What!*" Old Man Williams planted his hands on the table and scowled across the table. His mouth was a thin line, and shock etched deep lines into his face.

His youngest son met his gaze calmly enough, although Rosie detected a faint wobble to Mason's lower lip. "You want to know why I didn't come home? Look in the mirror. Look at how you're judging me. Like I'm cow dung."

"Masey, cow dung is yuck." Caleb offered another blob of banana. "Narna is good."

This time, Mason took it. "Thanks, mate. It's good to see I have one friend in this house." He placed the banana on his plate and took a tentative bite of the sandwich. But his shoulders were hunched like he was expecting a blow at any second.

It was obvious to Rosie that although he did his best to act like he didn't care, Mason was very much concerned about his family's opinion of him.

"I don't believe it," his father spluttered.

Mason huffed. "As if I would lie about my sexuality."

"It doesn't bother me." Luke stood up, walked around the table, and hauled his brother up and into his arms. "You'll always be my brother."

Mason sniffled, pulled back from Luke, and gave a watery smile. "I have a partner, Tyler, but I wasn't certain he'd be welcome here, so I left him at a motel in Bourke."

Luke clapped him on the back.

"That explains why you were on the bus and didn't charter a plane," Rosie said, then ate the last of her sandwich. *Gosh, this is fascinating.* She snuck a peek at Mr. Williams.

The old guy appeared to have calmed down. In fact, he

was staring at the opposite wall as if he was boring a hole through the plaster to a place only he could see. He had an odd expression on his face, like he'd been slapped with a dead fish.

"Call him and tell him we'd like to meet him. Wouldn't we, Dad?" Luke's voice was more statement than question as he returned to his chair.

Luke's father squeezed his eyes shut. When he opened them, there was such regret swimming in the blue depths that Rosie reached over and patted his hand. He turned towards his youngest son. "I'm so sorry, Mason, if my prejudice kept you from us all these years. I've been a fool. A bigger fool than you can imagine. I want you back in our lives."

"Really? Aw, thanks, Dad. It means a lot to me." Mason's voice came out choked.

"How did you meet Rosanne?" Mr. Williams said to his youngest son.

Mason shrugged. "Online. Where else? I never thought I'd come back here." Then he reddened as if he'd just realised his admission. "Sorry, Dad. I know I should have visited. But I wasn't certain you'd even want me to. When I discovered Rosie was from Sturt's Crossing, I felt it was a sign. That it was time for me to be honest and see whether we could be family again."

"Well, you don't know how glad I am, son, that you took the chance. You like Sydney?"

"Love it. I couldn't live anywhere else." Mason gave a hesitant smile. "But I wouldn't mind coming back more often, if that's okay with you?"

"I'm not going to make the same mistake twice." His father nodded. "I'll be happy to see you. Both of you. Just don't make it too long between visits next time."

"I won't." Mason grinned. "Thanks."

"Good. That's settled then."

"Let's move on, shall we?" Luke ran a hand over his chin.

"Geez. Look at the time. We need to get back on track with this business idea, or it'll be Christmas and we'll still be sitting at this table."

Trying not to laugh, Rosie muttered, "Sorry."

"Don't apologise," Luke said sharply.

Rosie lifted her gaze from her son's busy hands as he squeezed more mushed banana between his fingers, and met Luke's eyes.

"I'm the one being impatient. I've got a lot to do today," he explained.

"I can imagine." She grinned. "I am sorry that we landed on you unannounced, but I did come bearing a gift." She pointed at Mason, relieved when Luke smiled.

She leaned forward, gazing earnestly at Mr. Williams and then Luke. "Now, about this deal. It's quite simple really. With the money I get from the sale of Aunty Claire's land, I can repay my mortgage and remodel my house into guest accommodation. *And* fund the documentary Mason will make that will land Sturt's Crossing on the world map. Of course, we'll be asking for donations from the station owners whose land we'll be showcasing."

Luke's forehead wrinkled. "I don't see how a doco will send tourists flocking to our region."

Rosie waved a hand in the air.

Her son imitated her. A blob of mushed up banana landed on Luke's shirt.

"Ooopsie," Caleb said and chuckled.

Luke sighed.

Rosie giggled and handed over a napkin. "The documentary will be teamed with our business idea. A treasure hunt for the long, lost, legendary Bloodwood gold nugget."

"I've never heard of it." Rolling his eyes, Luke dabbed at his shirt.

Mason sniggered. "That's the beauty of the entire project,

bro. We've come up with a fabulous idea. Think of it as a cross between a mystery weekend with clues that need to be solved, a survivor adventure, and an outback tour. We're targeting specific demographics of course. Say the eighteen to thirty-five year-old bracket. We'll do a loop encompassing all of Corner Country, kinda following in Sturt's footsteps a bit. Give it a historical twist, too. Tyler's crunched the numbers and says it will be tight for a while, but this project is a sure thing."

"We won't be deceiving anyone. Our website and advertising campaign will make it very clear that the nugget is fake. We're trading on the lure of adventure, the spirit of competition and we'll be using camels," Rosie said.

Caleb nodded his head solemnly. "Mummy, I like camels."

"Camels?" Luke added slowly, "I've been considering entering the camel market, more along the lines of milk and exporting to the Middle East, though. Not some high-risk pipe-dream."

"There, you see?" She reached over and squeezed his hand. "It was meant to be."

Luke gently slid his hand out from under hers.

She flushed, feeling like he'd rejected her. Caleb yawned as his eyes fluttered shut. Hugging her boy closer, she rubbed his back as he snuggled into her breasts. When she glanced up, she caught Luke staring. A frisson feathered across her skin.

He shook his head and scowled like he didn't like the direction of his thoughts. "I'll make you an offer for Blackbird Tor. This property was never meant to be split up. I think Grandpa thought this would be the way to bring Aunt Claire back into the family."

"Well, that didn't work," Rosie said tartly and stared pointedly at Old Man Williams.

The old buzzard frowned and looked at the ceiling.

Rosie turned her shoulder to him and said to Luke, "Can you meet Ford's price?"

Luke nodded, his lovely mouth set into a grim line. But there were shadows in his eyes that told a different story.

"Does this mean I can have a shower now?" Mason switched a hopeful gaze onto his father. "I need to get my suitcase out of Rosie's car."

"Later boy. We haven't finished discussing your business plan." Old Man Williams slapped both hands onto the table, waking Caleb who began to grizzle. "Flat Rock Station will be returned to its former glory. But you two are barking up the wrong tree."

"Huh?" Rosie pressed a gentle kiss to her son's soft hair and caught Luke watching her again. Her tummy muscles clenched. *Oh, oh.*

The station owner leaned back in his chair and looked smug. "This venture of yours is going to need something a lot more concrete than an imaginary nugget. What you need to find is the richest opal seam in the world, reputed to be located in Blackbird Tor. And Luke is just the man you need, young woman, to help you do so."

CHAPTER 6

*D*uring the long drive from Flat Rock Station back to Sturt's Crossing, Rosie's head buzzed with all sorts of wild ideas, snippets of remembered conversation and, heaven help her, fevered images of Luke Williams kissing her.

Everywhere.

What would his hands feel like touching her body? Would his palms be rough, smooth? Goosebumps shivered over her skin. It had been so long since Rosie had even thought about sex, she wondered whether this intense attraction to a man she barely knew was the result of years of neglecting her physical needs.

Caleb had had enough of being trapped in his car seat and enough of sitting in a hot car. He cried most of the way home despite Rosie offering him his water sipper which he promptly tossed onto the seat beside him. She tried a game of *'I spy,'* and played his favourite songs on the stereo. Nothing worked. He was overtired and needed his bed.

And he wasn't the only one.

By the time she pulled into her driveway, the sun was setting, Caleb was snivelling, and Rosie's head was pounding. She fairly stumbled into the house, Caleb in her arms, the heavy tote bag over her shoulder and tottered to the couch where she collapsed.

"What a day!" She sighed, placing her son onto the lounge beside her.

Her house, having been shut up for so many hours, felt stifling. Rosie could barely breathe. Caleb wasn't impressed either. He opened his mouth and shrieked blue murder.

"Bath, fresh clothes, a quick meal, and bed for you, young man." Holding Caleb's hand, she wandered through the house, opening windows and switching on the ceiling fans.

As soon as the sun had fully set, the night air would cool off the heat of the day. Perhaps once Caleb was settled, she'd be able to think logically about Old Man Williams startling announcement. There'd been a wicked glint in his eyes when he yakked on and on about the opal seam that unsettled her. Made her think he had more on his mind than finding "buried treasure."

Personally, Rosie had never heard of an opal seam, but then that didn't mean squat seeing how she'd been too busy wallowing in her personal mess of a life. There was one person that might know, and that was her sister, Rachel. Being the local vet, she heard all manner of rumours and gossip.

It was close to ten o'clock before peace had been restored and Caleb was finally asleep. Rosie, herself, felt like she'd been put through an old-fashioned wringer. After running a bath and chucking in her last vanilla scented bath bomb, she stripped and climbed into the hot water with a relieved sigh, her mobile clutched in one hand.

Eyes half-closed, she listened to the phone ringing on the other end and was about to end the call, when her sister's familiar voice answered. "McDonald's Veterinary Clinic." Her sister had never bothered to change the name of the practice she'd taken over when Tommy McDonald retired.

"Rach, it's me."

"Rosie! Is everything all right? Is Caleb okay?" Anxiety made her sister's voice sharp.

Rosie yawned. "Yes, all good here. I'm sorry for the late call but I haven't had a chance to ring any earlier."

"How did your meeting go? Did Mr. Williams agree to your proposal?"

"That's sort of a yes and no answer." She sank lower so her tense shoulders were covered by the hot, scented water. "God, that feels good."

Rachel laughed. "Should I ask what you're doing? Or rather who with?"

"I'm taking a bath. Alone," Rosie said tartly.

"I think you should start dating again. Maybe go to Brissie or the Gold Coast for a couple of days. Or Bourke. There's bound to be more guys there over the age of twenty five but under forty." She giggled.

Immediately, Rosie's mind filled with the image of Luke smiling and how for a few brief moments, the chill in his grey eyes had warmed her all over. She squirmed and muttered, "I'm too busy. Anyway, dating doesn't figure in my plans."

She sat up, sloshing water over the side onto the lino-covered floor. "I need to ask you something. Have you ever heard of an opal seam or opals being found in this area?"

"Rosie, what are you up to this time?"

"Are you going to answer me?"

Her sister's sigh was drawn-out and gusty. And loud.

Rosie shifted her phone away from her ear. "Well? Have you?"

"I vaguely recall Snake's dad talking about opals with a couple of old prospectors. But that was ages ago before he handed over running the pub to Snake and retired to grow his own hops for beer. I was shopping in the general store at the time and the blokes were standing about, yarning and blocking the aisle. I only remember because I thought it was one of Snake's dad's tall tales. You know how he would say anything to try and get people to come and stay in the town."

"Ummm." Rosie stared at the peeling paint on her ceiling.

"What does this have to do with selling the land?"

Rosie unveiled the events of the day and when she finally fell silent, her sister instantly scoffed, "I think he said it to stall your sale to Ford. It's obvious the Williams will do anything to try and get hold of that land again."

"You have to admit, Rach, if we can actually find proof the seam exists, the discovery will put Sturt's Crossing on the map. Loads of people will come to town and that's gotta help the economy here, right?"

"Transient workers usually save their dosh to take back home. You really think people would want to move here for good?"

Trust her sister to be practical.

"I guess." Rosie thought for a minute. "But if it was really big, a mining business could open up. There'd be employment."

"And environmentalists will be out in full insisting the land isn't ruined. Not to mention what impact mining has on the water table and the pasturalists."

Rosie stepped out of the cold bath. "I'm certain everything can be worked out to everyone's satisfaction. At the very least, we'd get heaps of tourists wanting to try their luck. And they've got to eat and have a place to stay which translates to money being spent in the town. Have a little faith, Rach. All I have to do is bring home the bacon."

CHAPTER 7

The next afternoon, Luke sat opposite Anne Bishop and sweated despite the frigid air blasting from the air-conditioner wedged in the one window the bank manager's office possessed. The building itself was old, probably built early 1900's and made of corrugated iron. With the passage of years and shrinking of population in the town, it had been halved by a brick wall built down the middle. The bank consisting of a reception area and this cramped office occupied the western side. The other side housed the only butcher in town. The result - the smell of raw meat often wafted inside this part of the building. Hard to take on a hot day.

Lips pursed, the middle-aged Ms. Bishop turned yet another page then squinted over the top of her glasses at her computer monitor. "I'm not convinced, Luke, that you can cover the repayments of an additional loan."

He bit down hard on the hasty protest trembling on his lips. He knew it would do him no favours to get hot under the collar. The bank manager was only doing her job and, in the past, she'd done everything she could to ease the burden of the locals' finances by re-structuring their loans. A country woman at heart, she didn't want their town to become nothing more than empty streets and abandoned properties.

She stopped scanning the papers in front of her, clasped her hands together on the formica desk, and peered at Luke through her thick glasses. "I am sorry, Luke, but if you can't provide any collateral then I can't send through your request to head office. There's no way they'll agree to either an extension on your current loan or even another mortgage."

"Collateral," he repeated slowly, turning over his father's words in his head.

If there really were opals on Blackbird Tor surely that would be sufficient collateral to sweeten the deal? He'd done a bit of homework, working late into the night pouring over everything he could find on the net about opals and mining.

When he'd discovered how many tourists streamed into Lightning Ridge every year, he'd allowed a glimmer of hope to glow. An opal seam would be good not only for the town, but also for the property owners. Some of them could get on board, offering farm stays and the like. With tourists came workers, tradesmen, and more opportunities for everyone. Problem was, if there really were precious gems out there waiting to be dug out of the hard earth, then the price of the Tor would sky-rocket.

How would he afford to buy the land back then?

But if he didn't try, then Flat Rock Station and his family heritage would be lost.

"It's possible I may be able to get you what you need." He stood and held out his hand.

They shook.

"I hope so, Luke. The last thing I want to see is you and your father walking off Flat Rock Station with nothing but the shirts on your back." Ms. Bishop shuffled the papers into a neat pile. "Unfortunately, that possibility is on the cards if you can't meet your debts very soon."

"I understand." After thanking the bank manager for her

time, he retrieved his hat from where he'd placed it on the desk and walked from her office into the bank reception area. Deep in thought, he didn't hear the cheery greeting thrown at him at first. It wasn't until a thin, carroty-headed, young woman stepped in front of him that he registered he'd been hailed.

"Maggie. Sorry I didn't see you." He quickly swiped his hat off his head.

Maggie quirked a quick grin then wiggled her ginger eyebrows in a suggestive manner toward the manager's now closed door. "Any good?"

He shook his head.

The downside of living in a small town like Sturt's Crossing meant everyone knew everyone else's business. Which was one reason Luke kept mainly to himself whenever he came to town, unless it was to catch up with two of his old school mates. The only two who'd remained in the area. He repressed an inward shudder when he recalled one particularly rowdy catch up around three years ago. In fact, he'd been with Maggie's older brother, Glen and another mate, Jacko, at the time.

By the way Maggie Hayes's green eyes sparkled, Luke had a sinking feeling she was privy to everything that had happened that night, including the crazy idea that had won him a dare against his two best mates. He wondered how much contact Maggie had with Rosie Turner these days. Those two had been inseparable in school.

"Haven't seen much of you lately," she chirped as she waved over a couple in their late sixties to join them. "You remember my mum and dad. They used to run the general store until Glen and I took over. These days it's just me, since Glen took a droving job up through Queensland."

Luke greeted the older couple then added, "Lots to do on the property. We haven't been able to employ any casual labourers for over six months."

Maggie clucked in a sympathetic manner. "I hear you. There's not much happening in town either. Business is slow in the store, and there's next to no employment. We've had two families move away only this week."

He stood feeling more than a little awkward at the calculating way Maggie kept eyeing him off, as if she was adding up his worth as a single man. "I better be off."

About to move away, Maggie caught his arm. "Has Rosie been to see you? She's got this great idea to attract tourists to our area."

"She called in yesterday," Luke admitted.

Maggie and her parents waited but he didn't elaborate. Really, it wasn't anyone's business what he and his old man decided to do with Flat Rock Station. Helping out a little schemer like Rosanne Turner was not in anyone's best interests. Unless Maggie wasn't fully in the know…

Luke cleared his throat. "Whatever you do, don't invest in her pipe-dream. You'll never get your money back."

The Hayes exchanged glances. Maggie's father frowned. "Rosie is doing her best to help out this town. Can't you see that, Luke?"

"Help herself you mean." The words came out harsher than he'd intended.

Maggie glared at him while her parents took a step back as if not wanting to be in his vicinity. "You've got no right saying things like that! Rosie's always helped anyone she could. Why, when she inherited that money from your aunt, the first thing she did was pay off her parents' mortgage. She also paid for university educations for her sister and brother."

"And she helped pay for the damage to our store's roof after that freak storm five years ago damn well tore this town apart," Mr. Hayes said.

"Her husband—" began Luke, only to be cut off by Maggie.

"Neil is a total douchebag. But that's not Rosie's fault. Her only fault was standing by a guy who didn't deserve someone as kind as her. She sold her engagement ring to help my parents. You're an idiot if you think otherwise, Luke Williams." Maggie whirled around and grabbed her parents' arms. "Come on, Mum, Dad. The teller's free now."

They all stalked to the counter.

Feeling like a leper, Luke crammed his hat back on his head and pushed out the front door. He stood on the cracked pavement, gazing down the too quiet street. There were an awful lot of boarded up shops and abandoned houses lining the main thoroughfare through their small village. *I'm not the only one that needs this chance of a future. If something doesn't turn up soon, this town has had it.*

So he'd been wrong about Rosanne Turner. What if she did have good intentions and had had nothing to do with her crook of an ex-husband? She wasn't the only one who'd made decisions in their past that they'd regretted. He had two huge regrets; one concerning his aunt, and the other his brother. From now on, he intended to carve out quality time for those he cared about instead of pouring all his energies into the property.

Maybe he should give her the benefit of the doubt. They'd all played together growing up. With such a small population, even the school kids had been close knit with the girls filling the numbers on the footie and soccer teams. Although younger than him, Luke had still had a fair bit of contact with Rosanne. And since she and Maggie had been best friends and Maggie had been a great one for following on the heels of her older brother, Glen, Luke was surprised to realise how many of his school-day memories actually contained images of the ex-Mrs. Turner.

Then of course, there'd been that momentous first day of term in his last year at high school that was carved indelibly his brain. That moment when the realisation little Rosie Brown had grown up. The impact of her sweet, sexy smile, and the glow of her shiny blonde hair had hit him like a punch in the gut.

But that was the year his mother and brother left him behind. The year when he realised few women could be trusted to live the life that he loved. Now it looked as if both Rosanne Turner and his future hinged on whatever was buried under Blackbird Tor.

If anything.

Checking out the rumour wasn't much of a gamble and really Luke had nothing to lose. He'd discover for himself whether Blackbird Tor held the cards they needed.

First, though, he intended to legitimise the verbal agreement made yesterday with a certain gambler's wife and which he'd had drawn up by his solicitor in Bourke and who'd emailed it through to him this morning.

It didn't take long to find Aunt Claire's old home since Sturt's Crossing consisted of barely twenty-five, wide, red-dirt streets and lot of boarded up houses. The only street in town that was tarred was the main road that led east to Bourke in one direction, west onto The Cut Line that led to Tibooburra and Sturt's National Park that linked up with Wanaaring Road that headed south to Wilcannia.

Luke parked out the front and sat for a minute looking at the house—an old Californian style bungalow built in the 1920's.

Not much had changed since Rosanne Turner had inherited the property. In fact, the building looked more run-down than Luke remembered. There were cracks in the red brickwork, the iron roof needed re-placing, and most of the gutters were completely rusted away.

His lips twisted.

Rosie Turner and her husband obviously didn't believe in preserving the old lady's memories. Too busy blowing the rest of her inheritance on living the high-life. He used his anger to strengthen his determination. Picking up the envelope that contained the legal agreement, Luke swung out of his vehicle then marched up the dirt path.

A little of his resentment faded as he noticed the front lawn was mowed and the narrow garden edging the sagging front wire fence had been weeded.

He stepped onto the porch then damn near broke his ankle when his right foot dropped through a rotting floorboard. Wincing, he jimmied his foot out and sighed at the sight of his torn jeans. A careful placement of his foot onto the boards beside the new hole in the floor, revealed nothing more painful than a minor wrench. The last thing the station needed right now, was Luke laid up as well as his father.

Why hadn't she fixed this place up? Aunt Claire would roll over in her grave if she saw the condition of her home. Then he remembered what Maggie had said earlier that day in the bank.

His shoulders hunched as shame spiralled through him. If what Maggie and her family said was true (and he had no reason to doubt them) then Rosanne Turner wasn't the wastrel her ex was and had been looking out for others as best she could. He tapped the envelope against his jean-clad leg thoughtfully. He couldn't believe how much he was looking forward to seeing her again. How relieved he'd felt at hearing she wasn't as shady as her husband.

Taking a deep breath to tamp down his edgy excitement, he knocked.

Nothing.

His fist clenched, Luke hammered on Rosanne Turner's front door. The Christmas wreath nailed to the timber shook with each blow. Green, red, and silver tinsel dribbled down onto his boots. Where the devil could she be? At close to four in the afternoon and hot enough to roast a chicken where it stood, surely she wouldn't be running around outside somewhere with her little boy in this heat?

He stopped his thumping to press his ear against the

timber but could hear no sound of movement inside the house. Shoving his Akubra back off his forehead to the top of his head, he stepped away and planted his hands on his hips. Now what? Should he wait for a while and see if she turned up, or scribble a message on the back of the envelope and come back another day?

If she didn't come home until nightfall, either she or her son could fall into the hole and injure themselves.

I better stick around, just in case. Damnit! Why is life so complicated? He edged around the hole and slumped in the wicker chair, stretching his legs out before him, prepared to wait it out. The last thing he wanted to do today was drive back to the station only to have to drive into town tomorrow to get the blonde babe's signature.

Besides, he wanted to watch her reaction when she read the agreement he'd had drawn up.

Hell, he just wanted to be near her.

He yawned and flapped uselessly as about a dozen or so flies buzzed around his face. As he remembered how he'd left his father and brother heading out to the barn to check on the lamb's progress, he grinned. A little alone time together and maybe they could re-connect. It sure was something he hoped would happen between himself and Mason and he'd added it to his mental 'To Do list'.

The sound of a car bumping and rattling up the road chased his drowsiness away. *Finally.* A car door squeaked open and Luke's pulse notched up a gear. *No, make that five.* He sighed as he acknowledged the edgy anticipation stiffening his body's involuntary response. This attraction to Rosanne Turner was something he didn't need right now. Actually, if truth be told, something he didn't need ever. Although the blonde babe had a murky past, Luke could tell she was a woman who still had dreams in her eyes and hope in her heart.

And he was not going to play any part in either of them.

After seeing how broken the Old Man became after mother scampered, Luke had decided it would take a very special woman to make him want to walk down the aisle. No, it was a bachelor's life for him. And as for this crazy desire sizzling through him? As soon as Rosanne Turner's signature was on the paper he held, he wouldn't need to ever see her again.

Pity, that thought made him feel as lonely as a stray dog.

CHAPTER 8

osie popped little Caleb out of the car first, placing him on a thick towel she'd laid over the grass. He pushed his plastic tip-truck over to the side of the towel and began to fill the tray with dirt and twigs.

He was such a good boy.

Rosie cranked open the tailgate and began to unload all the gear she'd bought this afternoon, onto the ground. Under her breath, she recited the items as she lifted them out. *Two shovels; one square edged, one round point. One pick, not too big or heavy for me to use. Two empty jerry cans for spare petrol.*

All second, possibly fourth hand going by the age of them, but they were all she could afford. As it was, the cost had eaten into what little money she had left. The camp stove, gas bottle, and two-man tent she'd borrowed off her sister half an hour ago. Rachel had enlivened her visit by remunerating every possible disaster that could afflict Rosie should she continue with what Rachel termed her latest fantasy.

Fantasy! Huh! Rosie smirked. If it didn't include a certain cowboy then she'd never call it a—

"What the devil's all this crap?" said Luke's astounded voice from behind her.

She spun around and there stood her fantasy cowboy, Akubra pushed back revealing his handsome face, strong nose and a jaw-line lightly sprinkled with reddish stubble. He wore a black T-shirt that could have been painted on and which he'd tucked into worn blue jeans with a black leather belt and his scuffed leather boots. His forearms bulged with firm, rounded muscles and that flat stomach.

Oh my.

"Mummy's going camping. Mummy, says me sleeping with Milly and Jim," Caleb squealed. "Wanna play trucks?"

"Do you mind toning down your language?" Brought back to reality, Rosie gestured toward her son who had pushed to his feet and was toddling as fast as he could in Luke's direction.

"Sorry." Luke eyed the little boy now clinging onto his jean-clad leg and staring up at him in a fascinated manner. "Er… What does he want?"

"Pick him up." Grinning, Rosie walked back to her car and reached inside to grab three buckets and a large wooden sieve. "He probably wants his nappy changed. I'm still working on the toilet training thing."

"Ugh. I don't do nappies, Rosie."

Rosie stomped from around the back of the car and dumped the stuff in her arms onto the ground. "Excuse me?"

"I could call you sweetheart."

"How about my name?"

"Mrs. Rosanne Turner," he drawled as if knowing she'd be irritated by his emphasis on her former married state.

Her face flamed. She pointed at Caleb. "My son. He's tired. He's had a couple of big days."

The smirk on his lips slid away. "What if I drop him?"

"Then I'll kill you with my bare hands." Rolling her eyes, she trooped back to her car and struggled to heave out a Porta-potti. She had dragged it to the edge when she heard the sound of Luke's footsteps approaching.

"What do you think you're going to do with that?"

Rosie pushed a curl damp with sweat out of her eyes and turned around. Her heart performed cart-wheels beneath her rib cage.

Luke was peering past her into the car, Caleb clasped firmly in his arms. He straightened and they both stared at her. Oh heavens, how natural did the two of them look together.

If she'd never gone off to travel the world could this have been her life? *Reality check, Rosie. Reality check. I'd never have had Caleb and that's something I'd never change.* And what's to say, Luke would have given her a second glance?

She raised her chin and tapped a finger against the porta potty. "Seriously? You want me to explain how the human body works?"

He grinned. "I may need a refresher course on one certain aspect and, babe, in case you're confused, it's got nothing to do with that contraption sitting in your car."

"Try it with some other girl. I'm not interested."

He leaned closer. "You sure about that?"

She leaned backwards, the movement arching her back and pushing her breasts into prominence. He looked.

And looked.

Until she could have screamed.

Tension crackled between them. She was so hot she could have combusted on the spot. Her body tingled and tightened. When he licked his lips, she knew he'd noticed her peaked nipples. His face had this lean, hungry sharpness to it that heightened her own arousal. How would it feel to have his mouth on her skin?

Luke dragged in a harsh breath and turned away. His shoulders were taut. The urge to press against him and wrap her arms around his waist was so intense, Rosie had to clench her fists so she wouldn't give in. She swallowed over the whimper humming in her throat.

Not a good idea, Rosie.

"You're not going anywhere near that tor, so don't even think about it." His voice was so harsh, she jumped.

"Since it's my land, I can do whatever I like." Disappointment and frustration boiled like a campfire billy inside her. She blinked back tears.

Why him?

Of all men, why did it have to be Luke Williams to bring her body back to life? There was no future with this cowboy. He obviously found her attractive, but his opinion of her and her ex was dirt low. And he wasn't the kind of guy to have a short fling with—even she knew that would be a bad idea. He wore *"unattainable"* like armour.

"How about we go inside out of this heat and discuss this sensibly?"

He was right. Maybe she had a case of mild heat stroke making her so wobbly on her feet and woolly with her thoughts. Rosie nodded.

They picked their way over the gear spread out like a garage sale over the grass.

"You think you've bought enough?" His voice was amused.

"I've probably forgotten something vital. Its years since I've been camping in the bush." She stopped on the top step and pointed to the broken floorboard. "What happened here?"

Luke snorted. "I could have broken my leg. Then I'd have to sue you."

"Join the queue."

"Don't worry, I'll fix it."

"I don't need or want your charity."

"I wasn't thinking of doing it for free. I'll send you a bill."

"Smart arse. You think you've got an answer for everything."

"Yep. Just about." He winked, his silvery eyes twinkling. A tiny smile tugged at the corners of his mouth.

She sidled past him on the porch and unlocked the front door, then led the way into the lounge room. "If you wouldn't mind popping Caleb on his play mat and keeping an eye on him while I open up the house, I'd appreciate it."

"No worries."

A few minutes later, she returned. Holding out her hand she said, "Come on, munchkin. Its clean-up time." Then to Luke, "I won't be long."

"Not a problem. I'll go outside and check your gear. See what you've missed."

She paused. "I thought you declared my land was off-limits for me. Not that I care one fig for your opinion."

"I've changed my mind." Luke pushed to his feet. "Remember, I've known you since school and I also remember you're not that good at listening to advice. There's only one way to handle this problem. We go together."

CHAPTER 9

"I had my solicitor draw up an agreement based on what we discussed yesterday," Luke said, resting his head against the back of the couch where he sat. He stared so intently at her, Rosie wanted to squirm feeling as if any second he'd pounce.

She dragged her gaze away and looked at the envelope he'd placed on the coffee table beside her like it was a live bomb. She played for time, taking another sip of the iced tea she'd made earlier that day.

Since Luke's startling announcement about them taking off to Blackbird Tor together, he'd refrained from mentioning it again. And she still hadn't decided on how to respond. On one hand, she had to admit the idea of not going out into the bush alone was appealing, but then on the other hand, she wasn't certain of his motives.

The memory of how her ex-husband had constantly manipulated her was like a bitter shadow in the room.

Sitting on his play mat and clad only in a pair of cotton shorts over his training undies, Caleb was busily stacking plastic building blocks into a tall structure. Every so often, he'd turn around and favour Luke with a grin. It sure looked to Rosie that Luke's fatal charm had even won over her little boy, who usually was especially wary where men were concerned.

"What you're really saying is that if we do happen to find gemstones on *my* land, you don't trust me not to up my current asking price." Hearing that clarification spoken out loud, should have stoked rage in her heart, but instead all she felt was exhaustion mingled with despair. Why had she expected Luke to be different? To not look at her with suspicion? To not want something from her?

Neil had tainted her forever.

Heaven help her, she'd truly believed that somehow, she could find a way to whitewash her past and move on into a different future.

"You've got it all wrong. I don't want any surprises for either of us." Luke's mouth thinned.

With carefully precise movements, she placed her glass on the table, picked up the envelope and opened it. She reached for the pen, flipped the two-page document over to the signing page, then scribbled her signature and the date.

"You haven't read it." Frowning, Luke surged to his feet and crossed the room in three long strides.

Rosie stuffed the papers back into the envelope and handed it to him. "I don't go back on my word. And I have nothing to hide."

"For Pete's sake." He snatched the envelope off her then ripped it into several pieces, allowing the fragments to float to the thin-carpeted floor.

Caleb sent his blocks flying as he wobbled to his feet and trotted over to inspect the mess.

"What did you do that for?" Rosie gaped at the pile of paper.

Her son sat down in the middle of it all and grabbed handfuls to throw over his head. "Raining."

Luke bent down and nudged Rosie's chin with his

knuckles. His gaze held and searched hers. "We need to trust each other if we're going to be partners." He shook his head slowly, and a broad smile lit up his face.

"Same Rosie. Impulsive and honest as the day is long. I thought you'd changed but I was wrong. I'm sorry for misjudging you. Next time, read all documents before you sign. It just might keep you out of trouble, although I doubt it. You attract trouble like a magnet." The words might have been harsh, but his voice was warm.

She jerked her head, dislodging his disquieting touch. Why was he being nice to her all of a sudden? Far easier to keep him at a distance when he was glaring at her with ice in his eyes.

Now… She gulped.

Now, he was far too damn attractive, and so close she could smell his tangy after-shave and feel the heat of his body. There was a sparkle in his eyes that made her think his actions were a bigger deal than what they really were. She made a show of reaching for her glass, so he'd move away. When he did return to his seat on the opposite side of the room, she had to deal with her damn disappointment.

"I'm not going to clean up that mess."

Luke shrugged. "I'll do it later after the little guy's lost interest."

"I'll hold you to that promise."

"Good."

They stared at each other. There was challenge in the glint of his eyes, purpose in the firm curve of his lips. Rosie felt as if the stuffing had been knocked out of her, grateful she was sitting down. How long they would have remained in stalemate if someone hadn't knocked on the door, Rosie didn't know.

"Expecting someone?" Luke quirked an eyebrow and the moment was broken.

"Not that I know of." Rosie set aside her glass and left the room on trembling legs to answer the door.

Without thinking, she swung the door wide. A familiar man of around fifty or so and dressed in khaki bush clothes that strained over his large stomach, stood on the porch, a scowl on his olive-skinned face.

"Malcolm!"

"Mrs. Turner." He motioned toward the door. "May I come inside? I must speak with you urgently."

"Of course." Rosie smiled and stepped back. Mindful of Luke sitting in the lounge room, she remained in the hallway, and lowered her voice. "What can I do for you?"

"I've heard you've received another offer for Blackbird Tor. Since I offered first, and may I say the figure we discussed is more than fair, you have no right to accept another offer until our negotiations are complete," he said, breathing heavily through his nose.

"Your offer was contingent on my obtaining an access road to the property."

"Well? Have you?" His black eyes snapped like firecrackers. "Mrs. Turner, I want that land. I'll take you to court if I have to prove you're reneging on our deal."

Luke appeared behind Rosie. "I understand Rosie has yet to sign any agreement with you, Malcolm."

"Luke Williams." Ford's mouth turned down. "I should have known you'd try to sneak your way into this poor woman's good graces. You realise, he's only after the Tor. No Williams can be trusted."

"I don't know if you're referring to my mother or my father here, but either way, I'd be very careful what you say next." Luke moved closer, subtly shifting his body so he stood between Rosie and their furious visitor.

Rosie said, "I wasn't able to obtain the access agreement. I believe that makes your offer null and void, and that means the property remains on the market."

"This is not fair," Ford all but howled. "I would have negotiated that deal for myself, but I knew there was no way Williams would agree to anything to help me out."

"Exactly why are you so keen to buy the Tor?" Luke folded his arms.

"A man in my position needs to keep expanding." Ford craned his neck to peer around Luke to point at Rosie. "You haven't heard the last of this, young woman." He slammed out the door and stomped off the porch.

"Oh God! If he tries to sue me… I have no money to fight him." Rosie wiped her wet cheeks.

"Hey." Luke turned around cupped her face in his warm hands. "I spoke about this with my solicitor. It's all cool. There's nothing for you to worry about as long as you didn't sign any papers. You didn't, did you, Rosie?"

She shook her head. "I also didn't give him a definite answer. I told him I'd think about it."

"You see?" Luke raised his eyebrows. "Makes me wonder why he really wants the Tor."

"Do you think he knows about the opals?" Excitement chased away her anxiety. Could they be real afterall?

"Could be. What do you say, Rosie?" Luke grinned. "Are you up for a road trip?"

CHAPTER 10

It took another full day to organise their expedition
to Blackbird Tor and the morning after, at 5:30 a.m.
on the dot, Luke pulled up in front of Rosie's house with Jet
panting out the rear window. Her house locked, her gear on
the porch, Rosie was ready to leave.

They spent the next thirty minutes loading his Land
Rover, although Luke insisted on leaving a lot of her stuff
behind, saying it was too old to be of any use. Besides, he'd
told he he'd already packed what he considered necessary.

As the sun rose over the horizon bathing the land in
bright, golden light, Rosie sat in the passenger seat as Luke
drove the car through Sturt's Crossing's quiet streets.

Her eyes misted with tears as they passed the vets,
reminding her that her son was tucked up safely at her
sister's house on the outskirts of town. It had only been one
night and already she missed Caleb terribly. When she and
Luke had made their plans, it had all sounded so easy. Now,
having slept very little the night before, she wasn't so sure.
For one thing, her son might fret for her. She'd already texted
her sister three times this morning. Her mobile pinged. Rosie
snatched it up and read the screen.

"All good? How's your son doing?" Luke slowed as he turned the car off the highway and onto the gravel road that led to Flat Rock Station.

Rosie huffed out a breath, half relief, half woeful sigh. "He slept through the night. Rach says he's already up and playing with her kids, Milly and Jim."

"He's in good hands."

"I know. I've never been apart from him for more than a couple of hours. This is a big deal for both of us."

Luke reached over and squeezed her fingers briefly. "With luck, we won't be away too long. Dad's given me a rough mud map of the area where he believes there's a cave which goes deep into the Tor."

"I hope there's no bats."

"There's always bats, Rosie. Don't you watch movies?"

Rosie smiled, feeling a little of her anxiety ease. Luke was proving to be a good travelling companion; competent, calm and easy to get along with. "How reliable is his information though?"

Luke shrugged. "Dad seems fairly confident. He reckons he heard the story from an old bushman when he was a kid and was so fascinated by it, he went out and looked for himself."

"But he said he didn't find it."

"Well, he was young, twelve or thereabouts. He rode out on his horse with supplies for only one weekend. He had school and Grandpa would have given him a hiding if Dad had wagged it. Grandpa believed in discipline and he wasn't one who tolerated excuses."

"He sounds horrible."

"He was fair, though, and kind underneath. I don't remember him much. I think I was about four or five years old when he died. The horse he was riding stumbled because of a wombat hole. Grandpa went down hard, hitting his head on a granite boulder. It was three days before they found him."

Rosie shuddered, thinking how terrible it would have been dying alone. "Poor man."

"Yeah, wasn't good for anyone. Grandmum was devastated and handed over the property to Dad soon after. She's enjoying her retirement home on the Byron Bay, having made new friends, and spends her time playing lawn bowls. Nowadays, I carry my sat mobile with me every time I set foot off the homestead."

The outback was a vast and mostly lonely place with kilometres between towns and properties. Far too easy to get lost and never be found again. Rosie rubbed her arms, more grateful than ever that she wasn't making this trip alone.

She stared out the window at the passing scenery— scrubby low-growing bushes and sparse clumps of pale green grass contrasting starkly with the rich, red earth. A small mob of sheep were packed in a tight bunch under the shade of a desert bloodwood tree. "How's the lamb?"

"Getting better every day. Haven't found his mother though so Mason and Dad have been feeding him. Mason's named him Snowy and the lamb follows him about like a dog. Stands on the veranda and bleats through the screen door until he comes out." Luke laughed.

"Are you glad to have your brother home?"

Luke shot her a quick glance. "The weird thing is, it wasn't until I saw him again that I realised how much I missed him."

"I think he's happy to be back too," Rosie said. "Are we going to stop at the homestead for a break?"

"Nah. I'm taking a different road that will bypass the homestead and knock an hour off our travel time. If we stop, I know those pair will keep us talking for ages. Thought we'd keep going and make the most of the daylight. In the side pocket of your door, there's a topographical map of the property. I've marked the roads in red. Actually, they're more like dirt tracks than roads. It's gonna be a bumpy ride. Hope you've got a strong stomach."

Rosie fished out the map and opened it on her lap, comparing it with the mud map Luke handed to her which he'd had stowed in his shirt pocket. With her fingertip, she followed the red line Luke had marked. "I wasn't expecting a picnic. Don't worry, I'm a lot tougher than I look. Besides, I love camping. Every school holidays, Mum and Dad would pack us up and off we'd go. Each time, we'd find somewhere new to explore. All we had was an old Toyota Land Cruiser, a massive tent, and blow up mattresses."

"What? Your family really roughed it then? Bush dunnies and showers?"

"Mostly. Money was tight, so it wasn't often we camped in caravan parks with amenities."

"I've brought along a canvas shower bucket for us to use. But don't worry, I'll turn my back."

"A true gentleman," cooed Rosie, her body heating at the thought of Luke watching her soaping herself, butt naked.

"Or we could shower together. Save water, you know." He turned and winked. A broad grin spread over his face. "You're blushing."

"It's a hot day and shouldn't you be watching the road?" She pointed toward the windscreen.

Luke snapped his gaze back and swerved sharply to avoid a deep pothole. "Good call. I don't mind camping myself."

"Are you sure your dad and Mason will be okay by themselves?"

"Between the two of them they should be able to handle things for a few days. I've arranged for the district nurse from Bourke to call in tomorrow to check on the Old Man."

"I hope we find what we're looking for."

"Don't worry so much, Rosie. I've got a back-up plan if this doesn't work out."

"Your camel idea?" Even to herself, she sounded skeptical.

"Hey, its high in protein and delicious. You should try some."

"I'm a vegetarian."

"Camel milk is also popular with people on the alternative life-style band-wagon. I'll ensure it's one hundred percent organic. I've already got Mason working on a marketing campaign."

"I think my idea is a lot better. At least mine will generate trade for the town."

"Did I say I only had one idea?" He grinned at her. "Make that two back-up plans. You did say you intend to use camels."

"Lucky you." She chewed a nail. "If we don't find the seam … I'll have to sell the Tor and if you can't get the money, I'll be reduced to accepting Ford's offer. But I didn't like the way he acted the other night."

"Yeah, me neither. Wish I could work out what he was really up to." He sighed. "Rosanne, you don't have to tell me what's at stake. I know."

There was no sign of a smile on his face now and Rosie was immediately regretful she'd reminded him of their problems.

Curled up on the back seat, Luke's dog sneezed, making Rosie smile. "Maybe we could find another alternative if this treasure hunt is a total loss."

"That's what I'm banking on, Rosie."

Five and a half hours later, the vision of Blackbird Tor filled the windscreen as they drove steadily closer. A flat top outcrop of granite and ironstone, stubbled with scrubby bushes and stunted trees, rose above the landscape like a sacrificial slab.

Rosie shivered and felt compelled to turn around and stare back the way they'd come. Red dust billowed up in the air for a long way further back then she would have expected, but if anything caused the excessive dust cloud it was hidden by a bend in the track. She frowned.

"Anything wrong?" Luke glanced in the rear-vision mirror.

There was nothing now, only the dirt kicked up by their own car as they bounced down the rough road. Could have been a willy-willy.

"No. I just had this weird feeling for a second that there was someone behind us."

"Almost there. Let's pull over for minute and check that map again."

Rosie wound down the window the moment Luke killed the engine. About a gazillion flies buzzed inside. Now that the air con was off, the interior of the car quickly heated. It didn't help that she'd dressed for the occasion in beige, thick cotton cargo pants, a long sleeve button up cambray shirt of summer blue, and sturdy hiking boots. But she knew sun burn had its own dangers.

"The outback, I love. The flies I absolutely hate." Rosie flapped a hand in front of her face, shuddering when a fly crawled behind her sunglasses.

Luke handed over a tube of roll-on fly spray. "Try this but mind your eyes and mouth." He examined his father's mud map then looked out the window again. "There appears to be a flat area over to the east of the Tor not far from this track. We'll set up our base camp there and begin a sweep of the area to the west until nightfall."

"Yes, sir, captain." Rosie gave a mock salute.

"It's good you've realised who's the boss here." Smiling, he set the Land Rover into motion once more, but this time at reduced speed. Fifteen minutes later, he pulled up in a clearing. "Okay, this is it. Let's get the tent up before we start searching for the cave. I don't want to be fooling around with pegs and ropes in the dark."

Luke let Jet out and filled a deep enamel bowl with water for his dog. Then Rosie and Luke set about unpacking the basics from the back of the vehicle while Jet watched them from under the shade of a tree. It wasn't long before the tent was erected.

Rosie dumped her duffle bag inside and took a very long look at the two air mattresses laid out along opposite walls. There wasn't all that much space in between. They'd only have to roll over and they'd be lying side by side.

She rubbed her hands together. Maybe she'd snore, and he'd be turned off. Maybe he snored, snuffled like a wild pig. Maybe... Oh gosh, maybe she'd experience the most momentous night of her life. *I can't believe I'm thinking about having sex with him!*

Knees like jelly, she stepped out of the tent to find Luke waiting for her, the tiniest of smiles peeping about his lips.

Heat inflamed her face. Her mouth dried as a delicious tingle spread over her body.

"Ready?"

She nodded.

He handed over a backpack to Rosie and she shrugged it on while he did the same with a much heavier looking pack.

"What on earth have you got in there? The kitchen sink?" She settled a bush hat onto her head and popped her sunnies on, hoping he couldn't read her thoughts about their sleeping arrangements.

"A lot of *'just-in-case'* gear. Let's go. Come on boy," Luke said, snapping his fingers. His dog rose and trotted to his side.

Maps in hand, they set off, trudging toward the base of the tor where they began a painstaking search of its ridged sides.

Hours later, the sun was beginning to sink toward the horizon and they'd found nothing that looked remotely like a cave. Luke mopped his sweaty forehead with his sleeve and re-settled his Akubra over his head. "I'm impressed. No whinging, no whining about the heat. Apart from the flies that is."

"I need this as much as you, Luke." Rosie unclipped her water bottle from the side of her backpack to take a gulp but didn't stop walking. "Anyway, I told you. I like it out here." She tilted her face to the sky and smiled as even in those few seconds, she felt the sun's savage bite.

About to lower her head, she froze, squinted then pulled off her sunnies for a better look. "Hey, Luke. See up there? About five metres over to the right of that octagonal shaped boulder. Is that a shadow caused by the folds of the cliff, or the entrance to a cave?"

Luke stared hard for several minutes before turning toward her. "I can't tell from here. We need to get closer and it's a good two-thirds up the side of the Tor. Think you can do this?" He indicated the steep and rocky ascent with a sweep of his hand.

"Try to stop me." Jaw firm, Rosie strode past him and began to scramble up the side of the cliff.

CHAPTER 11

It was a difficult climb. Breathing heavily and sweating like a pig, Luke kept his attention divided on their objective and Rosie working her way steadily ahead in front of him, ready to grab her should she lose her footing. The climb seemed to take forever, and those last five metres felt like five hundred because every so often, their feet would slide out from under them due to the loose pebbles and rocks littering the side of the tor. They had to grab hold of larger rocks to stop themselves from sliding all the way back to the bottom.

Luke risked a glance down to check on his dog and saw Jet laying in the shade of a rosemary bush sleeping. He'd left water for Jet and told him to "stay" deciding he didn't want to risk his dog falling and injuring himself. It was bad enough knowing Rosie was with him, but he'd known he'd be wasting his breath if he even suggested she wait below.

What a woman. He thought about his second plan and smiled. A life lived alone had suddenly lost its appeal. The spectre of his parents' failed marriage had disappeared, routed by blonde curls and a pair of lovely sherry-brown eyes. The rest of her wasn't bad either. Her determination and zest for life humbled him, brought him to realise there was more to living than hard work. He wasn't conceited though, there was a good chance she wouldn't have a bar of him. But he wasn't blind either. He could tell she was attracted to him, hopefully as much as he was to her.

He eyed her nicely rounded bottom outlined by her pants with appreciation as she stretched out for a firmer handhold, bracing her body with her feet.

"Why did you marry him?" The question that had been burning in his gut even since he'd laid eyes on her again burst from his lips.

"Huh?" Rosie panted. She scrabbled with her hands and a small shower of pebbles rained down on him. "Sorry."

Luke shook dust from his eyes. "Your husband, why did you marry him?"

"You're asking me that now?" She sent him an astonished glance over her shoulder and heaved her body up another metre. "He was good-looking, still is actually, charming, and I was very naive. I think in retrospect he happened along at a time when I was ready to fall in love."

"You loved him." His gut wrenched savagely.

"Well, duh. I married him, didn't I?" She gasped. "Luke, I can see it. There's a small ledge. I'm almost there."

"Be careful."

"Ooomph!" She lost her grip.

Slid.

Luke grabbed her around the hips, stopping her from falling any further. "Get hold of something."

She gripped a large rock, that looked solid enough. "I'm good."

By dint of Luke pushing her on her backside and Rosie climbing again, she reached the ledge and swung up over the top. A few seconds later, Luke joined her where he pulled her away from the crumbling edge to sit with their backs against the cliff wall.

They stayed that way, their chests heaving as they regained their breath.

Slumped against the rocks, Rosie took a swig from her water bottle then offered it to Luke.

Not a hint of a breeze stirred the dust and trees below. Heat seared off the rocks surrounding them. The silence grew between them. Thickened. Would she tell him? Explain away those years of remaining with a guy who wasn't worthy of her? How would he deal with it, if she admitted to still having feelings for the ratbag?

He passed the bottle back to Rosie and she took another drink. He couldn't believe how desperately he needed to know the circumstances of her marriage. Maybe if he started first; let her know she wasn't the only one who could make mistakes.

"I should have visited Aunt Claire more." He leaned back against the hot rocks. "When I was still at school, I'd go there every afternoon with Mason and spend an hour or so. Then we would hurry back to the school gate where Dad would pick us up to drive us home. I liked her. She was a very gentle woman who'd made the best scones I've ever tasted. Why she and Dad wouldn't speak to each other, I have no idea. All I did know was that if Dad found out we were spending time there, we'd be in big trouble. So neither Mason nor I told him."

He shifted. "But when she died, I couldn't believe how long it had been since I'd last seen her. If I'd made the time, if I'd made more of an effort, maybe she would never have died alone, without her family."

"She had us, Luke. Mum and Aunty Claire were very close."

"I can't tell you how grateful I am for that."

"It was her heart, you know."

Luke nodded. "Dad had an attack last year."

"Yes, I heard about it. He looks like he's recovering well, though."

"Having Mason turning up and then you with your crazy idea, I think you've brought life back into the old man." Luke shot her a grin.

"My idea is more desperate than crazy." Turning the bottle round and round in her hand, she said, "Neil has left me badly in debt. I know I stayed married to him for eleven years, but I didn't love him for that long. I soon realised he'd married me only for my inheritance. I was still a fool though. I wanted a marriage like my parents, so I kept thinking, if I tried a little harder, if I could somehow help him with his gambling problem, then I could make it work. I thought if we had children it could be a way to bring us together." Her voice was quiet, tired, like she was over holding it together and despite his empathy for her past pain, euphoria rose.

This is the woman for me.

Rosie covered her face with her hands, mumbling, "We'd been married for three years before he told me he'd had a vasectomy because he couldn't stand children. We had separate bedrooms after that."

Turning toward her, Luke caught Rosie's hands in his and drew them away from her face. Her eyes glistened with unshed tears. "You still stayed with him."

"I was weak. I didn't want to admit I'd made a mess of my life and I felt like I was the failure. He began to have affairs. I pretended it wasn't happening until he started sleeping around with a couple of women from around here. My hometown. Then he attempted to force himself onto my sister. But Rach dealt with him."

"Geez! I had no idea." Luke swallowed over the fire and fury burning in his gut. "He should have cherished and respected you. You didn't deserve a scum bag like him."

"I knew my marriage was over, but I wanted a child so bad and I didn't want a rotten husband to be the father." She sucked in a deep breath. "Actually, I'm surprised you didn't hear the gossip since I told my sister everything when I was in hospital giving birth to Caleb."

Luke shook his head. "I take it all this happened two or three years ago. I had my hands full then trying to do whatever I could to feed our stock." He gave a sudden short laugh causing Rosie to glance at him, her eyes wide.

"Sorry. Just remembering one or two decisions in my past I'm not that proud of. One of them is not spending enough time with the people I care about. Go on, please. I'd like to learn more about you."

"Are you game?"

"I'm always game." He winked, glad when her expression relaxed and a little of the lost look in her eyes faded.

"Okay, here goes. I sold the last of Aunty Claire's jewellery I'd hidden from Neil, went on line and found this clinic that specialises in helping gay couples and single women become pregnant." The admission poured from her lips.

"Strewth!" Luke felt like his heart leap-frogged into his mouth.

"It was Maggie who gave me the idea. You remember Maggie Hayes, my best friend from school?"

Luke nodded numbly.

"She suggested I find a sperm donor. She said she'd heard about it from her brother. It was easier than I thought and luckily worked first time. I had to fill out this form with all these questions, you know, like what eye and hair colour I preferred. Personality traits, build, blah, blah I'd like in the father." Rosie rolled her eyes.

Cold sweat broke out across Luke's forehead.

Rosie leaned closer and stared. "Are you okay? You look a little pale?"

"I'm good." His voice sounded strangled. He cleared his throat, trying again. "Where was this clinic?"

"In Bondi."

"Strewth, Rosie you're not going to believe it! I donated sperm to some place in Bondi about three years ago because of some stupid dare with Glen and Jacko one night at the pub. We were in Sydney for the weekend, celebrating Jacko's buck night. Do you think…"

They stared at each other for sixty seconds.

"It was you I was thinking about when I filled out those forms. Well, the you I remembered from high school," she said slowly. Suddenly, she shook her head, sending her blonde curls dancing about her face. "No, way. That would be too much of a coincidence."

"Stranger things have happened." Luke squared his shoulders and smirked. "Could be, I'm that little fella's dad."

She gave him a shoulder push and grinned. "Get over yourself." Her lips twisted. "I don't regret what I did."

"Does Neil know?"

"I never told him what I did, and I haven't spoken to him since he left town the day Caleb was born. I guess he thinks I had an affair." She shrugged.

"I admit, I did wonder. I wouldn't blame you. You must have been lonely."

"I was."

Luke squeezed her hand and admitted wryly. "I also wondered whether there was a guy in town who'd stake claim on you."

"I am not some acres of land, Luke Williams."

"No, you're worth a lot more than the best property in the district."

Her face pinkened. "I let Neil do a lot of awful things to other people. I failed in my marriage."

Still with her hands in his, he nudged her chin a little higher and stared intently into her eyes. "You didn't fail, Rosie. Your ex-husband is a fool along with a lot of other things. I think you're the most beautiful, the sweetest, and the strongest woman I've ever met. Not to mention the possible mother of my child." He smiled, allowing his gaze to drop to her breasts before looking into her eyes.

"Luke Williams, are you flirting with me?"

There was such a humbling expression of vulnerability on her face that Luke wanted to pull her into his arms and shield her from the world. His chest swelled so tight he thought he would burst. "I've never been more serious in my life."

Rosie stared into Luke's eyes, searching for shadows, for even one hint of evasion but didn't find it. His gaze was crystal-clear, as if she was looking straight into his heart. She'd told him more than she'd ever told anyone, even her sister, knowing the odds were Luke could view her as a loser, someone to be pitied, a dupe. Or worse, someone who'd been involved in her ex's shady schemes.

She saw none of that in his eyes.

Rather, she saw certainty, respect and hope.

Did he mean … ? They'd only met up with each other again a few days ago but the attraction between them was strong. They had a history, bound by their shared love for both the town of their birth and the beauty of the land surrounding them.

And there was the possibility he was Caleb's father.

A remote possibility, to be sure.

She looked out over the vista laid before them, the strain of the climb beginning to tell with aching calf and thigh muscles. Her clothes stuck to her sweaty body and she had no doubt her face was covered with red dust. Hardly sexy but the way Luke looked at her made her feel like she was queen of all she surveyed. Her blood thrummed hot and heady through her veins as she considered a future she'd never thought possible.

Could she take a risk? Dare she take a risk? And now there was Caleb to think about too.

"Do you want to do a paternity test?" She held her breath. What would he say?

"Listen, Rosie. Whether or not I'm Caleb's real dad doesn't matter to me. He's part of you and for me that's enough."

An image popped into her head of the protective way Luke had held her son like he was someone precious.

She wet her lips, saw the searing heat glittering in his eyes. "Are you going to kiss me now or am I going to have to make you?"

His mouth quirked into a smile, deepening the dimple in his cheek. He leaned closer. She leaned in until their lips touched. Gentle at first, Luke moved his mouth tenderly across hers before taking her in a kiss that fired her heart and branded her soul.

A long shuddering sigh broke from her throat. She gripped his shoulders and pressed her body against his. Every part of her skin tingled. Images of making love with Luke filled her mind making her head whirl.

His lips left hers to travel along her jaw line to her ear where he whispered, "I want more than one kiss from you, Rosie."

Heart thumping almost painfully against her ribs, Rosie took the leap. "Me too. I'm not big on playing games where guys are concerned. I have too much to lose."

Luke raised his head and gazed into her eyes with an intensity that shook her to her core. "I do believe my game-playing days are over. Are you ready, babe?"

Rosie knew he was asking more than if she was prepared to keep on with their search. "Only if you'll walk by my side."

"Always."

"And Caleb?" Her voice trembled.

"Any man would be proud to have him as his son." Luke

shifted and rose to his feet, then bent down offering her his hand.

She took it.

His fingers interlocked with hers with a surety of touch that swept away the last lingering doubt in her mind. This cowboy was a man of integrity as solid as the Outback itself. Vitality frizzled through her veins and Rosie leapt to her feet, ignoring her aching muscles. She snuggled into his side, delighted at how her curves fitted into his hard leanness.

"I knew you were trouble the moment I saw you." Luke hugged her tight.

"What can I say? It's what I'm good at."

He laughed. "Let's move. This is the best day of my life. Look."

Rosie followed the direction of his pointing finger. No more than one metre from where they stood was a narrow opening.

"It *is* a cave. Come on." Smiling, Rosie led the way, hugging the side of the cliff with one hand and holding Luke's with the other.

"Wait a sec, I'll get your torch out of your pack."

Rosie paused while Luke unzipped a side pocket. He switched the torch on before handing it over.

"I'll go first. Keep the light trained on the ground and take your time. I don't want to have to hoist you out of a hole. And hang onto my belt." Luke eased his way through the fissure in the cliff wall.

Rosie took a deep breath, looped her fingers through the back of his belt, and followed. They shuffled forward, taking care not to snag their backpacks on the rough surface of the narrow tunnel that twisted and turned ever deeper into the Tor. Blackness soon swallowed all trace of daylight and Rosie shuddered, knowing she would never have ventured this far inside if Luke hadn't been with her.

He kept up a quiet reassuring monologue, probably

sensing she was ready to bolt for the exit the further they crept.

"It's getting hard to breathe," Rosie said.

"I noticed. Don't panic and you'll be fine. The good thing is there's only one way in and out, so no fear of us getting lost."

She gulped. Her hands were damp with sweat and not all of it was from the heat.

"I think we're heading downwards." Luke stopped and shone his torch over the walls in front of him.

"Is that a good thing?" Rosie rested against his back, gaining confidence from his bulk.

"No idea, Rosie. I don't want to go too much further though. I'm not risking your life in climbing down the Tor after nightfall."

"Give it another fifteen minutes."

"Fine, but no longer." Luke pushed forward again. "Hang on. The tunnel is beginning to widen, and I think it's getting steeper. Let's hope ... Stop!"

Unable to halt her momentum, Rosie cannoned into his back, her body weight jolting him forward a few centimetres. His boots scraped over loose pebbles, he pitched forward, stumbling, the torch light wobbled over the walls. His free hand flailed over rocks hunting for a firm grip. She knew the instant the ground beneath his feet gave way.

He began to fall.

Rosie dug her boots into the dirt and hauled backwards on his belt for all she was worth. Her arm felt like it was stretched to the limit as Luke teetered on the edge of a hole, God-only-knew how deep. Terror was as loud as bat wings beating in her ears. She tossed her torch aside. With her other hand, she groped along the side of the rock wall, searching until she found an outcrop of rock she could grip. Using it as leverage, she pulled backwards.

Swore.

Prayed.

Her own feet began to slide forward.

The thin beam of light afforded by her torch on the ground, revealed Luke was hanging onto a boulder to the right of him with both hands, his torso twisted at the waist. It was all Rosie could see of him. The rest of him looked like he'd been swallowed by the earth.

"My hands are slipping. The rock is too smooth," Luke gritted out. "Rosie you need to let go of me."

"Don't you dare, Luke Williams. Ever. Ever. Ever dare leave me." Fear, panic, grief, and a whole mountain of love flooded through her, escalating an adrenaline rush she'd never thought possible.

Giving her the strength of the desperate.

Her hand tightened over his belt in a grip that not even wire cutters could loosen. She grunted and pulled. Every muscle in her body strained. She kept on pulling. Heaved his body a bit further out of the abyss.

Panting, Luke said, "I've got hold of a better rock. Ease up a bit, babe, or that boy of ours will never have a brother. I can take it from here."

Rosie stopped pulling but didn't let go of his belt. Not until Luke had hauled his fine arse out of that bloody hole and had shimmied back onto firmer ground. Then she flung her arms around his neck and allowed herself to cry.

They knelt in the dark, locked together, body mashed against body, their hearts thudding like one massive drum roll.

"Shush, babe." Luke lifted his face from where he'd buried it in the curve of her shoulder and neck. "It's all good."

"You could have died."

"But I didn't. Thanks to you. God, I could have lost you, Rosie." He pressed soft lips to the side of her shaking mouth. "Okay, listen. We need to stop breathing so hard, not much oxygen down here. Easy does it, Rosie babe. Shallow breaths."

Rosie rubbed her wet face against his shirt to dry her tears and nodded. She counted to sixty, slowing her frantic pulse, and gradually felt the tightness in her chest fade.

"So much for our treasure hunt," Luke said as he gingerly cupped himself. "What's worse, you damn well cut me in two."

"Don't be such a baby. I thought you had bigger balls than that," Rosie quipped.

Luke chuckled, then sighed. "Doesn't look like we can go any further without better equipment. The cave isn't safe. Not that we've found anything. Let's get out of here."

"I'll grab my torch. Yours, I'm sorry to say, is long gone." She reached around him and found the torch. As she lifted it, the beam swept over the tunnel walls.

"OMG! Luke! Look at that. The rocks. I think I can see crystal of some kind."

Luke turned around and taking the torch from Rosie, adjusted the brightness of the beam and performed a searching sweep around them.

Red, green, turquoise, and golden fire sparkled in the light.

"Well, stuff me sideways with a dead goanna," breathed Luke. His voice rose with jubilation. "Opals. Rosie, we found the seam."

CHAPTER 12

The last rays of daylight were shrinking fast towards the western horizon by the time Rosie and Luke stumbled from the cave's entrance.

"Fresh air." Rosie drew the hot, dusty air deep into her lungs, gulping it down.

"Yeah, I'm with you, babe."

Hand-in-hand, they stood on the tiny ledge enjoying the moment, still high from the excitement of their find. Darkness was deepening over the land, the shadows of the trees and shrubs below elongated and impenetrable. There was a waiting stillness about the land that sent a shiver down Rosie's back.

A faint bark sounded.

"Jet. Poor fella. Must have been wondering where the hell we got to. Getting down isn't going to be easy. We're high enough up to still have some sunlight but once we climb lower, we'll need the torch to guide us the rest of the way. I'll go first, and we'll have to take it slow."

"Is that your only speed?"

Luke's white teeth flashed as he grinned. "I have a feeling you'll soon find out for yourself. Follow me."

Luke wasn't joking when he said they'd take it slow. On the climb up, Rosie hadn't registered the toll on her body at the time, being too focused on reaching her goal. But coming down was a totally different matter. After their near miss inside the cave, she ached in places she'd never known existed, so sore did she feel. Her arms and legs shook from the strain. She longed for the tent and all the way down, fantasised about curling up on that mattress, wrapped in Luke's arms.

Safe.

And then tomorrow she'd be home with her son.

Her future lay before her, just as sparkling as the gems they'd found but infinitely more precious. With her head filled with hopes and dreams, she climbed down the side of the Tor, more in blind faith as she followed Luke's instructions.

"We're here, Rosie." Amusement warmed Luke's voice as he steadied her with both hands grasping her waist.

Jet barked.

"Sorry. I'm absolutely pooped." She swayed, her knees buckling.

"Shit. I bet you're dehydrated." Luke scooped her up into his arms, backpack and all. "Come on, boy. Lead the way to the camp."

Eyes half-closed, head whirling, Rosie dreamt of a long, cool drink followed by a long, cool shower. Luke's arms were strong around her. She could feel the flex and pull of his muscles as he strode effortlessly through the scrub. Canvas brushed against her skin as they entered the tent.

"Here you go." Luke settled her gently onto the mattress. "I'll leave the torch with you while I light the kerosene lamp. Now, take this bottle of water and drink every last drop."

Rosie nodded and took the bottle from Luke.

"Rest up. You've had one hell of a day. I'll get us

something to eat and set up the shower so we can have a bit of a wash."

"Sounds good." Rosie smiled, delighted when his grey eyes darkened like storm clouds. Tilting the bottle, she drank as Luke left the tent. Never had water tasted so good. After drinking her fill, she shrugged off her backpack and flopped onto her back.

The sounds of Luke moving about outside filtered through the canvas walls and it wasn't long before light spilled through the tent flap from the kerosene lamp.

Her dizziness gone, she sat up and reached for her pack then opened the top zip. Holding her breath, she drew out the lump of rock and walked out of the tent.

"Isn't it beautiful?" The opal sparkled under the bright yellow light of the kerosene lamp.

"It's not bad." Luke moved to her side and smoothed a finger over the glowing colours. "I reckon it could be a black opal and with all this red in it, could be worth a tidy sum of money."

She grinned at him. "Oh, Luke. If that's true, we've not only helped ourselves, we've saved the town."

"Life can't get any better than that, babe." He planted a kiss on her cheek. "Strewth, I need to eat." He strode off to his car where he yanked open the tailgate.

Jet growled.

Dry grass crackled underfoot but the noise sounded some distance away.

Rosie shot a glance around the camp area. Luke was poised near the tailgate of his Land Rover. He was motionless. Listening.

Jet padded toward the edge of the spool of light, ears pricked, head low, the ruff at the back of his neck bristling, a low growl rumbling from his throat.

They were not alone.

"Who's there?" Luke called out.

A shadow flickered behind a clump of scrubby bushes. "No need to get your knickers in a knot, Luke. Only me, your friendly neighbour."

"If you're so friendly, Ford, why not join us here in the light?" Luke turned around to look at Rosie. He made shooing motions with his hand, then pointed to the tent.

Rosie shook her head. No way was she going to cower inside.

"It's true then? There's opals in that Tor." Ford's voice sounded flat, expressionless in a way that made Rosie's blood run cold.

"No way of knowing how big the seam is yet. We couldn't get very far." Luke glared at Rosie, jabbed his finger toward the tent again. "Could be what we found was an isolated outcrop. This area is a long way from Lightning Ridge and Quilpie."

"I heard you mention black opals. That makes sense; the Tor's got both granite and ironstone in her. She could well have boulder opals too."

"Now who's dreaming?"

"You should have sold me the land, Rosie."

The crack of a gunshot split the night.

Rosie ducked. Something hot burned across the top of her head.

"Stay down!" roared Luke as he dived around the side of his car. "Ford, you've made a big mistake."

Rosie dropped to the ground, her head throbbing. Blood dripped into her eyes. Squirming over the ground like a snake, she wriggled lightning fast out of the pool of light and into the shadows near the back of the tent. She still held the opal, the evidence they needed to prove their claim. She shifted to a crouch, pulse jumping, getting ready to run. Heart racing, she wiped wet, sticky liquid off her face with the back of her sleeve.

Ford shouted, "That husband of yours was no good.

Blasted idiot and his get-rich-quick schemes. I invested every dollar I had in some so-called property boom. I've got nothing left. Now there's this crazy stand-over bloke threatening to break every bone in my body if I don't cough up the dough by the end of the week." Three more shots were fired in rapid succession, each one pinged into the metal of the four-wheel drive.

"Stay out of sight, Rosie," Luke called.

The interior light of the car flicked on. Two seconds later, Rose saw and heard the flash of returning fire from near the driver's side. Two shots in rapid succession. Luke must have retrieved the shotgun he kept strapped beneath the dashboard.

Ford shot at the car, shattering what sounded like the front headlight.

Rosie melted a little further away from the camp and began to circle around toward where she believed Luke was hiding. There was no way of telling how much fire power Ford had brought with him. And Luke only had his shot gun with limited ammunition.

A cowboy who worked on the land didn't usually have that much reason to be armed to the teeth.

It wouldn't be long, and Luke would be out of bullets, and they were a long way from help of any kind. They needed to get out of here; sooner rather than later.

Automatic fire ripped the tent to shreds. Rosie noted Ford was careful not to take out the lamp. With no moon yet rising over the horizon, he needed that light to keep check on their movements and to give him a point of reference.

Keeping well in the shadows beyond the camp, she made the stand of three bloodwoods and poked her head out of cover to search for Luke. The faintest flicker of a shadow moving revealed he was on the other side of the clearing, having used the cover of Ford firing at the tent to change his position. Then Luke took out the lamp. The kerosene inside the glass container exploded, sending sparks and embers high in the sky.

Rosie flattened herself to the ground as Ford decimated the area near where the flash of Luke's gun had been seen with a hail of automatic fire. *Oh God.* Luke, where was he? Were they both going to die out here? She remembered how his grandfather had lain for three days before he was found and sobbed quietly. Her fingers of her right hand dug like claws into the dirt as if by doing so, she could hold onto life itself.

Ford stopped shooting.

Smoke and cordite stank the air. Rosie struggled not to cough and give away her location. She needed to move further from the clearing. Maybe she should make a run for the Tor; hide in the cave until Luke dealt with this maniac.

No. Rosie was fairly certain Ford had Luke pinned down. The moment Luke attempted to move, Ford would cut him into pieces.

It's up to me. I have to do something. But what?

Gingerly she raised her head, trying to see in the darkness and smoke that clouded the camp area. Her eyes stung and watered. She blinked and rubbed her face again with her sleeve. She wasn't far from the Land Rover. A glimmer of starlight glinted on the metal and she saw the passenger side door was open.

Pretend you're a stealth ninja. Her teeth clenched to stop herself from crying out, she inched carefully over to the car. Holding her breath, she raised herself up and felt along the floor of the Land Rover. There had to be something in here she could use. They'd certainly packed enough gear.

Her groping hand found cold metal. Long. Narrow. The hilt of a knife. Carefully, she traced its length and shape. Not just any knife. Luke's heavy hunting knife.

Well, she knew for a fact that she was no soldier and definitely no killer. *But if I can't use this on Ford, maybe there's something else I can use it on.* Ford drove the latest BMW X series four-wheel drive and it would have a touchy alarm system including tyre pressure monitoring. She could attempt to jimmy the lock or smash a window to open a door, or maybe slash a tyre to set the alarm off. With luck, the noise would be all Luke needed to get the advantage.

She visualised Ford's approximate location and what she remembered of the campsite and surrounding area. The ground had been rough, littered heavily with rocks and boulders, and she believed the track Luke had taken had been the only obvious way to the clearing. That meant the rancher could have left his vehicle back on the road.

Now, all I have to do is find his car.

CHAPTER 13

Luke strained his eyes, searching the darkness for Rosie. Had she been hit? Bile scorched his throat. Damn Ford and his reckless behaviour. Fear and fury bubbled like acid in his gut. If she was hurt…

No, he had to hope and pray that she'd gone to ground. And was staying put. *Hell.* Who was he kidding? Knowing Rosie, she'd wouldn't be sitting on her butt doing nothing. She'd try to help. But how?

First off, he needed to work out exactly where she was.

"You must be running low on ammo by now, Luke. Trust me, I can keep this up all night. Why don't you and the woman come on out where I can see you? All I want to do is take a look at what you've found," Ford yelled.

Luke didn't answer. He wasn't going to make this any easier for Ford if he could help it. He sank lower behind the knee-high outcrop of rock, one hand resting on his dog's back. His gaze slowly tracked what was left of the campsite.

Where the devil had she got to? The last time he'd seen her she'd been making way toward his car. He had a feeling she intended to look for something to use as a weapon.

Jet turned his head, looking off to the side. There was no

aggression in his body, rather his tail gave two thumps on the ground. *Rosie.* It had to be her.

By the way Jet slowly turned his head, Luke knew his dog was trailing her movements. She was heading away from the campsite. Hopefully out of harm's way. But she was definitely up to something.

Maybe she intended to provide the distraction, Luke desperately needed. He was down to four bullets, but he hoped he wouldn't have to use them to take his opponent down. *I need to get closer to Ford's position. Be ready for it.* He gripped Jet's fur harder as his dog whipped his head back towards the older rancher and barred his teeth.

Luke whispered, "Easy, boy. With me."

Hunched over and keeping his gun aimed in Ford's direction, Luke began his tortuously deliberate journey to bring him closer to the other man's position

The minutes crawled past.

Luke paused to wipe sweat from his face. His blood pumped thick and fast. Ford had ceased firing but judging by Jet's fixed stare and the aggression he could feel in his dog, the bloke hadn't moved.

Luke allowed his dog to lead him forward another metre and stopped to listen.

How close was he?

It was quiet.

The usual night reptiles and insects had fallen silent, chased away by the gunfire.

A shrill alarm shattered the night.

"What the..."

The expletive came from Luke's left, no more than two metres away. He dived forward, shifting his hold on his rifle so he now held the barrel. "Go boy."

Jet leapt, snarling, and latched onto Ford's shadowy form. The man howled as Jet's teeth sank into his arm.

Luke smashed his rifle butt into Ford's shoulder. Bone

cracked, eliciting another scream from the older man and he sank to his knees. His weapon fell from his hand.

Luke kicked the gun out of reach and gave Ford another wallop on the back for good measure. "Stand down, Jet."

His dog immediately released his hold and sat on his haunches, teeth bared inches from Ford's face where he'd collapsed into the dirt.

"Rosie! Where are you?" Luke hollered.

"I'm coming!"

Ford raised his head and Luke leant down and slammed a fist in his face.

"That's for trying to hurt my girl." He patted Ford down, relieving the man off a knife then waited, his rifle pointed at his head. "Don't even think about moving."

"OMG! Luke. Are you okay? Where's Jet?" His babe burst out of the bushes.

"Rosie?" One handed, Luke reached out and pulled her against his chest.

She clung to him like she'd never let go and his world righted.

Having taken Ford prisoner, Luke decided they needed to hand him over to the authorities as soon as possible. After ensuring he was bound securely with rope and guarded by Jet, Luke and Rosie broke camp, salvaging what little was left and stowing it in the Land Rover before they headed home.

"I'm beginning to think you do only know one speed." Rosie giggled from where she was curled in the passenger front seat, a blanket tucked around her.

"Hey, can't risk hitting a roo. We've only got one headlight," Luke reminded her. "We're coming up to the homestead now."

Rosie yawned as they turned onto the drive and struggled out of her blanket cocoon.

Jet barked from where he guarded Ford on the back seat.

As they came closer, a light turned on inside the house. Soon, the entire front yard was lit by floodlights. Luke pulled up close to the steps and turned to Rosie. "Brace yourself. I have a feeling this is going to be a long night. When Constable Anderson turns up to take custody of Ford, he'll want us to give written statements. And the Old Man is gonna want to know everything that happened. In detail. I have a feeling our alone time will have to be put on hold."

She leaned over and pushed a lock of his hair from his eyes. "Sooooo, do you want me to tell him everything?"

He kissed her quickly on the lips. "Some things need to stay sacred, babe."

"Mmmm, like your penchant for taking it slow." Smiling, Rosie lifted the rock from her lap and waved it about close to Luke's nose. "I can't wait to see your dad's face."

"Something tells me this opal isn't the only thing that's gonna make him happy."

"Not as happy as me."

Luke smiled. "Or me."

"What's going on? Did you find it?" Mason bellowed as he raced out the front door and clattered down the steps in his slippers and a satin, lavender kimono. "Holy crap! Is that bullet holes? Hey, Dad, you've gotta see this!"

Chuckling, Luke slid out of the car and strode around to her side to open her door. Holding out his hand, he said, "Ready?"

"I've never been more ready." Her fingers gripped his. Love and hope made her feel like she floated to the ground. Arms around each other's waist, they stepped onto the veranda where Old Man Williams waited.

He had the biggest grin on his face Rosie had ever seen.

She said, "We're home."

"There's a guy all tied up in the back of the car!" howled Mason, from where he was peering into the rear of the four-wheel drive. "Wow. Life sure isn't dull around here."

CHAPTER 14

They stood on the steps of the tiny, weathered sandstone church, a small group of people now bound into family, tighter than fencing wire. Members of the township were gathered in bunches and chattering to each other just outside the gate.

Her wedding day. To Rosie's eyes, it looked as if just about everyone who lived in Sturt's Crossing and the surrounding district had turned up for the ceremony, whether they'd been invited or not.

A wedding was always a cause for a celebration. Coupled with the news of the opal seam and Mason's documentary that was gaining increasing downloads and interest on the internet, everyone's hope for the town's future was riding high.

Surrounded by her family and friends, Rosie's chest tightened with heightened emotion. This time she knew she had the wedding, and would have the marriage, of her dreams.

Rosie's parents were part of the "grey-nomad" community of retirees with RV's or campervans travelling around Australia. They'd arrived yesterday armed with the wedding dress Rosie ordered online and which had to be picked up from Ballina. Mid-length of white Thai-silk, adorned with sparkling crystals around the heart-shaped neckline and low-dipping back, she'd teamed it with the bouquet of Sturt-desert peas Luke had presented to her. The dress fitted Rosie perfectly, clinging to her curves like a glove.

Dramatic, simply sophisticated, and downright sexy, or so Luke had whispered in her ear before sliding his warm lips along the line of her throat. She hugged herself, thinking of that moment, her blood heating as she imagined all the similar moments to come.

Her brother had flown in from his job in Mount Isa landing on the primitive airstrip usually reserved for the Royal Flying Doctor service, with fifteen minutes to spare. And just as well, as the plane had to detour to nearby Bourke to pick up the pastor and Mason's partner, Tyler. Her sister, Rachel, and her husband, Chris, had offered to host the wedding breakfast at their house and their two children had performed their jobs of carrying the two wedding rings with a seriousness beyond their years. For a wedding organised one week ago, everything had gone like clockwork.

"Not bad for a cowboy who only knows one speed." She curled her fingers around the firm strength of her new husband's forearm and smiled lovingly into his face.

Luke snorted. "This is nothing, babe. Wait until you really see me in action."

The stern, suspicious lines that had marked their first encounter had disappeared. His beautiful eyes were no longer colder than a snow storm. Rather they glowed like guiding starlight. Never would she grow tired of looking at him, no matter how old and wrinkled they both became. She'd found her soul mate and one who understood and accepted her for all her quirky, crazy ways. One who understood there may be times when her impulsive nature would land them in hot water. He'd not only stand by her, but she knew with all her heart, he'd fish her out every time.

"I have the most handsomest husband in the world. And the smartest." Pride resonated in her voice.

Several people snickered.

Her brother, Nick, laughed and slapped Luke heartily on the back. "Atta boy."

Luke's best man, Glen Hayes, wrapped an arm around his shoulder and gave him a mighty bear hug.

Red rose richly on Luke's cheekbones, but his delighted grin spoke volumes. "And I have the bravest and prettiness woman in all of Australia."

Standing beside them with Caleb snug in his arms, Rosie's brand-new father-in-law snorted. "In my day, newly-weds didn't stand about gas-bagging when there was food wasting on the table. Now, are we going to eat soon? I'm famished, and this little fella here is chewing his finger down to the bone."

"Poor baby," murmured Rosie running a fingertip over the curves of her son's ear. "I think he's teething again."

"Now she tells me!" declared George Williams in a dramatic tone. "Notice how she didn't share that little titbit until after I offered to take care of him until these two get back from the Haymans."

Everyone laughed except Rosie.

"Maybe we should postpone?" Rosie eyed her son with concern and laid the back of her hand on his forehead, checking for any sign of a fever.

George rolled his eyes. "I'm teasing you, girl. Caleb and I'll get on like a house on fire. You'll see. No need to fret and your sister says she'll call in every other day."

"Thanks, Rach." Rosie's gaze met her sister's.

Rachel drew Rosie into her arms and hugged her close. "He'll be fine. Go and enjoy your honeymoon with your hot guy."

Rosie stepped back to hug her tearful mum and then her beaming dad. Luke struck up a conversation with Rachel, something to do with his precious camels.

Maggie looking lovely in a satin sheath of ice-blue, elbowed her way through to the front. "I'm getting in position for the bouquet tossing." She grinned.

Feeling happier than she thought she deserved, she drank in the familiar faces surrounding her. She turned around, facing the road, about to toss the bouquet over her shoulder, then hesitated.

An angular woman in her mid-fifties, with faded blonde hair and dressed in tailored linen beige slacks, open nude-sandals, and a white blouse stood a little apart from the other townsfolk. When she realised Rosie had spotted her, she hurried down the path, stopping a few feet from the circle of well-wishers.

"He certainly is a beautiful boy. He has your lovely blond hair." Her voice was throaty and distinctive.

Rosie frowned. She was certain she'd never met this woman before, but her voice sounded familiar, like an echo from her past. For some reason, Aunty Claire's funeral popped into her mind.

Rosie's father-in-law's jaw sagged toward his chest for a moment before he blurted, "Stone the crows! Eleanor!"

"Hello, George."

"Oh my goodness." Rosie's mother leaned over and clutched Rosie's wrist, her eyes round with surprise. "I don't believe it." She nodded at her husband. "Look, David, it's Eleanor Reynolds. You remember, she was in the same year at school with me and Claire Williams. Well, I'll be! I haven't set eyes on her since 1982. The year George married Marlene Wilson and refused to invite his sister to their wedding."

The small group of family and friends gawped at the newcomer who stared them down with a cool composure Rosie admired. Whoever this woman was, it was obvious from the avid expressions and furtive mutterings whipping about like a willy-willy, she was a woman no one had expected to ever see back here in Sturt's Crossing.

Whether it was Rosie's recent brush with being the centre of gossip and innuendo or the stiff posture of the older woman that aroused her compassion, she wasn't certain. All she knew was that she felt compelled to offer Eleanor a show of friendship.

She stepped forward and held out her hand, ignoring her beloved cowboy's warning, *"Rosie."* "How lovely to meet one of mum's and Aunty Claire's school friends."

Eleanor Reynolds smiled and squeezed her fingers. "Thank you." Her eyes travelled over the group to settle on Luke's father. "How are you, George?"

Never one for small talk, he barked, "What are you doing here? You said you'd never return."

"I did come back once. For Claire's funeral, which I noticed you didn't attend." Her voice was cool but there was no accusation in her tone.

Rosie linked her fingers with Luke's, her gaze darting from the stranger to her father-in-law and back again. Anticipation bubbled. She just knew she was about to finally learn what had kept him apart from his sister all these years. Maybe the rift could be mended?

Even though darling Aunty Claire was no longer with them, Rosie couldn't think of a more perfect way to end her wedding.

Everyone shuffled closer.

All eyes were on George Williams still clasping Caleb on his hip and glaring at the stranger in their midst.

Small towns.

Close-knit communities.

Where love, hate, friendship, and good-natured rivalry were national sports.

"You know why," George said hoarsely.

Luke sucked in a sharp breath.

Did he know? Had he guessed but never mentioned it in loyalty to his father? Rosie spared a glance into her new husband's face.

He muttered, "The food will be getting cold. Let's all make a move."

Rosie whispered, "Nice try, honeybun, but I'm not going anyway until this is sorted." She elbowed him. "Shush. Not now."

Everyone held their collective breath, including Rosie.

"What are you doing with a cane?" Eleanor indicated the walking stick hooked over George's arm.

"Heart attack. Last year."

"Harumph! I see you're still breathing which goes to prove only the good die young."

"She was my only sister." A tear rolled down George's ashen cheek.

Eleanor gazed up at the sky for a few seconds before looking back. "And she was my only love."

The small group gasped. Hand over her mouth to smother her own surprise, Rosie leaned into Luke's side and he instantly wrapped an arm around her waist.

"I wanted to marry you. If it wasn't for Claire... She kept us apart."

"That's a pack of nonsense, George. You couldn't accept that she was gay." Eleanor's voice rasped thick with tears and pain. "And that I was gay. You wanted someone to blame."

"God help me. I did blame her." George blinked several times. His Adam's apple bobbed up and down as he gulped several times. "You look well. What have you been doing all these years?"

Eleanor gave a twisted smile. "I had one other love; seeing the world. I went off to Melbourne and trained as a nurse." She shrugged. "None of us got to live our heart's desire. Neither you, Claire, nor me. But we did live, George. You married Marlene and had a family. Claire had her close friends here in Sturt's Crossing, a lovely goddaughter, and she enjoyed being a school teacher."

George looked over at Luke and then glanced at Mason standing close-by with his partner and lover, Tyler Jenkins. "I've been lucky."

"More than lucky. They appear to be fine young men, George. You'd never have gotten any kids out of me." Eleanor gave a short laugh. "I've had a good life, better than I thought I would have when Claire refused to run away with me. She wanted to pretend our falling in love had never happened. She found it too difficult to publically admit her sexual preferences."

"I didn't support her." George shook his head.

Eleanor's eyebrows rose. "It was 1982. Not exactly the opportune time for coming out of the closet."

George shuffled his feet, looking shamefaced.

"Why are you back here?" Rosie piped up into the silence that had fallen while her family stood agog, not wanting to miss a single word. Even the well-wishers outside the fence were silent and the pastor was standing on his tip-toes, so he wouldn't miss a thing.

"I'm retired now, and I felt it was time to come home."

George cleared his throat. "I'm glad you came. We were friends once, Eleanor. Before I fell in love with you."

"Yes, we were." An earnest expression settled on her face, making her look older, tired. "I'd like us to be friends again, George but it will only happen when you make peace with your sister. Think of it as a gift of love."

George averted his gaze to stare where a flock of five white cockatoos had settled on the church roof. Tears flooded his eyes and Rosie laid a gentle hand on his shoulder. Her father-in-law stared at her.

"Your son gave me the gift of love. And my cowboy is so very much like his dad." She smiled.

"You're a wonderful girl. My son is a lucky man." He squared his shoulders. "I don't even know where my sister's buried."

"I can show you." Eleanor Reynolds held out her hand.

Rosie's heartbeats quickened. Would George take it? Or would he turn away and continue to live with his regret and lost dreams? Could he step into a future that was so different to his past?

He sighed. "Here. Do you mind taking little Caleb for a bit? I won't be long."

Rosie nodded and took her son from his arms. "Take as long as you like. We'll be here -waiting for you."

Luke reached out and gripped his old man's hand. "Good one, Dad."

Mason fished a cotton hankie from his pants pocket and blew his nose.

Together, George and Eleanor began to walk in the direction of the cemetery. Then he turned around and looked directly at Rosie. "Eleanor is right. I have been blessed. Two great sons, a lovely daughter-in-law, and a beautiful grandson that I'm sure is going to be the first of many." He winked.

Luke laughed. "I'm working on it, Dad."

They walked amongst the tombstones, the small community of Sturt's Crossing watching. Then Eleanor Reynolds' clear voice floated back to them. "Every Christmas Claire sent me a card with photos of your family. I can't believe how much Caleb looks like Luke at that age."

George snorted and bellowed, "That's because Caleb is Luke's son."

Luke and Rosie exchanged glances and smiled.

"Should I tell him about the sperm donor part?" Rosie said in a small voice, her heart thudding like crazy and skipping every second beat.

"Hell no." Luke hugged Rosie and Caleb close to his chest. "As far as Dad is concerned, since we're married that makes

Caleb my son. If, and when, we ever do that paternity test, the outcome won't matter. Either way, he's my son and the greatest gift you could ever give me."

Rosie snuggled close, breathing in his masculine scent and loving the firmness of his body against hers. Like a rock. Protective. Immovable. And pretty much irresistible where she was concerned. She giggled. "I'm sure I could give more gifts, if we ever manage to snag time alone."

"Babe, you just leave that to me. As soon as the speeches are over, we are *on that plane*." Releasing his hold, he hustled her off in the direction of their wedding breakfast and the new life that waited for them—together.

All honest reviews are appreciated. Reviews can help readers find books and increase a writer's visibility. Increased visibility can lead to more sales, allowing me to continue to write my stories.

Thank you to any who have the time to let others know what you enjoyed about my book.

These three small town romances have been re-branded and revised and now form part of my Edge of the Outback Romances which have been bound together to form a box set published as Sweet Country Romances.

For this series, I drew on my love and awe for the Australian Outback and recalled wonderful memories of the years I spent travelling and working around Australia.

During this time, I worked on a cattle station in the Northern Territory, weathered two cyclones, spent a week on a deserted tropical island, sailed the Barrier Reef, camped off the beaten track miles from nowhere, squatted and worked on the gemfields of outback Queensland as well as explored the Top End of Western Australia. I also lived for a time in Alice Springs where I'm positive I felt the heart of our great country beating beneath my feet.

And out there far from the smog and lights of cities, it's amazing how close the stars of the Milky Way appear to be and how brilliant they sparkle.

There truly is no place like home.

Science Fiction / Space Opera Romance

Darkon Warriors series:

Legend Beyond the Stars
The Portal
Awakening the Warriors
Star Pirate's Justice
When Stars Collide
Bargain with the Enemy
Touring the Stars
The Slave Trap

Mars Academy Series:

Stranded
Cosmic Fire

Apocalyptic Romance
Paying the Forfeit (Search for Home)
Storm of Fire (Search for Home)
Quest for Earth (Search for Home)
Don't Look Back (Warders of Earth)

**Contemporary / Small Town Romance: Bindarra Creek
Makeover (A Bindarra Creek Romance)**

Desire for Love
Cotton Field Dreams (A Mindalby Outback Romance)

Contemporary Romance
Scent of the Jaguar (A Deadly Forces Romance)

Fantasy/Ancient Worlds Erotic Romance: Bound by Love

AUTHOR BIO

Suzanne Gilchrist can't remember a time when she didn't have a book in her hand. Now she dreams up stories where her favourite words are…'what if' and 'where'? After several years travelling around Australia and Asia, Suzanne settled in the Hunter Valley, Australia with her family, two dogs and a cat.

Writing as both S. E. Gilchrist and Suzanne Gilchrist, she loves combining romance with adventure and suspense across different writing genres including science fiction, apocalyptic, exotic locations and contemporary small towns. Several of her books have been shortlisted in writing contests.

Suzanne takes a keen interest in the environment and animal welfare and loves bushwalking and spending time with her family. She is a member of the Romance Writers of Australia, co-runs the Hunter Romance Writers group and is the organiser behind several group writing ventures, including the best-selling *Bindarra Creek Romance* series, the *Deadly Forces* series and the *Mindalby Outback Romance* series.

Published by Escape Publishing (Harlequin Australia)
Suzanne is also an indie author.
For more information, please visit her website and sign up to her newsletter: www.segilchrist.com.
Or follow her on Facebook:
https://www.facebook.com/SEGilchrist/

Her twitter handle is: @segilchrist1

ACKNOWLEDGMENTS

I would never have realised my dreams of being a writer without the motivation and support of my family, friends and the wonderful writing community, Romance Writers of Australia.
Thank you to my face-to-face writing group for their support and generous sharing of knowledge, Hunter Romance Writers – a wonderful bunch of ladies who are just fun to be around.

A big thank you to Patti from Paradox Book Covers & Formatting for her box-set cover and formatting skills.

EXTRACT FROM SCENT OF THE JAGUAR

CHAPTER 1

The storm had hit hard and fast, not long after take-off from São Paulo de Olivença, a municipality in the western section of the Amazon Basin. Several passengers had drifted off to sleep, lulled by the drone of the engines and the stuffy tin-can air.

However, an afternoon nap was the last thing on Bernie's agenda. Not with so many anxious thoughts squirreling through her mind. Inside the cramped restroom, she pressed her pounding forehead against the cold glass, recalling her father's phone call. The storm interference had transformed his voice into a bubble of white noise, his frantic words difficult to make out.

She'd only deciphered, 'get to the US Consulate...Jaguar hunting you...' before the call had been cut off and he was gone.

Her father had too much respect for her profession to believe a wild animal would make an archaeologist give up the prospect of a new dig. Especially one as exciting and wreathed in mystery as this. So, the Jaguar had to be a person. But what *had* he been talking about?

Bernie hadn't waited to find out. Whatever was going on

had germinated fear in her father and, as an ex-marine, he wasn't a man easily intimidated.

She'd galvanized into action, leaving messages for the professor and the guides she'd intended to meet up with tomorrow. If she'd been alone, she would have risked continuing her journey to the dig—jaguar or no jaguar—but not when she had her younger sister, Kit, with her.

Within three hours, they were in the air, flying back to Manaus. Now worry plagued her that she'd made the wrong decision by insisting they change their plans. Maybe heading to a remote area of the jungle would have been a safer bet than isolating themselves on an airplane.

The Jaguar could be here, with them. He could be anyone. Waiting to spring his trap, to take her down. Or worse…Kit.

After splashing water onto her clammy face and patting it dry with a paper towel, Bernie exited the cubicle. She paused, shrugging the strap of her compact backpack into a more comfortable position over her shoulder. The plane dipped then levelled out. Her belly rolled, and she pressed a shaky hand to her protesting stomach.

A female flight attendant appeared out of the small galley, a frown marring her attractive features. "Please return to your seat. Didn't you hear the pilot request everyone remain seated until we're through the turbulence?"

"Sorry, I'm on my way now." Giving the woman a tight smile, Bernie headed down the aisle. She studied each passenger as she passed, her body tense, palms damp.

The guy in the front row gnawed at his fingernails while darting furtive glances behind him. Apparently ignoring him, his companion had her nose buried in a magazine. Across the aisle, a middle-aged African-American couple had their heads bent over a sheaf of papers, their voices low in discussion. The row behind held a Brazilian family of four, the kids tossing potato chips at each other and squabbling. In the next row, two men appeared to be napping while another guy bent over, tying his shoelaces.

Any one of them could be the Jaguar.

Her footsteps faltered, her eyes zeroing in on a lean-faced man with dark auburn hair in the process of stowing a duffle bag in an overhead locker. He looked down, the tender smile on his tanned face softening his profile for a moment, before he took his seat and became obscured by the headrest. As recognition hit, her heart stalled for a second before it kicked into high gear.

Zane MacIntosh. He'd turned up at the dig in Mexico last year with a group of possible benefactors then become part of their team for three weeks. How exactly he'd achieved that feat when everyone else had to go through a long-winded screening process, remained a question she'd like answered. Anger and bitter disappointment burned through her with such force, she charged down the aisle to confront him without a second thought.

"You stole that gold amulet and I intend to prove it."

~End of Excerpt~